Selected Praise for

MEGAN HART

"*Naked* is a great story, steeped in emotion. Hart has a wonderful way with her characters…. She conveys their thoughts and actions in a manner that brings them to life. And the erotic scenes provide a sizzling read."
—*RT Book Reviews*

"*Deeper* is absolutely, positively, the best book that I have read in ages! I cannot say enough about this book. The writing is fabulous, the characters' chemistry is combustible, and the story line brought tears to my eyes more than once…. Beautiful, poignant, and bittersweet… Megan Hart never disappoints me, but with *Deeper* she went above and beyond."
—*Romance Reader at Heart*, Top Pick

"*Stranger,* like Megan Hart's previous novels, is an action-packed, sexy, emotional romance that tears up the pages with heat while also telling a touching love story…. *Stranger* has a unique, hot premise that Hart delivers on fully."
—Bestselling author Rachel Kramer Bussel

"*[Broken]* is not a traditional romance but the story of a real and complex woman caught in a difficult situation with no easy answers. Well-developed secondary characters and a compelling plot add depth to this absorbing and enticing novel."
—*Library Journal*

"An exceptional story and honest characters make *Dirty* a must-read."
—*Romance Reviews Today*

"[Hart] writes erotica for grown-ups. She doesn't write sex just to titillate and she holds her characters to a higher standard. *[The Space Between Us]* is a quiet book, but it packed a major punch for me…. She's a stunning writer, and this is a stunning book."
—*Super Librarian*

naked

MEGAN HART

HARLEQUIN® MIRA®

Recycling programs for this product may not exist in your area.

ISBN-13: 978-0-7783-1574-2

NAKED

For questions and comments about the quality of this book, please contact us at CustomerService@Harlequin.com.

Printed in U.S.A.

This book wouldn't have been written without the constant support of my family and friends. Thank you, all. Thanks especially to The Bootsquad for the encouragement and motivation to continue when it would have been easier to play the Sims. Also to my BFF Lori who keeps telling me I can't quit writing, because she needs more books. And finally to everyone who asked me if Alex Kennedy was going to get his own book, this one's for all of you.

* * *

I could write without listening to music while I do it, but I'm so glad I don't have to. This is a partial list of what was on my playlist for *Naked*. If you like the songs, please support the artists by purchasing their music.

Justin King, "Reach You"

Kelly Clarkson, "My Life Would Suck without You"

Lorna Vallings, "Taste"

Hinder, "Better Than Me"

Staind, "Everything Changes"

Sara Bareilles, "Gravity"

Tom Waits, "Hope I Don't Fall in Love with You"

Chapter
01

"Alex doesn't like girls." Patrick said this like a warning.

I'd been staring at the man from the corner of my eye, framing him as part of the overall picture here at Patrick's annual Chrismukkah party. Alex was prettier than the bunches of Martha Stewart–inspired poinsettias and twinkling fairy lights, but so were all the men here. Patrick had the hottest friends I'd ever seen. Seriously, it was like a convention of hot men. After Patrick's admonishment I looked Alex over again more closely, mostly just to jerk Patrick's chain. He was so easy that way.

"Is that his name?"

Patrick gave a low snort of disapproval. "Yes, that's his name."

"Alex what?"

"Kennedy," Patrick said. "But he doesn't—"

"I heard you." I pressed my lips to the rim of my wineglass, warming it. The rich, strong scent of red wine wafted under my nostrils. I could taste the aroma on the back of my tongue, but I didn't sip. "He doesn't like girls, huh?"

Patrick pursed his mouth and crossed his arms. "No. Jesus, Olivia, stop ogling his ass."

I raised an eyebrow, mirroring Patrick's earlier expression. An old habit and one I knew irritated the shit out of him. It seemed like that kind of night. "Why do you invite me to your parties if it's not to ogle men's asses?"

Patrick huffed and puffed and frowned briefly before he must've remembered what that did to the lines around his mouth, and he forced his face to neutral smoothness. His gaze followed mine across the dining room and through the archway. Alex had his back to us, one arm on the mantelpiece of the living-room fireplace. He had a glass of Guinness. He'd been holding it for as long as I'd been watching, but I hadn't seen him drink from it even once.

"And you feel an especial need to point this out to me…why?" I sipped more wine and stared him down.

Patrick shrugged. "Just thought I'd make sure you knew."

I looked around at the half-dozen men helping themselves to the buffet, and then through the arch to the living room where another dozen men chatted or danced or flirted. Ninety-nine percent of them were gay and the other one percent was thinking about it. "I think I know better than to expect to get laid at one of your parties, Patrick."

Before I could comment further, a pair of thick, muscled arms gripped my waist from behind and a tight belly pressed along my back. "Run away with me and see how long it takes before he notices we're gone," said a deep voice directly into my ear.

I twisted, giving in to laughter at the tickling touch of a beard on my earlobe, and turned. "Patrick, you didn't tell me you were inviting Billy Dee Williams to your party! Oh, wait…Billy Dee would never wear that sweater. Hey, Teddy."

"Girl, don't you be making fun of this sweater. Mama McDonald sent me this sweater and her boy Patrick got one just like it." Teddy dropped Patrick a wink. "Difference is, I'm man enough to wear it."

I got a hug, a squeeze, a kiss and a pat on the ass all within the span of seconds before Teddy moved on to provide the same for Patrick. Patrick, still pouting, swatted at the bigger man and pushed him away while Teddy laughed and swiped a hand over Patrick's hair. Patrick scowled and smoothed his ruffled feathers, but allowed Teddy to kiss his cheek a moment later.

I gestured with my wineglass. "He's trying to tell me not to ogle an ass."

"What? I thought we were all here to ogle men's asses."

Teddy shook his, I shook mine; we did The Bump and dissolved into the sort of laughter helped along by a liberal helping of holiday cheer. Patrick watched us with his arms crossed and eyebrow lifted. Then he shook his head.

"Pardon me for trying to be a friend," he said.

Patrick and I had been friends for a long time. Once, long ago, we'd been more than that. Patrick thought that gave him the right to be my aunt Nancy and I let him because…well, because I loved him. And because there was never been too much love in my life to turn any small bit of it away.

This, though, seemed a little excessive even for Patrick. Teddy and I shared a glance. I shrugged.

"I'm making a run to the kitchen for some more wine, loves," Teddy said. "Do you want any?"

"I'm good." I held up my glass, still half-full.

Patrick shook his head. We both watched Teddy make his way through the crowd. Only when he was out of earshot did I turn back to my ex-boyfriend.

"Patrick, if you're trying to tell me in a not-so-subtle way that you fucked that guy—"

Patrick's short, sharp bark was so different from his normal laughter it startled me to silence. He shook his head. "Oh, no. Not *him*."

I didn't miss the way he cut his gaze from mine. That more than anything told me an entire story that needed no words. Hell. It didn't even need a picture to make it clear.

My grin faded. Patrick had never made a secret of his private life, and I'd heard more stories about the men he'd slept with than I ever wanted to. Patrick didn't get turned down, at least not often. I watched the red flush creep up his perfect, high cheekbones.

I looked again across the room at Alex Kennedy. "He turned you down?"

"Shh!" Patrick hissed, though the music and conversation was so loud nobody could've overheard us.

"Wow."

His mouth clamped tighter. "Not another word."

I looked again across the room at Alex Kennedy, still standing with one arm on the mantel. Now I paid attention to the crease in his black trousers and the way the soft black knit of his sweater clung to his broad shoulders and lean waist. He wore the clothes well, but so did all the other men here. From this distance I could see darkish eyes and longish medium-brown hair that looked as though he'd run a hand through it one too many times—or just rolled out of bed. Hair like that took lots of product and effort to look good, and his did. I had an impression of handsome features more than an actual view, and some of that was assumption. Alex was very pretty, there was no doubt about it, but if Patrick hadn't gone all "don'tcha dare" on me, I probably would've looked once, maybe twice, and never again.

"How come I've never met him?"

"He's not from around here," Patrick said.

I looked back at the man Patrick seemed so desperate for me to ignore. Alex appeared to be locked in deep conversation with another of Patrick's friends, their faces intense and serious. Not flirting. The man across from Alex drank angrily, his throat working.

I didn't need to lift my hands, thumb to thumb and pointer to pointer, to make a frame for the picture I was composing. My mind did that automatically at the same time it filled in the details of their story. *Snap, click.* I didn't have my camera, but I could imagine the shot, just the same. I framed Alex in my head, slightly off center and a little out of focus.

Patrick muttered and poked me in the side. "Olivia!"

I looked at him again. "Stop being such a mother hen, Patrick. Do you think I'm an idiot?"

He frowned. "No. I don't think you're an idiot. I just don't want…"

Teddy came back just then, so whatever Patrick wanted got swallowed behind a tight, hard smile. I recognized it, along with the look in his eyes. I hadn't seen it for a long time, but I knew it. Patrick was hiding something.

Teddy slung an arm over Patrick's shoulders and pulled him

close to nuzzle at his cheek. "Come on. The cheese tray's been decimated and we're almost out of wine. Come to the kitchen with me, love, and I'll give you a little treat."

Until Teddy, Patrick had never stayed with anyone longer than he'd been with me. I adored Teddy despite this, or maybe because of it. I knew Patrick loved him, though he hardly ever said so, and because I loved Patrick I wanted him to be happy.

Patrick's hard glance cut across the room again, to Alex and back to me. I thought he might say something more, but instead he shook his head and let Teddy lead him away. Me, I took another ogle at Alex Kennedy's very, very fine ass.

"Livvy! Merry holidays!" This came from Jerald, another of Patrick's friends, and a man who'd done some modeling for me more than once. I traded him some nice head shots for his portfolio in exchange for using him in some stock photos I needed for my graphic design business. "When are you going to take more pictures of me, huh?"

"When can you come in?"

Jerald grinned with perfect white teeth and a smile as straight as he was not. "Whenever you need me."

We chatted for a few minutes about when and where, and for what, and then Jerald gave me a hug and a squeeze and a kiss before abandoning me in search of someone with a penis. That was all right. I didn't need Patrick to hover over me to make me feel at home. I knew most of his friends. The ones of recent acquaintance viewed me as a curiosity, a relic, the woman who'd been with Patrick before he came out, but they were friendly enough. Liquor helped, of course. Friends who'd known Patrick and me since college, on the other hand, could all still laugh about the good times that had happened when Patrick and I were a couple without the half-disguised gleam of pity his newer, gay friends often gave me. Booze helped that, too.

Wineglass in hand, I made my way over to the buffet to load my plate with all sorts of delicacies. Squares of Indian naan bread paired with spicy hummus, cubes of cheese dipped in cranberry honey mustard, a few purple grapes still clinging to their stem. Patrick and Teddy knew how to throw a party, and even the Saturday after Thanksgiving, I still had room for food as good as they served. I was debating about sampling the slices of rare roast beef settled next to the crusty French rolls or the waistline-conscious strawberry walnut salad when a tap on my shoulder turned me.

"Hey, girl!"

I stopped with a roll in my hand, halfway to my plate. I knew Patrick's neighbor, Nadia. She'd always gone out of her way to be friendly to me, not that she had any reason not to be. I'd always thought Nadia's overtures of friendship had less to do with me and more with her, and tonight was proving that suspicion correct.

"I want you to meet Carlos. My boyfriend." Nadia had a pretty smile in an otherwise unremarkable face, but when she used it I wanted to take her picture. It transformed her.

"Meetcha," Carlos mumbled, his eyes on the food, though Nadia's hand held him in such a tight grip he couldn't actually grab any.

"Nice to meet you, Carlos."

Nadia gave us both an expectant look. Carlos and I gave each other the once-over, his dark eyes traveling over my entire face before meeting my gaze. He glanced at Nadia, whose fingers were curled into the crook of his elbow. Her skin was very white against his. I think we both knew what she wanted, but neither of us was going to give it.

I didn't know I was black until second grade. Oh, sure, I'd always known my skin was darker than my parents' and brothers'. My features not the same. They'd never hidden the fact that I was adopted, and we celebrated not only my birthday but the date I became part of their family. I never felt anything less than loved completely. Cherished. Spoiled, even, by two much older brothers, and parents I'd know later were trying to overcompensate for the cesspool their marriage had become.

I'd always believed I was special, but until second grade I'd never understood I was…different.

Desiree Johnson moved to my school in Ardmore from someplace closer to inner-city Philadelphia. She wore her hair in hundreds of tiny braids close to her scalp and clipped at the ends with plastic barrettes. She wore T-shirts with gold shiny lettering, and soft velour track pants, her sneakers startlingly white and huge for the size of her feet. She was different, and we all stared when she came into our classroom.

The teacher, Miss Dippold, had told us only that morning we'd be getting a new student. She'd taken care to mention how important it was to be kind to new students, especially those who weren't "the same." She'd read us a story about Zeke, the pony with stripes who'd turned out not to be a pony at all but a zebra. Even in second grade, I'd seen the end of that one coming from a mile away.

What I hadn't seen coming was Miss Dippold's command to me to shift my desk so Desiree could sit beside me. I obeyed, of course, atingle with delight at being chosen to befriend the new girl. Was it because I was the class's top speller for that week, with my name on the board and first-in-line privileges for recess? Or had Miss Dippold noticed how I'd lent Billy Miller my best pencil, since he'd left his at home again? My desk scraped along the floor, curling small shavings of polish off the wood as I moved it aside so Randall, the janitor, could fit in another desk and chair for Desiree.

It was none of those reasons, but one I'd never have guessed.

"There," Miss Dippold said when Desiree had settled herself into the new desk and chair. "Desiree, this is Olivia. I'm sure you'll be best friends."

Desiree's barrettes clacked against one another as she turned her head to look up and down at my pleated skirt, knee-high socks and buckled Mary Janes. My hair, twisted into tight curls and held back with a matching headband. My cardigan sweater.

For a second-grader, Desiree already had a lot of attitude. "You *got* to be kidding me."

Miss Dippold blinked behind her huge tortoiseshell glasses. "Desiree? Is there a problem?"

She gave a world-weary sigh. "No, Miss Dippold. Nothing wrong with me."

Later, just before lunch, I leaned to take a peek at the drawings she was making on her notepad. Mostly swirls and circles, shaded with pencil. I showed her my own doodles, which weren't as elaborate.

"I like to draw, too," I said.

Desiree checked out my drawings and snorted. "Uh-huh."

"Maybe that's why Miss Dippold thought we'd be friends," I explained patiently, still trying. "Because we both like to draw."

Desiree's brows rose up to meet her hairline. She looked around at the others, classmates who were getting restless in anticipation of sloppy joes and afternoon recess. She looked back at me, then took my hand and laid it next to hers. Against the pale gray desktops, our fingers stood out like shadows.

"Miss Dippold didn't know anything about my drawing," Desiree said. "She meant it's cuz we're both, you know."

"Both what?"

Now she gave an exasperated sigh and rolled her eyes at me. Her whole tone changed. "Because we're both black."

It was my turn to blink rapidly, trying to take all of this in. I looked around the room, at a sea of white faces. Caitlyn Caruso was adopted, too, from China, and she looked different than the other kids. But Desiree was right. She'd pointed it out as if I should've known all along.

I was black. This revelation stunned me into silence for the rest of the day, until I went home and took down all our family albums to flip through page after page of photos. I was black! I'd been black my entire life! How had I never noticed it before?

The answer was simple—my parents had never said so, never made it a big deal. I'd been brought up to appreciate diversity. I had little choice. Born to a white mother and a black father, I'd been adopted as an infant by parents in a mixed marriage, though of religion, not race. My nonpracticing Jewish mom had married my fallen-away Catholic dad and they'd raised two sons together in a haphazard clash of holidays until they divorced when I was five. We never talked about the color of my skin, or what it meant, or if it should mean something.

Desiree didn't stay long in our class. Her family moved again a few months later. But I never forgot her for pointing out to me what I should've known my whole life.

But here's the thing about people like Nadia, who pride themselves on being color-blind—in the end, all they see is color. Nadia hadn't introduced me to her boyfriend because we both liked to draw, or we both listened to Depeche Mode, or even just to be polite. Carlos and I knew it.

Nadia didn't get it. She chattered on between us, dropping names as if I should know them, referencing hip-hop songs. Carlos caught my gaze and gave me a small shrug she didn't see. He looked at her with obvious affection, though, stopping her finally with a single murmured, "Baby."

Nadia laughed, looking confused. "Huh?"

"If you don't let me eat some of this food, I'm going to pass out."

"Carlos works out a lot," Nadia confided as her boyfriend began to decimate the buffet table. "He's always hungry."

I was saved from having to comment by the kerfuffle arising in the living room. I'd still been aware of Alex Kennedy at the corner of my vision. He hadn't strayed from the fireplace. The man he'd been talking to had raised his voice and his hands, gesturing and pointing. Accusing.

This would not be the first time drama had exploded at Patrick's house; throw a party for a bunch of queens and there are never enough crowns to go around, as he was fond of saying. I wasn't the only one who turned to watch, either. Alex, instead of engaging in the back-and-forth, only shook his head and lifted his beer to his lips.

"You...you're such an asshole!" cried the other man, voice wobbling in a way that made me cringe in sympathy and embarrassment for him at the same time. "I don't know why I ever bothered with you!"

It was easy enough for me to see why he'd bothered. Alex Kennedy was a smoking-hot piece of yum. He stood, stoic, in the onslaught of another round of insults and accusations, until finally the other man stormed off, followed by a few clucking friends. The entire incident had taken only a few minutes and had turned only a couple of heads. By far not the most exciting or dramatic argument ever to hit one of Patrick's parties, and in fact likely to be forgotten by the end of the night by everyone but the two men involved.

Well, and me.

I was fascinated.

He doesn't like girls, I reminded myself, and dug into the roast beef, diet be damned. And when I looked up from the carnage of my plate, Alex Kennedy was gone.

It was a good party, one of Patrick's best. By the time midnight rolled around, I'd had my fill of goodies and gossip and had to hide my yawn behind my hand so nobody would accuse me of being the old lady I sometimes felt I'd become. Karaoke had begun in the living room, where so many people were dancing both the menorah in the window and the Christmas tree in the corner were shaking.

Was that…? Oh, no. It was. I covered my eyes with a hand and peeked through my fingers as a man took center stage to sing along with Beyoncé's runaway dance-club anthem from a few years before. The one about putting a ring on it. Oh, and he was dancing, too, keeping perfect time without missing a step. He probably had his own clip up on YouTube. Everyone clapped and shouted, but I looked to the corner by the fireplace for the object of his attention. Yep. Alex Kennedy.

Somehow I didn't think a ring had ever been put on any part of him but his cock.

"Perk up," Teddy advised, and filled my glass with wine I didn't want. "Party's not over yet."

I groaned and leaned against him. "Maybe I should just head home."

He shook his head with a laugh and patted his pocket. "Got your keys."

I lifted my glass. "If you hadn't insisted on keeping this full…"

We both laughed. I'd spent so many nights in their guest room his insistence on me staying had almost nothing to do with the fact I'd been drinking. Now, though, as I watched through the arched doorway to the living room-cum-dance floor, I wished I'd been smarter and not planned ahead to spend the night; I wished I could walk from here, but it was too cold and dark and too long a way. I wished I could hitch a ride with someone, but though a few guests had already left, most were still in full-on celebration mode and none of them lived out my way.

I hid another yawn. "I think I need some coffee."

Teddy frowned. "Poor Livvy. Always working so hard."

"If I don't, nobody else will do it for me." I shrugged.

"Well, I'm impressed. Striking out on your own. Quitting your job. Patrick didn't think you'd stick with it." Teddy looked momentarily uncomfortable, as if he'd spilled a secret.

"I know he didn't."

"He's proud of you, too, Liv."

I wasn't so sure Patrick had a right to pride in my accomplishments, but I didn't say so. Instead, I let Teddy hug and pet me a little, because he's like a cuddlier version of the Borg from *Star Trek*. Resistance is futile. Not only that, but I'm a sucker for a big man in a Santa sweater; what can I say?

I handed him my glass of wine. "I'm going for some coffee. Or at least a Coke or something."

I could've just gone to bed, but with the party still in full swing it was unlikely I'd be able to sleep. Patrick's kitchen was kitschy cute, complete with a swinging-tailed kitty clock and retro-looking appliances. Well, except for the space-age espresso machine, the fancy kind that steamed milk and used those special pods. I'd never learned to use it and in fact didn't dare touch it in case I dialed something wrong and sent us all back to the Stone Age. I'd be the one to step on the butter-fly.

I knew he had a regular coffeemaker someplace, but a search of the cabinets didn't turn one up. Patrick never got rid of anything—and I mean never, not his favorite T-shirt or a lamp with a broken switch. Hell, obviously not me. He hoarded belongings and people like the Zombpocalypse was coming and the only way to survive was by building a new civilization out of outdated wardrobes, nonfunctioning appliances...and past lovers. I knew he still had that coffee-maker.

Maybe on the screened back porch, plastic-sheeted now for protection against the winter. Patrick had stored a couple dozen boxes of miscellaneous crap there, promising Teddy he'd sort through it, but never doing so. His espresso machine was new, so there was an excellent chance he'd simply moved the old machine aside.

Bracing myself against the cold, I pushed open the back

door and went onto the porch. I hissed out heat and broke at once into goose-pimply shivers. I didn't turn on the overhead light, but went for the first stack of boxes. Didn't find the coffeemaker, just a collection of porn mags I flipped through with numb, fumbly fingers and shoved back inside the box. It was the closest I was likely to get to an erection tonight, and don't think I didn't mourn that fact just a little.

Starting my own business had been great for my ego and sense of satisfaction. It'd been hell on my bank account and my sex life. No time to date, no time to invest in another person, even if I'd found someone I thought would be worth making an effort for. No time even for casual flirting, since working for myself meant I was alone most of the time. My other two jobs, the ones I'd kept so I could cover my mortgage, weren't exactly conducive to meeting men. Taking school and sports team photos required a lot of traveling, and though I met many a DILF—a dad I'd like to fuck—most of them were married. My job at Foto Folks was fun and paid well, but my clients were invariably middle-aged women looking for "boudoir" shots or moms who brought their kids to get pictures taken in front of giant stuffed bears. I'd developed a severe allergy to feather boas. I was run-down, but I was happy. I was tired and sometimes stressed, but I was doing what I loved.

I was also officially undersexed.

"C'mon, Patrick, where'd you put it?" I moved toward the porch's far end, around the sheet-covered wicker furniture and behind a large stack of lawn chairs. "Ah, bingo."

Coffeemaker, filters, even a zipped plastic bag of coffee beans. He really never got rid of anything. I laughed and shook my head, and turned at the sound of the back door opening behind me.

Freeze-frame.

Two silhouettes appeared in the doorway. Men. The smaller one shoved the bigger one against the wall. Oh. I got it. I was ready to clear my throat and announce my presence when the taller man turned his face toward the light.

How could I have ever thought him commonly, regularly handsome? Alex Kennedy's profile made me want to weep, if only because there are too few people in this life who are so beautiful while also being so real. In full light everything on his face had lined up just right. Here, now, with shadow splitting him in half, I could see his nose was too sharp, his lower jaw a little too undercut for perfection. His hair fell over his forehead, and he grimaced as the man in front of him dropped to his knees and unzipped Alex's trousers.

I still had time to call out a warning. They were far gone, maybe drunk or maybe just so deep in their lust they weren't paying attention to anything else, but I could've stopped them if I really wanted to. I didn't.

"Evan," the low, creamy voice that must belong to Alex said. "You don't have to do this."

"Shut up."

The shadows morphed into figures again, one standing tall, the other crouched at his feet. The light from the streetlamp down the alley was barely bright enough to illuminate anything, but it was enough to show me what was going on. And, I thought, to block me from their view if they'd bothered to look, since I was in the far corner and settled deep in shadow. So long as I kept quiet and still, chances were very good they'd never even know I was there. They would come…and then go.

Evan yanked Alex's trousers down past his knees. I stifled my sudden harsh breath with my hand. I couldn't see cock, but I'm not too proud to admit I looked for it. What I could see was Evan's hand stroking. His shoulder moved, a lump of black against gray. Alex's head tipped back with a dull thud against the wall.

"Shut up and take it," Evan said.

Maybe he meant to be menacing or sexy, but Alex only laughed and put his hand on Evan's head. Did I imagine the twist and twine of his fingers in the other man's hair? It was impossible to see, but in the next second, when Evan's head jerked back, I thought it must've been from his lover's grip.

"Are you fucking serious?" Alex said around his laughter.

The next noise Evan made didn't quite hit menacing. I didn't find it very sexy but Alex must have, because he loosed his grip enough to let Evan's head bob forward. I heard the soft, wet noise of a mouth on flesh.

Damn.

"Fuck, that's good."

"I know how you like it," Evan said, softer this time, without the attitude.

"Who doesn't?" Alex laughed, low and slow and a little drowsy.

If it makes me a pervert to get excited watching two people fucking, then sign me up and send me the T-shirt.

More soft, wet sounds. I was sort of soft and wet myself at that point, and the only thing stopping me from reaching between my legs was that I was frozen in place with fascina-

tion—and of course, knowing I wasn't watching some sur-
reptitious gay porn, but real live men getting off.

I squeezed my thighs. Wow. That felt good. I did it again,
putting pressure on my clit that wasn't as good as a fingertip
or a tongue would have been, but the slow and steady clench
of muscle nevertheless started the buildup of pressure inside
me I recognized.

I blinked, my eyes adjusting further to the darkness. I could
see the flash of Alex's eyes as he looked down at Evan, then
the gleam of Evan's smile as he pulled away from Alex's cock.
Alex put his hand on Evan's head again. Evan got back to the
business of cock sucking.

Alex moaned.

Evan made a muffled noise that didn't sound nearly as
nice. I heard more shuffling. The floorboards creaked.
Another dull thump on the wall made me open my eyes, and
I watched Alex's silhouette arch.

He was coming. I had to close my eyes, turn my face. I
couldn't watch this, no matter how sexy it was, no matter how
kinky and perverted I was. I wasn't cold anymore, that was
for sure.

"No," Alex said, and I opened my eyes.

Evan had stood. There was distance between them, a space
of light in the darkness of their two shadows. I watched
Evan's move forward again, a little, and Alex stepped to the
side.

"No?" Evan repeated, voice querulous. "You'll let me suck
your dick, but you won't kiss me?"

Zip. Sigh. Alex's shape moved in what looked like a shrug.

"You're a fucking asshole, you know that?"

"I know it," Alex said. "But so did you before you brought me out here."

Evan, incredibly, stamped his foot. Even Patrick at his queeniest never stamped his foot. "I hate you!"

"No, you don't."

"I do!" Evan opened the door and I shut my eyes tight against the sudden spilling of light. "You can just forget about coming home!"

"Your place isn't home. Why do you think I took all my stuff?"

Ouch. That stung even me. If I were Evan I'd have hated Alex, too, just for the smug tone.

"I fucking hate you. I never should've given you a second chance!"

"I told you not to," Alex said.

Evan swept out. Alex stayed behind for another minute or two, his breathing heavy. I kept as still as I could with my heart pounding so fast it made stars behind my eyelids. I was sure he'd hear me, but he didn't.

Alex went inside.

I discovered I didn't need coffee to keep me awake.

Chapter 02

Patrick pounced on me in the kitchen, his expression fierce. "Where were you?"

I gestured at the back porch. "I went looking for your coffeepot."

He crossed his arms over his chest. "It's right there on the counter."

The party was still going strong, but I'd had enough. Too much drama for one evening. If I hadn't had a few too many glasses of wine, screw the drive, I'd have gone home to sleep in my own bed. As it was, I was coming down from the adrenaline high and could barely manage not to slur my words.

"You know I can't use that one. Too complicated."

He eyed me. "Are you drunk?"

"No. Just tired." I hugged him, surprising him for a second, I think, given the way he jumped. Only for a second, then his arms went around me. Held me tight until I pushed him away. "I'm going to bed."

"Already?"

"I'm wiped out!" I knuckled his side and Patrick tried not to laugh, but gave in. "What is your problem, anyway? Why'd you come in here like the back end of your broom was on fire?"

My joke annoyed him. "Very funny. I was looking for you, that's all. You disappeared."

"Uh-huh." I yawned behind my hand. "Well, here I am. No big deal, Patrick, sheesh."

He grabbed my hand and squeezed it. "I just wanted to make sure you were okay, Liv. Is that so wrong? Making sure my best girl's all right?"

"You haven't called me that in a long time." My fingers, trapped in his, twisted. He let me go.

"I mean it, and you know it."

If you've ever loved someone for too long to stop, you know how I felt just then. Standing in the kitchen Patrick shared with someone else, bleary from exhaustion and red wine, I refused to give in to melancholy. I kissed his cheek instead and patted his ass the way I always did.

"I'm going to bed."

I went up the back stairs. Narrow and steep, with a sharp bend halfway up, they were difficult to navigate even clear-headed. The sound of the music faded but the bass *thumpa-thumpa* continued as I climbed the stairs and went through what Patrick and Teddy called "the back room," which had one door leading in and another leading out, and down the long, narrow hall. Like the stairway, the hall had a jog in it, sharp to the left. I loved old houses for their nooks and crannies, and this was no exception. It had been cut into apartments when Patrick and Teddy moved in, but they'd been renovating back into a single dwelling. I touched the wallpaper in the hall, revealed when they'd stripped off a layer of tacky 1970s paneling. In the dark I couldn't see the tiny sprigs of lavender flowers against the pale yellow background, but I knew they were there.

Once I'd taken a photo of the view down this hall. The light from the window at the end had sketched shadows beneath the light fixtures, which weren't fancy enough to be considered antique, just old. I'd captured a misty, fuzzy figure in the corner, something like the shape of a woman in a long dress, her hair piled high on her head. Trick of the light, perhaps, or optical illusion. It was just out of focus enough for me to never be sure. But nights like this, when I thought I might stumble from weariness or too much cheer, I imagined I felt her comforting hand helping me along.

I went from doorway to bed in a few steps, shedding my clothes and diving onto the soft mattress with its mound of covers and pillows. I tossed them on the floor without ceremony, knowing Patrick would squawk, but too tired to pile them neatly on the trunk beneath the window. I reached to the nightstand and ruffled around inside, past the box of tissues, the lip balm, and found the small square box of earplugs I kept in there the way I kept a spare box of "girl" things under the bathroom sink.

In half a minute I had blessed silence, though an occasional surge of bass from downstairs still vibrated my stomach a little. I pulled on an oversize T-shirt from the bottom nightstand drawer and snuggled beneath the heavy comforter, the extra pillow tucked firmly between my knees to alleviate the pressure on my aching back. I couldn't hear my sigh, though the dull thud of my heartbeat still sounded in my ears.

I couldn't sleep.

My sophomore year of college, I shared a room with three other girls. The dorm I'd chosen had been overbooked. I'd been given the choice of living in a different building, farther away from my classes and the cafeteria, or moving into a converted study lounge for the semester. It hadn't been so bad. The larger room meant we'd all had a bit more space, and the lounge was in the corner of the building, so instead of the one small window the regular rooms had, we had four large panes of glass. The downside was the complete and utter lack of privacy. Forget about having a guy over; it was impossible even to masturbate without an audience.

I don't know about the other girls, one of whom was a devout Christian whose missionary position had nothing to do with sex, but I have always been, and suspect I always will be, an avid fan of getting myself off. I'd learned the trick back then of rubbing off on a pillow tucked between my legs, just this way. Of using the slow, steady push of inner muscles to bring myself close, slowly, and finishing myself off against the pillow. I hadn't come that way in a long time—I lived alone now and could strip down naked and do it on my dining-room table, if I wanted. Not that I ever did.

But I hadn't forgotten how to do it, how to press and release and inch my hips forward and back, just so. I gave half a second's thought to embarrassment and tossed it aside in the name of orgasm. After all, I hadn't burst in on them, or sneaked up to peek through a window. The show on the porch had been dropped in front of me like nondenominational holiday gift, and I've never been one to return a present just because it didn't fit quite right.

The memory of Alex Kennedy's groan slid over me in the darkness and straight to the pit of my belly, inside me. Down to my clit. I shifted ever so slightly against the pillow. How must it feel to be the reason he made that sound?

I was suddenly tipping closer to the edge. I shifted again, tightening my inner muscles and holding, then releasing. Slow, sweet waves of climax began deep inside me. I turned my face into my pillow and bit the softness to stifle my own groan. I rode the waves of pleasure with my eyes closed tight.

Of all the pictures my mind had taken that night, his face was the one I could still see.

The house was quiet when I woke. I stretched under the weight of the blankets. The tip of my nose and cheeks had gone cold, and that didn't bode well for how the rest of me would feel should I venture out of my warm cave. Patrick and Teddy's house was old and heated unevenly, and I'd forgotten to open the register the night before. This could mean only my room was chilly, or that the entire house was shiver-inducing; it really depended on what they'd done with the thermostat before they went to bed.

My stomach rumbled. My bladder, the most effective alarm clock I would ever have, reminded me of all the wine I'd drunk. Worse, my mind insisted on replaying the activities of the night before in vivid black on black.

Had I really made myself come while thinking about Alex Kennedy getting a blow job? It would seem I had. I stretched again, feeling softness beneath me, warmth around me, the brush of smooth fabric on my belly where my T-shirt had bunched up. I waited for shame, or at least embarrassment, but nope. Nada. I was thoroughly depraved.

This more than anything got my ass out of bed, because one could really be appropriately depraved only with an empty bladder and a full stomach. I took care of the first easily enough, skip-hopping down the cold, bare wooden floor of the hall and into the bathroom, where I could actually see my breath, and the hot water from the sink scalded my hands. I gave a longing look at the bathtub, an old-fashioned claw-foot tub Patrick hated and I coveted.

Downstairs, the kitchen was gloriously warm. Heat flooded up from the open grate in the floor from the furnace directly below. In another twenty minutes I'd probably be sweating, but for now I gloried in it. I also reveled in the shelves of leftovers from the party the night before, everything tucked away in plastic containers and stacked neatly according to size and shape. Patrick's work. I could only guess how late he'd stayed up, tidying, before Teddy forced him to bed. On the upside of that, I could be sure none of the food would give me food poisoning. Patrick was a stickler for keeping his buffet table appropriately cold or hot, depending.

Chicken pot stickers called my name, the little bastards, not even trying to pretend they didn't know I was trying to lose a couple of pounds. The chocolate cake I could ignore, but not the little dumplings of fatty, sweet-and-sour goodness. I pulled the container from the fridge and turned to put it on the table—and almost ran smack into a bare chest.

The container of pot stickers hit the floor and bounced. I screamed. Loudly.

Alex Kennedy smiled.

"Damn, you're pretty," I said.

He blinked, his smile getting wider. He crossed his arms over his very fine, naked stomach. "Thanks."

I thought about bending to pick up my breakfast, but doing
that would put me at his feet, and that wasn't a place I was
sure I could stand to be. Not after last night, and what I'd seen.
He cast a glance at the container by his toes, then at me. Then
he bent to pick it up.

Alex at my feet, on the other hand? Very nice indeed.

"Thanks." I took the container and eased past him to put
it in the microwave. I looked over my shoulder. "Want some?"

He laughed and shook his head and took a step back. And
then I realized something sort of funny, sort of strange. He
was…uncomfortable?

I was used to finding half-naked men in Patrick's kitchen
the morning after a party. True, I'd never watched any of them
come down someone else's throat, and then used that thought
to give myself an orgasm, but he didn't know about that.

"I'm Alex. Patrick let me crash here last night."

"I'm Olivia," I offered, and waited for a reaction. Not even
a blink.

"It's nice to meet you, Olivia."

He cleared his throat and shifted from foot to foot. His bare
toes were as lovely as the rest of him. For the first time I
noticed his pajama bottoms, printed with Hello Kitty faces,
a faded pair that looked well loved and often worn. They
covered more of him than my thigh-length T-shirt did of me,
and I wished for a robe or at least a sweater, though I was no
longer the least bit cold.

I gave them a look. "Nice."

Alex laughed, staring down at his toes. The glance he gave
me was amused, a little embarrassed, but not much. "Thanks.
They were a gift."

The microwave dinged and I removed the container, holding it out. "You sure you don't want any?"

He shook his head, even though his tongue crept out to dot his bottom lip. "I think I'd better go with oatmeal."

I pulled a fork from the drawer and poked it into a dumpling. "Please don't tell me you're going to make me feel guilty because I'm not up this early to run a mile and a half."

His laugh sounded more genuine this time. "Hell, no. I'm not going for a run. Not in this weather, anyway. Or, well…not ever."

I swallowed a bite of delicious. "Thank God."

I went to the fridge again for some orange juice. Teddy squeezes it fresh and never leaves the pitcher empty. I pulled it out and offered some. Alex nodded. I grabbed a couple of glasses and set them on the table, then poured. His expression prompted me to check if I had something in my teeth or hanging from my nose.

"What?"

"Nothing," he said. "It's just…"

I sat at the kitchen table and waved him to a seat, too. He pulled the glass of juice toward himself and sipped. I waited.

"Just what?" I said, when it seemed he'd stalled.

"Patrick didn't mention he had another person staying here. That's all."

"Ah." I dug into another pot sticker, which shouldn't have been so tasty washed down with orange juice, but was. "He didn't tell me you were staying here, either. In fact, he said…"

Both of us seemed to have come down with a case of bite-your-tongue-itis.

Alex quirked a brow and sat back in his chair. The kitchen was warm, but he was shirtless, and goose bumps dappled his skin. An image of myself leaning across the table to lick his nipples sent a flash of heat through me that didn't come from the furnace chugging to life beneath our feet.

"What? Tell me." The man I'd seen last night at the party, the one in my room, was back. His voice melted, gooey caramel on soft ice cream. I wanted to lick it.

"He said," I told him, carefully not looking at him but at my food, "to stay away from you."

"Did he?"

I knew my laugh sounded forced, but he didn't know me. "Yes."

"Why?"

I licked soy sauce from a finger and caught him looking, his eyes narrowed but not angry. Interested, maybe. Intrigued. "Because Patrick likes to make sure I don't get into trouble."

Alex snorted lightly and drank more juice. "He thinks I'm trouble?"

"Aren't you?" It sounded like flirting. It felt like flirting, but I knew better than to flirt with a man who was into guys. I'd learned my lesson on that a long time ago.

"I guess that depends," he said. Then, "Yeah. I am."

We both laughed at that, somehow companionable in our assessment of his character via the conduit of Patrick's warning. "I thought so. You look like trouble."

Alex's fine brown hair had been carefully groomed last night to look like a mess, but now it fell in genuine disarray over his forehead and into his eyes. When he bent to stare at the table, tapping his fingers on it, his hair obscured his face. I wanted to brush it off his forehead.

"Emo bangs," I said.

He looked up at me then and pushed the hair out of his eyes. "Huh?"

I gestured. "Your hair. Those long bangs, like one of those emo kids who wear skinny jeans and black fingernail polish."

He laughed again, for real this time, and long. "I guess that's a sign if nothing else is, huh? Time for a cut?"

"I don't think so. I like it." I speared the last pot sticker and held it up to him. "Sure you don't want it?"

"What the hell." He plucked it from the fork and ate it from his fingers.

I watched his lips close over his fingertips and suck away the soy sauce. Warmth swirled inside me, which was stupid, but hey, a girl can look even if she can't touch. We both finished our orange juice at the same time.

Then we sat in silence. Alex might be trouble, but he sure wasn't chatty. Not that I got a snobby vibe off him or anything, as if he just didn't want to talk to me. More like he wasn't sure what to say.

"How do you know Patrick?" It was ask or leave the kitchen for the chilly wilds of upstairs, where I'd have to dress and go into the colder outdoors to head home. Besides, I wanted to know.

"We met in Japan."

"You work for Quinto and Bates?" That was the law firm where Patrick worked.

He shook his head. "No, I was brought in as a consult with Damsmithon Industries while Patrick was there for the international business meeting."

"So you're not a lawyer." I swirled a finger in the remains of the pot sticker juice in the bottom of the container. I wasn't hungry anymore, but couldn't resist the savory tang.

He laughed. "Hell, no. But Patrick and I hit it off, hung out after the meetings. Kept in touch. When I told him I was coming back to the States he said I should stop by to see him."

All of this didn't sound like it should go along with the image of Patrick's face and his warning to me about Alex being trouble. "So...you're friends?"

"What exactly did Patrick say about me?" Alex's bangs fell down again, and he didn't brush them away.

I paused for a second before answering. "Not much, actually."

Which wasn't like Patrick at all. He usually had something to say about everybody, and if he didn't have anything, sometimes he made stuff up. I pondered this while Alex got up and went to the fridge. Patrick had warned me away from Alex, but hadn't given me details. No gossip. Strange.

Alex brought back the pitcher of juice and a tinfoil-covered plate of cookies that had escaped my notice. He offered them to me first, and don't think I didn't notice that he had manners. I didn't pretend to myself or him that I shouldn't eat any cookies. It was too late for that. Come January I'd be moaning about the size of my ass, but so would everyone else I knew, whether it was warranted or not.

I picked up a gingerbread man with a huge erect cock. "Hmm. Normally I bite the heads off first, but..."

Alex snorted and picked up one for himself. "Now there's a dilemma."

We were still laughing when Patrick came down the back stairs. He wore a silk kimono and a bleary expression. His blond hair stuck up in corkscrews all over the place. He gave us both an imperious look from his spot on the last step.

"We can hear you all the way upstairs."

"Sorry." Alex sounded contrite.

I didn't bother. "Oh, Patrick. C'mon. It's, like, noon already. Get your lazy ass up and about."

Patrick yawned broadly and swept past me, then turned to give me a real glare. "You didn't even make coffee?"

"Your fucking machine is too complicated," I told him fondly, though of course he knew that, and of course he was still miffed that I hadn't started it brewing for him.

"I'll do it," Alex said, and was up and around the table before either Patrick or I could do more than blink at each other in surprise. "I should've thought of it, man. I'm sorry."

I raised a brow at this sudden leap to obsequiousness, but hell. I didn't know the guy beyond what? A warning, a karaoke serenade and a drunken blow job in a dark room. He hadn't quite seemed the servile type to me, but then I was forever being surprised by what I didn't expect.

"Thank you," Patrick said a little stiffly. "Alex, this is Olivia Mackey. Olivia, Alex Kennedy. Olivia is an independent contractor with her own graphic design company, and Alex does consulting for several international corporations."

Coffeepot carafe filled with water in his hand, Alex turned while Patrick made the cocktail party introductions. He and I shared a look past Patrick's kimono. I gave Alex a tiny shrug. I didn't get it, either.

"We met," I told Patrick. "What is up with you?"

"I'm just being a good host."

"Thanks, Patrick," Alex said, and set about making the coffee.

He figured out his way around Patrick's kitchen, faltering only once, when he opened the wrong cupboard to pull out the coffee pods, and found the spice jars, instead. I turned in my chair to watch him. He was no casual houseguest. He knew how to make himself at home.

Patrick and I could hold entire conversations without words, but this morning he was deliberately not giving me the right signals. Or he was misreading mine. He could be selective that way. Before I could get him to tell me what the hell was going on, Alex turned from the coffeemaker.

"Anyone hungry for pancakes?"

"I couldn't," I exclaimed.

Just as Patrick said, "Alex, you're a darling."

Patrick looked at Alex. Alex looked at me. I looked at Patrick.

"Actually," I said, "I should get going. I've got some work to do—"

"On Sunday?" Patrick asked incredulously. "What's the point of working for yourself if you can't take the weekend off?"

I stood and stretched. "The point of working for myself is that I can work whenever I want."

"Yeah, and work whenever you have to." Alex leaned against the counter, one long leg crossed over the other at the ankles.

I nodded. He understood. Patrick, who worked eighty-hour weeks but also took a month's vacation every year, understood the importance of hard work, but would probably never comprehend why I'd quit a stable salary to go out on my own.

I hugged my former boyfriend and kissed his cheek. Patrick softened, finally, his embrace unwilling but inevitable. He held my face still and looked into my eyes.

"Don't work too much, Livvy. It's the holidays."

I put my hands over his on my cheeks and carefully peeled away his fingers to release his grip. "You want me to take back all the presents I bought you?"

He laughed the first real Patrick laugh I'd heard in a few days, and squeezed me close. He whispered in my ear, "Remember what I said."

Most of the time when Patrick hugged me I could take it for what it was—a physical expression of the affection and love between two friends. Platonic friends. And then there were the times when I breathed in the scent of him, the cologne I bought for him so many years ago and which he'd never switched from, even though he could afford something trendier and more expensive. When I felt the press of his body along mine and I had to close my eyes and remind myself to let him go, and when I found it almost impossible to do so.

Still locked in Patrick's arms, I forced myself to open my eyes. Alex's gaze found mine over Patrick's shoulder. With that scrutiny as motivation, I patted Patrick's back quickly and stepped away, hoping my nipples weren't hard through my T-shirt or that my cheeks weren't as flushed as they felt.

Patrick caught my wrist before I could get entirely away. "Stay for a while. It's Sunday."

"Patrick…"

He didn't let go. "Alex, tell Liv she should stay."

"Olivia. You should stay." Alex, still leaning, smiled.

I smiled, too, even as I turned and gave Patrick a good, hard poke. "I have a life, Patrick."

He scoffed. "What are you going to do today? Hang around that cold apartment and fiddle with your pictures? She's a photographer," he added for Alex's benefit, and jabbed at my ribs.

"Cool. What do you take pictures of?"

"Everything!" I said over my shoulder as I tried to dance out of the way of Patrick's poking fingers.

I looked at him, hard. Last night he'd warned me off Alex as though my mortal soul depended on it, and now he was begging me to hang around for the day. Of course, he often persuaded me to stay longer than I'd intended, and often I let him. But I did have work to do in my studio, which wouldn't paint or clean itself, and which had been sadly neglected since I'd bought it six months before.

"Patrick…"

Knowing he was manipulating me didn't make it any easier to resist him. When he flashed me the familiar pout, the one that had always swayed me, I sighed. I glanced at Alex, who was watching us both with an expression I could only describe as intrigued.

"Alex is making pancakes," Patrick said.

I looked at Patrick. Patrick looked at Alex. And Alex… Alex looked at me.

"I am," he said. "And I'm really good at it."

I knew enough to admit defeat.

"Fine, but I'm taking the first shower, and I don't care if you run out of hot water," I told Patrick, who smirked how he always did when he got his way.

Upstairs I bumped into Teddy coming out of his bedroom.

"You're staying?"

Another man might have hated the fact I was still so much a part of Patrick's life, but not Teddy. But then I'd never seen him hate anything. Teddy fully believed in that crap about lemons and life.

"Yeah. Just for a little while. I do have to get home tonight."

He laughed. "You should move back up here, Liv. It wouldn't be such a long drive then."

I rolled my eyes. "You're as bad as he is. Annville's only half an hour away, for crying out loud."

Teddy had spent his entire life in Central Pennsylvania, a place where crossing the Susquehanna River could be considered entering a whole new world. He grinned. "But it's Annville."

"Pfft." I waved a hand. "I'm taking a shower. I hear there are pancakes in the making."

Teddy rubbed his stomach. "Yum. Our guest, I assume, not our beloved Patrick."

Patrick never cooked. "Yeah. Hey, Teddy…" I paused and leaned against the doorjamb to my room. "What's the story with him, anyway?"

"Alex?"

"Yeah."

Teddy shrugged and his smile became a tiny bit strained. "He's a friend of Patrick's. He needed a place to crash. He's only going to be here for a few more days. Nice guy."

That answer floated between us, a bit of fluff on a current of not-going-to-bring-up-certain-topics. The topic in question being why Patrick felt he had any right or interest in my love life, or lack thereof. I shrugged, finally, because sometimes you simply have to put aside things that have no answer.

"Taking a shower," I said, and Teddy left me so I could.

Forty-five minutes later, my stomach full of pancakes and turkey bacon and good, strong coffee, I was attempting to kick Alex's ass at *Dance Dance Revolution* and failing pretty miserably.

I had Teddy beat, and was pretty well matched with Patrick, but Alex…he was a superstar.

"My feet keep slipping on the dance pad," I complained, out of breath.

"I'll set myself to advanced," Alex offered with a wicked gleam in his eye. He was practically rubbing his hands together and twirling an imaginary mustache. "You can stay at basic."

I wasn't going to turn down that offer. "You're on."

"I knew I shouldn't have let you start playing," Patrick said from his place on the couch, where he was reading a thick paperback novel.

At the sound of affectionate amusement in his tone, I looked at him while Alex used the Wii remote to switch the settings. Patrick, bundled under a heavy quilt, had gone back to his book. Teddy'd disappeared, probably to play *The Sims* on his computer upstairs. And Alex and I were playing *DDR*. It was a picture of lazy Sunday bliss, so why did suddenly it all feel so…wrong?

"Olivia?"

I turned at Alex's question and flashed him a smile I couldn't be sure looked real. "Yeah. I'm ready."

He tilted his head the tiniest bit. "You want to take a break?"

Patrick must have heard concern in Alex's tone, because he looked up again. "What's the matter?"

"Nothing." I waved a hand. "Too many pancakes. Let's go."

Alex had changed out of his Hello Kitty pajamas and into a pair of faded jeans and a long-sleeved T-shirt, but his feet were still bare. He tapped one against the dance pad, but didn't start the next song. He looked from me to Patrick.

"Okay. If you're sure."

"Sure. Let's go."

But there was no way I could beat him, even with the different levels set to make it more to my advantage. I was distracted by the sudden, unexpected wave of nostalgia and something else, something I couldn't parse. My performance was sucktastic.

"I think you're letting me win," Alex said.

Patrick scoffed from the couch. "Olivia never lets anyone win. Take your victory and savor it."

I gave Patrick a narrow-eyed glance. His teasing had a ring of truth to it that sat wrong with me. "I should get going."

This got Patrick's attention, and he looked up. "Now? I thought you'd stay for dinner, at least. Alex says he's going to cook lamb chops."

Alex laughed. "Dude."

I looked at him. "Now you know the real reason he's letting you stay."

My teasing, too, had a ring of truth to it, but Patrick didn't seem to care.

"It's okay. I like to cook."

In the background, the music of the game blared on and on, though I couldn't blame my inching headache on that. I looked at Patrick again, settled so neatly on his couch with his book, and his friends around him, catering to him. Giving him whatever he wanted. Patrick annoyed me sometimes, the way anyone can on occasion. I hadn't hated him in a long time, but I remembered, suddenly, how it felt to hate him.

"I'm sure they'll be delicious, Alex, but I can't stay. It was nice meeting you." I reached for his hand, and he took mine. Shook it firmly and let it drop.

He put his palms on his hips. "Maybe I'll see you again."

"Well, if you ever come back to visit Patrick, I'm sure you will." I was already turning to go.

"I'm staying in the area, actually. I got another consulting job. Just short-term."

I paused. Patrick looked up. He put down his book.

"You didn't tell me that."

"My contact with Hershey Foods just got back to me," Alex said. "I'll be here for about six months. Maybe eight, depending."

This caught Patrick's attention and he sat straight up. "Where are you staying?"

"Not here, don't worry." Alex laughed. "I've got a room booked at the Hotel Hershey for a week, but I'm looking for a place to rent for the rest of the time."

The sound of heels echoing on the wooden floors of my too-empty extra apartment rang in my ears, along with the *ka-ching* of a cash register. "I have a place you might be interested in."

Both men gazed at me then. Patrick's brows had raised. Alex looked assessing.

"I bought a building," I explained. "An old firehouse. I live on the second floor, but the ground-floor apartment is vacant and partially furnished."

"You told me you didn't want to deal with the hassle of having a tenant." Patrick's tone, faintly accusatory, put a small curl in my lip.

Alex, on the other hand, let his gaze drift back and forth between the two of us before his mouth tipped up a fraction at the corners. "Where's your place, Olivia?"

"Annville."

I said it just as Patrick said, "The middle of nowhere."

"Annville," I repeated, "is about twenty minutes from Hershey. Same distance as from here."

"Sounds great. When can I see it?"

"How about right now?"

Alex smiled. "Perfect."

Chapter 03

Alex drove a crappier car than I expected. I hadn't noticed the baby-shit-brown sedan parked along the street in front of Patrick's house the night before. It probably looked much better in the dark.

"Rental," he explained when I stared at it.

I'd parked my own car with the pride of privilege in Patrick and Teddy's narrow driveway in front of the garage. "Mine's around back. I'll pull out and wait for you so you can follow. Oh, and let me get your cell number in case we get separated."

He had a crappy car but a very, very nice and shiny new iPhone, the latest model. "Yeah, I'd better take yours, too."

There was nothing strange about this exchange. Hell, random strangers gave each other their numbers all the time. Texting had replaced normal face-to-face conversations. Pretty soon we'd all just implant chips in our heads and never leave our houses. Even so, tapping his long and unfamiliar number into my phone felt somehow intimate and strangely permanent.

"Now you," Alex said, and held up the phone's camera. "Smile."

"Oh, you're not—"

Too late; he'd taken the shot, and held it up to show me how I had a place now in his list of contacts. I was smiling, my head half turned, and the light was better than I'd thought, the picture clear and crisp. I'd be in his phone forever, or until he deleted me.

Alex unlocked his car with the keyless remote. He'd put on a black wool peacoat with an upturned collar and a long, striped scarf. With his tousled hair and long bangs he could've been a catalog model, and I mentally snapped a few shots of him looking into a sunset, maybe standing next to a golden retriever, advertising something sexy like cologne or designer sunglasses. Not that I ever got those sorts of jobs, but someday I might.

He caught me looking and smiled as if he was used to being stared at. "Ready?"

"Yep. Follow me."

He put a hand over his heart and gave a half bow. "Wherever you may go."

My mouth opened, flippant words ready to spill out, but somehow they got tangled up on my tongue and all I managed was a smile. It had been quite a while since any man had left me speechless with something as simple as a grin and a few words. No wonder Patrick had warned me off. Alex Kennedy *was* trouble, unfortunately of the best kind.

And he didn't like girls, I reminded myself. "I'll be in the silver Impala."

I kept my eye on him in the rearview mirror the entire trip, but Alex had no trouble navigating the sparse traffic and keeping up with me. We pulled into the alley next to the three-story building that had once been the firehouse on Annville's Main Street, and parked in the lot behind it. He got out before I did, and tipped his head back to look up at the building.

"Sweet."

I felt a rush of pride as we both took a minute to look at the building's brick backside. The iron fire escape wasn't pretty, but even so, the building was impressive. And I owned it. The whole thing, just me.

"So, this is Annville," Alex said.

A car crept slowly along the alley and kicked up a stray grocery bag I snagged to toss in the trash. While living in Harrisburg I wouldn't have bothered, but since moving to the small town I'd taken more pride. "Yep. In all its glory."

Alex, hands in his pockets, turned around in a circle to give everything another once-over. "Nice."

I laughed as I turned the key in the back door's lock. "It will be quite a change from your international globe-trotting."

"That's okay. I grew up in a small town. Not as small as this," he amended, stepping through after me and stomping his feet on the mat. "But believe me, I wasn't raised a world traveler."

The long, narrow hall led to a three-story foyer with the wide, wooden spiraling staircase to our right and the door to the ground-floor apartment to the left. Directly ahead, a front door opened onto the sidewalk along Main Street, and tall windows let in a lot of light. Alex looked up, smiling, and let out a whistle.

I looked over my shoulder at him as I opened the door to the flat. "Come inside."

It wasn't anything special—a living room, dining area and kitchen, with a bathroom and two bedrooms that had been carved from what had once been the garage housing the fire trucks. It was darker than my place, not having the big second- and third-floor windows, but it did have immense, broad beams in the ceiling, and a nice, open layout.

"What do you think?"

Alex walked around, checking out the wooden floors, the plastered walls. He tested the spring-cushioned love seat left behind by the previous tenants, and peeked into the kitchen while I watched. He looked into one bedroom, then the other, and finally the bath. The whole tour took about seven minutes. He turned to me with a broad grin.

"I'll take it."

"Really? That fast, huh?"

"Sure. It beats sleeping on someone's couch," he said. "I like it."

"You don't even know the price," I pointed out, though I hadn't planned on charging much since the place did need some work and something was better than the nothing I'd had from it before.

"Name it."

I thought. "Four hundred a month?"

"Sold."

"Should I have asked for more?"

Alex looked around. "Probably. That couch adds a lot of value. The smell, especially."

"It doesn't smell!" I cried, horrified. "Does it smell?"

He laughed. "I'm kidding you, Olivia. It's fine. So…you want first and last month's rent? A security deposit? Got paperwork to sign?"

I hadn't thought that far ahead. "Umm…"

Alex came forward, hand out. I thought he meant to shake, but when he took mine, he didn't let go. He pumped my hand slowly, smiling. "Maybe we should just spit on our palms."

"Wow. No. How about we skip that part. First and last month's rent is fine, if you have it."

"I have it." Alex squeezed my hand and let go, then looked around again. "When can I move in?"

"Whenever you want."

"Sweet." He turned to me. "Next week? It'll take some time for me to get some things shipped here. Buy a bed. That sort of thing."

"That's fine. I'll get you a copy of the keys."

Alex studied me. "You sure you don't need references or anything like that?"

"Why? Because you're trouble?"

Alex laughed. "Right. That's me."

"I can handle you," I said.

"I'm sure you can." Alex's stomach rumbled suddenly and loudly. After the pancake orgy earlier I'd have thought I wouldn't eat until the next day, but of course my own stomach had to answer his. "Let me take you to dinner."

"It's only three o'clock."

"Late lunch, then." He grinned. "Where do you want to go?"

"Alex…I really need to get some work done."

"Olivia," he wheedled, a man totally used to getting his

own way. "I heard your stomach rumbling. You can't deny you're hungry."

I'd known him for less than forty-eight hours and already I'd seen how he looked when he came, tasted his cooking, had my ass handed to me playing *Dance Dance Revolution,* and now I was going to practically be living with him.

I let Alex take me to dinner, too.

It was hard to eat while laughing, and he wasn't giving me much chance to do anything else. Alex had stories, and if I could tell that many of them were exaggerated for effect, it was also easy to believe them. He'd been all over, done so much, that I felt like a real country mouse beside him.

"What is your story, really?" I said over slices of cheesecake and mugs of espresso. "How'd you make it here from Japan?"

"I came from Holland, actually. Before that I was in Singapore. Went to Scotland, too."

I made a face. "Smart-ass. You didn't come to Central PA just to visit Patrick?"

"Well…" Alex shrugged. "He invited me, for one thing, and it was on my way back home. Plus I had a lead on this consulting gig. It all worked out."

"Where's home?"

"I'm from Ohio. Sandusky."

"Cedar Point!" I said. "I've been there."

"Yeah. That's the place." Alex drank some espresso and leaned back in the booth. He still wore the long scarf, though his peacoat was scrunched in a pile by his side. "I thought I'd get back there for the holidays, but it looks like I'll be staying here instead."

"How come?"

This time Alex did more than glance at me. He gave me the full weight of his gaze. "I haven't been back in a long time. Sometimes, the longer you stay away from something the harder it is to go back there."

I knew that already. "Yeah. I guess you're right. So…you don't get along with your family?"

A pause, a breath. He raised a brow.

"Too personal?" I asked.

"No. Just not sure how to answer."

"You don't have to," I said.

He shook his head. "No, it's okay. Have you heard the expression 'home is the place where they have to take you in'? Or whatever it is?"

"Of course." I licked the tines of my fork and then dragged it through the chocolate syrup on my plate.

"Well, let's just say I'm more of a 'you can never go home again' type of guy."

"Wow. That's too bad."

"Yeah. I guess so. I used to not get along with my family at all. My dad was…" Alex hesitated again, then kept going before I could tell him once more he didn't have to speak. "He's an asshole. I was going to say he *was* an asshole, but I guess he still is. He doesn't drink anymore, but he's kind of an ass, anyway. I think that's just who he is."

I sipped at the last of my coffee. "But?"

"But he's trying. I guess. Not that I think my dad and I are ever going to go on that big father-son fishing trip or anything," he added.

"You never know."

"I know," Alex said pointedly. "But at least he talks to me

when I call home. And he cashes the checks I send. Well, hell, he always did that."

Alex laughed. I laughed a second later, thinking I should feel a little awkward about this sharing but...not.

"People change," I said.

"Everything changes." Alex shrugged and looked away. "Shit happens. Anyway, I'd been working overseas for a long time. Sold my company a few years ago and wasn't doing a whole lot. I went back home for the summer and...fuck."

A harsh word, a little out of place for the circumstances. It put me on the edge of my seat. It sounded good, coming from him, as if he said it a lot. He must've been keeping himself in line until now. I liked thinking he might be letting go.

"Let's just say I remembered all the reasons I'd left home in the first place." He flicked his bangs from his face with a practiced jerk. "Anyway, I got some offers to do some consulting, got a start with a new company. Traveled for a while, went back overseas. Worked for a while in Japan. That's where I met Patrick. But the job ended and I had to go somewhere. Thought I'd travel around my homeland instead of being a stranger in a strange land."

"I love that book."

He looked at me. "Me, too."

"So, what, you're not working at all? Just going wherever you want, whenever?"

"Sleeping on a series of couches." Alex paused to bite some cheesecake. "I'm sort of a professional houseguest."

"That sounds..." I laughed.

He laughed, too. "Shitty?"

"Sort of."

He shrugged. "I'm good at making a pain of myself by abusing hospitality."

"I don't see that about you at all." I thought of how he'd moved around Patrick's kitchen, making himself at home, but not overstepping. "Besides, people wouldn't invite you to stay if they didn't like you."

Alex dragged his fork through the cheesecake and kept his gaze there. "Sure. I guess so. But now I don't have to worry about it anymore, right?"

Warmth eased over my cheeks at that, and I couldn't keep my smile tucked away. "I guess not. I've got your first and last in my pocket, and it's pretty much already spent."

"I guess you're not treating for dinner, then." He reached to jab his fork through the last bite of my cheesecake, and while I might've stabbed out the eyes of anyone else who dared do such a thing, I could only laugh at him.

"No way. You invited me."

I don't think it's possible to know someone in just a couple days, a few hours. I didn't believe I knew him then, no matter what I'd seen or said. But at that moment, I believed I could know him. More than that, I believed I wanted to.

"That's right, I did. The person who asks should always pay for the date."

He looked up at me with those dark eyes, that soft, smirking mouth, and I once again found myself without words and wondering how he managed to strike me so stupid with nothing but a glance.

"C'mon," Alex said as he got up from the table. "Let's get out of here."

And I followed.

★ ★ ★

The first clue I had that Alex had actually moved in was the different car in my parking lot. It wasn't a new car, but whoa. Bright yellow Camaro with black accents? Not at all what I'd have picked for my new downstairs neighbor. It looked to be from the mid-to-late eighties, the only reason I could guess that close being that my brother, Bert, was something of a muscle car buff and would often wax poetic about a certain type.

I pulled in beside it and stepped out to look it over. The car itself was in fine but not pristine condition, the interior a little more worn. This wasn't even a showpiece car. This was a butch, wheels a-rollin', smoke-out-at-a-traffic-light sort of car.

I liked it.

It had been only a few days since we'd sealed the deal without the spit on our palms, and I'd put the cash Alex had paid me with to good use—toward groceries and some bills, and added a new photo printer I didn't need but really wanted. I hadn't seen him since Sunday, though he'd left a message on my voice mail telling me he'd be moving in sometime this week. Judging by the car and the boxes stacked up in the front entry, he'd made a good start.

His door opened as my foot hit the first stair, and I turned, setting the heavy printer box on the railing to rest my arms. "Hi."

"Olivia." Warm and gooey caramel, smooth and yummy, that was his voice. "Hey, can I give you a hand?"

I'd have said no but for the fact I'd been stupid and tried to carry not only my three bags of groceries but also the printer, and my arms were already shaking. "Yeah, that would be great. Can you grab—"

He'd already lifted the heavy box from my hands. "I got it. You go on ahead."

I shifted the plastic bags in my two fists and led the way up the stairs to my own door, unlocked it and pushed it open. "Thanks. You can put the box over there on the dresser at the foot of the steps."

I pointed to one of the dozen dressers I'd collected from thrift shops and used furniture stores. Patrick called it a fetish. I called it a practical use of space and an appreciation for re-cycling. The one I meant was long and low, about thigh-height on me. I'd covered it with a collage of articles and photos cut from the stash of photography magazines I no longer subscribed to. It fit just right against the wall under the metal spiral stairs leading up to the loft, and because of this was covered with all the junk I meant to take up there and consistently forgot.

Alex set the box next to a collection of hardback novels I'd picked up at a library sale and hadn't had time yet to crack open. "Big Jackie Collins fan, huh?"

I laughed. "Hey. Some books are bad because they're bad. Some books are good because they're bad."

He looked over his shoulder at me. "People, too."

Before I could answer that he'd stepped back to look up through the spiral stairs, his hands on his hips. "What's up there?"

"Just the loft."

"Can I see it?"

"Sure." I followed him up the winding stairs.

At the top, Alex let out a low, impressed whistle. "Sweet."

Downstairs, the large open space and elevated ceilings dwarfed my few pieces of furniture. But I'd made this space up here comfy and cozy with a jumble of thrift store and salvage pieces—a curving sectional that had come from a hotel lobby, a low coffee table and dozens of cushions. The floor-to-ceiling windows that let in so much light below were bisected a few inches from the ceiling by the loft's floor, and I'd hung sheer colored scarves and strings of beads in front of them. A cheap paper lantern from IKEA dangled in a corner.

"I read up here." It wasn't really big enough to do much else.

Alex ducked reflexively as he stepped to the loft's center. He wasn't in danger of bumping his head, but the ceiling was so low up here it felt possible. Grinning over his shoulder at me, he sank onto the sectional and bounced a little, then put his hands behind his head and his feet on the table.

"Awesome." He looked at the pile of books stacked on the floor next to the sofa. "More Jackie?"

"Probably." I tilted my head sideways to check out the titles. Lots of science fiction, some romance, a couple of mysteries. "I think there's a little bit of everything there."

Alex lifted the book from the top of the pile. "Robert R. McCammon?"

"*Swan Song.* Have you read it?"

He shook his head. "No. Should I?"

"It's scary," I told him. "You can borrow it, if you want."

Grinning, he tucked the book into his fist and stood. "Thanks."

Alex was tall but not big, not broad, more lean than anything. Yet he took up an awful lot of space. He stretched up one arm and placed his hand flat on the ceiling, and the lines of his body shifted. A hip went down, a knee bent. Once again I pictured him in a catalog. He had a face that could convince people they wanted stuff they couldn't afford and didn't need.

"Well, I'd better get back," he said after a spare few seconds.

"Lots of unpacking?" I asked over my shoulder as he followed me down the stairs.

"Umm…no." He laughed. "I don't have a lot of stuff."

"But you got a new ride. I saw it out back."

Alex laughed again. "Yeah. Fucking Bumblebee. What can I say? I got my first hard-on for the Transformers."

"Better that than Rainbow Brite, I guess. Or the Smurfs."

We laughed together and he looked around my apartment again. The layout of my place was a little different than his, with more open space and higher ceilings, plus the loft. It was brighter, too.

"Nice place."

"Thanks. I can't take much credit for it. I bought it already made into apartments. Hey, would you like some hot tea? I just got some chai."

"That would be great."

I left him to make himself at home while I heated the water and put away my groceries. I had no doubt he would, and though I was more one to guard my privacy, that was surprisingly okay with me. By the time I came out of the kitchen with two mugs of steaming chai, he'd made the tour around my apartment.

"You took all these?" Alex reached for the mug without looking at me, his gaze fixed on the photos I'd hung in stark glass frames without mats.

"Yes."

We studied them together. I warmed my hands on my

mug. He sipped. He said nothing for so many minutes I began to feel nervous, as though I wanted to speak. Had to speak. I bit my tongue, determined not to ask him what he thought.

"This one." He pointed to a shot of me and Patrick at the far end. "You didn't take this one."

"Oh. No." I'd hung it there because it was a favorite, a candid shot of us in happy times. Our hands were linked, my head on his shoulder. We looked like a normal couple.

Alex sipped more chai.

"I should take it down, I guess." I made no move to do so.

He looked at me then. "Why?"

"Well…because…it's a lie." It wasn't what I'd expected to say, but once the words came out they felt right. "That picture isn't real. It was never real."

Alex handed me his mug and I took it automatically. When he lifted the frame off its hook I made an unexpected noise of protest. He gave me a look and took the single step up onto the level where my dining table was. He put the photo facedown on it.

"Now, it's down." He reached for his mug and I handed it to him. "Feel any better?"

"No." But I laughed a little. "Thanks."

"Hey, do you have any plans for tonight? I know it's Friday. You probably have something going on."

I had to work the early shift at Foto Folks the next morning. "Actually, I don't."

"I rented some movies. And, like a d-bag, didn't remember I don't have a TV yet."

"Ah. So you're going to use me for mine, is that it?"

"I'd be ashamed to say yes, but it's the truth."

I sipped from my mug as I pretended to think about it. "What did you rent?"

"The new Transformers movie. And *Harold and Maude.*"

"Yeah, wow, because those two are so similar," I told him with a laugh. "But I haven't seen the Transformers and it's been years since I watched *Harold and Maude.* Sure. I'll let you use my TV."

"I'll buy the pizza, how's that?"

"Sounds like a plan."

We made arrangements to meet later, and Alex showed up at six o'clock with a large pizza from the place down the street in one hand, a bunch of DVDs in the other. I hadn't done more than change my clothes into Friday-night-stay-at-home sweatpants and a T-shirt, but he'd showered and shaved, and wafted through my door on a delicious cloud of garlic and cologne. I wondered if I should've made more of an effort.

"Dinner by candlelight?" he asked as he set the pizza on my dining table.

"Oh…no. They're not for ambience." Lighting candles was something I did on Friday nights when I wasn't out and about, a habit left over from my childhood, when my mom had made a point of lighting candles even if she'd done very little else to usher in the Sabbath. Big change from now, when her life revolved around it.

He gave me a quizzical look. "Are you Jewish?"

I shouldn't have been surprised he guessed—a world traveler would probably have encountered some Jews somewhere along the way. "Not really. Sort of."

"Oookay."

I laughed, self-conscious. "It's complicated."

"Fair enough. It's not any of my business." He glanced at the candles. "They're pretty, though."

"Thanks." My mother had given me the candlesticks. I don't think she knew I used them. At least I'd never told her. "What can I get you to drink?"

Moving right along. Alex got the hint. "Water's good."

"You sure? I have some red wine. In a bottle even, not from a box."

He made an impressed face. "Fancy. But no, thanks."

"Do you mind if I have some?"

My question seemed to surprise him. "No, of course not. It's your house."

He'd been gracious enough not to push me on the religion issue; I gave him the same treatment about the drinking. We piled slices of pizza on our plates and ate in front of the television while the Transformers blew up a lot of stuff and Harold fell in love with Maude. We laughed a lot and talked over the movies. We sat at opposite ends of the couch, but our feet met in the middle, nudging every so often.

It was the nicest night I'd had in a long time, and I told him so.

"Get out of here." Alex flipped a hand at me.

"I'm serious!"

"Well. Good. I'm glad."

A few glasses of red wine had left me mellow and languid. "It's nice, just hanging out with you, Alex. No pressure. None of that stupid back and forth stuff."

He was silent for a few seconds as the credits rolled. "Thanks. It's nice hanging out with you, too."

I yawned under cover of my hand. "But it's late, and I have to get up early tomorrow."

"Work?"

"Yeah. Think of me while you're still snuggled down under the blankets in the morning."

He laughed and got up, held out a hand to help me up, too. "Oh. I'm sure I will."

Our fingers had linked, but now he let me go. I watched as he popped open the DVD player to take out the disc, and slipped it into the paper rental sleeve. He caught me looking as he turned.

"We should do this again," I said. "It was fun."

I wasn't drunk, but I was tired and more than a bit fuzzy. I couldn't quite read his smile or the expression in his eyes— something was there that looked like amusement. Something beneath that, too deep to decipher.

"Yeah. I'd like that. Good night, Olivia." Alex didn't move toward the door.

This was the point of the night where, with another man, I'd have been tipping my face up for a kiss. Hell, this was the part of the night where I'd already have decided if he was going to spend the night or be kicked out. Instead, we both laughed at the same time. Alex stepped away. Whatever tension I'd imagined—and it had to be imagined—faded.

"Good night, Olivia. See you."

"Night," I called after him as he let himself out the door. "Catch you later."

The door clicked shut behind him. I gathered the trash and put the leftover pizza in the fridge, then padded into my bathroom for a hot shower so I wouldn't have to wake up so early the next morning. Usually the steam and water relax me enough so that I'm boneless by the time I come out, ready immediately for sleep, but not this night.

My soap-slick hands slid over my skin. Nipples tight. An ache between my legs. I wasn't making myself come with Alex's face in mind, his long, lean body…the sound of his moan. I wasn't sliding my hands over my breasts and thighs and belly pretending they belonged to him. I was absolutely not lying in darkness on my bed with my legs spread, a finger in my cunt and another on my clit, working my body into ecstasy while I pretended it was him.

All right, so I was. It was impossible not to. He was beautiful and sexy and the closest I'd had to a date in months. That was by choice, since plenty of men asked me out but very few impressed me. And he wasn't into women. I'd seen evidence of that with my own eyes, even if Patrick hadn't warned me off him.

Yet my body gave it up for him, my mind swirling with thoughts of how wrong it was. How stupid and useless. My mind knew better, but my pussy didn't care. I slid fingers deep inside my hot, slick flesh and felt the clamp and grip of my internal muscles as I spasmed. My clit throbbed, pressure building while I tapped a fingertip in a slow beating rhythm on top. Teasing. Holding off.

Until at last I thought once more of his voice, my memory conveniently merging the sound of his groan with my name, and the way he said "fuck me." In my head it had become a command, not an exclamation of surprise. And as I surged up and over and down into the spiral of heat and pleasure, I wished he would say it to me for real.

Chapter 04

"I haven't seen you in forever." Patrick frowned. "You never return my calls and I sent you about four dozen pings at Connex and you ignored me there, too."

I fiddled with my camera settings and took a few shots of nothing just to test them. "I've been busy with work. I haven't even logged in to Connex lately. What sorts of pings?"

"I invited you to our New Year's party. Teddy thinks I'm crazy for having another party so soon after the last one. But what can I say? I like parties. Besides, I don't want to go out anyplace around here for New Year's Eve and nobody invited us anywhere." Patrick shrugged. "You'll come."

"What if I have plans? Turn to the left a little. Hold up the cup. Look like, c'mon, Patrick, look like you're enjoying it." I peered through my lens to frame the shot I was supposed to use in an ad for a local café. "I've seen you look more enthused about watching *Lawrence Welk* reruns."

"What do you want me to do, look like I'm getting ready to fuck the mug?" Patrick frowned and lifted the cup higher and forced an entirely false grin onto his handsome mouth. "Is this better? How's this, Olivia? Ooh, coffee, I'm so horny for you…"

I snapped a couple of shots just to annoy him with later, when he saw how ridiculous he looked. "Quit being a jerk. C'mon, I need this for tomorrow."

"Nothing like running behind schedule." Patrick licked the mug.

I snapped another shot and thought I might frame that one as a gift. "It's a last-minute job, and I can't afford to turn them down."

He shot me a glance, then put his pout into place. "How's this?"

"A little less constipated, but yes. Good." Finally I got something that would work. It wasn't art, but it would do. Patrick put the mug down while I transferred the pictures to my computer.

"You'll come, right? And dinner on Friday. You haven't been over since the party." He flipped through the large album of photos I'd chosen as my best, to show off to potential clients. "Oh, I like this one. Why don't you do more of these, Livvy? They're so good."

I glanced at the picture, a nude I'd taken at a photography workshop I'd gone to the year before. "Because I'm not an erotic photographer and I don't have much use for nudes."

"She's pretty."

I gave him a look. "Yes. She is. She's a model."

He flipped a few more pages. "I like this one, too."

A landscape. Nothing special. I could add text to it and play with the dimensions to use in brochures or Web sites. I shrugged.

"You don't take compliments very well."

I laughed and began toying with the pictures I'd taken of him. "I want to make my living doing this, Patrick. I don't have any grand ideas of becoming a famous artiste. The work's good. Yes. I get it. I'm not setting up shop at the street fair to sell my prints, okay?"

"You could have a gallery show. Your work is good, as good as some of the stuff I've seen hanging up downtown. You know I have a friend of a friend—"

"Stop," I told him firmly. "Patrick, I love you, but I'm not having a gallery show. And besides, I know people, too, you know. It's not like I couldn't get something going if I wanted to."

"So why don't you?" He leaned against the large wooden chest of drawers I'd salvaged from the back alley.

I thought about warning him he'd get his designer jeans dirty rubbing up against the old wood, but decided against it. As fussy as Patrick could be, he liked to pretend sometimes he wasn't, especially when we were alone and sort of reverted to the way we'd been as a couple. When he'd had to be what he felt was "manly."

"Because I don't want to." I shrugged again.

"You should do it anyway."

Now I turned to look at him full-on. "You know, you can leave anytime."

Patrick-my-boyfriend would never have flipped me the finger. Patrick-my-boyfriend had insisted on using tools and playing sports. He'd farted and burped a lot more back then. I couldn't say I wasn't happy he'd let go of that.

"You don't go that way, remember?" I said with a glance at his middle finger.

He snorted and stood up. "You'll come to dinner."

The past two Fridays I'd spent watching movies with Alex. "I might have plans."

"What on earth could you be doing on a Friday night that would be better than games and food and drinks at my house?" He paused. "Do you have a date?"

"I love how you make that sound like science fiction." I sighed, giving up trying to work on the pictures with him there. "As a matter of fact, my tenant and I are probably going to be watching the entire BBC production of *Pride and Prejudice*. The Colin Firth version."

Patrick gasped and recoiled. "What? You...with him? But..."

He looked so shocked and hurt I shouldn't have laughed, but I did. "He's never seen it."

"Liv!"

"Patrick!" I mocked.

He shook his head, frowning, brows pulled low over his blue eyes. "I knew you renting to him was going to be bad."

"What's bad about it?"

Alex had been great. He took the big garbage cans out to the Dumpster in back, had cooked dinner for me twice the week before, and hung out watching old movies with me. He had a great sense of humor and didn't play his music too loud. He also liked to do yoga, shirtless, and that was a bonus. I'd found myself unable to sleep for thinking of him, but I didn't want Patrick to know that. I sounded a little too gushy, too perky, but my focus was on the computer screen and not my tone of voice. Patrick's silence alerted me to my faux pas, and I turned to look at him.

"Don't be like that," I told him.

"Well, you haven't called me, like, in a week," he said. "I thought you were going to come over to watch *Supernatural* on the big screen. You know Teddy bought the Blu-rays."

"I've had to work, Patrick. I can't just throw all that aside all the time." I tried to sound gentle and it came out annoyed. Probably because I *was* annoyed.

Patrick just glared. He was jealous. This realization punched an incredulous laugh out of me. He hadn't been jealous of the past three guys I'd dated, but he was jealous of this?

"Oh, Patrick."

We knew each other well enough that some things didn't need to be spelled out. He frowned and kicked at the floor. "I guess you'll be spending Christmas with him, then?"

"Instead of you?"

He crossed his arms and looked dour.

"I do have a family, Patrick. My dad's invited me home with him and Marjorie. And my brothers have, too."

"And you're going to go?"

"I think so. I don't see them that much." My brothers had invited me for past holidays and I'd declined, not wanting to make a trip either to Wyoming or Illinois in the winter. I believed them both when they said they'd miss me, but I was also sure they weren't heartbroken. We'd all grown up. They had families. Kids. Our family had never been as close as some and never as distant as others. What we had worked, at least for us.

"What about your mom?"

"My mother doesn't celebrate Christmas, remember?" I

gave him my full attention, and a scowl. It had certainly been a bit of an issue when we were dating. Not as much as the eventual revelation that he preferred sausage to tacos, but it had caused some tension.

"I can't believe you're blowing me off for someone else."

"Get out." I pointed at the door, but not before Patrick danced closer, just out of reach, to smack his lips at me. I didn't want to smile or laugh, but I had to. "Out! I have work to do! Isn't Teddy waiting for you?"

"Teddy's always waiting for me."

"And I'm sure he has dinner all ready for you when you get home, too. Don't be late, hanging around here. Go on. Go." I shooed him. Patrick grabbed at my hand but missed.

I liked him this way, acting silly as he had when we'd been together long ago, before sex got in the way and he thought he had to be something he wasn't. He was different now. We both were. But Patrick was really different with his new friends, his new partner. It might have been the "real" him, but this silliness was part of him, too. Time had passed, wounds had healed. In many ways Patrick and I were closer than we'd ever been as a couple. I knew in every part of me that mattered that if we'd gone ahead and done it, married, we'd have been miserable and divorced—or worse, miserable and *not* divorced—in less than a year. I was happy my Patrick had found his place in the world with someone who loved him the way he deserved and wanted to be loved, and I didn't mope around wringing my hands, wishing for my prince to come. Or I tried not to.

Then I was feeling sad and nostalgic again and hating it. Part of it was the time of year, when I felt caught between my different worlds, anyway, but part of it would always just be...Patrick.

"Just don't forget about me," he said.

"Oh, Patrick. As if I ever could." I stood to give him a hug and a kiss he didn't deserve, but I couldn't deny. "Now. Get out. I'm busy."

"Call me," he demanded.

"I will! I will. Now go!"

"Liv..."

"Yes, my dear one?" The words were sweet, my tone a little bitter.

"Nothing. Never mind." Then he went out and closed the door behind him.

I turned to my computer and lost myself in work. It was better than being lost in anything else.

I wasn't brought up stupid.

On the contrary, both my parents were part of the sex, drugs and rock-and-roll generation. Fans of the Grateful Dead. I had two much older brothers who hadn't thought a lot about shielding me from the movies they watched or music they listened to. I knew about sex.

After my parents divorced, when I was five, my dad remarried almost immediately. His new wife, Marjorie, an enthusiastic member of Sacred Heart Catholic Church, had brought with her my two stepsisters, Cindy and Stacy, both a year or so older than me. My mom stayed steadfastly single, rarely even dating. My parents were cordial to one another as they shared me, neither ever making me choose, and if there was always a little bit of tension with my dad over my place in his new household, it was made up for by my mother's complete indulgence in me. We were best friends, my mom and I.

I had my first "real" boyfriend at fourteen, gave my first hand job a year later. Most of my friends had lost their virginity by the time we were sixteen, but I waited another year before I gave it up in my boyfriend's basement at a graduation party for his older brother. I wasn't scarred by screwing him, even though we broke up shortly after that. I knew enough to use a condom and was smart enough to go all the way with a guy who'd already proved himself adept at getting me off. It was as fine a first time as I could ask for.

My life changed my senior year of high school. My mom, who favored flowing gypsy skirts and long, unbound hair, had always been a reader, but her choices of material had changed over the past year from Clive Barker and Margaret Atwood to thick, leather-bound copies of the Tanakh and journals on Jewish commentary. I knew about Judaism, though we'd never practiced anything more religious than spinning the dreidel. But now...well, they say there's nothing like the enthusiasm of a convert. My mother, born and raised Jewish, wasn't technically a convert, but she was definitely enthusiastic.

Suddenly, most of what we'd done together as a family disappeared, tossed out in the garbage along with an entire pantry of food she deemed unfit to eat. She put away half her dishes to keep them unused for a year, the time it would take to make them kosher again. The others she koshered by pouring boiling water over them, and maintaining a completely meat-free house.

Suddenly we were Jewish *and* vegetarian. My mom had always been a devout carnivore. The Friday-night dinners I could've dealt with. The candle lighting, the baking of challah. But giving up cheeseburgers? No way.

I moved out to live with my dad and Marjorie, who took me in, but not quite without making it seem as though I were a burden. It was her duty, I heard her whisper to a girlfriend once, when they were gathered for coffee. Her Christian duty. It bothered her more that I hadn't been baptized than the fact I was black—which was good, because there was always the chance I might accept Jesus Christ as my savior, but I could never change the color of my skin.

I loved my dad and didn't mind having to share a bathroom with my stepsisters, or having a small, dank bedroom in the basement. I didn't mind the prayers before meals, because at least they were giving me plenty of bacon, ohhh, bacon. Every morning, bacon and eggs. I didn't even mind church so much, because the altar boys were cute.

My mother didn't like any of this, but caught up in her own journey, she let a lot of things slide. So long as I was with her for the holidays she wanted to celebrate, she didn't mind what I was doing the rest of the time. If I was there to light the menorah, she was all right with me going home to my dad's to stuff the stockings. I was smart enough not to tell her about the youth group Marjorie encouraged me to join, or how my dad had been hinting that it might be a good idea for me to get baptized.

I escaped salvation by heading off to college. Where I met Patrick my sophomore year. He lived in my dorm, and the first time he smiled at me, I imprinted on him like a duckling. Tall, fair-haired, ruddy-cheeked…and Catholic. As in can-name-all-the-martyred-saints Catholic. I was smitten.

I like to think of life as an infinite jigsaw puzzle with so many pieces that no matter how many you fit together, the picture's never finished. Meeting Patrick was the culmination of a hundred thousand choices. He was the end of only one path, but it was the one I took. No matter how it ended, he was the choice I made, and while I'd always felt I would never waste time in regretting it, I was beginning to think I might.

I thought I knew what love was with a handsome boyfriend who was a very good kisser. I thought I knew what it was for three years, all through college, even when all my friends were fucking like bunnies and the sheen of chastity was wearing off. Love is patient, love is kind, right? Love forgives all things?

That's what I believed then. I wasn't so sure now.

Our senior year, Patrick got down on one knee and asked me to marry him, with a princess-cut diamond ring in one hand and a bouquet of twelve red roses in the other. We set a date. We planned a wedding.

And two weeks before we were due to walk down the aisle at my father's church, I found out Patrick had been lying to me all along.

I hadn't been raised stupid, but I'd sure ended up feeling dumb.

The week passed. I heard the sound of voices as I passed Alex's apartment, and I saw his car come and go, but I didn't see him. I ended up watching *Pride and Prejudice* alone and somehow blaming Patrick for that.

The week before Christmas is busy for most people, even those who don't celebrate the holiday, and I had a to-do list as long as anyone's. I hadn't put up a tree, but I had bought presents. I'd be spending the day with my dad and his family, though my brothers and their wives and children weren't going to be there. I'd also picked up a slew of last-minute design jobs for after-Christmas sales promotions, and a few portrait sessions for friends looking for down-to-the-wire stocking gifts for friends and relatives.

The little girl in my camera's viewfinder didn't have wings, but she was a little angel. Four years old, mop of curly black hair, stubborn little rosebud mouth and a pair of crossed arms. A tiny, badass version of Shirley Temple, including the dress with the bow at the waist.

"No! No, no, no!" She stamped her foot. She pouted. She glared.

"Pippa. Sweetie. Smile for the picture, please?"

Pippa looked at her daddy Steven and stamped her foot again. "I don't like this dress! I don't like this headband!"

She tore the bow from her hair and threw it on the ground, and to make sure we all knew just how much she hated it, stepped on it with her patent leather shoes.

"I blame you," Pippa's other daddy, Devon, told me.

I raised a brow. "Gee, thanks."

Devon laughed as Steven grabbed up the bow and tried to salvage the look. "She's stubborn, that's all. A lot like you."

"Pippa, princess, please—"

"Oh, and her daddy spoiling her has nothing to do with any of that?" I murmured, my attention focused on the scene playing out in front of me. *Point and shoot. Click.* I captured the battle between father and child with a press of one finger.

"Don't take pictures of this!" Steven demanded.

Pippa, laughing, dodged his grasp and ran around the studio. Her shoes pounded the old wooden boards, the beat of freedom. She ran fast, that little girl. Just as I always had.

Devon laughed and sat back, shaking his head. I snapped

picture after picture. Pippa running. Steven grabbing her up, dangling her upside down, her pretty dress flipping up to show the rumba panties beneath, and her springy curls sweeping the floor. Daddy and daughter snuggling close. Then, two daddies with their little girl, the love among them a visible, tangible thing I didn't control or edit, but merely captured.

"Pippa, do it for Daddy," Steven said. "I want a pretty picture of you to give Nanny and Poppa."

That rosebud mouth pursed again and the small, fine brows furrowed, but at last Pippa gave a sigh better suited to a little old lady. "Oh, okay. Fine."

He settled her on the upturned wooden crate and arranged her hair and dress, then stepped back. I framed the shot and took it. Perfect. But even as I tilted the camera to show the digital image to Devon, I knew this wasn't the one I'd tweak and polish to give them for their wall.

Small arms hugged my knees and I looked into an upturned face. "Lemme see, Livia! Lemme see the pitcher."

I knelt beside the little girl and showed her the photo on the screen. She frowned. "I don't like it."

"Shh," I whispered conspiratorially. "Don't tell your daddy that or he'll make you sit for another one."

Even at four, Pippa was smart enough to figure out when a smile was a better weapon. She giggled. I joined her. When she hugged me, her small, soft cheek pressed to mine, I smelled baby shampoo and fabric softener.

"Why don't you go play with the dollhouse," I told her. "Let me show your daddies the pictures."

"I wanna see the pitchers, too!"

"You will," I promised, knowing there was no way to keep

her from it, but not willing, as her fathers were, to indulge her every whim. "But first I have to put them on my computer. Go play."

"She listens to you," Steven said with an exhausted sigh as Pippa skipped off to the corner where I'd placed my old doll-house. "Thank God."

I shrugged and slipped the memory card from the back of my camera. I took it to the long, battered table I used instead of a desk, and pushed it into the card reader plugged into the back of my Macbook. My photo program opened, showcasing the series of pictures I'd taken. Steven and Devon pulled up chairs on either side.

"Look at that one," Steven said about the one showing the three of them. "Gorgeous, Liv. Just amazing."

The heat of pride flushed my cheeks. "Thanks."

"No, seriously. Look at that." Devon pointed to one of Pippa, backlit in front of one of the studio's long, high windows, her dress belled out around her knees as she spun. "How do you do it?"

"Practice. Talent." I clicked on the shot to enlarge it, and toyed with some settings to bring out the contrast of light and dark. "Mostly practice."

"Anyone can take a snapshot. But what you do is art. Really art." Devon sounded awed. He turned from the monitor to look at me. "She draws, you know. Pippa does. The pediatrician says kids her age are just barely making stick figures, but she's already drawing full bodies."

"I don't draw," I told him gently, and kept my focus on the screen.

"I'm just saying," he answered softly.

We worked together for a little while on the photos they

liked best, until I'd cleaned them up and added them to a disc for them to take home. I added the raw shots, too, in case they wanted them for any reason. I lingered on the one of Pippa in front of the window.

"Can I use this in my portfolio?"

"Of course. Absolutely." Devon had taken the disc and put it in his bag, while Steven went to check on their daughter.

"Thanks." I'd get a print made later. For now I looked again, only for a moment, before clicking it closed and removing the memory card to place back in my camera.

"You know, Liv…" Devon hesitated until I glanced at him, and then he looked across the room. "You know you're welcome, anytime, to see her. Not just when we come over for pictures or when we invite you. That was our agreement, wasn't it? That you'd always be welcome to be a part of her life."

I followed his gaze with my own. Pippa had rearranged the furniture in the dollhouse, putting beds in the living room and an oven in the attic. She giggled as Steven took one of the dolls and made it speak to the one in her hand.

"I know. Thanks."

Devon meant well, so how could I tell him that I didn't want to invite myself into their home to watch them raise my child? That I appreciated being kept a part of Pippa's life, but that I didn't expect or even crave anything more than what I already had? She was my child, but I was not her mother.

"Thanks again for the pictures." Steven settled a check on my desk.

I didn't pick it up. He'd have written it for too much, again, and I didn't want to be ungracious by arguing with him about the amount. I liked taking pictures, but I liked paying my bills, too. Besides, taking his money made this not a favor, but a job. I think we both preferred it that way.

"Livvy, are you coming to my birthday party? It's a pretty princess party." Pippa twirled. "And I'm going to have a piñata."

I laughed and tugged one of her long, silky curls. "A pretty princess piñata for Pippa. Perfect."

She tipped her face to look up at me, her eyes squinched shut with glee. "Yes! And all my friends are coming."

"Then I guess I should come, too. Since I'm your friend."

Pippa hugged my thighs just briefly before dancing off again. "Yes, yes, you'll come to my paaarty. And bring a present."

"Pippa!" Steven said, exasperated.

Devon chuckled and met my eyes. I think he understood me more than his partner did. Steven, hovering just a little too close, watched me. He didn't say anything, but he didn't have to. I could imagine how he felt. So I stepped back and watched Pippa, who twirled again, already chattering at her daddy about where she wanted to go for dinner and what she wanted to watch on television when they got home.

"I'm going to take Pippa out to the car. Get her strapped in the seat. Devon?" Steven lifted Pippa's coat, an entirely impractical white, fur-collared jacket. "You coming?"

"Yep. I'll be right along."

Devon waited until the sound of Steven's boots and Pippa's patent leather shoes echoed away down the concrete stairs. He shrugged into his own coat, a soft brown leather that hit him at midthigh and belted at the waist. Something in the way he turned his head as he tied the belt caught my eye, and I lifted my camera to take a shot.

It blurred, but I took another as he glanced up at me with a self-conscious smile. I'd missed what I was looking for, something elusive I couldn't have described in words. "Look back at your hands."

The moment was lost, though, and I pressed the button to view the blurred shot, thinking how I could fix it. Devon peered over my shoulder. He laughed.

I looked up. "See? It takes practice."

"And talent," he told me.

Devon is a tall, broad man with skin the color of dark caramel. He shaves his head and wears a cropped goatee, and when he flexes I always expect to hear the purr of ripping fabric as he pops the seams on his shirt. He's also one of the most gentle men I've ever met.

"You should come in and let me take your picture. Just you."

Devon raised a brow. "Uh-huh."

I punched his arm gently. "I like taking portraits when I'm not at Foto Folks. It would give me material for my portfolio, anyway."

"We'll see." He smoothed the front of his coat. "I meant what I said, Liv."

"About coming over? I know." My camera made a nice barrier between us. I didn't want to disappoint Devon, and I knew that's what would happen. He wouldn't understand my feelings about his daughter. Nobody seemed to.

"It's just…we're family, you know? All of us. I lost my parents years ago and my sister doesn't speak to me." Because he was gay, he didn't have to say aloud. "Family's important. I don't want you to think you're not welcome to be a part of her life."

I nodded. "I know, Devon."

"Merry Christmas, Liv."

"Thanks. Same to you."

He touched my shoulder gently and left, closing the door behind him. When he'd gone I sat back in my chair and opened the file with the photos I'd taken today.

Devon's family had disowned him at age seventeen, when they'd found out he was gay, and he'd never reconciled with his parents before they passed away. He'd made his own family, gathered friends around him to love and be loved in return.

Pippa was my child, but not my daughter. Steven had requested we not call me Pippa's mother, and that I sign all parental rights away upon her birth. I'd had no objections. I hadn't counted on Devon's love for family making this so complicated.

I took a last look at the photos of the little girl and her parents, her real and true parents. She looked like me and even acted like me a little, and I was blessed to know her. But I was not her mother, and never would be. I took one last look at the photos, and then I closed the folder.

Chapter 05

I didn't take the photo of Pippa along to my father's house to show him on Christmas Day. We never spoke of her, or mentioned my pregnancy, which had been unexpected and definitely not welcomed by most people in my life. Instead I took bags full of gifts for Cindy's and Stacy's children, four of them apiece, nieces and nephews I didn't bother putting "step" in front of.

We had a big ham dinner. We opened gifts. My brothers both called, and I spoke to them. I fended off questions about my love life and bragged about my work—not the part at Foto Folks or the photos I took at schools and for sports teams, but the brochures and ads I'd created for personal clients. I relaxed and enjoyed my family and hoped they enjoyed me, too.

I declined the offer to spend the night, and drove the hour and a half home with my iPod blasting everything I could play that wasn't a Christmas carol. I pulled my car next to Alex's in my parking lot at just past midnight.

It had been over a week since I'd seen or spoken to him, and I thought about knocking on his door as I passed. Not that he was required to check in with me or anything. In fact, so long as the rent was paid on time, we really didn't have to interact at all. But we had, and I missed it. I peeked and saw a line of light beneath his door; I took a deep breath and knocked. He didn't answer, and my courage fled. Rather than knock again, I started up the stairs, and had made it just inside my door when I heard his voice.

"Olivia?"

The best part of skiing is that first moment looking down the mountain. Getting ready to push off. To speed and swoop. To fly. This felt like that moment.

"Hi, Alex. Merry Christmas."

He wore a pair of jeans and an unbuttoned, long-sleeved shirt over nothing else, his hair rumpled and one cheek creased. "Merry Christmas. I heard you come in."

"Did I wake you up? I'm sorry."

"No, it's okay. I was in a post–Christmas dinner stupor."

"Do you want…to come in?" I held the door open wider.

"It's late. That's okay. I just wanted to give you this." Alex held up a small box wrapped in silver paper with a crisp blue bow.

I looked at it and then at him. "You got me a present?"

"Sure. It's that time of year."

"But I didn't get you anything."

"That's okay. Just open it."

"Well, come in, then." I stepped back and he followed, but not too far inside the doorway. The box had been wrapped so I could simply lift the lid without removing the paper. Inside, nestled on a soft bed of pretty fabric, was a bracelet made of polished stones. "It's beautiful!"

"I'm glad you like it. I know it's not much—"

"I didn't get you anything," I reminded him. "It's pretty. You shouldn't have, Alex. Really. But thank you."

"I just wanted to give you something," he said. "Prove to you I'm not a total douche bag."

I was startled into laughter. "Oh, God. I don't think that."

"No?"

"Of course not." I paused. "Should I?"

He studied me, brow furrowed. "I just thought... Never mind."

"Thought what?"

He waved a hand. "Nothing. Really."

I wanted to press him for an explanation, but didn't. I slipped the bracelet on my wrist and held it up to tilt it back and forth, admiring it. "Thank you."

Neither of us moved. I hefted a tote bag full of leftovers Marjorie had packed for me. "Are you hungry?"

Alex put a hand on his stomach. "Wow. Um...no. I don't think I'll ever be hungry again."

I laughed. "Until tomorrow."

A smile drifted slowly across his mouth. "Yeah. I'm sure I'll want to eat again tomorrow."

"All right, then." Again we stayed still, him a step inside the doorway. "Sure I can't convince you to take a slice of Christmas ham?"

"Hmm...I didn't have any ham. We had something called a turducken, if you can believe that."

"You did?" I laughed some more. "Wow. Patrick always said he wanted to make one of those for Christmas."

"Well…yeah," Alex said. "He invited me over."

I could think of nothing to say to that but, "I've never had one."

"You should try it. Well, I'm going to bed. See you, Olivia. Merry Christmas."

"Thank you for the bracelet."

"You're welcome." He smiled over his shoulder at me as he left.

I closed the door behind him and leaned against it, not sure why knowing Patrick had invited him over for Christmas had been such a big deal, only that it was.

If Patrick's Chrismukkah extravaganza had been an orgy of food, music and drama, his New Year's Eve party was much quieter. Still plenty of food and music, but the guest list had been cut way down. Teddy's sister, Susan, and her teenage son, Jayden, Nadia and Carlos from next door, and a few of Teddy and Patrick's friends I'd met but didn't really know. Patrick's brother, Sean. Me.

And, of course, Alex Kennedy.

He came in the back door, arms laden with packages wrapped in silver paper tied with blue bows. I turned from the counter where I'd been slicing cheese and laying out a new supply of crackers. My heart gave a stupid little skip of surprise.

"Alex!"

"Olivia." His smile flashed white teeth that had never seen braces, I'd bet, because they were just endearingly imperfect enough. "Happy New Year."

He saw me looking at the bundles he carried. "Patrick said you all exchange New Year's presents."

We did. Small things, usually. None of the elaborately wrapped gifts in Alex's arms looked small.

I grabbed at the one getting ready to topple. "Let me help you."

"Thanks."

We piled the presents on the table. I gave him a sideways glance. I was used to the men in Patrick's house looking pretty and smelling good. Truthfully, it had sort of spoiled me for men in general. Tonight Alex wore jeans, faded just right, and a black fitted T-shirt beneath the heavy peacoat he shrugged off and tossed onto a chair. His hair fell down a little into his eyes as he straightened the packages. I didn't want to stare, but did anyway.

Dinner was simple but good, and the conversation flowed as sweetly as the wine. I sat next to Sean and across from Patrick, Alex at the other end of the table. Maybe I liked leaving the conversation up to everyone else. Or maybe it was still the season making me quiet and watchful. It wasn't until I saw Patrick touch Teddy's hand that I realized it was more than simply holiday blues.

There wasn't anything sexual about the touch. That I'd seen plenty, in the days when Patrick in his newfound gayness had fucked his way through half the city and not been too ashamed or too tactful not to include me. The way Patrick touched his lover's hand was comfortable, a gentle, brief squeeze.

My eyes burned. Next to me, Sean leaned to say something to Teddy's sister on the other side of me. Everyone was laughing at something I'd missed while I'd been taken up with unexpected jealousy. When I glanced down the table to the end, Alex met my eyes.

In his gaze I saw a mixture of emotions, most of which looked like some form of pity. It stung. It left me naked.

It also lasted only seconds before he was laughing, too, ignoring me and my plight, but instead of being grateful for his compassion, I wanted to poke him with a fork. Alex Kennedy, the man who'd had a diva breakup anthem tossed in his face at a holiday party, then let the singer blow him on a back porch, didn't have the right to judge me.

"So, Liv," Sean said when he turned back to me. "What've you been up to lately?"

"Yes, Liv. Tell everyone what you've been doing."

Suddenly the focus of the entire table, I found my mouth inconveniently empty of food, which meant I had to fill it with words. "Oh…I've opened my own studio."

"Recording?" Jayden, who'd been kicking everyone's butt on a popular guitar-playing game, asked.

"No, photography. It's more of an advertising business. Graphic design for local places. Brochures, Web sites, that sort of thing. I take pictures for the work, rather than using stock photos."

"But some of your pictures have been used on those sites, right?" Patrick sounded proud, and I didn't really mind the nudging.

"Pretty much anyone can upload pictures to a stock photo place, but yeah. Some of mine have been very successful." I'd made more money on selling the rights to some of my images than I could using them exclusively. It wasn't art. It was business.

"Don't listen to her. She's a great photographer. I have some of her landscapes hanging in the living room," Patrick said.

"You took those?" Sean looked impressed. He leaned a little closer. "Wow."

I tried to think why this should be such a surprise—I had almost married his brother, after all. It wasn't like Sean had never met me before. But back then my camera had been a hobby. Now it was a job. Or, I thought as I caught a whiff of his cologne, he was paying more attention to me than he had back then. I sniffed surreptitiously. He smelled nothing like Patrick, but spicy and masculine just the same. Beneath the table, his knee nudged mine again. This time, I thought it was on purpose.

This close to him, I could see the white flecks in his blue eyes, identical to Patrick's. Like his brother, Sean had thick blond hair and a mouth that curved just so, and also like his brother he had broad shoulders, a lean waist and a flat, flat belly that begged any straight woman with half a libido to lick it.

Unlike his brother, though, Sean Michael McDonald wasn't gay.

"Yes. I took those."

The conversation moved on after that, but I'm not sure what we talked about. I didn't look at Sean again. I didn't have to. I knew all too well that he was right there.

After dinner came the opening of the gifts and more wine. I kept my glass full by mostly pretending to sip. Alcohol's never good mixed with self-pity, especially on New Year's Eve at an ex-lover's house to which you have not brought a date.

The rule of the gifts was that they had to be small. Hand-made, or inexpensive. Nothing too fancy, and everyone was to bring an extra to pass out in a grab bag exchange. I got a great new pair of soft driving gloves, a more-than-fair exchange for the gas station gift card I'd tucked into the basket of goodies to be passed around. There were personal gifts, too, obviously, and I made out well there, as well, but better for me was watching the faces of Teddy and Patrick as they opened the gift I'd brought for them both.

"Liv, this is…amazing." Teddy stroked the sleek mahogany frame. "Beautiful. Really."

"When did you take this?" Patrick asked softly.

"Over the summer." We'd gone to a local park to have a picnic dinner and listen to a band play on the riverfront. I'd captured the two of them sitting with the river behind them, their gazes locked and mouths almost touching. Getting ready to kiss.

They hadn't noticed me in that moment, and behind the shield of my camera I'd convinced myself I hadn't felt like a third wheel. Now I couldn't help remembering that I had. Beside me, Sean shifted until his thigh nudged mine again. Behind me, I felt the warmth of his arm snake along the back of the couch. The hairs on my neck stood up.

Alex was watching me.

I forced myself to focus on Patrick. "I hope you like it."

"Love it," he said. "Look, Teddy, it will go right there."

As they talked about the perfect place to hang the picture, Sean's fingertip whispered along the back of my neck. I shivered. He leaned close to whisper in my ear. "Cold?"

I turned, just slightly, away. "A little."

"Maybe you need a sweater or something."

As other gifts were opened, the room rang with laughter. Patrick certainly wasn't looking at us. In the past there had been many times when everything around me disappeared but the sound of Patrick's voice, or the sight of his face. Almost the same voice murmured next to me, now. Almost the same eyes looked at me.

There was still a moment when it could have gone a different way. If Sean hadn't shifted again to press his thigh to mine in a move more blatantly sexual than Patrick had ever made on me, or if I'd come with a date the way I'd planned...or if it hadn't been New Year's Eve and I hadn't still been in love with the one man I would never have.

"Actually, I'm going to grab something to drink."

"Want me to come with you?" Sean smiled an easy, quirking smile that would've charmed me senseless if it hadn't been almost identical to his brother's.

"No. I'll be right back." My own hard-edged smile must've put him off, finally, because I escaped to the kitchen without a tagalong.

I didn't want a drink, really. I needed some fresh air to clear my head. I was absolutely not going to give in to the glums, not tonight, not ever. Not again. I was fine.

I was fine until I shrugged into my coat and found the small, wrapped package in my pocket. I'd meant to give it to Patrick some time when we were alone, not in front of the group. I'd bought him a button featuring the stabbity knife from his favorite cartoon, *Kawaii Not*. He'd gotten me hooked on the quirky, sick-sense-of-humor artwork, and it was one thing we still shared that he didn't with anyone else. I'd wrapped the button in nondenominational paper and scribbled his name across it. I'd wanted to make sure, so fucking sure, he knew how casual and careless a present it had been. An afterthought. Not important.

But feeling it there, the button's round edge through the cheap paper, I knew I was the only one who'd have ever thought it was important, or meaningful.

By the time I got out the back door and down the porch steps, I was crying. My vision blurred. Tears froze on my cheeks. They burned, and I stumbled. I drew in a hitching, labored breath that seared my lungs. I made it all the way down the path and past the detached garage before I burst into raw, hateful sobs. I stopped, a hand on the bare wood, to swipe at my eyes.

"Fuck!" I cried when I saw I was not alone. "Where'd you come from?"

Alex, bundled against the weather, stood beneath the eves. He'd been leaning, but straightened now. In one hand he held a cigarette that wasn't lit.

"I went around the front of the house. Olivia? Are you all right?"

"Do I look like I'm all right?" I'm sure I meant to answer him calmly, but the words shot out of me, riding the backs of more sobs. I pounded the garage wall. "No! I am not all right!"

I covered my face and sobbed into my gloves. The noises in my throat became like those of rusted gears, grinding against each other until the whole machine broke down and stopped. I became aware of a firm hand on my shoulder and then an even firmer chest against my cheek. I hadn't realized he was so tall until my head fit just beneath Alex's chin. His coat smelled good. The hand not holding the cigarette stroked down my back.

I'm all for equality of the sexes and everything, but I bet there are few women out there who'd have been able to resist the allure of the comfort Alex offered. Strong arms, manly chest. I didn't want words or advice. I didn't even really want to tell him what had happened, only wanted to stop feeling so bad. When I finally drew away, my sobs had stopped but I didn't feel any better.

"It's the most wonderful time of the year, my ass." Alex put the cigarette between his lips. "Holiday time is shitsville."

I tucked my hands into my pockets. "Yeah."

He nodded. That was it. No explanation. No further assurances.

I looked him over. The streetlamp made his eyes seem darker, his skin paler. I watched him lip the end of the cigarette, then take it out of his mouth and draw in a breath of frigid air.

"Are you smoking that? Or not?"

"Not," he said. "I quit."

"So what the hell are you d–doing out here?" I said around chattering teeth. "It's freaking freezing."

"Ah…old habits. You know when you smoke you always have an excuse to duck out of a place when you want to."

"I'll keep that in mind." I scrubbed at my face, not just to wipe away tears but to get some warmth circulating. "I should've gone out with that guy I met at the coffee shop. He wanted to take me to some package deal at the Hotel Hershey. Dinner and big band dancing. I'm sure there would have been plenty of chocolate, and a guy to kiss at midnight. Do you know how many years it's been since I had a date to kiss at midnight?"

"Can't have been that many."

My laugh sounded faintly of the same grinding gears my sobs had. "Too many. And not because I haven't had offers!"

"I wouldn't have assumed that."

Surreal. All of this. The night, the conversation. The man in front of me lipped his cigarette again, then let it dangle from the corner of his mouth.

"I didn't have a formal dress, but that's not why I didn't go."

Alex watched me with a faint smile for my babbling.

"Go ahead and ask me why I passed up a night at the Hotel Hershey to come here, instead."

"Oh, I know why," Alex said.

My shoulders slumped. I blinked my sore and swollen eyes. "You do?"

"You love him."

If anything should've made me cry that night, it was those three words, said as simply and matter-of-factly as that. Maybe I was cried out by then, dehydrated. Frozen. All I could manage was a shake of my head and a sigh that blew my breath out in a long plume.

The crack of fireworks came from down the street. A church bell tolled. Tears welled up again and clogged my throat.

"Dammit," I whispered. "It's midnight."

"Happy New Year," Alex said.

Then he tossed aside the cigarette, pulled me into his arms and kissed me.

Chapter 06

*H*is mouth, warm and soft, pressed mine for about five seconds before I managed to react, and by that time he'd pulled away just enough to murmur against my lips, "I don't have any chocolate. Sorry."

I stepped back and put a hand over my smiling mouth. "It's all right. You didn't have to do that."

He fixed me with a steady gaze. "What makes you think I didn't *want* to do that?"

Alex doesn't like girls, Patrick had said.

"Well, thank you," I told him. "I'm sorry I cried all over you and burdened you with my blabber. Again. It's not the best way to start the New Year."

He put his hand on his stomach and gave a silly little half bow. "My pleasure. Really. Knight-in-shining-armor shit always makes my New Year. It's my fucking resolution, actually."

I'd been sure I wouldn't laugh for a good long time, but now I did. Loudly. It hurt my throat, but felt good just the same. "You should go back inside. Aside from being freezing out here, you're missing the party."

He looked over his shoulder, across the yard, to the house. "Right. The party. I think I'm heading home, actually."

I nodded. "Ah. Okay."

"You okay to drive?" He moved a little closer and put a hand on my shoulder.

"I wasn't really drinking. I'll be fine."

His fingers squeezed gently. "You sure? I can drive you."

"No, really. I'm okay." I shivered and clamped my teeth against further clattering. "I'm going to go. I'm an icicle."

He laughed and released me. "So much for global warming, huh? You wouldn't know it by this weather. Drive carefully, Olivia."

"I will. And, Alex," I said as he turned toward the sidewalk. He looked back at me. "Thanks again. And Happy New Year."

He tipped an imaginary hat. "I told you, it was my pleasure."

He'd already disappeared around the corner of the house when I got my feet moving. I was going to go inside, get my things and head home. No more sitting too close to Sean's brother, no more mooning over what might have been and never was.

"Where were you?" Patrick cornered me the moment I walked in through the back door. "It's past midnight. You missed the toast."

"I needed some air."

"What the hell are you doing?" Patrick closed his eyes and turned away, held up his hand. "Never mind. I saw you."

I saw betrayal on his face, clear as any expression I'd ever seen there. What picture would tell this story? "Saw me what?"

"With him." Acid dripped from his voice, but he kept it pitched low, with a glance through the kitchen door toward the living room.

"Who? Alex? Jesus, Patrick…it was just—"

"Whatever." He cut me off with a slash of his hand.

I stopped being sorry just then. Patrick, staring at me with fury burning in his gaze, was jealous. And I, seeing this for the first time, thought of how many other times over the past few years he'd steered me away from or out of potential relationships, knowing I loved him and trusted his judgment as my friend.

"You have no right." My voice wavered alarmingly.

"I have every right! This is my house!"

"It was a New Year's kiss from a friend. Hell, Patrick, you've gone down on guys when I was in the same room!"

He couldn't deny that, but he wasn't going to let that make a difference.

The look he gave me said it all, and then he looked away. His throat worked as he swallowed. I tried to remember if I'd ever seen him this angry with me, and couldn't. We seldom fought. Patrick and I were always best friends.

"What a really shitty thing to do to me," he said finally.

"To you? I didn't do it to you, Patrick. Or to anyone. If anyone has a right to be upset—" It was my turn to swallow against burning words. "I think I should go."

He blocked the doorway. "You can't rush out of here. Everyone will want to know why."

"Do you think I care?" Tired, worn, and still too much in love with him to be able to be this close without wanting him, I stood my ground but didn't touch him. "Really, Patrick? Do you think I give a flying fuck what anyone here thinks?"

"I thought you were staying over. It's New Year's Eve. Tomorrow we'll have pancakes and…" He faltered.

"I'm not staying. And really, I think I should go. It's better."

"I fucked him, Olivia," Patrick said tightly after a half a moment. "Just once. Teddy doesn't know."

"God, Patrick. Just…oh, my God. When?"

He shook his head, then gave it up. "Christmas."

"In your house? With Teddy there? What the…" I swallowed hard. Jealous didn't even describe it. "How could you? And you're angry with *me?* What a shitty thing to do!"

"Teddy knows I sometimes sleep with other guys—"

"Yeah, he knows. That's the point, isn't it? That he knows who they are? And when you're doing it? Fuck, Patrick, I wish I didn't even know this." About his arrangement with Teddy, about his sex life. About everything.

"Don't you tell him."

"Do I even know you?" I whispered.

Patrick cleared his throat. "Don't tell Teddy, Liv. Please."

"Why would I? I love Teddy. Why would I hurt him like that? Why would you?" I added, and rubbed my hand across my eyes. This was one big basket of fucked-up. "Why would you tell me this now, anyway?"

"I didn't tell you. You forced me to tell you."

He wanted to tell me, or he wouldn't have. I'd just begun to warm up from being outside, and now I went cold again.

From down the hall, Teddy's loud laughter drifted. I swallowed a sour taste. I crossed my arms, more jealousy stabbing me all over, in tender places I didn't even know existed.

"Fuck you, Patrick. That's why you don't want me hanging around him. You're not jealous of him, you're jealous of me?"

"I'm not jealous," he growled. "I'm just trying to protect you."

"From what? Clue me the fuck in, okay? Because it seems to me you're not trying to protect me from anything. You're just trying to… Fuck. I don't know what!" I swallowed years of longing. "I am not a fucking coffeepot!"

"What the hell's that supposed to mean?" Patrick reached for me.

I pulled away. "It means…it just means… What do you want me to do? Make him move out? Not be his friend because you couldn't keep your dick in your pants? What the fuck do you think is going to happen, Patrick?"

"Nothing," he said sullenly.

I shook my head. Patrick stepped back. I waited for him to say he was sorry, or to make some effort at touching me again, but I was glad when he didn't. Nothing he said or did could make this right, or make it go away.

"I'd better leave."

He didn't try to stop me this time. I pushed past him and into the hall, where I waited for him to come after me. He didn't. I went down the back stairs and grabbed up my coat. In the front room, the squall of *Rock Band* had been replaced by the sound of party horns on the television. They'd tuned in to the Times Square celebration. The television was showing a local news program, coverage of the post-midnight New Year's festivities. In Central Pennsylvania we're big fans of dropping strange things from the sky on December 31. The newscaster was talking about the giant Lebanon bologna being donated to feed the homeless.

At home, Alex's apartment was dark and quiet, no light beneath the door. This time, I didn't knock.

"Halllp!" The small figure behind the towering stack of boxes and bags overflowing her arms cried out, but too late.

I managed to catch a couple of the packages, but most of them hit the floor at our feet. Sarah sighed and stared. I laughed, and she shook her finger at me.

"You'd better hope there was nothing breakable in those."

"Why on earth would you have bought anything breakable for me?" I crouched to help her gather up all the things she'd brought. "Where do you want all this stuff?"

"On the table."

Sarah'd been the one to find the long dining-room table set up in the center of my studio. I called it vintage, she referred to it as antique, but it had cost a hundred sixty bucks at the local church's resale shop and came with a set of ten chairs. Only two of them had been reupholstered, and the others were all stacked along the wall, waiting their turn. When it was finished the whole set would be fantastic and impressive, just the sort of thing I'd always dreamed of having in an office of my own.

We settled the packages on the table's scarred surface. Sarah regarded them critically. "I feel like there should be more."

I looked at all she'd brought in with her. "More than this?"

She clicked a blue-painted fingernail against her teeth as she mused. "I guess we'll see when they're all open."

I rubbed my hands together. "Then let's open them up!"

Sarah laughed and grabbed a hair band from around her wrist, then used it to pile the mass of her blue-and-purple hair on top of her head. She pushed up the sleeves of her slim-fitting, silver spangled T-shirt and put her hands on the hips of her black skinny jeans, just over the black leather belt with its rhinestone-encrusted buckle. She was studying the array of goodies she'd brought while I was studying her, and when she caught me looking, she laughed.

"Sweet, huh?"

"What made you decide to go back to blue?"

She grinned and ran a hand over the unruly strands of mul-tihued hair. "I dunno. Orange and red was a little too harsh and green won't stay in. I like the blue and purple."

I did, too. I'd tried dying my dark hair a few times, but without stripping the color from it first, nothing would show up. I'd given up on trying to bust out of that box. "I like it, too. I told you that before."

"I know, I know." She waved a hand. "I just wanted to try something different."

I laughed. "Because everyone else has blue-and-purple hair."

Sarah made a face and gave me the finger. "Fuck you."

I blew her a kiss. "Not today. I have a headache."

She guffawed, the bold, bright laughter that turned heads, and slapped her thigh. "Do you want to see what I brought you or not?"

Of course I did. My studio had been bare and gutted when I bought the old firehouse. Sarah, whose design work I'd have admired even if she wasn't my friend, had agreed to help me turn it into the professional-looking space I desired. In return, I'd promised to do her brochures and Web site and other graphic design-type stuff. Oh, and to take her picture whenever she wanted, which was usually every time she changed her hair. So that was pretty often.

I didn't care. She always let me put the best pictures up on my Connex page, the one I kept for the rest of the world and not just friends. She was always willing to pose for me, too, if I had an idea in mind for something special. Sarah loved to dress up and put on makeup, but didn't have any hang-ups about how she looked, or at least not as many as a lot of the "models" I had access to did. And she was okay with doing crazy stuff and looking silly, which most models definitely were not.

She pulled a length of material from the first bag. "Picked this up at a yard sale at a Mennonite place last summer. Isn't it gorgeous?"

She held out the end for me to feel. Soft, auburn velvet, delicately embossed with a faint pattern of trefoils. She caught my gaze.

"For the side wall." She pointed to the long, plain, windowless expanse. "I'm going to tack up some furring strips, top and bottom, and shirr this in between. I have some other stuff, too, some sheers. You'll be able to hang your portraits and stuff over it."

She started opening other packages. Bolts and stray pieces of material spilled out onto the table.

"Sarah, that's too much. I can't take your entire fabric supply. I was just going to paint the walls."

She sighed and turned to me. Sarah's a good five inches shorter than me. Despite this, she has no problem staring me down. "Liv."

"Sarah."

"If I were craving chocolate, would you buy me some?"

"Umm…yes?"

"If I broke up with my boyfriend, you'd take me out dancing, right?"

"Of course."

"I love fabric. I have a fabric addiction. I crave buying yards and yards and bolts and bolts of material." Sarah pointed at the pile on my table, then gestured around the room. "All of this? Is from two boxes in my storage unit. Do you want to know how many boxes I have?"

"Okay. I get it!" I laughed, but she wouldn't let me go.

"Guess, Liv!" she demanded.

"Ten."

"Thirty," Sarah confessed in a whisper, as if she was ashamed, though her grin gave her away as anything but. "Thirty boxes of fabric, Olivia. Take this off my hands. Please. So, help a sistah out here."

The faux "urban" accent had grated my ears coming from Patrick's neighbor, Nadia, but from Sarah it made me laugh. "Fine. But I owe you."

"Of course you do," she said matter-of-factly. "Don't worry, I'll make you pay."

Together we sorted the fabric into piles. She'd picked all complementary fabrics, even colors I'd never have thought would go together, but did. Purples with reds and rusts, browns and blacks together. She lined up the fabrics and pulled out a single box of nails.

"Huh," she said, looking at the box. "These won't do much good without a hammer."

"Or the furring strips."

She looked around the room. "And a ladder. And hey, don't

you have any big, strong men to help with this? Especially ones who'd be happy to work shirtless?"

I sighed. "Yeah. Right. Believe me, if I had a big, strong, shirtless man in my life who liked to use tools, don't you think I'm bringing him around you. I'm keeping him for myself."

"Selfish bitch." Sarah chuckled and hopped up on the table to swing her legs back and forth.

"I'll see what I have in the back room as far as tools go. I have a ladder there, too."

"Make sure you don't have a hunky handyman back there," she called after me as I headed to the rear space I used as a storage place, dressing room and small kitchen.

I flipped the switch on the wall, which turned on an old standing lamp I'd put in the corner. I needed to replace the overhead fixture. The small circle of light from the lamp wasn't enough to really see what was in all the boxes, some of which I hadn't even opened since moving in. I knew what was in most of them. A few contained untold mysteries, probably not of the Orient, but you never knew. I was pretty sure I'd stashed a toolbox someplace on one of the shelves.

After a couple moments scrambling, I found a box of tools, but not of the hammer and screwdriver variety. I unsnapped the locks and lifted the hinged, plastic lid. From the other room I heard the sound of Sarah's phone and low-pitched laughter.

Inside the box lay a huge, flesh-colored cock, complete with balls and a handy-dandy suction cup to keep it secured to a table or wall. Beneath it in other compartments were all sorts of sex gadgets—a butt plug still in its original package, boxes of novelty condoms in flavors and shapes, sample packets of lube with names like Slippery Nipplez and Cherry Popper.

This box had been a bridal shower gift to me from a group of college friends. It had gone with me from my dad's house to my first apartment, the one I'd meant to share with Patrick but had ended up living in alone. And now, somehow, it had found its way with a bunch of my other crap to the storage room in my studio.

I looked at it for a while. It had been a joke when I got it, and had become more of a joke later, though I'll admit it had taken me a long time to see it as funny. I'd put it away when I couldn't bear to see it, not because of the contents but because of what the gift had been meant to celebrate.

I ran a finger along the monstrous dong and shook my head, laughing. Something like this was too funny to be kept locked away. And after all this time, if I couldn't break out the huge rubber penis my friends had bought me in antici-pation of an unexpectedly canceled wedding to my gay boy-friend, I really needed a better sense of humor.

"Sarah!" I cried, clasping the dong to my crotch and striking a pose in the doorway. "I have something for you! Woo-hoo!"

Yeah. I twirled it like a lasso. Then I jerked my hips back and forth, fucking the air like a porn star on ecstasy. "Come and get it!"

Of course I hadn't looked before leaping through the doorway. Of course I'd assumed the pizza man had come and gone, and that Sarah was alone in the office. Of course I was wrong.

Of course it was Alex standing next to Sarah, their mouths agape and eyes wide. Sarah looked back and forth from him to me and shot me a look I knew meant she thought I'd been holding out on her. She recovered first.

"Thanks, Liv, but I've already got one like that."

"Me, too," Alex said after half a moment. "Mine's not as big, though."

Sarah guffawed and jerked a thumb at him. "I like this guy."

I stood in front of him with a gigantic rubber penis in my fist, and I couldn't find anything witty or smart to say. "Hi, Alex."

Sarah gave him a long up and down perusal. "Hello, Alex, owner of a huge cock."

I clapped the hand not full of pseudocock to my forehead. "Thank you, subtle Sarah."

Alex didn't seem perturbed by the implication we'd been discussing him. He gave Sarah his hand. "Alex Kennedy."

"Sarah Roth." She fluttered her eyelashes at him, and he laughed.

"Nice to meet you, Sarah." He looked at me. "I brought you a rent check."

Sarah's brows disappeared into her hairline. "Rent?"

"Remember I told you, I got a tenant?"

She snorted laughter. "Uh-huh. You sort of left out a few details on that one."

I realized I had the dildo in a death grip, as if I were strangling an anaconda. I had no place to put it so I set it on the table, where it nestled among the piles of fabric. The three of us stared at it.

"That's a shame," Sarah said after a minute. She plucked up the dong and swept the fabric out of the way, then suction-cupped it to the table surface. "There you go. *Much* better."

We all stared at it again.

Alex cleared his throat. "That's, um, impressive?"

Sarah gave the dildo a flick with her finger that set it bobbing like a metronome. "Well, listen, I'm out of here. Have fun, kids. Liv, I'll make a run to the hardware store."

"You don't have to go," Alex said. "Not because of me."

She snapped her fingers at him. "Hell, no. I need a trip to the hardware store. I have a serious jones for a new nail gun. Besides, I have plans."

"What plans?" I asked suspiciously. "You didn't mention any plans before."

Sarah held up her phone. "I didn't have them before, but I do now. And you've got company now, anyway. Alex." Smirking, she gave him another obvious assessment. "Maybe he can help you pound something. Ta, kids. Liv, I'll call you later. Alex, nice meeting you. Hope to see you again."

"You, too," he said, and watched her go before turning back to me with a slightly incredulous look. "I feel a little like I've been run over by a steamroller."

I laughed. "That's Sarah for you."

"Here." He handed me an envelope, which I put into my pocket. He looked around the room. "Great space."

I'd forgotten he'd never been up to the studio. "Thanks. It's the reason I bought the place to begin with."

"I don't blame you." He glanced over his shoulder at me. "You see the potential in things a lot, Olivia."

The compliment moved me, set me back a little. "Thanks."

He smiled. "So, I got a call from Patrick."

"Yeah?"

Alex's smile twisted a little. "Yeah. Apparently I'm supposed to avoid you?"

"Apparently." Something in his voice and expression tipped me off that something was a little strange. "What did he say?"

"Umm…" Alex looked discomfited. "A lot of shit."

"And…what did you say?"

"I told him he was a prick and to fuck off."

I raised a brow but believed he was telling the truth. "Wow."

Alex frowned. "Look, Patrick doesn't own me. Fuck, he doesn't own you, right?"

"No."

He shrugged. "I'm not really into being told what to do. For my own fucking good or not."

"He told you it as for your own good?" I crossed my arms over my chest. "Wow."

Alex shrugged again, but gave me a look softer than his last words had been. "Don't worry about it. I think he got the picture."

I cupped my elbows in my hands. "He was a little pissy that we've been spending so much time together. Thinks we're becoming BFF or something."

It didn't seem right talking about Patrick with a giant pink penis between us. I yanked it free from the tabletop and put it in a chest of drawers along the wall. Alex didn't say anything while I did so, and I kept my back to him as I pretended to look for something in one of the drawers.

"What's the story with you two, anyway?" he asked, mildly enough. I could imagine his dark eyes. Gray, not brown as I'd thought.

"I don't think I have a story."

"Olivia," Alex said seriously, "everyone has a story."

"Patrick and I used to be a couple." It was the short version.

"I know that part already."

I chewed the inside of my lip. "It was years ago. Obviously. Before he was gay."

Alex tilted his head, gave me an assessing look. "You don't think he was always queer?"

"No, I…" Alex had stumped me for a second. "Right. I meant before he came out. Before he admitted it, I guess. We were a couple when Patrick tried to be straight. How's that—is that better?"

He didn't seem to mind that I sounded harsh. "And now? What are you now?"

I sighed. "Now…I don't know what we are. Friends, I guess."

Alex made a skeptical noise, then gave an exaggerated look around. "And, moving right along…nice studio."

"You said that already."

"I know."

I laughed. It was easy to laugh with Alex. Easy to put aside the discussion of Patrick I didn't want to have, anyway. "It's a mess. Sarah was here to help me spiff it up."

"And I chased her away. I'm sorry." He put a hand on his heart and looked pained.

"Oh, don't you feel bad. Now that you're here I can use you. I've got a ton of junk that needs to be hauled around," I said with a grin. "There's no way I'm tackling anything fancy without Sarah here, but I can paint the walls with stain blocker mildew stuff and clean out the back room."

"Manual labor?" Alex looked skeptical. Then he cracked his knuckles and rolled his head, cracking his neck. He hopped from foot to foot. "Manly stuff, huh?"

I snorted. "Oh, yes, manly stuff. Because clearly I'm so entrenched with gender stereotypes."

I couldn't interpret his long, studying look, or the half smile that followed it. I'd amused him again, but I couldn't tell why. I gave him a look of my own.

"You're not too pretty to work, are you? Afraid of getting your hands dirty?"

"No, ma'am. I can even use power tools on occasion."

I snorted lightly. "I bet you can."

Alex gave a pointed glance at the drawer where I stashed the dildo. "I bet you can, too."

We both burst into laughter, utterly companionable and uncomplicated. My giggle fluttered into a sigh. He watched me, his dark gray eyes alight.

"What?" I said, wondering at the scrutiny.

"Patrick's an asshole."

I frowned a little, not wanting to head back toward that dark mood. "He can be. But so can anyone."

Alex grunted. "Hell, yeah, that's the truth."

Alex had never been anything but nice to me—supernice, really, above-and-beyond nice, but I knew he had firsthand experience with being a bit of a prick. I'd seen it myself. But that wasn't my business. I tried to judge people on what they did to and for me, not for anyone else.

"C'mon. I want to get this space painted by the end of the day so when Sarah comes back again we can hang the drapes. Because believe me, if it's not finished, she will kick my ass."

"She's a little tyrant, huh?" Alex followed me into the back room and let out a low whistle. "Cool."

I looked at the wooden shelves constructed from thick barn beams and heavy planks of wood. They reached ten feet high, halfway to the raftered roof. Once they'd been used to store equipment and supplies for the firehouse, but now most of them were bare or cluttered with the jumbled mess of everything I needed for the studio or couldn't fit in my living space downstairs.

"This room is what sold me. When they put this place up for auction, the Realtor didn't even want to show me this part. Apparently the former owner'd run out of funds before converting this floor to living space. There was water damage, broken glass. The first time I came up here, I found a dead bird."

"No wonder she didn't want to show you."

It seemed I laughed with him more often than anything else. "Right. Well, I made her, anyway, because to spend that sort of money on two apartments, even with the rent potential, seemed like a very bad choice."

"And you're not into making bad choices."

I flung him a look. "I think we can both agree I've made a few."

"But not in buying this place." Alex tipped his head back to stare up, up to the roof, where four-foot beams held the weight of the tiles. Then he rubbed his hands together again. "Great. What first?"

"First I want to seal the bricks and paint the studio walls. Give everything a nice, fresh start."

"Groovy."

"You don't have to help me, you know." I nudged past him to get at the buckets of sealant and paint, the brushes and drop cloths. "You must have better things to do."

"Nope."

I handed him a brush. "Why do I find that hard to believe?"

"Because I'm so damned pretty," Alex said with a straight face. "And charming."

I tapped his chest with my paintbrush. "That's it."

"Believe it or not, Olivia," Alex said, as he exited the back room after me, each of us carrying a bucket and a brush, "that can actually be a disadvantage."

"Oh, yeah? How so?" I paused to look around the room, seeking the best place to start. I had several buckets of clear brick sealant and a few cans of the dark gold paint I'd picked for the room's other walls. The floor, of scratched and scarred wooden planks, wouldn't be hurt much by splotches of paint, but as I didn't have the money to refinish it for a while, I flung down a drop cloth in one corner.

"For one thing, everyone assumes you already have plans when you don't, so hardly anybody ever invites you places." Alex set his bucket of sealant down by the front wall, between the long, floor-to-ceiling windows. "It's annoying."

I spread out my drop cloth and opened my paint can. "Oh, yeah? Should I hold you while you cry?"

Alex guffawed. "Am I that pathetic?"

"Sort of, yeah." My tone said the opposite. I straightened, watching as he bent to open his bucket. He'd shoved his sleeves up high on his elbows and I took a long, satisfying look at his forearms. I'm a sucker for a nice pair of wrists. The tendons underneath are very sexy to me.

I watched as he lifted the heavy bucket and bent to pour some of the sealant into the low pan, then soaked the roller in it. And yes, I was staring at his ass, because, please God, never let knowing it's stupid get in the way of ogling a fine rear end.

I poured paint into my own pan and dipped my roller. "Why don't I believe you?"

"It's that damn reputation of being an international playboy." Alex shot a grin over his shoulder. "Thought I'd give being a domestic playboy a try."

"How's that working for you?"

"Not so good," he admitted, and began coating the bricks with sealant. "It's not as exotic, that's for sure."

Again I submitted to laughter and reveled in it. "Everyone's got their talents."

We painted for a while in casual silence. The room got hotter. I turned to ask him if he wanted something cold to drink, and stopped short, slapped to silence by what I saw.

He'd lifted the hem of his shirt to wipe his face. His belly was tight, taut, with a single line of hair trailing from his navel into the waistband of his low-slung jeans. His belly button was perfection; I remember that, thinking how could a dip and hollow of flesh be so perfect?

"Don't move," I said.

The picture in my head had already appeared. All I needed was to make it happen. I wiped my hands on the seat of my jeans, not caring if I left streaks, and got my camera from its place on top of the dresser by the door. Alex, surprisingly obedient, had frozen, his shirt still lifted, his face turned toward me, one hip cocked.

I looked at him through the safety of my viewfinder, making him a picture and not a person. Light shafted in the windows on either side of him. I couldn't forget how I'd seen him once before, cut in half by shadow.

"Turn your face."

He did. The effect wasn't quite the same, the room was too

bright, but I captured the motion with a series of rapid shots as he moved. They'd be blurry. I didn't care.

"So fucking pretty," I muttered, and thought I heard him make a noise low in his throat. But I was so caught up in what I was trying to capture, I didn't pay attention.

I moved closer, aware as I always was how my position could change the picture. Click. Move. Shift, click. I didn't pause to view the pictures on the digital screen—didn't want what I was getting to interfere with what I saw in my head. Not yet.

"Lift your shirt again. Wipe your face."

That wasn't as good as it had been the first time. He was too self-conscious. I stepped closer, studying him. "No. Take it off."

This time I couldn't pretend he didn't make a sound. Alex twitched. I thought he'd say no, but then he reached over his shoulder to grab a handful of the shirt on his back, pull it upward and over his head. He clutched it for a half second before tossing it to the floor.

"Beautiful." I grabbed one of the dining-room chairs, seat tattered, carved wood dusty. I dragged it toward the window to his left. "Sit."

He laughed from deep in his throat, but moved without protest. With my camera still in one hand, I used the other to push him gently toward the light. Pliable, he moved, and I saw his smile, but focused on everything else.

"I have an idea…it's just…" I could not express it in words. Hardly ever could. "Tilt your chin just a little…yes. Perfect. Stay like that."

My camera whirred. Alex stayed still. I took another picture and moved nearer to get close up. Very close.

"You smell good. What is it?"

"It's called Whip. I get it from Black Phoenix Alchemy Lab," he said slowly, on an exhale.

"It's good."

The first time I'd ever seen him I'd thought how good-looking he was, but it had been a standard sort of pretty. Watching him get head from another man, seeing him come, remembering how it felt to climax with that picture in my head, layered that impression with a sexuality I hadn't been very good at ignoring. Dangerous to me, that sexuality, because I'd been burned by that flame and would be forever scorched.

Yet now I leaned closer. Looked into his eyes. "Will you do something for me?"

He swallowed, meeting my gaze, and breathed out without saying anything. His assent came with a nod. I wanted to touch his face, but kept my hands tight on the camera, which made all of this safe.

"Will you take off your shoes and socks?"

He laughed, not nervously but with a small hint of surprise, then bent to do what I'd asked. He straightened, his gaze bold and inquiring and anticipatory.

"Perfect." I moved back a few steps. "Look out the window. Think about something…sexy."

"Wh-what?" He stuttered the word with a laugh.

I looked at him over the camera. "Don't tell me you can't do sexy."

"I can do it."

Of course he could. He looked out the window, his body language shifting subtly. He slouched a little, one bare foot in front of the other, a man at ease with his body in a way that made him a natural model. I took a profile shot of him looking far away.

When he put his hand up to his chest, fingertips just over his nipple, I almost dropped my camera. I kept myself from squeaking only by biting my tongue. *Focus. Focus and snap the shot.*

It's not real.

If you look at it through a lens, it's not real.

Alex leaned back a little more in the chair, then gave me a lazy glance. "Yes?"

"More."

The quality of his laughter changed. Got slow and low. This man had had an audience before. Maybe not one with a camera, but he wasn't shy about being watched.

"How much more do you want, Olivia?"

"What can you give me, Alex?"

He shifted, his hand sliding down his chest and belly to the button at his waist. Neither of us spoke. I held my breath, but couldn't tell if he was holding his.

This was not the sort of picture I normally took. Yet here we were, him before me with his hand ready to unsnap his jeans, and my camera ready. I licked my mouth. I raised the viewfinder to my eye and made it all not real.

"Yes," I told him in a hoarse, low voice I wished didn't shake. "Do it."

He unsnapped and unzipped. He reached inside. His back arched, just a little, as his hand disappeared inside the denim.

He made another noise and closed his eyes, bit down on his lower lip. I caught the flash of teeth. His hair fell forward, shielding him.

Click.

Snap.

Nothing through the viewfinder is real. Except, of course, when it all is.

His hand moved. I knew what he was doing, but the angle I shot from showed only a man, head bent, face closed in concentration. Naked chest. Naked feet. I moved, circling. His jeans had slid lower, showing the dimples at the base of his back and a hint of his ass.

I pulled a stool in front of him. Got on it to shoot down, now the shot consisting of muscled, broad shoulders and the top of his head. I didn't tell him how to move or what to do.

Our breathing was very loud.

I got off the stool to take a few more shots. Standing in front of him, I looked at his face, not at his cock in his hand. I wasn't touching him, but I imagined I could feel him against me. I could smell him. I thought if I breathed in, I could taste him, too. I think I made a sound. Alex opened his eyes. They were naked, too.

I knew why Patrick had warned me.

This could go no place good. I would end up embarrassed, rejected. This wasn't about a photo now. I put my eye to the camera again.

He breathed out. "Do you want…"

"I want all of it. Yes."

He sighed and shivered. His hand moved, stroking. And through the tiny square of glass, I watched him, and I made the pictures in my head real.

I moved closer, meaning to take another shot. His hand captured my wrist. I didn't pull away. Inches apart, I looked into his eyes and saw an invitation that became a request when he took my hand and placed it under his.

He moved mine along his cock, very, very slowly. Up. Down. He was so hard, so hot beneath my palm.

It wasn't the first time I'd had a man's cock in my hand, but I'd never been holding a camera with the other. I'd never been helpless to pull away, frozen in my own arousal. I lost myself in his dark gray eyes.

He took my camera from my hand and put it on the windowsill. Alex pulled me closer. His hand moved mine, faster now, and he let out a small groan.

He took my other hand, now empty, and put it on the back of his neck, where it curled in the softness of his hair. My fingers twined, tightly, instinctually, and he moaned at the pull. His head tipped back. His hand moved mine faster.

I couldn't pretend this wasn't real anymore. It was all too real, too much, too focused. Who did this sort of thing?

Apparently, I did.

He let go of my hand when I moved it on my own, and when I pulled his hair again he gritted his teeth with a strangled gasp. I had never felt this before, power like this. To stand over a man who by all previous accounts should not have been aroused by my touch. To feel his cock stiffen more in my hand and hear the pace of his breath quicken… To watch him close his eyes…

"Look at me," I said.

He did.

I did not fall into orgasm from that look, but I came damn close.

I let go of his cock and stepped back, two steps. Four. He shuddered and made a sound of protest, but he didn't move.

"What the fuck," I said with a quaking, shaking voice, "is going on?"

"Olivia—"

I shook my head and stepped back again. "Why are you fucking with me?"

"I'm not—I'm sorry," he said quickly. "I just… Believe me, I didn't think this would happen."

The breath hissed out of me and my shoulders slumped a little. "I think you'd better go."

"I like you, Olivia."

"You don't even know me."

With a sigh, he took a step away. I didn't like the distance between us any more than I had the lack of it, but again I stayed still. Alex put his hands on his hips.

"I could get to know you."

"I don't think that's a good idea."

He looked too sure of himself, too cocky. A man used to having his own way. "Why not?"

"I don't think we got started the right way, that's all." I gestured at the chair, my face heating.

He looked at the chair, too, and then back at me. "I'm sorry. That was… Believe me, I didn't plan that."

I knew he hadn't, any more than I had, but it *had* happened. Unexpected, utterly sexy…but unacceptable. And there was more to it than that.

I swam for a minute in his gaze. I rocked a little bit, my entire equilibrium a mess. This was something I wanted and couldn't convince myself not to want.

I should've told him what I'd seen, him with Evan. Told him I knew about him and Patrick, too. But that meant admitting I'd been in the room, and how did I do that without sounding like some sort of crazy, horny pervo? Or a jealous ex-girlfriend?

"Patrick said you don't like girls," I said at last, lamely.

"Patrick," Alex said, "doesn't have a fucking clue."

Chapter 07

I hadn't stopped him from walking out. It took me a few minutes of warring with myself to decide to follow. I found Alex outside beneath the fire escape, another unlit cigarette dangling from his mouth. He'd shrugged into his coat, slipped on unlaced boots.

"Very James Dean," I said.

Alex didn't say anything.

I stopped myself from saying anything else. This, our second kiss, was harder, a little rougher, a lot sloppier. Alex pulled me closer. His hands found my ass, covered by the length of my thick wool coat, but I felt them there. Heat. All of him was heat, and hardness. The air was so cold it burned my throat when I gasped, but his breath warmed me.

He warmed me.

He'd propped open the back door and now we both moved through it, kicking the doorstop out of the way so the heavy

metal door clanged closed behind us. Still kissing, we went
down the hall, where he kicked open his door, too, catching
it neatly with one hand before it could hit the wall.

We stopped kissing then, for a moment. I needed to
breathe. I needed to give my neck a rest, too, from the angle.
He was taller than me, and I was wearing flats. I drew in a
shaky breath.

Alex put a hand to the top button of his peacoat. I shook
all over when he slipped the button from its mooring and
parted the wool, just so. I could see a piece of bare flesh
beneath. Another button slipped out of its slot beneath his
capable fingers.

More naked flesh.

Upstairs, I'd paused only long enough to pull on my coat
and boots. Beneath, I wore my paint-spattered clothes. I was
already naked under his gaze. I felt naked. I wanted to be
naked.

Alex undid another button. Now I could see his chest was
entirely bare. He took off his coat and tossed it to the side
while I stood unmoving. Without the frantic kissing molding
us together, my focus had scattered. I had too much time to
think.

Alex took the final few steps to cross the distance between
us. He looked down at me, his eyes searching mine. I thought
one of us should speak, but neither did. This time when he
kissed me it was slow and deliberate, no confusing his intentions…or his preferences.

His fingers crept over my hips to bunch the hem of my
shirt. Higher, a little higher, the fabric whispered over my
belly. Cool air brushed my skin. I shivered again, a fever chill.

"Touch me," he said.

His chest was warm when I splayed my fingers over the smooth skin. I put my palms flat over his nipples. I felt his heart beating, the rise and fall of his chest with every breath. I curled my fingers, the nails digging ever so lightly into his skin.

His groan arrowed straight between my legs. Alex put a hand over mine, the one over his heart. I thought he meant me to pull away, that I'd hurt him, but he only curled my fingers a little harder against him. My fingernails dented his flesh.

I could've cut him. Gouged. I could've made him bleed just then, and though it never would have occurred to me to do something like that in the midst of any sort of passion, I looked into his eyes and could see him thinking about it.

"Alex..."

He kissed me again. Alex had furnished the apartment with a flat-screen TV hung on the wall and a full-size futon covered with giant pillows in cases of all different colors. It was only a few steps away from us, but I wasn't sure I could make it even there. I thought I might just fall down on the bare wooden floor and pull him on top of me.

Somehow we made it at least a couple steps closer. He'd kept my hand a prisoner against his chest, but now Alex paused. He pulled away. He let go of my hand, let go of the bunched fabric at my hip. He stepped back and looked me over, head to toe. He looked at me, his smile wicked and sexy. His gaze knowing.

He didn't know me. Couldn't know me. But I wanted him to.

"I wanted to do this since the first time I saw you." His

hands closed on my hips again and slid beneath, across my belly.

He lifted my T-shirt off over my head. I wore a lacy bra that matched my orange satin panties, the color brighter against my skin than I remembered.

"Unzip," he said.

I did. The denim slid from my hips and into his hands, and he pulled my jeans off my legs one at a time while I rested a hand on his shoulder to keep my balance.

Alex's hands cupped my ass. He held me still as his lips tickled my stomach. My hand went from his shoulder to his hair.

His mouth moved over the satin of my panties. Wet heat from his breath filtered through the fabric. I glanced over my shoulder at the futon, waiting for us.

His hand in mine, I led him there, tossed aside pillows and pushed him down onto the cushions. I crawled up his body to straddle him. His cock pressed the front of his jeans.

I stroked him. Another stroke. Alex arched with a small hiss of indrawn breath. His eyes closed briefly, taking the pleasure.

I could feel him, hot and thick, but the material between us had to go. I unzipped, unbuttoned. I eased his pants down, though they were already so low I could see the jut of his hip bones.

I freed his cock and stroked it again, skin on skin. He shuddered and made a small noise I wanted to eat, that's how delicious it was. If I was going to do this, I wasn't going to falter. No hesitation, no worries. I knew what I was in for—which was more than I could say about a lot of things in life.

I lifted my body to slide off his jeans, then straddled him again. Alex put his hands behind his head. He watched me stroke him a couple more times, but then moved to capture my wrist in one hand.

"Wait." He pulled me down on top of him to kiss my mouth. We rolled, facing each other. His knee moved between my legs, his thigh pressed against my cunt. My panties slid against my flesh, hot and slick.

"I don't want to finish before we even start," he said into my mouth.

I licked the corner of his lips, which had a habit of twisting up when he was being wicked. "That wouldn't be so good."

His hand moved between us. His finger found my clit through the soft material covering it, and circled there. Pleasure stabbed me, unexpected. My body jerked.

Gray eyes stared at me. His fingertip circled, circled. "I want to make sure I remember what I'm doing."

"I think you're doing all right." Each word dripped from my mouth, slow and smooth.

His palm pressed flat to my belly. I lay back, nerves on fire. Alex slid his fingers along the hem of my panties and then beneath. "Like this?"

"Yes…" It was all I could manage to say.

"Good." His hand shifted, moved lower. His finger probed me gently. Slid inside. "This?"

"Yes."

He stopped just long enough to draw the satin off my body, only seconds passing, but long enough that when he touched me again it was electric. He lay on his side, propped on his elbow, staring at my face while his fingertips kept up their magic.

"Stop," I said after a moment, my voice quavering. "I don't want to finish too quickly."

He laughed and kissed me. Though I'd said for him to stop, he only slowed. He nuzzled my ear. "I just realized…I don't have any condoms."

I'd closed my eyes, giving in to the pleasure, but they snapped open now. I sat, my heart pounding so fast the room spun for a second or two. I grabbed his shoulder. I thought I might tip over then, from pressing my body against his hand, but I held off my orgasm with a few deep breaths.

"Well, shit," I said.

"Yeah, I suck." He kissed me until my mouth opened and I tasted him. His hand moved again. "I want to watch you come."

He could've recited the alphabet and I'd have found it arousing at that point, but those words were the sexiest thing any man had ever said to me. I reached between us to stroke him, and Alex bit the inside of his cheek.

"I want to watch you, too."

This had started sort of desperately, in a back-clawing, up-against-the-wall-fuck sort of way. It could've been awkward now that the urgency had softened, but it wasn't. I wouldn't let it be, and Alex didn't make it.

We wriggled and shifted until we were face-to-face, hands moving in time. My soft laugh eased into a moan. His laugh sounded a little strained and he bent his head for a moment, eyes closed, before he kissed my neck, my throat, the tops of my breasts.

His hand moved faster. I was skating close to the edge, my body tensing. My hand on him moved faster, too. In sync. He groaned, and I recognized the sound and his expression—I'd seen it once before, after all.

The memory, still so fresh, locked me up tight for a second, but only just that long. We kissed. His moan filled my mouth. He shook a little.

"So close," he whispered. His fingers slowed, perfectly easing me over the edge without forcing me over, letting me find my own way in my own time.

Orgasm flooded me with warmth and I let it sweep me away. Alex buried his face into the curve of my shoulder and followed a moment after me. His teeth found my skin but didn't bite, even though I arched into it, my body reeling with pleasure. He came between us, against my belly, the sensation startling and intimate.

Messy, too, but as I fell back with a satisfied sigh onto the pillows, I didn't care. "Wow."

He collapsed more slowly, ending up on his back, his shoulder pressing mine. "Mmm-hmm."

I took a few seconds to catch my breath, then turned to face him. "I haven't done anything like that since high school."

Alex laughed without looking at me. His gaze scoured the ceiling. He swiped a hand across his forehead, pushing sweat-damp hair from his eyes. "I always have condoms."

I settled deeper into the cushion, aware now of various sensations I hadn't noticed when he was making me come. How tight my bra straps were. How tired I suddenly was. I yawned.

He looked at me then. "Sleepy?"

I sighed with another yawn and sat up, testing my emotions. Nothing about this felt casual. Just the opposite, in fact. It felt like it meant too much. This night, this man.

I feigned the yawn this time. "I'd better get going."

I was up and off the futon and bending to look for my panties before Alex said anything.

"Wait. What? Wait a minute, Olivia."

I stood in my boots and bra, my jeans in one hand, my panties in the other. Alex had moved to the edge of the futon, one foot on the floor, one hand reaching. The light from the hanging lamp in the corner caught him one way, the shifting glare from the TV in another, and once again I saw him painted with shadows.

"Stay," Alex said.

I guess some creative people hear music, or poems or scraps of dialogue, in their heads. I take pictures. And in the span of those few seconds, that picture was taken.

Black boys, as the song says, are nutritious. White boys, the other song says, are so sexy. I'd dated my share of black, white, even Asian men and found the color of their skins to be what made the least difference between them. But one thing I found about white boys was that every single one of them loved my hair.

Alex wasn't different. He ran his fingers over the long, twisted locks I usually wore pulled off my face and hanging down my back. Now, after our romp on the futon, they had fallen out of the hair band and tumbled over my shoulders. I drew them over his chest, his thighs. That beautiful cock, which stirred a little at my touch. I looked up at him through the shield of my hair and thought about taking him in my mouth.

He pushed my hair away from my face, his long fingers stroking my forehead. "You're so gorgeous, you know that?"

I propped myself up on my elbows. "Mmm."

Alex laughed and pulled me up to kiss my mouth. "Don't make that noise like you don't believe me. I hate it when people can't take a compliment."

"Fine. I'm gorgeous." I ran my tongue along his jaw and nestled my face into the dip of his neck.

He wrapped my hair around his fingers, released it. Twisted it again. I looked at him with a raised brow. He laughed and let go.

"Sorry."

"It's okay. I like your hair, too." I ran my fingers through the softness, making sure to let it all fall over his face when I was finished caressing.

"Have you always worn it like that?"

I sat up. "Nobody's ever asked me that before."

He sat up, too. Cross-legged and naked, we faced each other, our knees touching. Alex grabbed a pillow for his lap, and I took one as well.

"You don't have to tell me."

I laughed. "No, it's fine. When I was a kid, my mom had no clue what to do with my hair. Natural hair wasn't really in fashion, even though my mom was a pretty natural woman herself. I'm talking gypsy skirts and head scarves. Birkenstocks."

"Patchouli?"

"You got it." I laughed again, stretching. Comfortable with him. "Anyway, she finally started taking me to a special hairdresser who dealt with black hair, and that was okay. We relaxed it for a while, when I was in high school. Then when I got to college I had sort of…not an epiphany, exactly. More like an identity crisis. I thought I'd try being black for a change—"

He looked so startled I had to laugh. "I'm adopted."

"Oh. Ah. Oh?" He still looked a little confused.

"My parents are white."

"Ah." He nodded. "Okay. I get it now."

"Yeah." I nodded, too, rubbing his knee with mine. "Anyway, when I went to college I figured it was time to explore this other identity. Not the one I was raised with. I joined a black sorority and the BCC, the Black Cultural Club."

"How was that?"

I laughed again, this time ruefully. "Well, I made some great friends, but it was hard. I wasn't black enough for a lot of them. Not the color of my skin and not the way I acted. It was tough, but I learned a lot about myself. Isn't that what you're supposed to do in college, though?"

"I didn't go."

"No?" Surprised, I looked into his eyes. "Not even community college?"

"Nope."

"Wow." That made his success more impressive, but it felt awkward to say so.

He shrugged. "I should've gone. Maybe I'd have learned something about myself."

I stretched out on my side, propping my head on my hand, and ran my fingers up the inside of his thigh. "I don't know that I wouldn't have learned it all, eventually. Anyway, that's when I decided to go natural with my hair. In the long run, it was easier than fighting with it all the time. It was flattering. And…it connected me. It might sound stupid to say so."

"No, it doesn't." He stretched out, too, so we were face-to-face again. "It makes sense. It's enviable, actually."

I laughed softly. "Sure."

"It is." Alex ran his fingers over my hair again, pulling a few of the locks forward, over my shoulder. "It suits you."

It seemed like the most natural thing to kiss him then. His mouth opened under mine. His tongue stroked. This time when I let my hair trace a path over his body, I did take his cock in my mouth.

I sucked him slowly. He arched. I gave in to the smells and sounds of his desire. I lost myself in it. I found my clit with my fingertips and got myself off as I made him come. When he did, he twined his fingers in my hair, and I smiled even as I took him down the back of my throat.

Minutes later, his heartbeat slowed under my cheek. His breathing matched it soon after. He snored a little from deep in his throat. It was cute. He went boneless and relaxed under me, and before I knew it, I was out like a light.

I woke to the smells of bacon frying and coffee perking. I stretched under soft blankets and my hands encountered a mountain of pillows. I sat up, rubbing my eyes on a futon in the middle of Alex Kennedy's living room. And I was naked.

I could see him, beyond the half-wall and arch, in the small, U-shaped kitchen. Well, I could see part of him. The cabinets hanging low over the countertop island that divided the kitchen from the dining area left a couple of feet open for pass-through viewing. I could see him from shoulders to thighs, a nice view of his briefs-clad ass and the apron strings dangling against it.

As for myself, the sheet I pulled up to cover my breasts might've made a nifty toga if I'd been talented enough to fold and twist it, but I didn't have that skill. I scanned the floor for my clothes and saw a sock, a boot, my shirt. A flash of orange told me my panties were hiding just beneath the futon. I reached for them as Alex appeared the archway.

"Good morning."

"Hi."

He had a spatula in his hand and the apron I'd viewed from behind turned out to have the cartoon torso of a bikini-clad woman with huge tits imprinted on the front. "Hungry?"

A man who wore Hello Kitty pajamas wouldn't balk at cross-gender bacon frying, but a surprised laugh burst out of me anyway. "Umm…"

He grinned and smoothed a hand down the apron's front to fondle the big cartoon boobs. "Nice, huh?"

"You know, my current circle of male friends has skewed me so far that shouldn't even have surprised me." I got my panties and slid into them, but couldn't find my bra. I could go topless, prance around in what my mom had always called *gatkes.* I had the scent of him all over me. I grabbed up my sweater anyway and slid it on over my bare skin. My nipples pebbled immediately against the soft fabric.

I caught his gaze as I used a couple of my locks to tie back the rest at the nape of my neck. His smile had frozen for a second, and if I'd looked at him a moment later I think I'd have missed his expression. "Alex?"

He waved the spatula. "Breakfast is ready, if you want it."

We faced each other from across the room. The morning after. Here it was. I looked for a reason why I shouldn't cross the distance between us and kiss him as if we'd been lovers for years. I didn't find one.

"Morning," he said against my mouth, and the hand not wielding the spatula rested comfortably on my ass, which he squeezed to pull me closer.

"I'm going to use your bathroom, okay?"

He gave me another small squeeze. The cartoon woman was getting an erection. "Sure."

I didn't shower, just used the toilet and sneaked a mouthful of his toothpaste to swish around in lieu of an actual brushing. I caught sight of my reflection and couldn't stop the grin— my mascara might be a little smeared and my hair a little wild, but damn, didn't I look satisfied?

Alex had set plates on the island and loaded them with scrambled eggs and bacon. The toaster dinged as I sat, and he pulled out slices of wheat toast. A stick of butter on a plate and a half-empty jar of peach preserves appeared as I sat in one of the wicker bar stools.

The kettle whistled and he lifted it to pour some hot water into my mug, then handed me a box of Earl Grey teabags.

"Wow, this is some service." I breathed in the good breakfast smells with a happy sigh.

"I'll be right back. You don't have to wait."

I dug into the food while Alex disappeared into one of the bedrooms, to come out a moment later wearing a pair of fleecy bottoms. Batman, this time. The apron, balled in one fist, got tossed onto the counter as he slid into the seat next to mine.

"Good?" he asked, watching me eat.

I nodded, mouth full. Our dangling feet nudged, then our knees. He was touching me on purpose, and it was okay because last night we'd been naked and sweaty and our mouths had been all over each other, and we hadn't fucked, not technically, but we'd done just about everything else.

"Olivia?" His brow furrowed. "You okay?"

"Sure. You?"

Alex didn't have an open face, one I could read easily. He

needed a translation I didn't know him well enough to make. When I looked at him, I saw a story. I saw a picture I wanted to take and capture and keep.

"Yes."

I poked my fork into the leftover bits of scrambled egg. Then I took a deep, slow breath and steadied myself before I turned on the stool to face him. "Listen. About last night…"

He looked at me solemnly without speaking, his gaze shielded and shuttered. He chewed slowly and swallowed. I watched his throat work and thought of the taste of his skin. I thought about a shadowed room and him in silhouette, a man on his knees in front of him. I thought of the sound of a groan.

"I never actually had sex with Patrick. We dated for four years and we were going to get married, but we never actually slept together." I cupped my hands around the barely warm mug and cleared my throat. This had to be said. I needed to tell him everything before anything went any further.

Alex nodded, but waited in silence for me to keep going.

"He told me it was because he wanted to wait. Because he was Catholic. And I believed him, because I loved him. He liked getting head from me, though. That was okay." I laughed again and sank into the cushions, a hand over my face. "God. It's all so obvious now, but then…I guess I just saw what I wanted to see."

"Or maybe he didn't want to admit anything else."

"That, too." I sighed. "Anyway, a couple weeks before we got married, I was putting away some laundry in his dresser drawer. I found a box of condoms."

"Ouch."

Even now, the memory turned my stomach. The betrayal of it. I knew right away they weren't for me.

"Yeah. So I confronted him about it. I thought maybe he'd deny it, but he didn't. I thought he'd tell me about some girl he worked with, something like that. I didn't expect him to tell me he was fucking his way through the city's gay population."

"He came out to you, just like that?"

"Just like that. He said, 'I'm a fag, Olivia, and I like fucking other men.' He looked scared when he said it, but he did."

Alex blinked and looked away for a second. "What did you do?"

"I didn't believe him for about two seconds, and then it all made sense. It all fit. And I just…lost it. I cried. I threw the box of condoms at him. They spilled all over the floor, and he went down on his knees to pick them up. I remember that…how he got on his knees to gather them up like they were precious. As if I'd thrown down a bunch of jewels and he wanted to make sure he got every single one."

I looked at Alex's face. "Then I told him the wedding was off, that I was leaving him."

Alex looked surprised, then not. "I thought he broke it off after he came out to you."

Maybe Patrick *had* talked to him about it. I shook my head. "No. That's what everyone thinks. But what really happened is Patrick begged me to still marry him. Told me his family would disown him, that we'd lose all the money on our deposits. He told me we had to get married. And I loved him, so…at first I said yes. I said I'd lie for him. That I'd live a lie for him."

"But you didn't marry him."

"No. We cleaned up the mess, put away the laundry and then…" I swallowed hard, remembering. The smell of cologne. The taste of Patrick's tears. "He kissed me. And he put his hands on me. He tried to make love to me. He said he wanted to prove to me that he could be a good husband, too. But I couldn't look at him that way, Alex. I couldn't have his hands on me. What he'd done…all I could think was that he'd said he loved me more than anything, and yet he'd lied to me all along. Himself, too, maybe, for a long time. But mostly to me."

Alex rubbed my shoulder, his fingers squeezing gently. "I'm sorry, Olivia. It was a shitty thing for him to do."

I put my hand on top of his, but not to remove it. I squeezed back. "Yes. It was. And it was even shittier when he told everyone I'd cheated on him."

"And you didn't tell anyone the truth?"

"I'd promised him I wouldn't. I thought that was fair, that he should come out to them himself. And I'd have been there for him, probably, if I hadn't been so angry…"

"It wasn't your job to hold his hand." Alex sounded angry himself.

"I know that now. But I'd have done it. Instead, he told everyone it was because of me. No wedding. No marriage. And he didn't come out to any of them for close to a year. By that time I'd come to terms with it, or so I thought. And by that time…

"By that time I'd been pregnant with Pippa, carrying a child I knew I couldn't raise, for a couple who would, and wanted to. My mother had disowned me, not because of the pregnancy, but because I was giving up the baby she thought I should keep.

"Well, by then a lot had happened. I'd heard from some friends that he'd finally come out. So one day, I called him up and asked him to meet me for dinner, which he did. We talked. We sort of…fell on each other's neck and sobbed, I guess. He'd always been my best friend, you know? It's hard to be in love with your best friend when you know it can never be more than that."

"Sure. I know." Alex squeezed my hand again and dropped his to his lap.

Now was the time to tell him what I'd seen on the porch and what Patrick had told me. I drew in a slow breath but didn't quite find the courage to do it. Alex leaned forward and for several long seconds did not brush his lips over mine. When he did, I felt the touch in every inch of me. Yeah, it's cliché, but it was true.

His hand cupped the back of my neck, his strong fingers pressing just right at the base of my skull. I shivered, my eyes closing in anticipation of a deeper kiss, which he didn't give me. I licked my mouth and tasted him.

"Alex…I have to tell you something."

He pulled away and let me go. "Okay."

And once again I didn't tell him the truth. Blame my body, which he'd played so well. Blame my heart, that stupid thing, which thought it could handle this. "I think you really need to get some condoms."

Alex blinked. Then he laughed. "I thought you were going to say… Never mind."

I touched his knee to get him to look at me. "What?"

He shrugged and drank his coffee. "I just thought you were going to tell me it was a mistake. Or something like that."

It might have been, but it had been such a damn long time

since I'd gone to bed with anyone that I wasn't going to ruin it with regret. The almost-sex had been great. I had no reason to think full-on fucking wouldn't be equally fabulous.

I stroked his knee a little higher, up to his thigh. "Do you think it was a mistake?"

He twisted my hair around his finger for a moment before letting his hand fall to his side. "No."

"Good." I took another breath, feeling lighter. "Alex, look…I'm not sure what this is or what will happen, but I don't like to spend time wishing I didn't do things after I've already done them. There's no point in that."

He nodded after half a second. "Agreed."

"Good." I leaned close, not quite kissing him but offering my mouth if he wanted to take it. "So what do you say we go buy some condoms?"

Chapter 08

*I*t's a law of nature that when you're buying something embarrassing you will run into someone you know. Tampons, yeast-infection cream...condoms. Add a post-orgasm glow, clothes that had clearly been worn two days in a row and what I was sure was the smell of illicit sex hanging over me, and there was no way I was getting out of Wal-Mart undetected.

Today it was Father Matthew from St. Paul's. He had a cart full of cold-care products and a very red nose when he passed me in the aisle, heading toward the pharmacy. It had been months and months since I'd gone to church, and I'd never been a full member there, but of course the condoms in my hand meant he recognized me right away.

"Olivia! How are you?" Father Matthew blinked behind his thick glasses. His hair stood up all over his head and he looked as if he should be in bed.

"Fine, Father, how are you? Got a cold?" The box in my

hand felt as if it might catch on fire any second. I gave myself a mental slap to the forehead for thinking I didn't need a shower before making the ten-minute trip to the store.

Behind me, Alex snorted laughter. He'd been fooling around just a moment before, comparing the brands and trying to do a price per orgasm comparison. I didn't dare look at him.

Father Matthew blinked, his voice like a foghorn. "Oh, yes, a pretty bad one. I won't shake your hand."

He looked over my shoulder at Alex and then back at me, clearly expecting an introduction.

"Um, Father Matthew, this is my…friend, Alex Kennedy."

"Nice to meet you, Father. I won't shake your hand, either."

The priest laughed, then sneezed and fumbled in the pocket of his heavy coat for a handkerchief. He honked into it and sighed. "Nice to meet you, Alex. I should get going. I want to go home and get into bed."

"Sounds like a great idea," Alex said, and if stepping on his foot wouldn't have been so obvious, I'd have stomped him into silence.

As it was, I put on a fake, bright smile and kept the condoms tucked close to my side. "Sorry you don't feel well, Father. Get better soon."

"Oh, thank you. And, Olivia, you know you're always welcome to come back to Mass." Father Matthew grinned and his gaze dropped momentarily to the box in my hand before he flicked his gaze to Alex. "Both of you could come. Are you Catholic, Alex?"

"Yes, Father, as a matter of fact."

Surprised, I turned to look at Alex, who'd put on a choirboy smile.

"With a name like that, I was pretty sure you were. Come to Mass," Father Matthew said. "We'd be happy to see you there. Happy New Year!"

He didn't push it more than that or wait for an answer I knew would probably be a lie, anyway. I liked him for that. I'd liked him when I went to church, too. It was the rest of it I didn't care for.

As Father Matthew ambled off toward the pharmacy, Alex pulled me against him so he could nuzzle my ear.

"Wow, I haven't had a close call like that since I was in high school."

I laughed and turned to poke him in the chest. "What happened in high school?"

"I was in the drugstore buying rubbers when my mother showed up in the next aisle. She wasn't buying rubbers, thank God. Epsom salts." He shuddered, then imitated a woman's voice. "'A.J., what are you doing here?'"

"What did you tell her?"

"I said I was buying bubble gum."

"And she believed you?" I laughed.

He shrugged. "She didn't ask any questions. That's all I cared about."

I studied the box in my hand, then tossed it into the basket he held. "Let's get out of here before the rabbi shows up. Do we need anything else?"

Alex grinned. He hooked another box of condoms off the rack and tossed it in. Then a bottle of silicone lube. The big one. I raised a brow.

"Let's hit aisle four," he said.

"What's in aisle four?"

"Snacks," he said matter-of-factly.

"You think we'll need...snacks?" I had to try hard to keep a straight face.

"I think you're going to need to keep your strength up," he told me with another smile that shot a bolt of liquid excitement right between my thighs. "Definitely."

He waited until we were back in his car before he asked me about the priest. "Do you go to church a lot?"

This was a conversation that would take a lot longer than ten minutes. "Not really," I said anyway.

"Huh."

I looked at him. "Huh, what? Do you go to church? Or were you telling Father Matthew a lie about being Catholic?"

He laughed. "No, I wasn't lying. If you call being born a Catholic, raised a Catholic and confirmed a Catholic being Catholic."

"But you're not, now?"

He shrugged. "I'm not anything now."

"Huh," I said.

Alex glanced at me, his mouth still curved in a smile. "What did you tell me before? It's complicated. But really, Olivia, it doesn't matter to me what you are."

I watched the fields turn to houses. In another minute he made the turn down the alley and into the lot behind my building. I picked at a piece of lint on my gloves. "I don't know what I am."

Alex turned off the car and twisted in his seat to face me. "Well, that's okay, too."

He kissed me when we got in the back door. It was the same place he'd kissed me the night before, still as cold, just brighter in the daylight. Alex was warm, though. Mouth and hands. The bags crushed between us.

"I have to go upstairs first. I want to take a shower," I said.

His eyes flashed in the light from the windows facing the street. "Do you want me to come up?"

Did I?

I faltered at the question, thinking of spending another few hours on his futon in the middle of his living room with the full light of day doing nothing to hide anything I might want hidden. My bedroom had dim, soft and romantic lighting and a nice comfy bed. It was also *my* bedroom, and I'd never had a lover in it. Somehow, that seemed to make all of this suddenly more intimate. More important.

"No?" he asked.

He was perceptive, scarily so. Why did he seem to see every thought I ever had, while I could only guess at his? I shook my head.

"It's not no, it's just…I won't take long. I'll come back down. Okay?" A kiss was supposed to soften the words, but I couldn't tell if it had or if he was just that good at faking. I thought maybe the latter.

"I'll leave the door unlocked."

I nodded and left the bags with him. In my apartment I closed my eyes, but could see only his face, the way he looked when he came. Deep, gray eyes, unreadable. His smile.

I lifted my arm and ran my nose along it from the elbow to my wrist. I could smell him on me. Taste him on my lips. My heart skipped, my thighs squeezed together involuntarily, and I actually made a sound of longing.

I wanted Alex. It didn't matter about anything else. My reasons. His. I'd meant what I told him about not wanting to regret, but now I understood I hadn't quite meant that, exactly.

I was sure I would regret this, sometime.

I simply didn't care.

He'd left the door open, just as he'd promised. I knocked, anyway, before I swung it open. I peeked around it, suddenly nervous and not knowing what I'd see. Naked Alex, waiting for me? I could only hope.

He wasn't naked, but his wet hair showed he'd showered, too. I'd put on a pair of jeans and an oversize button-down shirt over a cute camisole top. He wore jeans, too, and a pink button-down shirt with a very frayed hem. He hadn't tucked it in or even buttoned it all the way, and I got to see quite a bit of flesh as he turned from the counter, where he'd been setting out a bowl of pretzels.

"You're going to feed me again?"

"Strength, Olivia. I told you."

My mouth and throat went dry. It's one thing to know how to be a modern woman, full of confidence in her sexuality and totally okay with the casual fuck. It's another to actually be that woman.

"We should talk about something first, though," he said seriously, before I could reply.

"Uh-oh." I shook my head and took a step backward. "That doesn't sound good."

He didn't let me escape. He took my hand and led me to the futon, where the sheets and blankets and pillows were all tidied. We both sat. He didn't let go of my hand. He turned it over in his and traced the lines on my palm until I shivered. Then he looked at me.

"We don't have to do this."

It was the last thing I'd expected to hear. I almost yanked my hand from his. "If you don't want to—"

"I want to. I want to," he assured me, pulling me closer. "Believe me, Olivia. I do."

I scanned his face, which looked sincere and open, though those mingled expressions did nothing to help me figure him out. "So why did you say that?"

"Because…" He cleared his throat and shifted. I could see his bare chest inside the pink shirt. I could smell him.

He smelled good. I leaned closer, just a little. "What?"

"I haven't been with a woman in…well, a while." He said it as if it was a relief to get it out, all in a rush.

A woman, he'd said. It could have been a lie, but he'd made the distinction. If he'd said "anyone" I'd have turned around and walked away. That's what I told myself, anyway. That if he'd lied to me just then I'd have left.

"Me, neither," I said lightly.

His eyes searched mine and he smiled half a beat after I spoke. "You're funny."

"Sometimes."

His thumb traced a random pattern on my palm. "I just wanted you to know."

"Thank you." Our knees bumped. I toyed with one of the two buttons holding his shirt closed. When it came undone, I took care of the other and spread open his shirt to get a better look.

His laugh became a hiss when I circled a finger around one of his nipples. He buried his hands in my hair when I kissed his mouth. I moved onto his lap, straddling, cupping his face to hold his mouth to mine. We kissed that way for a while until I had to break for a breath.

I felt his erection under me and rocked forward on it. My clit rubbed the seam of my jeans as my crotch pressed his belly. I wore no bra beneath the camisole and my nipples rubbed the soft fabric. I wanted them to rub his bare skin.

He'd let go of my hair to grip my ass and pull me harder against him. He licked his mouth, then dipped his head to find my throat. My collarbone. His tongue left a wet path as he moved lower to the curves of my breasts.

He looked up at me. "Can we take this off?"

My shirt, he meant. "Only if you take yours off, too."

"Take it off me."

Such a sexy voice, all rough and ragged, but smooth as well. I slid the shirt over his shoulders, down his arms. It bound his hands behind him for a moment when it caught on his wrists, and I didn't push it farther right away.

"I can't use my hands like this," he murmured into my mouth.

My fingers had been inching the fabric down, but I stopped. "Maybe I like it that way."

It was only talk. I'd never tied up a man, or been tied up myself. The semi-sex Patrick and I'd had was certainly, in retrospect, not normal, but it was absolutely vanilla.

Alex tipped his head to look into my eyes. "Oh, yeah?"

I paused, straddling his lap, my arms around him and him unable to move his hands. "Do you like it that way...?"

"I like it any way I can get it."

I didn't take the shirt off his wrists. I kissed him a little harder, thinking about this. My breasts rubbed his bare chest with the thin camisole between us, and when I broke the kiss he was breathing hard.

This wasn't really the time to get into the game of "did you ever." But there's nothing sexier than knowing you're turning someone on, and with his cock so hard I could feel it throb through two layers of denim, Alex was definitely turned on. I tugged at the shirt, but didn't pull it off.

"What do you like about it?"

He blinked, then swiped his tongue along his lower lip, narrowing his eyes in thought. "Sometimes you just want to give it all up, you know?"

My voice cracked a little when I answered. "Give what up?"

"Control," Alex whispered, and closed his eyes.

He breathed out. I breathed in. He opened his eyes.

"Then again, sometimes you don't." He tugged the shirt off the rest of the way and grabbed my hips. He rolled us until he was on top of me, between my legs, his cock pressing me just right and his belly smooth and hard and hot on my skin where my shirt had pulled up. He cuffed my wrists, pulled my arms slowly over my head and pinned them there with one hand while the other went to the snap of my jeans.

"I could get away." Any fierceness I'd intended was ruined by my voice shaking with each word.

"You could," he said. "But you don't want to."

I did not, and so I didn't move when he opened my jeans and slid a hand inside. Over my panties, lace this time, chosen for effect more than comfort. He rubbed my clit and my hips moved.

One-handed, he managed to get my jeans down to my thighs. I couldn't help him, not with my hands pinned above my head, so I don't know how he managed to get them down farther than that. He used a foot, finally, pushing at the denim crotch until the jeans tangled around my ankles.

"Dammit," he said in a low voice.

I laughed, arching my back as his mouth found my belly. "So much for that."

He shoved the jeans off the rest of the way, nuzzled my skin and moved up my body to lean over me and stare into my face. His grip on my wrists loosened. "Put your hands together, palm to palm. Lock your fingers."

His hair had fallen forward, making him look rakish and impossibly sexy. He hadn't shaved and the subtle glint of stubble had me shivering, thinking of how it would feel on my belly when he kissed me again. I did as he said.

His breath soughed out as he looked at my clasped hands. "Fuck. That's…fuck, Olivia."

I arched again, offering my body to him without words, wondering just what he'd do. And what I would do when he did it.

"Don't let go," he cautioned, his voice dark and deep. "I want to see how long you can last."

A little alarmed, I stopped moving. "How long I can last before what?"

His smile soothed me. "Before you have to touch me."

Then without another word, Alex moved down my body to center his mouth over my lace-covered clit. He kissed me there. I jerked but kept my hands together. His low laugh blew damp heat over me, and I opened my legs for him.

He hooked a finger in my panties and slid them down, his mouth following. Kiss after kiss, first on my belly, then my thigh, then my knee. Both ankles. Up again on the other leg, until he'd centered himself again.

I stayed very, very still. It took an eternity for him to put his mouth to me again, and when he did my fingers slipped apart. Only for a second. I clutched them tight together.

"I know you like to win." He spoke against my skin. His tongue found my clit and circled there, and I felt his finger stroke me. "Don't you?"

"This isn't *Dance Dance*..." My words slid into a groan at the pleasure of his mouth.

He murmured laughter against me, and it felt so good I pushed myself against his tongue. His finger slid inside me, and that felt good, too. They call it eating out, but Alex didn't just eat me. He savored me.

He licked and stroked me until I trembled with climax, and then he eased off. The futon dipped as he knelt upright. I hadn't realized I'd closed my eyes until he stopped, and then they flew open.

He wasn't smiling when he unhooked his jeans and pushed them down to free his cock. He got out of them and knelt again, one knee between my legs and the other at my side. He stroked himself slowly, eyes narrowed in concentration.

My internal muscles clenched, my clit throbbing. Every muscle in my body had tensed, ready to tip over into orgasm, and now I hovered on the edge of pleasure. It would take only one more kiss, a touch, and I was sure I'd come.

He didn't touch me. He kept stroking himself, his face serious. He bit down on his lip and then let his head tip back. His hips pushed forward, thrusting his cock into his fist.

He made a pretty picture. Even with an orgasm tightening my body I had to frame him in my head. *Snap, click.*

His eyes opened and he looked down at me. I'd made a noise, sort of a growl. When he smiled I wanted to curse him out, except he looked so delicious I couldn't.

"I'm so fucking hard," he said, deliberately stroking. "I want to be inside you, Olivia."

My fingers slipped apart, just a little. I moved them from over my head to rest on my forehead, just over my eyes, though I could still see him. I wanted to see him. "You are so not being fair."

His laugh became a groan. "Fuck, this feels so good...but you'd feel better."

My clit throbbed again. Climax had not eased off; I was still so close I thought I could probably finish just by squeezing my thighs together. My cunt ached, empty.

"You're so wet," he said. "I'd slide so far in...and then out...."

He cracked open one eye, judging my response. I'd have laughed if I'd been able, but I couldn't find the breath. All of it was taken up with trying not to unlink my hands.

"Fuck it," I said after a second, and sat up, reaching for him. "You win."

I pulled him on top of me and we kissed wildly. His hands slid up my body to help me off with my clothes. Bared to him, I breathed out. Everything in me strained for release.

He sat up long enough to grab a condom from the box; smart man, he'd put it under the cushions. Foil tore. He didn't play any more games. Alex rolled the condom down over his cock and then moved back over my body. His mouth found mine. He covered me, one hand pressing the futon next to my shoulder and the other...oh, the other, fuck, guiding himself inside me.

He pushed into me slowly and stopped when I grumbled a small protest. He slid a hand beneath the back of my neck, fingers diving into my hair, and brought my mouth to his. Openmouthed, he kissed me and then stopped, breathing hard.

I blinked him into focus, his face so close I could count his lashes. Inside me his cock throbbed, and I shifted. My clit pulsed, but he didn't move. I shook, not on purpose, but unable to stop my body from finding its way.

He pressed deeper into me. Then just as slowly withdrew a shallow inch. It wasn't enough. I lifted my hips and clutched his ass to move him.

He sank into me, then pulled out. Thrust. Our teeth clashed in a hard kiss, but I didn't care about bruises. It felt so good nothing else mattered; it all fell away. We fucked hard and fast, and when I came I closed my eyes on starbursts of color like fireworks.

Alex came a half a minute after I did. He groaned my name, surprising me. I loved it.

A minute passed before he reached between us to hold the condom and pull out of me. He rolled onto his back with a loud sigh. I stared up at the ceiling, unable to form words, boneless and sated.

"I'm sorry," he said after another minute.

I'd been drifting, not quite sleeping but in a happy place. Now I pushed up on my elbow to look at him. "For what?"

He sat, too, then scooted to the edge of the futon to deal with the condom. He looked over his shoulder at me. "For…well, I said it had been a while."

I thought he was kidding. Was certain of it, in fact, until I saw his face when he got up to head for the bathroom. And there I sat in the pile of pillows scattered by our passion, confused.

I got up and followed him. "What do you mean?"

He was washing his hands at the sink. "I mean…it was…fast. That's all."

"Oh." I chewed my cheek. This was delicate ground. "Hey. Look at me."

He turned, expression neutral. I was used to that. I put a hand on his hip, pulled him closer, right up against me. Flesh to flesh.

"It was the best sex I've had in a long, long time."

His mouth fought not to smile. "When's the last time you had sex?"

"It's been a long, long time," I conceded, as I rose on my toes to kiss his mouth. "But that doesn't make any less fuck-tastic."

He put his arms around me. Kissed me back. Laughed a little. "Next time…"

I reached around to squeeze his ass. "Next time. Yes."

We spent the day naked or almost naked, watching movie after movie from his giant collection. He hadn't moved in much furniture, but he had enough DVDs to stock a rental place. We ate pizza from his freezer and he made me marga-ritas using Gran Patrón Platinum tequila with a price tag that made me cough, while the booze itself slid effortlessly down my throat. He didn't actually drink any, I noticed.

"You sure you don't want to go out?" Alex had pulled on a pair of loose, red silk boxers and lent me one of his soft and wash-worn button-downs. We'd made a table from a hard-sided suitcase, and sat on cushions from the futon. "We could head over to the Corvette. They've got wings on special there. Happy hour drinks, too, I think."

I was buzzed enough from the margarita, and I licked salt from the rim of my glass as I shook my head. "God, no. I'm stuffed."

He leaned to steal a piece of pepperoni I'd picked off my pizza, and stuck it in his mouth. "You should've said something, Olivia. I'd have made something else."

It took me a second to parse what he meant. "Oh…no, it's fine. I don't eat pepperoni, but not because…well, I guess it's because I never had it growing up. I'm not offended by it."

I hadn't actually thought about that—why I turned aside pepperoni and shrimp, two foods my mother would now rather be stabbed with an ice pick than eat. Why I'd eat turkey bacon and not the regular kind, or why I'd eat ham my dad sent home with me but never would cook it myself. I poked at the round red slices, which left a smear of orange grease on my fingertip, and instead of licking it off used one of the paper towels we had in lieu of napkins.

He wasn't asking, but I told him anyway. "My parents divorced when I was five. My dad's Catholic, my mom's Jewish. Both remarried. My dad's been pretty active in his church for a long time, but my mom has just recently over the past few years decided to become observant. That means she follows the dietary laws and keeps the Sabbath."

Alex topped off my glass with more frozen margarita from the blender, his attention taken up with not spilling, but he shot me a grin. "I know what it means."

I laughed self-consciously. "Well, mostly around here people don't."

He leaned to kiss the corner of my mouth. "You forget. I'm a world traveler."

I put a hand on the back of his neck so he couldn't pull away. I turned the kiss from something small and light to deep. Hot. He was smiling when I let him go.

"French kiss," he murmured against my lips before sitting back. "A little later I'll show you an Australian kiss."

I rolled my eyes. "Yeah, what's that?"

"It's just like a French kiss," he explained, "but you do it down under."

I groaned and flopped back on the pillows. "Did you learn any *good* jokes in your world travels?"

Alex stretched out beside me. "That's the best I have, sorry."

I turned onto my side, facing him. "That's okay."

"Do you have to work tomorrow?"

I made a face. "Don't remind me. But, yes. Not until four with Foto Folks, but I've got a few client jobs to take care of in the morning. Why?"

"Just wondering if you had to go to sleep early."

I returned his smile. "I should. I should go home soon."

"No," Alex said seriously. "Don't."

I groaned again and flopped onto my back to stare at the ceiling. "Alex…"

"Olivia."

I sat up and pulled my knees close to my chest, my arms linked around them. "I don't want this to get weird or anything."

He tugged one of my locks. "It doesn't have to."

I looked at the futon, pillows scattered and sheets rumpled, and the box with condoms spilling from it. I looked at our dinner. I looked at him.

"This has been great, Alex. Really fantastic. And unexpected."

"I'm full of surprises."

Of that, I had no doubts. "I think I should go now."

His eyes narrowed and he looked away for a second, then back. "I wish you wouldn't."

"Alex…" I sighed. I didn't want to leave. I wanted him to go down on me again, I wanted to fuck him again, and that, I knew, was only going to lead to trouble. And I had been warned.

"Olivia," he said again, patiently, "do you have a boyfriend?"

"You know I don't!"

"Would you like one?"

I rested my chin on my knees and studied him for a few long, silent minutes. He didn't look away. He didn't shift or twitch. Alex simply waited for my answer.

"Don't you think most people want someone?" I said finally. "Even the ones who say they don't?"

"Yes. I think so." He tilted his head a little. "So?"

"Do I want a boyfriend?" I squeezed my arms tighter around my knees, then looked deep into his eyes. "Are you offering?"

"I like you. You're beautiful—"

I laughed.

He raised an eyebrow. "You are. And talented. And fun to be around. I've never met a woman who liked the movie *Harold and Maude.*"

"We haven't even dated," I said.

Alex didn't glance at the futon, scene of our sexcapades. "We can date."

"Uh-huh." I chewed the inside of my cheek. "Maybe we can start with that."

He laughed. "Okay."

"Okay, now this is weird." I unlinked my hands to stretch out my legs.

"I told you it doesn't have to be."

"I haven't had a boyfriend in a long time, that's all."

"I haven't had a girlfriend in a long time, either. Probably longer than you haven't had a boyfriend." Alex ran a fingertip down my shoulder to my wrist, then pulled his hand away. He laughed, then held up a finger. "Wait here."

He jumped up and disappeared into the bedroom he never slept in, and came out a moment later with a frazzled silk flower on a green plastic stem. He dropped to one knee in front of me, a hand over his heart, and held it out. "Olivia. Will you do me the honor of being my girlfriend? Or not being my girlfriend, whatever you want to call it?"

I broke into laughter and took the pathetic flower. "Where did you get this?"

"It was in the bathroom vanity when I moved in. See? It's fate."

"It's disgusting." I let it droop in my hand.

"Hey, real flowers have bugs in them. Be glad I didn't bring you a beetle-infested rose or something. That would've been disgusting."

I couldn't keep a straight face around him. I tossed the flower aside and held out my arms for him to move closer. "This is crazy."

"I got your crazy," he whispered in my ear, before he kissed my neck in the tender spot he'd discovered.

I know he had to feel the way my pulse raced when his lips

skimmed my throat. I know he heard the sharp intake of my breath when his teeth nipped me there, and I'm certain he felt the tug of my fingers in his hair when I sank them in deep.

He unbuttoned my borrowed shirt and folded it back to reveal my bare breasts underneath. His lips moved over my collarbones on each side, then down over the slope of my flesh, pausing to suckle at one nipple, then the other. I sank back onto the pillows, my arms over my head, and gave myself up to him.

"You are too hard to resist." My voice hitched.

I felt his laughter against my skin. "I know."

Against my thigh, I felt his cock rise in the silk. He shifted, and the heat of it pressed my bare skin. The pillows slipped under me as I arched into his kiss. I've never felt small. I tower over my mother, can look my brothers in the eye, and stand only an inch or so shorter than my dad. I'm curvy and rounded and they're all spare and thin. Here in Alex's arms, I felt petite.

"I didn't realize how big you were," I said against his mouth.

He shifted my weight, just a little. "I'm not surprised, considering the size of your dildo."

I swatted his chest. "I've never used that thing!"

He laughed and eased me onto the futon, which had been stripped down to the bottom sheet. "Uh-huh."

I reached between us to grip a handful of silk-covered cock. The silk moved easily over him as I stroked, and his hiss rewarded me. "And that wasn't what I was talking about."

He pushed into my hand and buried his face against my neck to lick and suck gently. "Good. Because there's only so much my ego can take."

I snorted softly and let my fingers close over him a little harder. "Something tells me your ego can take a lot."

He looked at me then, not smiling, his gray eyes intense. "Smoldering" is what Sarah would have called it. She reads a lot of romance novels. Alex was definitely smoldering.

"See? You know me already," he said.

I pushed at his shoulder when he moved toward me for another kiss. He stopped. "You make it sound like you're hard to know."

His gaze softened. "I don't want to be."

He had a hand on either side of me, dipping the futon, and one of his knees fit just between mine. All he had to do was bend his elbows and straighten his leg to be on top of me, but Alex held off. I pressed my palms to his cheeks, holding him still while I studied every line and curve of his face.

"You don't want to be an international man of mystery?"

He shook his head, and my fingers slipped on his skin. His hair tickled me. "Not really. Not with you."

Heat flooded me, top to toe. I felt the blush, even though I knew the color wouldn't show on my skin. I gently pulled his mouth to mine. Lip on lip, a gentle brush. A small and tiny kiss made bigger by what he'd said.

I didn't ruin it by talking. I know when it's best to be silent. I answered with my eyes, my touch, instead. Another kiss. We moved together without needing to choreograph it, our bodies shifting in perfect time.

Alex rolled onto his back and I followed. I straddled him. I took a fistful of silk and pulled it down, baring him. His long arm found a condom from the half-empty box, and he handed it to me with another smoldering look.

I didn't take off his shirt, not even when I sheathed him

and pushed him inside me. My thighs gripped his sides, the shirt fell open, showing off my breasts and belly, the curves no diet would ever whittle off me.

His hand slid between us, his thumb pressing my clit. "Like this?"

I loved that he asked, and more than that, remembered. I'd had lovers who didn't know what I liked after a dozen times fucking. "Yes."

His other hand gripped my ass, squeezed. "Shift up a little bit."

I did, and gasped at the pressure on my clit. All I had to do was move, just a little, and his cock slid in and out with ease, while my clit rubbed his knuckle, and sometimes his belly. Perfect. Magic. I closed my eyes, head bent, pleasure rising in me again when an hour ago I'd have said I was spent.

It took longer this time than it had the others. We moved slower. Didn't rush. Time went liquid around us, and I melted with it.

"Yes," he said when the first tremors shook me. "Fuck, yes."

I opened my eyes to look down at his face, twisted with his own desire. His eyes gleamed, then his eyelids fluttered. He thrust harder inside me. My orgasm started in long, rolling waves and I made hardly a sound, but Alex knew it. He groaned. He slowed. The futon rocked under us.

He took my hand, slipped his fingers into mine. Linked, we came together. A gasp and a sigh, I wasn't sure who made what noise, only that we both did it at the same time.

The first few seconds postorgasm are always as different as the orgasms themselves. This time I rolled off him into a boneless heap, arms and legs akimbo, and shuddered out a breathless "whoa."

"Aw, shucks, don't say that just to make me feel better."

"I don't say things just to make people feel better," I told him. It wasn't meant to be serious. How could it have been, when I could barely string two words together?

"Me, neither."

Something in his voice turned my head to look at him. Alex stared at the ceiling. He licked his lips once, then again. He blinked rapidly, as if he had something in his eyes.

"Telling people what they want to hear just to make them feel better is no better than lying," he added offhandedly.

He looked at me. We didn't say anything for a second or so, and then I rolled toward him and kissed him. He kissed me back.

"So, if I ask you if a pair of jeans makes my ass look fat, and it does, you won't tell me it doesn't?" I traced my name on his chest with my finger.

Alex laughed and pressed my hand still against him. "I just won't say anything."

"Then I'll know my ass looks fat in those jeans," I told him.

"Yeah," Alex said, before he kissed me again. "But at least you'll know I wasn't lying."

Chapter 09

"You have a seriously warped idea of what's romantic," Sarah said from around a mouthful of sushi.

"You look so cute with rice falling out of your mouth."

She snorted and dabbed up the fallen crumbs with a thumb, then licked them off. She pointed her chopsticks, the ends stained with soy sauce, at me. "Dude says you have a fat ass and you get all squishy? Warped."

"He did not say I had a fat ass," I rebutted. Alex had, in fact, spent the next fifteen minutes telling me how much he liked my behind. And my in front. And all the other bits in between.

She shrugged and dipped another piece of spicy tuna into the soy-wasabi mixture. "Meh. Don't listen to me. I'm just jealous you're all getting laid and stuff, and I'm at home alone with my hand."

"Poor thing. Don't you have a B.O.B.?"

"Ran out the batteries on that sucker and haven't upgraded," my friend said with a grin. Then another shrug. "Battery-operated boyfriends can't take you out for sushi."

"I'm the one taking you out for sushi," I pointed out.

Sarah licked her chopsticks seductively. "Any chance of me getting lucky?"

I laughed so loud the other diners turned their heads to stare. "Um…no."

"Why, cuz you're all gooey and gushy over Mr. Alex Gigantic Magic Cock Kennedy? What did he do, give you his class ring?"

From anyone else it would've sounded like mocking, but I knew Sarah well enough to know she was teasing. "Don't hate."

She laughed when I imitated her, and stole a piece of salmon-avocado roll from my plate. "I can't help it. I'm jealous. Or envious, maybe. I don't wish you didn't have what I want. I just wish I had it, too."

"What happened to that guy you hooked up with from the motorcycle shop?"

She fixed me with a typical Sarah look, raised brow, curled lip, totally snarky. "He didn't like bunnies."

I stopped with a piece of sushi halfway to my mouth. "So? When did you get a rabbit?"

"I don't have a rabbit, but I totally can't get into a guy who hates bunnies. I mean, that's so…wrong. Who hates bunnies? And he didn't laugh at LOLcats.com, either. He said they were…" She lowered her voice, looked around. "Stupid. And lame."

"Ouch. Who doesn't like pictures of cats with funny captions? That *is* pretty lame."

"Yeah. I dumped him. And the sex was pretty bad. Really bad, actually. Do you know," she added, with another point of her chopsticks, "the last really great fuck I had was with a guy I will never, ever go to bed with ever again?"

Sarah's love life had more ins and outs and turnabouts than any of my other girlfriends. "Who was that?"

"Oh." She shrugged again, ate the sushi, drank some hot tea. "Some guy you don't know."

"Well, that's not fair. Why'd you bring it up if you never told me about him?" I finished my sushi and drank my tea, too, thinking about ordering some extra sushi rolls to take home for dinner. "And how do you know you won't ever get with him again if the sex was so great?"

Sarah laughed, again drawing attention, and shook her head. "Oh, God, no. Joe? No way. He is *so* not boyfriend material."

"Ah...so you're looking for a boyfriend."

Sarah raised a brow again. "Dude. Where have you been? I am *so* looking for a boyfriend. I want it all. I want a ring on my finger, I want babies. The works."

"Huh. Really? Why now, all of a sudden?" In all the time I'd known her, Sarah had always been such a free spirit, definitely more a "Flesh for Fantasy" than a "White Wedding" sort of woman.

"It's not all of a sudden. I'm just freer about admitting it. I don't want to be in a nursing home when my kids are in college, you know?"

"I know. And I'm older than you, so shut up."

"Yeah," Sarah said, "but you have a *boyfriend*."

The emphasis she put on the word split my mouth into an

inappropriately huge grin. I stifled it, but she saw. She poked my plate with her chopsticks, but grinned, too.

"You liiike him," she teased.

"What's not to like?" I said in my mother's voice. "He's very pretty. He's got a job, sort of, but even if he doesn't, he's got money. He's a good dresser. Great kisser. Anyway, it's only been a couple days. Too soon to make it into anything it's not."

"Don't forget great lay," she added, and poured more tea for us both. "You ordering takeout?"

"Yes." I pulled the menu toward me and held up the teeny tiny pencil as I looked over the list. "He is a great lay."

"Well, there you have it. All the makings of a great relationship."

I sighed and checked off an order for three sushi rolls and a couple sashimis. "Yeah...well. The boyfriend thing. It didn't work out so well for me before."

"Pffft. Wasn't your fault. Now, not having a boyfriend since then? Your fault."

"I've had..."

"Ah, ah," she said. "You've had a couple fuck buddies, and you've had dates. But no boyfriend."

I swirled my chopsticks through the dots of soy sauce on my plate, making letters. "Yeah. Well...I don't know if I want him to be my boyfriend. Once bitten and all that."

Sarah didn't tease this time. "You can't let what happened with Patrick scare you off men forever."

"Alex fucks guys." I said it flatly, but quietly, so nobody else would hear. "I saw him getting head from a guy at Patrick's Chrismukkah party."

"What?" Sarah's shriek echoed around the restaurant. "What the fuck? You didn't tell me that!"

I shrugged uncomfortably. "I didn't tell him I saw. It was dark. They didn't know I was there."

She paused. "Was it hot? God, I bet that was really, really smoking hot."

"Sarah," I said with annoyance. "Focus."

"Sorry." She shrugged, a typical Sarah move. "Bunny, all this means is that you like a little gay in your guy. Nothing wrong with that. You said yourself he's great in bed, and he's really into you."

I sighed again, anxiety I'd managed to tamp down before now rearing up in my throat. "What if it's not just a *little* gay?"

"Honey. He rocked your world and made you come so hard you saw fireworks. A gay man doesn't do that. I mean, a totally gay dude doesn't."

"Patrick—"

She cut me off. "It was never like that with Patrick. Unless you told me a lie. A bunch of lies. Don't forget, Bunny, I've sat with you through more than a few too-many-margaritas nights."

This was undoubtedly true. "No. It wasn't like that with Patrick."

"The sex was nonexistent, and he lied to you. Sounds to me like you're ahead by two already with Alex."

I thought back over every word we'd ever shared, me and Alex. Every nuance. "No, well, he hasn't lied, exactly…"

"Have you asked him if he's into dudes?"

"No."

Sarah spread her fingers, eyes wide. "So? Are you gonna?"

"I don't know. What do I do if he says yes?"

"Olivia, baby, honey. Sugar muffin—"

I broke into laughter. "Stop."

Sarah grinned. "Poopsie."

I slapped my forehead. "You're too much."

"Bunny, I am not enough." She preened and dissolved into laughter herself.

"Seriously. What do I do if he says yes?"

"Same stuff you've been doing with him, I guess. You already know he's okay with getting head from a guy. Which, by the way, I'm still sure was totally hot."

I finished the last of my tea and waited for the server to set down my take-out carton of sushi and hand me the bill before I answered. "It was. But that was before I knew I'd be sleeping with him. It's different now. I guess I have a hang-up."

"Who'd blame you?" Sarah looked sympathetic. She could be unflinchingly honest, but she was also the best friend I'd ever had. The best female friend, anyway.

"Patrick says he fucked him. He's all bent out of shape about me being with Alex—"

"Wait up." She held up a hand like a stop sign. "You told Patrick before you told me?"

"He was pissed off because we were spending time together, and because we kissed on New Year's Eve…"

"What? Wait!" Sarah frowned. "You didn't tell me that, either. You've been holding out on me!"

"You," I said, "didn't tell me about that last great lay you had."

She puffed a breath that blew her bangs off her forehead. "Okay. Fine. Whatever. So did you tell Alex you not only saw him getting head from some dude, but that Patrick said they fucked?"

"No."

"You'd better. If he admits it, then you have it out there between you. If he doesn't, you know he's a fucking liar and you cut your losses and get out while you still can."

"I don't want him to be a liar." The words caught in my throat, sticky like rice.

"Bunny, of course you don't. Just ask him. You'll feel better. Do it like a Band-Aid, just rip it off and get it over with."

"I should go," I said, catching sight of the clock. "Speaking of my own work. I'd like to actually do some, since I have to be at my other job the rest of the week."

"Foto Folks, photos of your mamas. Photos of your papas." Sarah sang the theme song from the company's superannoying commercial. "Pictures of fat ladies in tiaras and feather boas. Pictures that make you want to hurl!"

"Nice. Thanks. That's my livelihood you're mocking."

"Not forever. You'll be out of that place in a few months. I feel it. You'll have so much business you won't be able to handle all of it."

"From your mouth to God's ears," I said as I got up and counted out the cash, plus tip, to cover the food.

Sarah gave me a funny look, her head tilted. The light flashed on her multiple earrings, and in this light, her hair looked black, not dark blue and purple. "You been talking to your mom?"

I hadn't, not for a long time. Too long. But I'd been thinking about her a lot lately, from small things. Odd things, like the pepperoni pizza. "No. I should call her. Patrick tried to guilt me into it, but…"

"Oh, Patrick can fuck himself," Sarah said darkly. "Bunny, you know I love you, but that boy has got to step back."

I blinked, surprised at her vehemence. "What brought that on?"

She stood, gathering her coat and bag from the back of the chair. "I thought you were pissed at him. I'm on your side."

"Well, I am pissed off at him." We wove through the tables that had been empty when we came in, but now had plenty of customers. "I just wonder why you are."

In the sunlight outside, on the sidewalk, Sarah turned and gave me a sudden, hard hug. "I've always been pissed off at him. I just pretend otherwise for your sake."

I'd known she didn't like him, but this was news. I hugged her back, then looked at her face. "Why?"

"Because..." Sarah sighed. "Oh, Liv. Why do you think? Because I love you. You're my friend. Why else would I put up with him, unless it's for your sake? I sort of hoped..."

"What?"

Sarah shrugged, but looked me in the eye. "I sort of hoped you'd be done with him after this last thing. That maybe you'd... And then when you told me about Alex, I really hoped..."

It wasn't like her to mush words, but even with the mumbling and stammering, I knew what she was getting at. My stomach tightened again. My mouth thinned. "Wow. I didn't know you hated him so much."

"I'm sorry," she said quickly, then before I could say anything added, "Don't rush to his defense. Patrick's been pretty crappy to you, and if you're planning on forgiving him and being all merry la-la, huggy kiss and smooch with him again, I might have to smack you."

I blinked at her rapid-fire description of my relationship with Patrick. "I'm still mad at him, don't worry."

"And now you're mad at me, too." She made a face. "Sorry."

"No. I'm not mad. You're not wrong." I clutched my box of sushi tighter as a chill breeze kicked up the hem of my coat and made Sarah's hair, brilliant blue now, fly around her face. "I just... It's complicated with me and him."

"I know. I know." She hugged me again.

Sarah is a hugger. Anyone can fall prey to her embrace. I let her squeeze me even though she was right: I was angry. A little at her and a little at myself because I knew she was right.

"He's been a part of my life for a long time. I almost married him."

"But you didn't. And, pumpkin..." She sighed and hugged me again, patting my back. She pulled away. "I get it. I do. But I just hate that he makes you feel so...bad."

"He doesn't—" I stopped myself. I had never thought, or never admitted, that Patrick made me feel bad about anything.

"I'm zipping my lip. That's it, I'm done. You have to get home to that luscious new boy toy so you can screw him once more before you go to work and I...I must make my rounds cleaning lawyers' computers of virus-ridden Internet porn. Did I tell you I found some guy's stash of tranny panty hose porn? Man, that was a day I needed some bleach for my eyeballs."

"Yikes."

"You said it." She nodded. She hugged me yet again. She added a kiss to my cheek, though she had to jump up a few inches to reach it. "Let me know when you want to do some more work on the studio. Or if you need me for some shots or anything."

"I have a job lined up next week. I think I'll need someone with pretty hands."

She waved her fingers at me. "I gots pretty hands."

I laughed. "Go on now, go. I'll call you later."

"Later, gator." With a wave, Sarah headed off to her car. Her hair blew back in the wind. She walked as if she owned the parking lot, and she turned heads. I envied her that confidence.

I envied her ability to say what she meant, and mean what she said.

My phone rang as I watched her drive away, and I pulled it from my pocket. I knew the number, and I recognized the photo. But instead of answering Patrick's call, I thumbed the phone off and stuck it back in my pocket.

There wasn't much of a crowd for the afternoon service at Congregation Ahavat Shalom, but that was fine. Fewer people I'd have to make small talk with. I hadn't been to services here in months, either, but I took my usual spot in a pew near the front and to the side, where I could watch the rabbi. Most of the congregation sat behind me, and that was fine. I didn't always sing along with the prayers, at least out loud. I was still learning.

Today I was happy to hum along with the tunes without trying too hard to stumble along with the Hebrew. I knew it only phonetically, anyway, and had to read the English translation to get any sense of what was going on. But I didn't necessarily go to synagogue to mumble mindlessly without really trying to seek out meaning from the words. I could've gone to church for that.

"Shalom, Olivia." Rabbi Levin put my hand between both of his to shake it. None of that no-unmarried-male-female contact for our rabbi. "We haven't seen you in a while."

"Shalom, Rabbi. I liked your talk today." The afternoon service didn't usually feature a sermon, but Rabbi Levin had spoken briefly of fresh starts, new beginnings and how the recent New Year, the secular one, was a second chance for traditional Jews who celebrated their new year in the fall. "I liked what you said about celebrating the holidays of the community even though they might not technically be yours."

"We have to live in the world. Yes, it's important as Jews to maintain our heritage and identity. But at least here in Harrisburg, we don't live in a community where everyone worships the same as we do. It's important to recognize how we can merge the secular and religious aspects of our lives," Rabbi Levin said with a broad grin. "I'm glad you liked the sermon."

He touched my shoulder and moved off to greet the other congregants.

We have to live in the world. I could get behind that. Keeping hold of my identity, that was something I could get behind, too, if only I could figure out what my identity was.

The first few times I'd come to a service here, nobody'd known what to say to me. I overheard whispers suggesting I was maybe one of those "Ethiopian Jews" but nobody had the courage to come up and flat-out ask me. I knew how I looked, with my café au lait skin and hair in shoulder-length Nubian locks. I didn't fit in with these women in expensive pantsuits, the men in their handwoven talliths. They couldn't know I'd been raised at least half Jewish, with memories of lighting a menorah and spinning the dreidel as equally prominent as those of sitting on Santa's lap. I was scary to them.

In comparison, when I'd gone to Mass, the man next to me in the pew had turned and given me the handshake of peace with such wholeheartedness I worried he might crush my fingers. A gaggle of people had stopped me after the service to welcome me to the church and ask if I was a new member, or if I was considering joining them. They'd circled me, their smiles bright and sincere and just a little desperate. They were scary to me.

I didn't feel I fit in either place. The services were unfamiliar, as were the prayers. I took comfort in the ritual sameness of both church and synagogue, even though their messages were so vastly different.

Yet something drew me back to Ahavat Shalom, and I think it was the lack of overwhelming welcome. I didn't have to prove myself to anyone there. I didn't have to pretend I knew what was going on, because nobody asked me how I felt about God the way the church folks did. I didn't feel I had to step up and proclaim anything.

Maybe this was the year to figure out what I wanted to proclaim.

Maybe this would be the year to do a lot of things, I thought as I pulled into my parking lot and didn't see Alex's vehicle. Disappointed, I shivered as I left the car, and not just from the freezing air and gray skies promising snow. In the warmth of my apartment I stripped out of my coat and hat and gloves, and made a huge pot of Earl Grey.

Then I picked up the phone.

"Happy New Year," I said when my mother answered.

"Olivia! Happy New Year to you! I'm so glad you called."

I believed her, of course. She was my mom. She'd changed my diapers, bandaged my knees, held my hand crossing the street. She'd taken pictures of me before every school dance. My mother loved me, despite everything that had happened and how I'd disappointed her. I loved her, too, but I found it hard to forgive her for the things she'd said and done. Maybe she found it hard to forgive me, too.

Silence fell as I thought of what to say that wouldn't be too heavy. My mom cleared her throat. My gaze fell on the book I'd been reading.

"I picked up the new Clive Barker last week. I'm about halfway finished with it."

She paused. "I haven't read it."

"It's really good."

Another pause and clearing of her throat. "I haven't read him in a few years."

Oh. I hadn't forgotten the minefield of "don'ts" between us, but now I became extra aware of how treacherous every step would be. "I didn't know."

I should've. I might've, if we'd been as close as we used to be, but who could I blame for that? Her? Or myself?

"But tell me about you," my mother said. "How's the new business going?"

She had to have heard it from one or both of my brothers, or their wives, but I didn't mind. It let her pretend she knew more about my life than she did, so I could act as if we still spoke every day. I told her about the business, and my job with Foto Folks and with the school photo gig.

My mom, in turn, told me about Chaim's job, their new house, the synagogue, the trip they were planning to Israel.

She talked a lot about friends I hadn't met, and of the classes she was in charge of at their shul.

"I'm teaching the aleph class," she told me proudly. "Religious schoolkids, kindergarten and first grade. I love it."

"Good for you."

"You could visit, Olivia," she said finally, which was what I'd been waiting to hear since the conversation began. "We'd love to see you. Both of us would, Chaim, too."

That might be true. I didn't know my mother's husband well enough to say. "You could visit me, too. If you wanted."

"You know that's not possible."

The coffee in my stomach sloshed. "Well, I'd better get going. Happy New Year, Mom."

"Olivia—"

"Bye," I said, and hung up before she could say more.

At least we hadn't argued, screaming and accusing each other of awfulness. At least we'd been civil to each other. At least we'd managed that.

A knock on my door got me up off the couch, and I opened it to find Alex.

"Hey," he said.

"Hi," I said, and I let him in.

Chapter 10

*I*t was a good time to work at a photo studio catering to families with children. Most people had brought their spawn in for holiday portraits way back in October and November, which was also the busiest time of year for school portraits. I'd run myself ragged then, driving miles every day and coming home to work until the mall closed at night. Now I could sit back a little and relax.

Or so I thought. The mall wasn't as crazy crowded as it had been during the holiday shopping frenzy, but it seemed as if a lot of people had decided to redeem their gift certificates. And, thanks to some fancy marketing done by Foto Folks in the fall, a lot of women were coming in with vouchers for a free glamour session.

Every makeup chair was filled when I got there for my shift, and so were all the seats in the waiting area. They'd started signing people up for time slots and handing out short-range beepers the way they do in popular restaurants. Three of the four small picture-taking cubicles in the back were full, too, with the fourth just vacated by a woman in a feather boa *and* a tiara.

"Wow," I said, unable to stop myself.

Mindy, who did hair and makeup, had just finished with a customer and was ducking back to the coffeepot for a mug. "You're telling me. It's been nonstop in here since we opened."

A woman in a red pleather jacket covered in zippers—think Michael Jackson in *Thriller*, and you'd be only half as close to how ugly that jacket was—sauntered past us. From the waist up she was entirely glamazon—hair, fake lashes, bright red lipstick. The works. Below the waist, the part the picture wouldn't show, she was totally Mennonite. I mean complete with the flowered dress, white athletic socks and sneakers.

"What the—?"

"She's doing them for her husband."

"But that's… Isn't that against… They don't…"

Mindy filled her mug and added sugar and cream. "I don't know. But she came in, picked that jacket off the rack, told me just how she wanted her hair and makeup done. I'm not going to argue."

I wouldn't, either. It wasn't my place to tell anyone who came in how to dress or how much eye shadow to put on. "Hi, I'm Olivia," I said when I went into the cubby.

"Gretchen."

"So, Gretchen, did you have something particular in mind today?"

I fiddled with the camera while we talked. Gretchen did, indeed, have an idea of what she wanted. She described it to me, including the use of the large electric fan to get the windblown look.

"My sister-in-law Helen was in here before Christmas and she had this done," Gretchen explained. "I want what she got."

Just because I'd never do it didn't mean I couldn't understand the appeal. Gretchen, by the looks of her, didn't live a glamorous life. If I could make her feel pretty for just half an hour, give her pictures she could gaze at for the rest of her life, I'd do it.

"All right, let me see you up here on this stool." I posed her in front of the table, low enough so that she could rest her elbows on it and place her chin in one hand. Classic glamour pose. "Let me get the fan blowing."

We worked it hard, Gretchen and I. She was a trouper, too, bending and stretching and holding still when she had to. Her expression didn't change much. She looked half-terrified in some of the shots, sleepy in some others, but she was laughing in between so I knew she was having fun. Our time and my allotment of shots were almost up, though, when I took the picture that would be the best of the lot.

"Look at that one," I said more to myself than her. "Gorgeous. That's the one."

"Really?" Gretchen looked hopeful. "They look good?"

"Beautiful," I assured her. "Go on and get changed into your own clothes and meet me in the approval room—the small one with the door on the left. That's where you can see all the shots and pick which ones you want."

We use digital photography at Foto Folks, film being outdated and nearly obsolete except for hobbyists. Customers come to the approval room to look at the pictures on a large-screen monitor, then pick their packages right then and there. They can walk out with the photos within an hour if they want to wait. Most of them do. It's a far cry from the way we did it when I was in high school working for a local photographer. He'd have a studio session, then call the customers back in about a week later to see a slide show of the best shots, and it was another couple of weeks before they had their prints in hand. We really have become a drive-through society.

I slipped the memory card into the reader, and had opened up the ordering software to fill in all of Gretchen's information by the time she came in without the red jacket, her face scrubbed back to plainness. I pulled up the files and showed her each picture, one at a time.

She didn't say much until we got to the last one. She was laughing in it, her face turned a little, eyes downcast. It was nothing like any of the rest, all of which had a forced, plastic quality to them that shamed me, even though I knew it was what she'd asked for.

"I think this one is the best," I said.

Gretchen stared at it for a long, silent moment. "I don't like it."

I'd been so ready for her gushing praise I was already hovering the cursor over the add-to-order button. In fact, my finger slipped in shock at her words and I added the shot to her order. "Oops."

She shook her head. "That doesn't look like me."

It looked more like her than any of the others, but I wouldn't argue with her. "All right. We can choose different portraits."

"Wait, please." Gretchen touched my hand on the mouse to stop me from clicking back to the image I'd chosen.

She looked at it for a much longer time than I should've allowed her. I knew there were customers waiting, and Foto Folks based bonuses not only on portraits ordered but number of customers serviced. I wasn't just holding up myself, but my coworkers, who depended on me to make their handiwork look good enough to convince customers to buy.

"No. It doesn't look like me. I like that one with my chin on my hand," she said, and there was no convincing her otherwise.

Gretchen walked out of the approval room after ordering over a hundred dollars worth of photos, including wallets. I got the idea she was going to trade them with her friends, sort of like the kids did in school with photos I'd also taken.

"I'm so glad Helen suggested I request you," Gretchen said as I walked with her out to the front of the store. "I'm going to tell my other girlfriends about you, too!"

"Thank you, I appreciate it."

She was still bubbling and giddy as she left, and I considered I'd done my job pretty well. It was my turn to think about a run for coffee when Mindy tapped my shoulder. "You have a special customer."

I turned to look. "Teddy."

"Hey."

My stomach climbed into my throat. I managed a squeaky "hi." Unlike most every other time I saw him, Teddy didn't open up his arms to give me a hug. Awkward silence hung between us while Mindy watched, her eyes round and mouth open just a little. To be fair, Mindy's mouth was always open just a little. But it was open a little more today.

Teddy's smile should've warmed me more than it did. "I was hoping you'd be working today."

"I'm working most days."

"Yeah." He sighed. "Listen, Olivia. Patrick told me…about what happened."

This wasn't a private place and I couldn't have this conversation with him here. Didn't want to have it with Teddy, at all. I felt the frown tug the corner of my mouth.

"Did he?"

"Of course he did." Teddy looked sad, a big burly bear of a man who favored colorful sweaters and had been kind to me when he didn't have to. "What were you thinking?"

Past kindness didn't give him the right to scold me, though. "I wasn't thinking of anything. I told Patrick I was sorry. I don't know what you want me to say, Teddy. Did Patrick send you over here to be his messenger boy, or what?"

Teddy looked taken aback by my tone. "He's very angry."

Around us, makeup artists and customers moved back and forth. Most gave us curious looks. I glanced back toward my booth, where Mindy had taken the next customer.

"I have to get back to work."

"I think if you just apologized to him—"

"You know what?" I said tightly, turning on my heel to get up in his face a little bit. "This isn't any of your business, Teddy."

His mouth worked. I didn't give him the chance to speak. I dropped my voice low to keep some semblance of privacy.

"If he wants me to grovel, he's out of luck. I'm not going to beg his forgiveness, Teddy. I've done that already for a bunch of shit that wasn't my fault, and I'm not going to do it again."

Teddy drew himself up. "Well. I don't know what to say."

"Nothing would be a good place to start," I told him. "Because you don't know. You really don't. You think you know about me and Patrick, but you only know what he's told you, and I can guess that it painted him in a pretty flattering light, didn't it? Because that's the way he likes to think of things. He's not good at taking blame."

Teddy knew this, obviously, since he lived with Patrick, and loved him. "I think I know him well enough——"

"You don't know about us," I repeated. "You only know what he's told you, and I've heard his version of the story."

"Are you saying Patrick's a liar?"

"I'm saying," I said evenly, "that he has a version of the story. And I have one. And they're not exactly alike."

"Olivia, I've never tried to shut you out of Patrick's life——"

I cut him off again. "And I love you for that, Teddy, believe me. I do. But this is between me and Patrick. I know what he wants. More than an apology. He wants some sort of declaration of loyalty, he wants groveling, he wants me to roll over and show him my belly just to keep the privilege of remaining in his good graces. Am I right?"

Teddy shifted from foot to foot, looking supremely uncomfortable. "I don't know."

"I have to get back to work now." I shook my head when Teddy tried to speak again. "I appreciate you playing the part of peacemaker, I really do. But this isn't your job and it's not your business. It's between me and Patrick, Teddy. And I'm not sure I'm ready to resolve it right now."

"But, Olivia…"

"This is not your business."

Teddy had never seen me like this, and I could tell it startled him. Probably pissed him off a little, too, the way people get when they feel their good and noble intentions have been stepped on. He drew himself up with an audible sniff.

"I'm sorry you feel that way," he said. "I thought we were friends. After all I've—"

He cut himself off that time, maybe because the flash of anger I felt was reflected on my face. He backed off, and it was a good thing, because while I really liked Teddy a lot, if he'd tried to smack me down with how good he'd been to me I'd have said something I really would regret.

"I didn't tell Patrick I was coming here. I won't tell him I did, either."

"That's probably good."

I didn't thank him, and we parted with as much dignity as was possible, considering the circumstances. The confrontation had left my stomach twisted and churning, though. My palms sweaty.

"You okay?" Mindy asked.

"Sure." The lie tasted sour.

I should've been used to that.

There might be something I despise more than getting up early on a day I technically didn't have to. Puppy mills. Paper cuts on my tongue. The smell of sewage. But I really hate rolling out of bed when I could be snuggled down under my blankets, dreaming.

There was no help for it. I'd taken a job laying out a brochure-style menu for the coffee shop down the street. The owner wanted something simple in design but fancier than text photocopied on colored printer paper. I'd let it go too long, had gone back and forth with him on the pricing of the printing, which I'd stupidly agreed to negotiate. My feeling at the time had been one-stop shopping for the client. I'd do the artwork, the design and figure out all the details for printing and packaging, which basically entailed calling some local places and doing Internet research. No biggie. Except, of course, I was still working for Foto Folks and getting calls for fill-in work with LaserTouch Studios, the place that hired me for the school and sports team photos.

I fiddled with my mouse, changing the specs on the document one more time to get it to fit the requirements of the site the client had finally chosen—not because of superior quality, of course, but for the price. Said site didn't seem to understand the superiority of Apple computers, and though customer service had assured me several times my files should load, no problem…there were problems.

"Fuck it in a bucket," I said when the file timed out, midload, for the seventh time.

"Olivia?"

I turned, startled. "Hey, Alex. What's up?"

He came through the door I hadn't realized I'd left half-open. "I knocked downstairs and when you didn't answer I thought maybe you were up here."

"I am." I gave him a smile and twirled around in my office chair.

"Working? Or playing?"

He was still all the way across the room, but I could feel the pull and surge of sexual tension. We'd been together for a couple weeks now but he'd been in my studio only one other time, and look how that turned out.

"Working," I said. "What are you up to?"

He moved across the wooden boards with slow, deliberate

steps, and by the time he got to me, my thighs had already parted so he could stand between them. The chair moved from side to side as I tilted back in it to look up at him. He stroked my hair off my shoulders and his kiss was brief, but sweet.

"I came to see if you wanted to go to Chocolate Fest with me."

I raised a brow and hooked my fingers in his belt loops to hold him close. "Is it today?"

"Yep. I got tickets to the VIP session. All the chocolate you can eat, plus hors d'oeuvres and champagne and live music."

"Huge crowds. You have to fight for a sample bite of brownie from Sam's Club. It's pretty ludicrous."

"No crowds," he promised. "I have it on good authority that the VIP session is crowd-free. And champagne, Olivia."

I glanced at the screen of my laptop and sighed. "If I could get this damn file to upload, I'd be there in a heartbeat."

"Then we'll have to get that file uploaded." A smile slid over his mouth, into his eyes, making him a pirate. Sly and sexy, his hair just a little tousled in such a way it made me think about him rolling around in a bed. Or sinking my fingers deep into it, and pulling.

"Give me a few minutes to try again, okay?"

"Sure."

He didn't ask me if it was okay to look around, he just wandered the big room taking a peek at anything and everything. I kept an eye on him while I tweaked the file specs one last time and started another upload. I didn't have anything in here I didn't want him to see, no secrets, but I still felt a little strange about him helping himself to the stacks of thick, spiral-bound photo albums in which I kept copies of all my favorite shots.

He pulled one from the pile and took it to the chair by the front windows. The chair he'd been in before. He sat, fingers flipping through the pages. I was probably the only one of us who got tingly.

"Yes! Thank God!" I cried a minute later when the browser window showed the message "upload complete."

I typed quickly, entering the client's order information and checking everything one last time. I stabbed the enter key and twirled around in my chair with a loud "woo hoo!"

Alex looked up from the album, but I was already off my chair and doing a little victory dance. He stuck a finger in his place to watch me. I didn't feel stupid, even though he was laughing.

"Boom boom boom." I shook my butt, turned and shook it some more. Jumped around a little.

"Let's go back to my room?"

I stopped, hands on my hips. "I thought you were going to take me for all the chocolate I could eat."

Alex got up, put the album on the chair and snagged my wrist to pull me close. Right up against him. He wasn't naked, but might as well have been by the way my body reacted. He anchored my hips. We danced a little, more slowly than I'd done on my own. Less rump shaking, more slow grinding.

"You're a good dancer," I said.

"I know."

I swatted his shoulder, but when I tried to push him away he laughed and kept me pressed tight against him. "You're supposed to tell me I'm a good dancer, too."

"Oh, believe me, I was checking out those fine moves."

"Maybe we can go dancing sometime." I settled back into

the slow circling, our feet moving half an inch at a time. Sort of like being at the prom without the cheesy music or wrist corsages, and with more full-frontal contact.

"Any good places to dance around here?"

I let my hands drift down to his fine, hard ass, which I squeezed. "Sure. In Harrisburg."

"Not in Annville." Alex laughed and bumped his crotch against mine. "What a shocker."

I squeezed his butt harder. "Hey. I thought you said you were going to like being a small-town boy."

One of his hands slid up to center between my shoulders. Before I knew it, he'd dipped me so low my locks brushed the floor, but even though it took me completely by surprise, I never once felt he might drop me. Alex kept me there for a moment before pulling me back up into his arms.

"Was I serious about that?"

"I don't know, Alex. Were you?"

He pursed his lips and gave his head a thoughtful shake. "It sounds like the kind of thing a guy says to impress a beautiful landlord into letting him take a lease on an apartment."

"And here I thought you weren't a liar."

We stopped dancing, stood still. I had my favorite chunk-heeled boots on, so I could look almost right in his eyes. I felt his hands on my waist, his body all along the rest of me. We'd stopped dancing but it still felt as if we were spinning, fast and faster.

"Small-town boy it is, then."

My tongue dipped into the tiny well in the center of my bottom lip, wetting it. Offering it. His gaze fell there, watching, and his own lips parted. There was nothing small-town about the kiss he slid across my mouth.

My phone rang on the table. Sarah's ring tone, the dance beat of a popular techno song. Reluctantly, I pulled away to answer it. Alex chased me the whole way, so I was laughing when I took the call.

"What the hell is going on?" Sarah asked.

"Oh…nothing. What's up?"

"'Nothing' sounds like someone's got a hand in your panties."

"Umm…" I wriggled away from Alex kissing my collarbone, only to turn and have him nuzzle the back of my neck, instead. "No."

Sarah gave a derisive snort. "Uh-huh. Tell Alex I said hi. Or, hey, girlfriend."

"As if." I'd have given her a harder time but hey, I was distracted.

"Does he go down on you?"

"What?"

"See, I always figured gay dudes could get it up for a woman, but actually eating pussy was something different. I mean, putting your dick in something warm and wet seems like a no-brainer, right? But actually going pearl diving…"

"Is there a point to this conversation?" I managed finally to wriggle away from Alex's groping hands and teasing tongue, and even got a few steps out of reach.

He grinned, unashamed.

"Aside from my sudden, desperate need to dissect whether or not a dude can do a good job eating pussy if he's not really that into the chick, or if he can fake it till he feels it, or what? Other than that?"

"Yes, other than your sudden, twisted need to discuss oral sex. Was there a point?"

Alex had gone back to the album by the window, though he looked over at me when I mentioned oral sex. I turned so I didn't have to see his face.

I checked the progress of my order, had the e-mail to show it had gone through, and started closing all my browser windows. A few more messages had come in to my business e-mail and a few to my personal—but those were Connex notifications, nothing important I needed to look at now. I started shutting down my computer. Alex hadn't said what time we should leave, but I needed a shower and a change of clothes, and by the way we'd been fooling around earlier, I thought it might take me longer than usual.

"Actually, no."

Sarah's answer gave me pause. "No? Are you serious? You called me up to ask me about guys eating pussy?"

That definitely drew his attention. I pantomimed asking him what time we needed to leave. Eleven. I had a couple hours before then, which should've been plenty of time…if we didn't end up making out or fucking.

"Yes," Sarah said.

I closed the lid of my laptop and sat in the twirly chair to talk to her. "What about it?"

"What do you think about it?"

"I'm a fan, obviously."

Sarah laughed. "Hell, yes. Who's not?"

"What's going on with you?"

"I just… Say I'm taking a survey."

I didn't believe a word of it. "Uh-huh."

"So, what do you think? Can a guy perform adequate and/or exemplary cunnilingus on a woman he's not attracted to?"

"What the—" I cracked up laughing, certain she had to be

putting me on. "Adequate and exemplary cunnilingus? Are you kidding me?"

"I'm serious, Liv." She sounded serious.

I rocked in my chair and put my feet up on the desk. "Guys can fuck anything. I'm convinced of it."

"Not fuck. Eat out. I know they can stick their dicks in any hole and get off." Sarah sounded a little more sour than she normally did. "But…cunt eating. Dining at the Y. Muff-diving. Gorging on the hairy burrito."

"Ew," I muttered. "Gross."

"Can they? Do you think?"

I shot a cautious look at Alex, who no longer seemed to be listening. He'd moved on to another of my albums and was flipping pages, his expression engrossed and thoughtful.

"Do you mean just gay guys?" I kept my voice low, my back turned.

"No. Straight guys, too."

"Hmm." Patrick had never gone down on me. Disgruntled at the memory, I said, "I guess so. Why not? Why couldn't they?"

"That's what I thought, too." Sarah sounded unexpectedly defeated. She paused, then asked in a smaller voice, "Do you think it turns them on?"

"Sarah, sweetie. Is something going on you want to talk to me about?"

She sighed. "I met someone, that's all."

"What happened?"

"Nothing." Her laugh sounded more normal this time. "I mean, nothing. Dude's a dud."

"Ah."

"Well, anyway, I'll let you go. I just wondered what you

thought about all that. I've got some other people to call and ask."

"Are you for real?"

"Girl, you know it's true."

I groaned. "Don't start quoting Milli Vanilli tunes to me, please…"

Too late. She was already singing. I laughed. Sarah singing early nineties pop songs was always good for a chuckle.

"I'll be by this week sometime to help with the studio if you want," she said. "Have fun with Ahhhlex."

"We're going to Chocolate Fest."

"I hate you."

"You don't hate me," I told her. "You love me."

"And yet, I don't think I could eat your pussy," Sarah said, so matter-of-factly she might have been reciting the times tables. "Not even if you paid me."

"Good Lord, why would I pay you to go down on me?" I had to wipe my eyes from tears of laughter.

"Ding, ding! Survey says…! Because…hell, I don't know why, either. Goodbye, fool."

"For a Jewish white girl from the suburbs of Philly, you do a mean impression of Mr. T."

"Liv, I am blacker than you are," Sarah said. "Peace out, Girl Scout."

"Bye."

I thumbed off the call and turned. Alex, silhouetted in the window, didn't move. I reached for my camera and took a quick shot. Then he shifted, coming out of the light and into focus.

"Let me guess. Sarah."

"Yeah. Smile." I held up the camera and watched him move closer. "Too close!"

I got a picture of his eyeball, blurred, and that was it. I showed him in the view screen. "Ah, there's one for the fridge."

"It's better than the one where I have a bowl cut and a striped turtleneck on."

"When was that taken?" I teased. "Last year?"

Alex curled his lip. "Ha-ha, second grade. I told my mother it didn't match my brown corduroy flare-leg pants, but she didn't listen."

"Oh, the trauma."

His gaze shifted for a second before a hard smile split his mouth. "Yeah. I guess if that was the worst of it, I'd be a lucky guy."

He said the words lightly, but they felt heavy. I put my camera on the table and took his face in my hands. I kissed him. Not hard, not sexy. Just…sweet.

"I'm sure you looked hot even in a pair of cords and a striped turtleneck."

He raised a brow. "Of course I did. I was the hottest boy in second grade. And third. And fourth—"

I put a finger over his mouth. "I'm sure."

He smiled and kissed my finger. "That was a long time ago."

"Yeah?" We were moving again, not quite dancing, but swaying. It seemed we couldn't touch each other without turning it into something sexy. "How long? How old are you?"

"How old are *you?*"

"I'm twenty-eight." I had a strange thought. "You're older than that, right?"

He laughed ruefully. "Christ. Yes. I am."

"You don't look it."

He pulled a face. "Gee, thanks. Thank God I spent all that money on Botox and pancake makeup."

"You don't use Botox." I touched the feathered lines, very faint, at the corners of his eyes. "And I don't see any makeup."

His sexy smile sent tingles down to my toes. "Not today."

It wouldn't have surprised me to know he wore makeup. Or women's clothes. My circle of male acquaintances had been so gay-centrically skewed for such a long time I was more shocked by men who knew more about fantasy football than *Fantasy Island*.

I could've said something then, but again I held back. "Too bad. Guyliner's hot."

"Pffft. Guyliner. Is that like a manpurse, or moobs? Bromance?"

We laughed together. I liked the way he held me, not too hard or soft. Not as if he was trying to keep me. More like he knew I had no plans of getting away.

"We should get going," I murmured into his mouth. "I still need to change."

"What, out of this exquisite fashion statement?" He looked down at my nightgown and ratty cardigan, my knee-high leather boots.

I let him kiss me a few more times. "C'mon, I'll be late. That phone call set me back a good twenty minutes."

"Sounded important," he said offhandedly.

"She was taking a survey about if I thought men could orally please a woman if they're not into her."

He blinked, then laughed. "What? Why?"

I shrugged. "With Sarah, who knows."

"Yes," he said after a second. "Absolutely."

I gave him a look. "You sure about that?"

"Not from personal experience," Alex said. "But yeah. I'd say definitely. A man can do a lot of things for sex with a lot of people he's not really into."

I made another face and pulled away a little. This time, he let me go. When I turned to fuss with my laptop and camera, my phone, Alex stayed quiet. I didn't want to think about the things a man would do to get off, even at the expense of someone else.

"Olivia."

I didn't turn. "Hmm?"

Alex took my shoulder and turned me until my butt bumped my desk. He put a hand between my thighs. Parted them. He didn't look away from my eyes as he did it, or when he stepped between my legs. Or when he lifted the hem of my nightie an inch on my naked thighs.

I drew in a breath.

He smiled. He looked down, then, to his hands. "I got a hard-on the first time I saw these boots."

"New Year's Eve," I found the voice to say, though it came out weak and hoarse and full of longing.

"No." He shook his head. "The first time I saw you, you had these boots on. The Chrismukkah party. Patrick's house."

I'd worn the boots to that party, but not the next morning when we'd met in the kitchen. I let him push me back against the table. Let him push my nightgown up to my hips. "But why didn't you—"

"Hmm?" His question hummed over my thigh.

If he'd seen me then, if my boots had turned him on, if he'd wanted me that way, why had he gone outside to get head from Evan? I didn't want to ask. I didn't want to know.

He moved my panties aside with a finger and stroked. I shifted to let him pull the material down over my hips, and off. The table was big enough to hold all of me, and I stretched my arms over my head. Arched my back. I gave it up to him, right there, without question or worry about the size of my thighs, the thickness of my bush. Not a damn thing.

Alex leaned over me. He spread my legs, slid his hands beneath my ass, lifted me to his mouth. I was already wet. He made the sort of noise I make biting into a piece of double chocolate cheesecake…mmmm.

I gasped again when he sucked gently on my clit. Then he fluttered his tongue, oh so softly, before circling it. I rocked into his mouth, urging him on.

It was the fastest I'd ever come. With him. With anyone. With myself, even. I shot off hard. My hands slapped at the table's slick, polished surface, squeaking. I shook and shuddered. It was over in half a minute, nothing drawn out about it.

With the aftershocks rippling through me, I opened my eyes and smiled up at him. "Mmmm."

Alex slipped his hands from beneath me and stood up straight. I sat up to grab the front of his shirt and kiss him.

He laughed into my mouth. "That was unexpected."

I nipped his bottom lip. "Oh, I'm sure it wasn't that much of a surprise. Not for the hottest boy in every single freaking grade."

His hand cupped the back of my neck. "Careful. You might have me thinking I'm pretty good at that."

I pushed him to the side so I could hop off the table, and shook my nightgown down over my thighs. I picked up my panties and headed for the door, saying over my shoulder, "Oh, it was fine. But with a little practice, you could be *really* damn good..."

I started running when he growled and lunged.

I made it all the way to the front door of my apartment before he caught me. We didn't get much farther than that.

Chapter 11

"You were right. This was worth it." I looked around the half-empty ballroom. The one other time I'd gone to Chocolate Fest the crowd had been cheek to cheek—not the ones on our faces. Today, people circulated freely to sample from the fifty or so booths lined up in aisles.

And it was good stuff, too. Not just cookies or cake, but homemade candies from local gourmet shops and bubbling fountains for chocolate-dipped fruit. The champagne was cheap, but cold, and the hors d'oeuvres fancy but unnecessary, as far as I could see.

"Nothing but the best for you," Alex said gallantly.

I rolled my eyes, though his words were sweeter than any chocolate I'd tasted. He gave me an utterly satisfied smile and squeezed me closer as we walked, hand in hand. We both glowed with the radiance of the freshly fucked. I'd gone on my knees for him in the hall outside my door, taken him in my mouth. Sucked him hard until he came. Chocolate couldn't chase away the memory of his taste flooding me.

Not that I wanted it to.

I had Alex all over and up inside me. Smell, scent, all of it. He didn't have to touch me for me to feel him.

We got looks, of course. Even after America elected a black man as president, people still saw skin color. Alex didn't seem to notice. I'd lived with it my whole life and still I could never not notice the second glances.

We walked past the cakes decorated for the competition. People oohed and ahhed over the creations of sugar and almond paste and fondant. My favorite was the cake shaped like a lake, the ice made from melted hard candies, the snow of crystal sugar and marshmallows. Tiny fondant figures skated on top. It was a simple design compared to some of the more elaborate ones, but had been expertly crafted.

I was still looking at it as I moved on, not paying attention. I bumped into Alex. Stepped on his foot because he'd stopped all of a sudden.

"Ouch," he said mildly, staring at the scene in front of him. I burst into laughter I quickly hid behind my hand. "Wow."

"There must've been a theme," he said, nodding toward the next three cakes. "But damn if I don't think it's wrong to take a bite out of Jesus's face."

All three were life-size re-creations of Christ's head, complete with the crown of thorns and agonized expression. Small pieces had been cut, I guessed for the judges to taste, and all I could think of was the phrase "this is my body, that shall be given up for you."

"Why would anyone ever want a cake like that?" I studied it, wondering.

Alex laughed. "First Communion, maybe?"

I shuddered. "No, thanks."

"Did you have one?" he asked as we moved away from the cakes and toward the center of the ballroom, where the raffle prizes and silent auctions were showcased.

"A Jesus-head cake?"

"A First Holy Communion."

"No. Nor a Bat Mitzvah. You?"

He nodded. "Yep."

"Good Catholic boy," I teased. "When's the last time you went to confession?"

"Long time ago. Hey, look at this one." He pointed to a basket stuffed with picture frames and other photography goodies. "Want to bid on it?"

I looked at the basket, wrapped in crinkly, translucent paper, and then the card attached. "Oh, cool. I know Scott Church. I took a couple of his classes."

Alex peeked at the basket's contents, too. "Digital camera. Nice. I should get me one of those. Gift certificate for a full glamour photography session. Ha. Don't need one of those."

He slipped an arm around my waist and pulled me close for a kiss. "I'd rather have my picture taken by you."

"I think we could manage that."

"Liv?"

I looked up at the sound of my name, just as a tiny figure tackled my knees with a squeal. Laughing, I peeled her away before she could knock me over. "Pippa, hi. Watch out. Devon, hi."

Devon gave Alex a curious glance, then stuck out his hand. "Hi. Devon Jackson."

"And I'm Pippa." Today she wore a ruffled gown, her curls tied back with a matching bow. "I have a pretty dress."

"Yes, you sure do." Alex bent a little to admire it, then straightened. "Alex Kennedy."

"Where's Steven?"

"Home with a cold. Told me to get out of the damn house," Devon said with a grin. "I have friends who work for the New Horizons Adoption Agency. They told me to come on by, man the booth for a little while today."

"You can make a Valentine's Day card," Pippa said. "With glitter, and lace and glue!"

"We'll have to stop by and check it out," I told her.

She tipped her head back to give Alex a sly once-over. "You could make one for Olivia. If she's your valentine. Is she?"

Alex put his arm around my waist again. "She sure is."

Pippa laughed and danced. "Do you guys kiss? Do you? Ha-ha! That's funny!"

Devon laughed, too, and shook his head at her. "Pippa, you run back to the booth and take charge over there."

Giggling, she launched herself into my arms for a hug and a kiss, then darted off through the crowd.

Devon's once-over of Alex wasn't quite as blatant as Pippa's, but I saw it.

He looked over the basket display. "You bidding?"

"It's for a good cause. Yeah, I think so." Alex's fingers tightened on my hip before he withdrew. "Olivia, I'm going to go get some tickets, okay? I'll be right back."

"I'll be here." I watched him go, the crowd parting. Heads turned to look at him even when I wasn't on his arm. I looked back at Devon, whose mouth was still pursed, brow furrowed. "What?"

He laughed and rubbed my shoulder for a second. "Girl, don't get your panties twisted on me, now. Man owned up to being your valentine, that's all. And he's looking at you like he thinks you're tastier than any of this candy in here. And you…"

"Me, what?" I gave him an icy look that didn't intimidate him.

"We got ties, don't we?" Devon's broad shoulders blocked out the sight of anything behind him, but he wasn't being aggressive or scary. He looked concerned. "We're family."

"We're dating, that's all. I met him a couple months ago. He's been living downstairs."

"At your place?" Devon's brows rose, wrinkling his bald head.

"Yes."

He let out a low whistle. "Huh. So things are serious."

"I don't know about that."

He glanced over his shoulder to the ticket booth, where Alex was now charming the volunteer in charge. "He looks like he does."

Before I could answer, Alex came back with a string of tickets. "They were selling them in arm's lengths," he explained. "I got one for each of us."

Devon laughed. "I need to get back to the booth before Princess Pippa makes all the valentines and doesn't leave any for anyone else. See you all later. Liv, you call me, hear?"

"I will."

We both watched him go, and Alex handed me a strand of tickets. "What are you going to try to win?"

I ended up putting my tickets in all the baskets, while Alex put all of his in the photography basket.

"I don't have a camera," he said when I laughed at his choice. "I need one."

"You could just buy yourself one, Alex. I can't believe you don't have a camera."

He shrugged, his tickets gone. The session was ending, and we were going to have to leave to make room for the next wave. "I had a camera, but not a digital one, and it broke a long time ago. I just never got another."

"Maybe you'll get lucky and win that one, then."

He grinned. Took my hand. "I have a better idea."

When he looked like that I wanted to pounce on him, but I restrained myself since we were out in public. "What's that?"

"You can tell me what kind to buy. I bet you'll give me good advice."

I laughed. "Uh-huh. Okay, sure. When do you want to buy it?"

He shrugged as we waited in line to pick up our coats from the coat check. "Whenever."

He helped me into my jacket and shrugged into his navy peacoat, looking wickedly delicious. I watched him wrap his long, striped scarf around his neck. He had an effortless style the straight men I'd dated had lacked. It might be stereotyping, but it was true.

"Today?" I asked, thinking of a visit to Cullen's Cameras. I hadn't been in ages, and there was always something there I wanted to buy.

"Sure. Let's go."

"So…what sort of camera are you looking for? Point-and-shoot or something more expensive?" I eased the car into a spot in the parking lot at the camera shop and turned off the ignition.

"Whatever you recommend." Alex leaned back in the seat and shot me a sideways grin. "You're the expert."

"How much money are you looking to spend?"

"Money isn't an issue."

"Must be nice," I said.

Alex's smile didn't fade, didn't wither, didn't move. His eyes, though, went a little shuttered. "It is."

"Come on, then. You ready?"

"Always."

I shifted him a glance as I opened my door. "No kidding."

His laugh rang out and hung, frozen in the winter air, on the steam of his breath, almost like a physical thing I could reach out and touch. Like ice that would break if tapped. He shook his head as he closed the car door.

"You have a dirty mind, Olivia."

I scoffed. "Oh, that's a good one, coming from you."

I led the way to Cullen's Cameras, a tiny shop tucked among the houses of a residential neighborhood. I never knew how Lyle Cullen stayed in business, since he never advertised and the shop wasn't anyplace anyone would ever look for if they didn't already know it was there. But the business had been in his family for years and I guessed it had become more of a beloved obsession than a moneymaker.

I reached for the door, but Alex was there before me, holding it open. Gentlemanly. Inside I breathed the smell of dust and the hot air spilling from the old iron radiators. Underneath it the faint smell of chemicals from the darkroom. Alex sneezed.

I got my first camera for my birthday when I was three. It

was big and clunky, with a plastic view screen that showed pictures of farm animals when you pushed the "flash" button. Nobody told me it wasn't real.

It didn't really matter. The pictures I made when looking through the small plastic hole didn't have to exist for me to see them. I remember talking to my grandpa about the lady in the long dress in the corner. I asked him if she was an angel. Angels, to me at the time, were always ladies with wings and halos of tinsel, or babies in diapers who shot arrows to make people fall in love. That woman had no wings, but it was clear to me that viewing her through the lens and no other way meant she was special.

Grandpa only saw the barnyard when he looked. So did Grandma, and my parents, and everyone else I asked. After a while, when there were other toys to play with, I stopped asking about her. I didn't forget about her. I just moved on.

Cameras with removable, disposable flashbulbs that came in packs of six. Cameras I had to load and wind by hand, and later, when my parents saw how serious I was about photography, cameras with better lenses. My dad gave me his old Nikon, complete with the original neck strap in a 1970s hash mark pattern of orange and brown, and I discovered bulk packs of film stuffed into the toe of my Christmas stockings.

The best camera I got, the one I still used, was a Nikon D80 I'd bought for myself with my first check from Foto Folks. It had seemed a fitting use of the money, even though I'd had to cancel cable television for a few months. I hadn't missed the TV shows, and I used my camera almost every day. I considered it a good trade-off.

"Olivia. Hello." Lyle Cullen beamed at me as he came out of the back room. He rested his chubby hands on the glass

case displaying several cameras resting on soft blue velvet.
"Who's your friend?"

"Alex Kennedy." Alex held out his hand and the men
shook.

"Here for a camera, Alex?"

"Yes, sir. I am."

Lyle's broad grin widened. "Good, good. Let me show you
some lovely models. Tell me a little bit about what you want
to do with it, and we'll see what we can do for you."

Alex followed him to the case along the far wall, and I
listened with half an ear while Lyle asked what he was looking
for. The rest of my attention focused on the Nikon D3
seducing me from a narrow glass case where it sat like a jewel
in a crown. Which, in my opinion, it was. It might as well
have been a diamond or a ruby for the price, and for how
unlikely it was I'd ever be able to afford it. I stared at it long-
ingly as I tried to convince myself it wouldn't really take
better pictures, and I'd be so afraid of breaking or losing it I'd
never take it out of the box.

I wasn't convinced, but then I'd never been very good at
making myself believe I didn't want something when I knew
I did.

"Olivia? What do you think of this one?" Alex held up a
simple point-and-shoot digital camera. "It's waterproof. And
takes video."

If Lyle had suggested it, that meant the camera was a good
choice for the buyer. Lyle never tried to upsell just because
he could. I nodded and crossed to take a closer look.

"It's great."

"Mr. Cullen says it's good for taking to the beach or skiing,"

Alex said, and held the camera up to look at the view screen. "Smile."

I'm used to being on the other side of the lens, but that doesn't mean I don't know how to strike a pose. I flashed him a grin, a finger beneath my chin. He laughed at the picture he took and showed me. It wasn't half-bad.

"I'll take it."

"Very good, very good. Let me get you one from the back," Lyle said. "And for you, Olivia? Anything today? The D3 maybe?"

He knew of my lust for the D3, knew I couldn't possibly afford it, but he never failed to ask.

"You're tempting me, Lyle. But not today."

"What's the D3?" Alex asked when Lyle ducked into the back room to get his purchase.

"C'mere." I showed him. "It's gorgeous, huh?"

He left a beat of silence, proving he didn't see the difference between my dream camera and any other, before answering. "Sure."

I laughed. "It's a nice camera. Top of the line. Too rich for my bank account, though."

"Ah. It's a sell-your-firstborn sort of thing, huh?"

I hesitated, thinking of my firstborn. "No. Not that. Maybe I could sell a kidney, though."

Alex bent to peer into the case. "How much is it?"

"Too much," I said as Lyle came back.

Alex paid for his camera, along with a bunch of accessories, a case, an extra battery, a car charger, an SD memory card. He tricked that camera out like a show pony, and watching him, I couldn't even envy the money he was dropping as if it really was nothing. His excitement about the new toy was infectious. He started taking pictures as soon as we left the store.

He posed me in front of the car. He stood with an arm around my shoulders and held the camera at arm's length to take both of us—and laughed when the shot cut off the top of his head. He took a picture of me in the driver's seat, and one of himself in the passenger seat, and then he took an accidental picture of his crotch.

"Another one for the fridge," I said when he showed it to me. "Wow. I can't imagine not having a camera."

"I can't imagine you without one."

By the time we got home, Alex had already taken about fifty shots—of me, of the car, of the scenery. Of himself. Most of them were blurred and only a few were any good, but he had a great time. He cornered me against the car again when we got home, this time taking a picture of us in which both of our heads were cut off.

"Maybe I should leave this to you," he said.

"You'll get better."

Hand in hand we went to the back door, where a plastic bin that hadn't been there before waited. I recognized it right away because I'd been with Patrick when he bought the set at Costco. I let go of Alex's hand and bent to touch the top.

"What the hell?"

I opened it. A pair of gloves, a scarf. My small bag of earplugs. A sleep T-shirt. Balderdash, the board game I'd taken to share at the New Year's party. There was nothing I couldn't have lived without. I moved aside a box of crackers, and my heart twisted.

Patrick had sent back the photo I'd taken of him and Teddy. This was bad. Worse than bad. Even if we made up, even if this moved behind us, he'd ruined the gift I'd chosen so carefully. I could never give it back to him and I could never keep it for myself. It would always remind us of the fight. It would have been better for him to just throw it away than return it.

Alex's hand squeezed my shoulder. "You okay?"

I shook my head.

He sighed and enfolded me in his arms. "He's an asshole. Don't let him do this to you."

No soft words or kisses could change the way I felt. I picked up the bin and dumped it in the large garbage can and shoved the lid down. Alex watched me silently.

"Let's go inside," I said, subject closed.

Chapter 12

$\mathcal{I}$ hadn't gone without talking to Patrick for longer than a day or two since we'd made up after we broke up. Even when he went on vacation he called or text-messaged me, and when I went out of town I usually found time to check in with him, too. It had been weeks without a word, and then this. The return of everything that could possibly give me reason to see him again.

Well, fuck him. I wasn't going to put on a hair shirt and beat myself with a chain to get back in Patrick's good graces. I had other things to occupy my time.

I knew things were moving fast, but it was so easy to see Alex, to be with him, I wasn't sure how to slow it down. We didn't live together, exactly, but the doors between our apartments stayed open more often than not, with us going back and forth between. It showed me how easy it would be to convert the firehouse into one residence, an idea I'd tossed around briefly before realizing I didn't have the cash for renovations, and the only way to get it would be by renting the downstairs unit.

I had no reason not to be with him. He was funny. Sweet. He was a better cook, had better movie choices, was a killer at Monopoly. Every time I thought about pulling back, Alex did one more thing to bring me closer.

"I can honestly say I have never made matchstick carrots." Knife in hand, I sliced into the carrots on the chopping board and prayed I wouldn't end up with matchsticked thumbs. "I usually just chop them into chunks."

"They need to be thin to cook in the right amount of time." Alex eased in behind me, his hands on my hips, and nudged aside my hair to kiss the back of my neck.

My nipples tightened at that simple touch, and I leaned back against him. His cheek rested along mine. His hands moved flat over my belly. We swayed a little to the music coming from his iPod speaker dock. This was the third night in a row he'd cooked me dinner, and I had no doubts it would be the third we'd end up making love for a few hours before falling into exhausted sleep. In my bed, though. No more futon.

"Where'd you learn to do all this?" I gestured with the tip of the knife at the mess I'd made of the carrots.

Alex put his hands over mine and guided them as he answered. We cut together, making perfect, thin slices. "It was learn to cook or starve."

I paused in cutting and turned in his arms to look up at his face. "Most guys settle for pizza and sandwiches."

Alex grimaced. "Yeah. Well, most guys live like pigs and

dress like slobs. Besides, cooking someone a gourmet meal practically triples my chances of getting laid."

It didn't escape me that he'd said someone and not "a woman." Sarah's advice rang in my head, but I pushed it aside. I pushed him aside, too, to grab my camera from its place on the dining-room table. I'd never be much of a chef, but I could take a mean picture.

"Oh, no." He laughed, holding up a hand that covered his face in the first shot I took. "I thought you were going to be my sous-chef."

"Too many cooks."

Point. Focus. Shoot.

I caught him looking down, his smile tilted, his eyes half-closed. Alex shook his head and turned back to the cutting board to make the carrots into something beautiful. I tried my best to capture him doing it.

He scooped up a handful of the carrots and tossed them into a sauté pan already sizzling with olive oil and garlic. He turned them deftly with a wooden spoon. The smell was incredible, and my mouth watered as my stomach rumbled.

"I'm going to gain a hundred pounds." I pulled up a chair to stand on to get a shot from overhead. Steam whirled around him and the light from the stove hood cast funky shadows on his face and hands.

"I'll just have to help you work it off."

"Uh-huh." I hopped off the chair and kept my camera in the hand well away from spattering grease as I leaned in for a kiss. "How you gonna do that?"

He laughed and eased the pan off the flames. Then he backed me along the kitchen cabinets, up the single step to the raised dining area, and into the basket chair I'd hung from a ceiling beam with a large, heavy chain.

Wicker creaked as I sat. The thin cushion shifted as I leaned against the curved back. Watching him. Laughing. I clutched the chair's side with my empty hand and gripped my camera firmly with the other.

"What are you doing?"

He grinned and yanked the beanbag chair, most of its innards missing so it was flatter than it should be, toward my seat. When he knelt on it, my heart stuttered. I knew exactly what he meant to do.

Wicker creaked again as Alex pulled my panties off and pushed my loose skirt up my thighs. He put a hand on each side of the chair. It moved freely under his grip, and so did I inside it. He nuzzled against my thighs, then deeper, finding my clit with his lips and tongue and rocking the chair so he didn't have to move.

I closed my eyes to give in to it, but opened them after only a few seconds of pleasure. This felt too good. All of it. Not just the sex, and not just the food. Everything about being with him.

So I put my camera to my face. Focused. Snapped a shot of his head between my legs, and it blurred because of the way he rocked the chair. Alex looked up at the sound of the shutter, his mouth slack and wet, his eyes heavy lidded.

Another picture taken, as I was. As I couldn't help being. I saw his mouth and eyes, and he saw nothing but a camera where my face should have been.

It felt safer that way.

"Don't stop," I said.

He bent again to nuzzle and suck, to lick and nibble. To

fuck inside me with one finger, then two, then an impossible three that stretched me so I cried out and shook the camera. But I didn't stop taking pictures.

I didn't mess with settings or shutter speeds, not when Alex's mouth was working such magic on my cunt it was all I could do to look through the viewfinder. My finger twitched, *snap, snap.* When he turned to the side, I caught his profile.

Eyes closed, mouth open. Pressed against me. Some of him inside me.

I couldn't keep my eyes open when I came. Orgasm blinded me, though my finger kept its place and my camera whirred. Pleasure burst inside me and all around. I said his name, then again, louder, as a second wave of climax ripped me up and scattered me, petals in a breeze.

The chair creaked.

My wrist cramped from the camera's weight, my fingers holding it in a death grip. I eased it free and settled it gently on the end table next to the chair. Then I pulled Alex by the front of his shirt until I could kiss him.

"What would it take for you to drop that thing?"

He tasted of me, of my desire. I couldn't tell if he was hard. I could reach between us, grab his cock and find out, but for now I slid my fingers through his hair.

"I'd drop a baby before I dropped my camera."

He laughed. "That's what I thought."

We kissed, each kiss still new. Each felt it would always be new, after two weeks or two years, or two hundred. I knew it wouldn't always be like this. Nothing ever was. But that's how it felt.

"Does it turn you on?" he asked.

"What? You going down on me? Umm, hello, yes."

Alex laughed again. Pulled away. "Taking pictures."

I licked my mouth and tasted myself. I had no easy, ready answer. "Sometimes."

His hands slid up my thighs and stayed there. He steadied the chair, kept it from rocking. "That time?"

I cupped his cheek. "It's something I do..."

He shook his head a little. His shaggy bangs fell over an eye. I pushed them away.

"I mean, did taking those pictures, then, turn you on more than if I'd just been going down on you?"

I tried to see if he wanted me to say yes or no, but saw only myself reflected in his eyes. If the eyes are the body's camera, I wondered what pictures Alex was taking of me.

"I don't know."

"I liked it," he said.

"Did you?" I traced his ear, then both his brows. His lips. He opened his mouth to nip at my finger, and I laughed.

"It was fucking hot."

I raised a brow and sat back a little in the creaky chair. "Oh, really?"

He nodded.

"Like that day...before. When you came the day Sarah was in my studio."

"Yes. That day."

"I never would've guessed."

Alex smirked. "The hard-on didn't give it away, huh?"

I kissed him. I wanted every word we ever said to each other to come between kisses. And I wanted not to be afraid of that.

"Let me take your picture, Alex."

"Again?"

"Sit on that chair, there." I pointed to a straight-backed chair in better shape than the one he'd been in that other day.

He looked over his shoulder, but didn't hesitate. On his feet, on the seat, hand already at the button on his jeans. "Like this?"

"Just like that."

He popped the button and unzipped to free his cock. If he hadn't been hard when he was making me come with his mouth, he sure as hell was now. He shoved his jeans and his briefs down to his calves. His black T-shirt hugged his chest, and his cock, firmly held in his fist, brushed the hem of it.

"Push up your shirt." I already had my camera to my face. "I want to see your belly."

I'd used the camera as a barrier before. A shield. Watching him now through the small square of glass, I wasn't separated from Alex but brought closer. Joined, somehow. A part of what he was doing in a way I hadn't been when we fucked. Making a picture of him, I almost was him.

I moved behind him to get a shot of his perspective. "God, that's fucking gorgeous."

He grunted at my words. I took pictures. I moved around him as he fucked his fist.

It could've been porn, what we did. A closeup of his prick imprisoned by his fingers followed a shot of just his face. These pictures told an intimate and private story and yes, it was about sex, but it was about something else, too.

Trust.

I set the camera aside to kiss him and put my hand on his to help him along. He came in another minute. I was looking in his eyes when he did, and I had no trouble seeing what was inside them.

"I need to jump in the shower," he said.

The timer on the oven went off. We pulled apart. He grabbed me for one more kiss, then went into my bathroom while I headed for the kitchen. My cell phone rang as I pulled a pan of something cheesy and delicious smelling out of the oven and set it on the stove.

I grabbed up my phone. "Hello?"

"Hello, Liv. Did you get the stuff I left for you?"

Patrick. My appetite fled. I cocked an ear, listening for the sound of the shower running. Alex wouldn't be in there long.

"I threw it in the trash," I said.

"I can't believe you." The coldness in his words seeped all the way through the phone and straight to my heart.

"Did you call just to bitch me out again?" I leaned against the counter.

Patrick's laugh grated into shreds. "You're fucking Alex Kennedy. Aren't you?"

The floor dropped from beneath me. "What?"

"You are. I told Teddy it couldn't be true. But it is, isn't it? You really are. I can't believe you, Olivia! I told you about him!"

"You told me he doesn't like girls," I hissed. "Well, guess what, Patrick. He does."

"I told you he was trouble!"

"What's your problem?" I said evenly. "That I'm fucking Alex? Or that I'm fucking anyone?"

Silence.

"I like him, Patrick. A lot."

"Of course you do." I could hear the sneer. "Everyone likes

him. Everyone wants to get in his pants. He's a slut. It's what he does."

The phone slipped in my suddenly sweaty palm. "It's what you do, too."

"That's not the point," Patrick snapped.

"What is?" The dinner smells that'd had my stomach rumbling minutes ago now turned it.

"I just can't believe you'd go for him," Patrick said in a low, hard voice. "For fuck's sake, Liv, haven't you learned your lesson?"

"What lesson is that? The one where I don't fall in love with a gay man?"

More silence from us both. Patrick's breathing turned sharp and short. Mine had, too.

"You don't love him," he said finally. "Jesus, Liv. You barely know him."

"I'm not saying I do. I'm saying I could. You must think I could, or you wouldn't be in such a frenzy."

"I'm not in a frenzy. I just don't want to see you making a mistake—"

"Like the one I made with you?"

Dead silence.

I hung up the phone.

"Babe?"

It was the first time Alex had used an endearment for me. It cemented how far this had gone. I turned to face him, wet from the shower, his hair rumpled and dripping and a towel hanging low on his hips.

"We need to talk."

He nodded, as if he was expecting this. Every glimpse I'd had of what he was thinking disappeared, locked up tight behind those deep gray eyes. He ran a hand through his hair, slicking it back.

"Okay."

My phone rang again. I turned it off without looking at who was calling. "It's Patrick. I don't want to talk to him."

"Okay."

I put the phone on the counter and crossed my arms over my stomach. That didn't help the butterflies, but I kept them there anyway. The picture we were making needed a caption: "Argument Waiting" or something artsy like that.

I could do what Sarah had said. Frame my question like cropping a photo, already knowing the answer the way I knew which piece of the picture I wanted to keep and which to cut.

Knowing changed things. It had for me, and it would for him. I thought I could deal with knowing my current lover went both ways and had once slept with my ex. I didn't know if Alex could.

"Olivia?" He didn't move closer. Didn't touch me. His gaze caught and held mine.

Asking him would show me if he'd lie or tell the truth. I thought of the past few weeks. Sex and movies and dinner and laughter.

I didn't want to know if he would lie.

"It's about that word," I said. "You know, the one I said I wasn't ready to use."

Alex smiled, nice and slow. "Boyfriend?"

"That one."

"What about it?"

I crooked a finger, and he moved closer. I touched his damp skin. "I think we should reconsider the option on it."

"Yeah?"

I nodded and kissed him, breathed against his lips. "Yeah."

Alex put his arms around me and pulled me close. "What about girlfriend? Is that okay, too?"

"So long as you're not saying it with two snaps up." I demonstrated, snapping my fingers over my head.

He gave me an odd look, his mouth parted as though words were about to come out, but I stopped him with another kiss. This one deepened. His hands started roaming.

"Dinner," I said into the kiss.

"It's just as good cold," Alex said.

"So you didn't tell him?" Sarah spoke from around a mouthful of nails. Perched high on top of the ladder, she wielded both a hammer and a nail gun. I'd stopped worrying about what would happen if she fell.

"No." I was a little more worried about what might happen if she dropped something, since it would hit me right on the head.

Sarah shot another nail into the strip of wood, tacking up another inch of fabric. I held the ladder steady while she reached, pleating the material and adding another nail. She looked down at me.

"He told you he wouldn't lie."

"Everyone says they won't lie," I said. "And that's not really the point, anyway, because I believe him. I just don't want to know."

Sarah climbed down the ladder and we moved it over a foot. "But you already know."

"I know."

She hammered another few pleats, curiously quiet. I'd expected a much, much bigger discussion about this.

Down the ladder, move it a foot, up again. We worked without much talk for a few minutes. The next time she came down, Sarah leaned on the ladder and didn't head straight back up.

"You really like him, huh?"

"I do. Want a drink?"

She nodded and we both grabbed colas from the small fridge by my desk. I sipped mine, but Sarah guzzled hers with a lot of drama. She belched, pounding her chest.

"Nice one," I said.

"Thanks." She rolled the can in her palms, back and forth. "So…if you already know, why not just ask him? Doesn't it bother you to know he fucked Patrick?"

I'd had a few days to digest the information, mull it over. Chew on it. I'd had time to crop it or blow it up, and I'd chosen cropping.

I shrugged. "I'm more upset at Patrick for doing it. It's not like I was a virgin before I got together with Alex, Sarah. I know he had lovers. So did I."

She snorted lightly. "I don't think I could deal. Hanging out with someone who'd screwed someone I was screwing? I'm open-minded, but not that open."

"Look at it this way. I don't believe it will happen again."

"You don't?"

"Patrick wouldn't be such a bitch about it, otherwise." I laughed, not entirely lightly.

Sarah's laugh was more genuine. "That's the truth."

We both drank the rest of our sodas and tossed the cans in

the trash. I stopped to look around the room as Sarah climbed the ladder. It was really taking shape.

"Let me get a couple pictures of this. I want to make sure I have it properly documented." I got my camera.

Sarah struck a pose. "La, la, la."

I hadn't yet deleted the photos from the last time I'd used the camera, and when I turned it on, the last shot showed in the view window. Alex and me, kissing, the angle odd and shadows deep, motion blurred. We could have been anyone.

I studied it. "Is it wrong of me to want this to work?"

Sarah got off the ladder and gave me one of her patented hugs. "No, bunny. Of course not."

"Because…I really do."

She gave me another squeeze. "Then you should probably tell him you know. It's going to eat you up inside, otherwise. Worrying."

I sighed. "Yeah. I know."

Sarah grinned sympathetically. "If it makes it any easier for you, I think I might be in love with a guy who fucks women for money."

"What? I didn't even know you were dating anyone!"

"See?" she said. "Everyone's got issues."

Usually I didn't mind working the late shift at Foto Folks. The mall closed at 9:00 p.m. in the off-holiday season and we stopped taking appointments and walk-ins at eight to make sure we were always finished by then. More people came in the evenings, which meant more clients, which meant more cash in pocket for me.

Tonight, though, I was restless. I hadn't seen Alex since the night before, when he'd slept downstairs because he had to get up early for a meeting and didn't want to wake me. My bed had been empty without him and I hadn't slept well, anyway.

I'd woken to an early phone call from my mom—the annual birthday call. Sarah had already sent me an iTunes gift certificate. Cards from my brothers and dad had arrived in the mail over the past week, and I figured something would show up from my mom, too.

I wondered what Alex was planning.

Before I could find out, though, I had to get through one last hour of heavy makeup and fingertips to chins. Feather boas. I wondered if death by tiara was possible.

At last I was finished and had made a few nice tips, too. I raced home and followed the smell of garlic up the stairs to my apartment.

"You look good in my kitchen." I hung my coat and hat on the hook as Alex appeared across the long living room. He wore the naked lady apron, though he wasn't naked underneath it. Too bad.

"Happy Birthday."

"Mmm, birthday kisses, the best kind." We were schmoopy, we were mushy. We were the sort of couple I'd always wanted to be.

"How about birthday spankings?" Alex squeezed my ass.

"For you or for me?"

He laughed. "Your choice. It's your birthday."

"I'll think about it." I gave him a sly grin and let him rub up on me for a few more minutes.

"You got some packages, by the way. I put them on the chair."

"Ooh, presents!" I found the boxes, one heavy one from

Amazon.com and one much smaller with my mom's return address on it.

I tore into the heavy one while Alex watched, and pulled out three hardcovers. It didn't register at first, but then my eyes focused on the titles and I put the books back in the box and closed it.

"They're from Patrick," I said. "*Hitchhiker's Guide to the Galaxy* and the sequels."

Alex looked at the box, now at my feet. "Good books."

"He's trying to butter me up. Also," I said unkindly, "I already have those books, but they're at his house. So he's essentially just replacing what I already own because he hasn't returned mine. He'll send back a gift I gave him, but not something that belongs to me."

My words dripped so much like acid they should've burned through the floor. Alex nudged the box with a toe. I frowned.

"Open the other one," he said.

The box from my mother held a silver necklace. It was pretty, a Star of David with a heart in the center. I held it up to my throat and thought about if this was something I wanted to wear.

"Can you help me with the clasp?"

"Sure." Alex went behind me and lifted my hair off my neck, then hooked the necklace in place.

It nestled just right in the hollow of my throat. I touched it. "How's it look?"

"Pretty."

I glanced up at him. "So…anything else for me to open?"

"Ah, my little greedy one."

"That's me." No point in denying it. Anyone who says they don't care about presents is full of crap.

"Dinner first," he told me. "Presents after."

I made a face, but dinner smelled too good to resist. He'd made lasagna, salad, garlic bread. He'd set my rickety table with a pretty cloth, flowers, my best china, which wasn't expensive but nice. He'd even lit candles.

We talked and ate. We fed each other bites from our forks. We split a piece of Godiva Chocolate cheesecake. An hour passed, then half of another, and still we sat and ate and laughed without running out of things to say.

Alex's eyes gleamed in the candlelight. "You have such a great smile."

"All teeth." I ran my tongue across them. "I spent a long time in braces."

"I bet you looked cute."

"Pffft. What about you? What were you like as a kid?"

His smile didn't fade, but his gaze grew veiled. "I was an idiot as a kid."

"I'm sure that's not true."

He shrugged and got up to clear plates. I didn't pursue it. A month into a relationship isn't all that long, no matter how long it felt. He'd avoided talk of his family before.

Together, we loaded the dishwasher and set the pans soaking in the sink. He blew a handful of bubbles at me. I tweaked his ass as I passed. And then, finally, he turned me around as I bent to shove some leftovers in the fridge, and kissed me.

"Ready for your present?"

"That wasn't it?" I nibbled his chin.

"Nope."

"You are grinning like a fool, Alex."

He grinned even wider. "Come sit down."

He led me by the hand to the couch and settled me on it. "Close your eyes."

"Oh, this means it's a good one." I clapped and closed my eyes. I was grinning, too.

Getting presents is always so much better when they're given by someone who knows how to do it just right. He teased me a little with the setup. Drew out the anticipation. And then, whispering, "Open your eyes," Alex pressed something into my hands.

It was wrapped in pretty paper, tied with a ribbon and a bow. "Did you do this?"

"Yep."

"You wrapped this?" I stroked the knife-sharp creases in the paper and the professionally tied ribbon. "Is there anything you don't know how to do?"

"Open it."

I started to ease off the fancy paper, not wanting to tear, but Alex shook his head with a sigh and forced my fingers to rip and shred. In moments it lay on the floor and a plain brown box sat in my lap. I lifted the tape holding the lid with my thumb and the cardboard popped open.

So did my mouth.

"What...? No. Oh...no, you shouldn't have! You didn't? You did. Oh, my God!"

He'd bought me the camera I'd shown him in Mr. Cullen's shop. A five-thousand-dollar camera, the one I'd been lusting after for years. Alex had given me a dream.

"Hey...don't cry." He wiped a tear from my cheek but could do no more because I was squeezing the breath from him.

"I love you," I said.

We both froze, cheek to cheek, the camera box between us. I hadn't meant to say it, at least not like that. I'd meant I loved him for buying me the camera, the way you love vanilla ice cream, or horror movies. Not love the way you love a person.

"I love you, too," he said quietly and directly into my ear, so there was no way I could pretend I didn't hear him.

I pulled away. "Alex…"

"Olivia," he said with a slow and easy smile.

"Thank you for the camera."

Kisses lingered and I had to lean back to catch my breath again. "It's…amazing. It's too much."

"It's not too much."

"It's very expensive," I amended. "I wasn't expecting it."

"Duh," Alex said, surfer-boy style. "That's totally why I bought it for you."

I cupped his cheek. "Thank you."

"You're welcome." Eager, like a kid, he bent over it to show me the other things in the box. A camera bag, neck strap. Cleaning cloth.

"Alex," I said quietly so he'd look at me. "I have some things to talk about."

Chapter 13

"I have to tell you something I never mentioned before."
I set the camera aside and took both his hands.

His brow creased. "Okay."

I drew in a breath, thinking of the words and how to say them. Then I knew. I got up and went to the drawer in the cabinet along the wall. I pulled out a sheaf of photos and came back to the couch. I faced him, our knees touching. I gave him the pictures.

They weren't in order, but as he sifted through them Alex set the ones that were alike together. He looked at the ones of the infant on a blanket, then the shot I'd taken just a few weeks before. He glanced up at me.

"She looks like you."

"Yeah. She does."

He blinked and gazed back at the photos. "You and Devon?"

I shook my head. "No. I met Pippa's dad in a bar after I broke up with Patrick. He claimed to be shipping out the next day, and even though I knew that was probably a crock of shit, I wanted to believe him for a few hours. It was…a bad time in my life. I found Devon and his partner through an adoption agency. They wanted a baby, and I wanted to help them."

"I don't know what to say." He put the pictures all together in a pile but didn't hand them back to me.

My stomach sank and twisted, dinner sitting in it like a stone. "I wanted you to know."

"She's beautiful."

I turned my head to look at the picture on top of the pile, the one of her spinning with her dress out around her. "She is. But she's not my daughter, Alex. I'm not her mother."

He shifted on the couch and I dared a look at him. "But you've got pictures of her."

"Devon and Steven wanted Pippa to know me. They want me to know her. But I'm not her parent." I swallowed against dryness, waiting for judgment.

He nodded. "That's quite a gift you gave them. I only gave you a camera."

The laugh startled out of me. "Yeah, well, believe me, that was a better choice for me."

He smiled and kissed me. "Thanks for telling me."

"I had to. I didn't want you to find out later, because you would. She's not a secret in my life or anything. And if ever…well, I mean, it would come out, eventually. That she was my first."

Something softened in his gaze, and his mouth. His kiss this time was longer. Different. And when he pulled away, his expression was more open than I'd ever seen it.

"I'm glad you told me."

I took another deep breath. "My family took it hard. My dad and his wife won't talk about it. One of my brothers pretends he doesn't know, but the other one had fertility problems with his wife, so they're actually pretty cool with it. But my mother…"

He waited for me without pushing.

"She hates what I did. Hates."

"Because you gave the baby away?"

"You'd think a woman who adopted a kid would be more understanding, huh?" I shook my head, bad memories still tasting bitter.

"So what happened?"

A lot had happened, but it would take longer than a few minutes to share the story, and I didn't really want to get into all the details. "She disowned me for a while. Now she just refuses to talk about it. But we're not close. We used to be."

"I'm sorry, Olivia."

"It's not just that. It's her whole Orthodox thing. Since she became observant, there's not much room in her life for me."

"That sucks."

"Yeah. It does."

"I'm glad you told me." He paused. "Does it matter to you?"

"What?"

"That I'm not Jewish."

I laughed, hard and long. "God, no. Why would you think so?"

He touched my necklace with a fingertip. "It suits you. And I thought the candles, the pepperoni…"

"Those are my things." I thought of my mom, hair covered,

insisting I stand beside her to pray. Throwing away the plastic dish that had been mine since infancy because there was no way to make it kosher, and she had no room in her kitchen or her life for anything that couldn't be made kosher. "I don't expect you to go by what I believe. If I believe anything, which I'm not sure I do."

"I just wondered if it mattered if I was different, that's all."

I took his hand, our fingers linked. I touched them, his, mine, his, mine. "We'll always be different."

He kissed our fingers. "That doesn't matter to me, either."

We kissed, not passionately, though of course it was all still so new that every time we kissed I thought about fucking him. I rested my head on his shoulder. "I wish…"

"What?"

"That I could be just one thing. One way or another."

His hand stroked over my hair, toying with the locks. "Nobody's ever just one thing, Olivia."

I snorted softly. "Right."

"I mean it."

I toyed with the snaps on the front of his shirt. Cowboy chic had never impressed me, so why did Alex's snap-front Western shirt so enamor me? I pictured him with a cowboy hat pulled low over his eyes, a pair of boots, a swagger. I could picture him as a lot of things. That didn't make them true any more than picturing myself as Catholic did, or Jewish, or white. Or black.

Alex looked uncomfortable for a moment, took a breath, looked as if he meant to speak, and thought better of it. I gave him the time he'd given me. When he did speak, his voice was low and guarded, but he looked me in the eyes. "I have something to tell you, too."

I braced myself. I took his hand. Palm to palm, our fingers linked. "Okay."

"Is the reason Patrick's so pissed off at you because of me?"

"Part of it." My thumb stroked the back of his hand.

He let out the breath he must've been holding. "So…you know."

I nodded and went for broke. "I saw you the night of Patrick's Chrismukkah party. With that guy Evan."

Alex groaned. His head dropped back against the couch. "Fuck."

It had been easier than I thought, but then so far, everything with him had been. "And Patrick told me about you."

Now he looked at me, a brow raised. "He did?"

"He said you…were together," I said delicately. "Just once. And that Teddy didn't know."

Alex frowned. "Did he say we fucked?"

I nodded. He sighed. Ran a hand over his hair.

"We didn't. He wanted to. I let him blow me, that's all."

Unlike Clinton, Patrick didn't always differentiate. It made sense. It didn't make it any easier to know, but at least I believed it wasn't a lie.

"I wish he hadn't told you," Alex said.

My fingers tightened in his. "Why? Because you didn't want me to know?"

"No, because I should've been the one to tell you." He didn't try to kiss me, maybe afraid I'd pull away. "I should've known he'd spill it. He told me to stay away from you."

"He told me to stay away from you, too."

"But neither of us listened." His eye gleamed again. "Must be fate."

"I have a lot of…issues…about what happened with Patrick.

I didn't want to get into another relationship with a guy who might create those same issues."

"Fuck, I'm surprised you ever agreed to be with me in the first place."

I kissed him then, just as slowly and easily as he always managed to with me. "You aren't Patrick."

"No, I sure as hell am not."

I looked into his eyes. "All I want to know is that you'll be honest with me. That's it. Fat ass in jeans, kinky secrets, whatever it is."

"I won't lie to you, Olivia. Okay?"

I believed him.

I'd fallen, hard.

I waited to hit the ground, but every day I spent with Alex was just as wonderful as the one before had been. Not that we existed solely in a glitter-covered cloud of rainbows or anything. He annoyed me sometimes with his smart-ass answers, and my perpetual lateness made Alex snap in irritation. But those were normal things. Couple-type things, and I welcomed even the small arguments because they didn't derail us. We could survive them. What had grown between us wasn't going to melt away or dissolve. What we had was real.

I took dozens of pictures of him. Hundreds. He was good at posing, comfortable with his body, completely in touch with his sexuality. I'd won the photography basket we'd bid on at Chocolate Fest, and it included admission to one of Scott Church's workshops, this one held in Philadelphia. I could take one model. Of course I took Alex.

I had a copy of Church's last book for him to sign, and Alex flipped through it on the drive from Annville to Philadelphia. The Pennsylvania Turnpike is long and straight and mostly smooth, the view along it fields and neighborhoods. Pretty.

"Am I going to have to get naked for this shoot?"

I flicked him a glance. "You don't have to do anything you don't want to."

He laughed more self-consciously than I was used to hearing from him. "I guess it wouldn't be the first time I was bare-assed in a crowd. Just not used to having my picture taken that way, that's all."

Alex and I talked about everything. Life, the universe and everything, to quote Douglas Adams. We'd covered families and lovers, his list quite a bit longer than mine. I wanted to know about that, him being naked in a crowd, but decided against asking. He would tell me the truth the way I always believed he had, and I wasn't sure I wanted to know it.

"I've taken your picture lots of times," I pointed out instead.

"Totally different."

"You think so?" I shot him another look as I eased into the right lane, getting ready to exit. "Why?"

"I don't care if I get a hard-on when you're taking my picture. And I usually do. What if I'm programmed for that?" He sounded serious, but his smile gave him away. "What if I'm like one of those dogs with the bell, but instead of drooling, my cock gets hard when the flash goes off?"

I laughed. "Oh, Alex."

"Olivia. I'm serious. What if I'm the only dude there with a flagpole between his legs?"

"There will be lots of naked chicks there. I've no doubt you won't be the only dude with a chubby."

"Fuck, I'm doomed."

With my eyes on the road to make sure I didn't take a wrong turn, I couldn't see his expression. I didn't need to. I could read his voice. This realization put a smile on my face.

"You're mocking me, Olivia. Why mock?" He sounded sad, but I could hear his smile, too. "That's not nice."

"Baby, if I thought you were really worried about showing off your cock to the world, I'd never have asked you to come with me today. But," I said as I took a side street, then pulled into the lot of an old warehouse, "I happen to know you have nothing to be ashamed of. Or embarrassed about. An erection to these people will be just another day's work. I promise."

He ran his fingers down the length of his striped scarf, worn for fashion and not warmth, since March had gone out like a lamb this year. "It wouldn't bother you? Really?"

"If you get hard because you get off on being naked in front of other people, or because there are hot naked chicks with flat bellies, no stretch marks and big tits there?"

"Either. All."

I took his hand. Stroked each finger. Held it to my lips and kissed each fingertip. "Should I?"

"I don't think you should. No."

We hadn't talked about monogamy. I had no time for another lover, but I guessed it was possible that during my long hours of work Alex had found someone else to fuck. It didn't feel that way, but I wasn't stupid enough to assume I'd be able to tell.

"Fool me twice," I murmured.

"Huh?"

I shook my head. "Nothing."

His mouth thinned. "I'm not Patrick, Olivia."

"I love that you're so scary smart you get me even when I'm being vague."

His mouth twisted, not quite a smile but no longer a frown. "Maybe I want to know you'd be a little jealous, that's all."

I studied him, our fingers linked. More cars pulled into the lot. Women, some of them barely dressed, got out. I squeezed his hand. "You just said—"

He squeezed, too. "I know what I said. And you have nothing to be jealous about. But it would be nice to know…you might be."

I sat back in my seat to parse this. Work it through. "You want me to be angry about you doing something I asked you to do?"

"No. Yes. Fuck," he said. "Not angry."

This conversation had taken some strange twists I wasn't sure I could follow. "I asked you to be my model because you're good at it, and because you're so fucking sexy, Alex Kennedy, I wanted to show you off a little."

"Share me?"

I was getting so much better at reading his eyes. "You don't want me to share you?"

"I want you," Alex said in a low, hoarse voice, "not to want to share me."

Everything with us was still so new, explosive, supernova, that even this could turn us on. This, our first real discomfort. I leaned across the gearshift and took his face in my hands.

"I don't want to share you, ever. I want you all for myself. I am greedy and selfish for you, Alex. I want you to be all mine."

His smile teased my lips. His tongue stroked mine and our kiss softened. He pulled away.

"Okay," he said.

"Is that jealous enough for you?" I stroked a thumb over his eyebrows.

"Yes. Will you kick a bitch's ass over me?"

I laughed then. "Oh, seriously."

His smile widened. "Good."

I raised a brow. "Do you not want to be my model today? For real? We can leave."

"Nah." He looked out the window, toward the warehouse. "It's okay. I want you to take this class. It's all you've been talking about for the past couple weeks."

"Not all I've been talking about. We talked about *Star Trek* the other day."

He kissed me again. "But you want to do this."

I held him close when he would've pulled away. "But you don't have to. I can take this class without a model."

"But that means you'll be taking pictures of someone else."

"Yes," I said slowly, thinking of the last workshop I'd taken. Naked women, naked men, all posed in a puppy pile of bare flesh, tangled limbs, faces obscured. It had been sensual, but not erotic. I'd learned a lot that day I could use in my own work, which aside from the pictures I'd taken of Alex was rarely sexual. "But that doesn't mean—"

"It means," Alex said firmly. "Because, Olivia, didn't it ever occur to you, I might be a little jealous, too?"

There were only about forty people in the room, photographers with one model each. Some hadn't brought any. We sipped sodas and nibbled snacks while Church set up the first shot using his assistant, Sarene. He talked the whole time, explaining F-stops and shutter speeds and lighting and shadow. Cameras clicked in front of serious faces. Some people took notes.

"Fuck, it's like a morgue in here," Church said suddenly. "This is supposed to be fun!"

We all laughed. He talked some more, showing us simple techniques to get the best angles. He added models to the tableau. Alex wasn't the only guy there, but he was one of the first pulled up to take part.

Camera to my eye, I watched him put his hands on the hips of a pale-skinned girl with no ass but huge breasts. She wore only a pair of platform pumps and a black thong, though he was still clothed. They posed. My finger pressed the button and took the picture. Through the camera lens, it wasn't real.

"Fuck me if I'm wrong, but don't I know you?"

I took the camera from my eye to look toward the voice. "Oh, hi. We've met, yes. Olivia Mackey."

Scott Church, who was always Scott Church in my head, sometimes just Church but never only Scott, gave me a hug. "You've modeled for me, right?"

"I've been to your class before."

"Kick ass." He gestured for me to show him the picture I'd just taken. "Show me."

Most creative people are the same. We do what we do for love and sometimes money, but mostly we thrive on praise. We can't help loving our own work even if we sometimes hate it, but having someone else love it often means so much more. Church looked at what I'd done and nodded, then shifted a setting on my camera, pointed it at the group of models still posing.

"Try this."

I did. We both checked what I'd captured. This time, he gave me a thumbs-up. "See the difference?"

"Yep. Thanks."

He looked again. "I want to see this one when you're done tweaking it, all right? This one is good."

I beamed. "Thanks. That means a lot, coming from you."

He didn't have much false modesty, that Scott Church, but he also knew how to take a compliment graciously. "Keep going."

We worked for another hour or so. Clothes came off. I could tell a few of the models were shy at first, as were some of the photographers, but here's a funny thing about being naked—at first it feels awkward, but after a while it's all just skin, the same as we all have.

By the end of the workshop I'd taken over two hundred pictures and thought half a dozen were good enough to show off. Maybe more once I got them home and worked on them with Photoshop. It had been a great day.

Church hugged every woman as we left, planted wet kisses on our cheeks. Shook all the men's hands. He'd spent a good portion of the time critiquing and praising, not just teaching, and now as we all left he shouted out, "Damn, I forgot to mention this. I'm having a gallery show at the Mulberry Street Gallery in Lancaster next month. Come on out and see me. I'll probably have some shots from today in there."

I met up with Alex at the table where I was grabbing a last cola for the road and he was still shrugging into his coat. His hair had been mussed by another woman's fingers, and while I'd taken a few photos of her doing it, now the pin of jealousy pricked me into smoothing it.

He grinned. "That was fun. I can't wait to see the pictures."

"And nary an erection in any of them," I said wryly as we headed for my car, among the shouted goodbyes from the other workshop participants.

He laughed and slung an arm around my shoulders. "It was too cold in there for a woody."

"Huh. You weren't hot pressed up against all those other bodies?" I fixed him with a steely glare only half feigned as I opened my trunk to put in our gear.

Alex pressed me against the side of the car, his hands on my hips, his mouth seeking mine. "Nope."

"Hmm." I shifted my knee between his legs. "What about now? I feel something…"

He chuckled into my ear and pushed his crotch against my belly. "That's all because of you. Did you know how fucking sexy you looked with that camera?"

"Baby, we all had cameras."

"I was only paying attention to you."

I laughed, though a little breathlessly. "Uh-huh."

He pulled back to look into my eyes. "You're different when you have that camera, Olivia."

"Different, how?"

He shook his head, searching for words. "I can't explain it. But you're…bigger."

The day had passed while we were inside, and the metal behind my back was chilly, but I didn't move. I hooked my fingers in his belt loops and pulled his hips harder against mine. "I'm already pretty big."

"That's not what I meant." His hands skated up my sides

to rest just below my breasts. "I mean…it's impressive, what you can do. You make art. Fuck, that's sexy. That's all."

"Me and everyone with a camera."

He wasn't letting me demure. "Not everyone. Anyone can take a picture. But what you do is different. Don't you fucking tell me no." He cut in when I opened my mouth again. "Just take the compliment."

"Thank you."

We kissed for a few minutes, then a few more. The door of the warehouse opened, reminding us that though everyone else had left the parking lot, we weren't alone. Alex's erection nudged my belly, and my panties had gone hot and damp, my nipples tight.

"We should get going," I breathed into his mouth.

"Yeah."

We didn't move. The wind came up and blew his hair into his eyes. I brushed it away.

"I meant what I said," I told him suddenly. "About being greedy for you. Wanting you all to myself."

Alex twirled one of my locks around his finger and kept me pinned to the car. "Good."

"I love you." I thought it would come out stronger, with more purpose. Instead the words caught, snagged, tore a little at my throat so they jigged and jagged.

He heard them, though. "I love you, too, Olivia."

I couldn't fault him for stumbling on the sentiment when my own words had been spoken so roughly. I just held him tight, squeezing, my eyes closed as I pressed my face to his chest. He smelled good and felt good, and just then in that moment I knew without a doubt, without fear, that I was going to love him forever.

He stroked my hair. "Whatcha thinking?"

I tipped my head back to look at his face. "I'm thinking...I want you to meet my mother."

Chapter 14

*H*e blinked, then laughed. "Okay."

"She lives only about twenty minutes from here."

He nodded slowly and stepped back to let me move. "Okay. Sure. If you want."

I took a deep breath. Gave him a smile. "Yes. I want her to meet you."

"How come you didn't mention this before?" he asked once we got in the car and I pulled out of the lot.

I kept my gaze on the roads, not as familiar with them as I should be, and not wanting to get lost. "I didn't think we'd be stopping by. I wasn't sure how long the workshop would go, and it's Shabbat, anyway."

He made a scared noise. "Is your mother going to have a problem with me?"

"Probably."

"Fuck," he said, sounding a little stunned. "Really?"

"My mother has a lot of problems with a lot of things she can't change," I told him. My hands gripped the steering wheel too hard, and I had to force my fingers loose. "Don't worry about it."

He was quiet for a minute. "Well, she won't be the first mother to hate me, anyway. I kind of have that effect on mothers."

I snorted soft laughter as I navigated the streets of my mom's neighborhood. We passed the synagogue she went to. The small, unremarkable home that housed the *mikvah,* the ritual bathhouse. We were almost to my mother's house, and I was thinking I should drive on by. Not stop.

"How could anyone ever hate you, Alex?"

"It's a talent."

"Not one you've ever shown me."

"You're blinded by love."

With no traffic ahead or behind us, I slowed the car, just a couple minutes from the house. "My mother won't hate you. She might not approve of you as a choice for me, but she won't hate you for being you."

He was quiet for another minute, speaking only as we pulled into my mom's driveway. "That's good to know."

I turned off the ignition and looked at him. "We don't have to stay long. I just want her to meet you. I want you to meet her. It's sort of the thing you do, right? Once you're serious with someone?"

His teeth flashed as he grinned. "So, you're serious about me, huh?"

"Yep."

He looked toward the house, where the porch light

beamed. "I think we've been spotted. Too late to make our escape."

I peered through the windshield to see the curtains in the front room twitch apart. "No going back now. Think of this as a rite of passage. Meeting the crazy family."

He looked out the window, my hand tight in his, as the front door opened. "Nobody's family is crazier than mine."

"Olivia? Is that you?"

"It's me, Mom." I crossed the grass and went up onto the porch so she could hug me. It was the same embrace she'd always given me, but I wondered if it would ever stop feeling different.

"Livvaleh, what on earth are you doing here?" My mother used the pet name as if she'd always called me that, though she'd only started a few years ago.

I hated it. "I was taking a workshop close to here and figured since I was so close…"

"Come in. Come in." My mom gave Alex an up-and-down look as she stood aside to let us pass. "And introduce me to your friend."

"Mom, this is Alex Kennedy."

I'd forgotten to tell him she wouldn't shake his hand, so he held it out. Only for a couple seconds, though, not long enough to be awkward. My mother's husband, Chaim, came out from the kitchen with his white shirt untucked, his belly pushing out the front of it and the fringes of his tzitzit hanging below it. He pumped Alex's hand and avoided mine.

"Olivia's brought a friend to meet us, Chaim." My mother's smile could've lit up Broadway. "You're hungry, right? Come in. We just finished Havdalah. I've got brisket, some challah…"

Growing up, my mom's favorite dinner had been takeout from McDonald's. Now she'd become a regular Batya Crockerstein. She'd told me once that cooking the foods of her childhood reminded her where she came from. Apparently only the cooking did, not the eating, because Chaim's belly had been half as big the last time I'd seen him, while my mom remained her tiny, birdlike self.

"We just stopped by…"

"Nonsense," Chaim said in his big, booming voice. "You'll stay, eat. Tell us everything about what you've been up to."

Maybe he didn't mean to make me feel guilty about not calling as often as I knew I should, but I thought he did. Everything that had happened between my mother and me had been my fault, according to him. Honor thy mother and father, and all that stuff. That he wasn't my father didn't seem to matter.

"I could eat." Alex sniffed the air. "Smells great, Mrs.…"

He shot me a look and I filled in for him. "Kaplan."

My mother beamed and bustled through the living room into the kitchen, gesturing at us to follow. "Come on! Come inside!"

They had company, a family I didn't know. A young couple, the woman with her hair covered by a knit snood and in clothes that showed not a bare inch of extra skin. The man in a white shirt and black trousers like Chaim's, his beard full and dark and his sideburns curling. A baby slept in a stroller, while a toddler of indiscriminate age played with some blocks on the floor.

"Tovi, Reuben, this is my daughter, Olivia. And her friend, Alex."

Reuben's eyes widened. Was it my clothes, the tight-fitting

black T-shirt with a white skull, eyes in the shape of hearts outlined with rhinestones? Or was it the color of my skin, my hair? It could have been the way Alex slipped his hand in mine possessively, neither of us with wedding rings on our fingers.

"Nice to meet you," Tovi said clearly, shaming her husband into nodding a greeting.

"Sit, sit." My mother bustled around the table, laying out plates and silverware for us.

We didn't eat in silence. I didn't know the people they talked about, but my mother made sure to bring me into the conversation as often as she could. Alex, too. It was interesting to see him behave himself, reign in his flirting, keep the language clean and respectful. I almost expected him to tug his forelock.

He was doing it for me, and the thought sent warm fuzzies all through me. It made it easier for me to behave, so as not to embarrass him with family drama. And I was glad, too, to have a meal with my mother that didn't end in cold silence or shouting. It was nice to feel like part of her family again.

"So, tell me about the boy," my mother said as I helped her clear the table. Their guests had gone and Alex had excused himself to use the bathroom, while Chaim parked himself in front of the small TV in the living room with the remote. "How long have you been together?"

If I didn't pay attention to her thick stockings, long skirt, long sleeves or the wig covering her hair, I could pretend nothing had changed when she spoke like that. It was the same way she'd always talked to me when I got home from a date in high school, eager to hear how it had gone. She sounded the way my mom always had, and I wanted to reply the way

I would've back then. Too much had happened, though. It made me cautious.

"I met him in December," I told her.

My mom opened one of the two dishwashers under the counter and settled a plate inside it. "Use this one, it's *fleishig*. The other one's *milchig*."

One for meat, one for dairy, the same as her dishes and sil-verware and pots and pans. The mother I'd had growing up would've scoffed at the excess, but now I could tell she was proud to be so *frum,* so observant. Like making sure no molecule of meat and dairy mixed, not even by accident, not even in the freaking dishwasher, was going to send her straight to heaven.

"December," she said after a pause.

I could see her counting the months that had passed with this person in my life before she'd known. Once, I would have been on the phone with her after the first time Alex kissed me. Now months had passed without us speaking at all, and the man I'd brought to meet her was more than just a friend.

"Well," she said when I said nothing. "He seems very nice."

Alex appeared in the kitchen doorway. "Can I help with anything?"

My mom turned, startled at this male intrusion into the purely feminine domain. "Oh…thank you, Alex. But now, you go on ahead and make yourself at home in the living room."

Subject him to awkward conversation with Chaim, who was nice, but who wouldn't have a clue how to deal with this *goyishe boychik?* Not something I'd do to someone I loved. I wiped my hands on a dish towel and stepped toward Alex.

"Actually, Mom, we have to get going. It's kind of a long drive back, and it's late."

She turned. "Ah. You have to get up early tomorrow? Church?"

I sighed. "No, Mom. Just work."

Expressions flitted across her face, over her mouth pasted into its tight, fake smile. She wasn't happy I was leaving so soon, but she couldn't hide her satisfaction at knowing I wasn't going to church in the morning. For all she knew I could be going to Mass three other times the rest of the week. I could've told her I'd stopped going altogether, put her mind at ease, but there were topics we hadn't agreed not to talk about, and simply never did.

"I guess if you have to go, you have to go." She headed for the platter of brisket on the kitchen island. "Let me send you with some leftovers."

"No, Mom, really—"

She stopped me with a look. "Please. It's only me and Chaim here. We can't eat all of this. Even if I freeze it, there's enough for ten people. That Tovi eats no more than a bird, and her Rueben's not much better."

Alex patted his stomach. "I did my share, Mrs. Kaplan. I hope that was okay."

She looked surprised as she laughed. "Oh, yes. Of course. You did fine, Alex. Just fine. So you'll want to take some of this along, yes?"

"Yes," he said, though I was getting ready to protest. "I'd love some."

"Fine." I tossed up my hands. "I'm outvoted."

My mother dropped me a wink that was so much like her

old self, her *before* self, that my throat constricted. "Yes, you are."

She caught me in the yard as Alex put the packages of food, all wrapped neatly in so many layers of foil I could've received signals from space, in the trunk. "He's nice, Livvaleh."

I glanced over at him as he rearranged the stuff so it could all fit. "He is nice, Mom."

"He's not Jewish," she said wistfully, then held up her hands before I could reply. "I know, I know."

I frowned and hugged my arms over my stomach. "You know, it's not like I tried being Catholic to hurt you."

"I know that."

I didn't point out that by choosing her faith I'd be alienating my dad. "It's unreasonable for you to expect me to date only Jewish men. And sort of unrealistic."

"Unrealistic? Why on earth?"

I took her hand. Our linked fingers made tiger stripes. Light, dark, light, dark. "Mom. C'mon."

"I've always told you it's not the color of your skin that matters, it's what's inside."

I let go of her hand. "As long as inside I'm the same as you, right?"

"I just want the best for you, Olivia. The way I always have. You're my daughter." My mother reached for me again, but didn't touch. "No matter what's inside."

"Yeah, well, I'm not so sure what's inside, either, okay?"

"So then it's all right for me to be hopeful," my mother said. "Not unreasonable. Or unrealistic."

I looked toward her house, the light spilling from the windows, hearing faint sounds from the television inside. "You have to stop trying to fit me into your life."

She frowned. "I will always try to fit you into my life."

This had not always been true, and we both knew it, but I figured she'd spoken without fully thinking of what she'd said. "At least accept my part in it, then, instead of trying to make it something it's not."

"Which is what?" My mother's so small she only reaches my chin, but she looked so fierce I stepped back.

"I don't know," I answered finally, as Alex slammed the trunk closed.

She melted, sagging. "Won't this ever get any better between us?"

"I don't know that, either, Mom. I'm sorry."

She sighed and shook her head. "I can't help how I feel, Olivia. I think what you did was wrong—"

"Goodbye."

She stopped me with a hand on my arm. "I can't condone it. But you're my daughter and I love you. Isn't that enough?"

I wanted to tell her it was, that all the things she'd said and done had washed away in time's river. I couldn't. I put my hand on hers, hugged her close, then stepped back to let her go.

If it's hard for a parent to let go of a child who's grown up and gone distant, it can't be any easier for the child. It wasn't easier for me. I missed my mom, a lot. I knew that things between us would never be the same. I couldn't pretend, as she tried to, that the damage hadn't been done, that the words hadn't been meant or that they hadn't cut as deep.

"Will you call me?" she said at last.

"Sure. You can call me, too," I told her. "Phone goes both ways."

This must have pricked her in a place she didn't like, because she jumped a little. "Of course."

What I'd said was true, and yet I could tell she thought I was saying it just to poke her. This more than anything proved to me things hadn't yet changed so much between us that I could forget everything that had happened.

"Bye, Mom."

In the car I gripped the steering wheel tightly, waiting for her to go in the house, but she stood there until I'd backed out of the driveway. I stayed quiet as I drove down dark streets. Alex turned on the radio and I let the music fill the spaces between us.

He didn't try to force me into conversation. The drive home went fast for me, lost as I was in my thoughts. Turning them over and over in my head, playing out the scenes of days gone by. By the time we got back to Annville my fingers were stiff, my jaw ached, my head throbbed.

Alex helped me carry the food upstairs and put it away in my freezer. Utter silence would've seemed strange, but I can't remember anything we said. Just that words fell from me, wooden replies to his questions, and nothing more.

I lost it all when he put his hand on the back of my neck as I washed my hands at the sink. That gentle touch, the heat of him behind me, broke down the final wall I'd been struggling to keep my tears behind. One fell on the back of my hand. Then another.

When he turned me to face him I buried my nose against his chest and sobbed. I braced myself for Alex to tell me it was all okay, but he didn't say anything. He stroked my back and held me close, but he didn't try to shush me. He didn't ask me what was wrong.

"C'mere." He took my hand and led me to the sofa, where we tucked ourselves under the knitted afghan and snuggled deep into the pillows.

Sometimes, talking helps. Sometimes silence is better. He gave me that, and not in an awkward "I don't know what to say" way, but simple quiet.

Our breathing synced, in and out. The rise and fall of his chest beneath my cheek kept me grounded even when I closed my eyes against the hot fall of stubborn, relentless tears. We stayed that way for a long time. His chin nudged the top of my head as I fitted myself in his arms. Our legs tangled. My hand came to rest naturally on his belt buckle. Every piece of me had a place to fit with every piece of him.

"I haven't seen my parents in about two years," he said after a few more quiet minutes. "Haven't spoken to my father in that long, either. Got a card from my mom on my last birthday. That's it."

I held him closer. "What happened?"

"It doesn't matter."

I looked up at him. "Sure it does."

Alex smiled and touched my hair. "No. It really doesn't."

We'd been fucking for months, and I didn't know him. Not like I ought to know a man I'd found myself thinking about spending the rest of my life with. I knew every part of his body, I knew his favorite drink, I knew what he liked on his pizza. But what were those things? Trivia.

"Was it bad?"

"I don't want to talk about it, Olivia." Alex pushed me back, gently but firmly. "It's the past. It's over."

"You know you can talk to me about it—"

"I said I didn't want to." He got off the couch. "I'm getting a drink. You want anything?"

I watched him head for my kitchen, where he knew where everything was and had no hesitation in helping himself. I got up to follow him. He poured another glass of juice and finished half of it, then poured the rest down the sink.

"I'll buy you another bottle," he said when he saw me looking.

"I'm not worried about it."

He shrugged and put the glass in the dishwasher. "Fine."

We were having an argument, and I wasn't sure why. "Do you want to come to bed? It's late, and I have work to do tomorrow."

"I thought we'd maybe go somewhere tomorrow," Alex said.

"We went somewhere today. I have work to do and tomorrow's the only day I have to get it done. Plus I have to do laundry—" I broke off at the sight of his face, mouth twisted, brow furrowed. "What?"

"Nothing. I just thought we could spend the weekend together. Not working."

Annoyed, I wiped at a splash of juice he'd left on the counter. "Well, sorry, but not everyone's a self-made millionaire with a lot of money in the bank who doesn't have to work more than a few hours a week."

His expression hardened. "I worked fucking hard to build my business, Olivia."

"And I'm working hard to build mine!" I slapped the damp dish towel into the sink. "Jesus, Alex, don't you think I'd rather stay in bed all day and watch movies with you than get up so I can get my life straightened out?"

"I'd better let you head to bed, then. Like you said, it's getting late."

I was so stunned he was actually walking out that I let him get all the way to the front door before I stopped him. "You don't have to go."

He took a few seconds to turn. "I have some stuff to do around my place, anyway. And I don't want to keep you up."

"Please," I said. "Keep me up."

A reluctant smile twitched at his mouth. Encouraged, I moved in for the kiss. He opened at the press of my lips on his. His hands fit naturally on my hips. Without stopping the kiss I hooked a finger in his belt and stepped him back toward my bedroom.

I took off my shirt when we got through the door. I started unbuttoning his next. I pushed him back on the bed and he fell with a laugh, then pulled me on top of him. We rolled among soft sheets, scattering pillows.

He kissed his way down my body and undid the snap of my jeans with his teeth. His hand slid inside, over my satin panties. His finger probed, stroked, just the way I liked it.

Alex, his own jeans mysteriously undone, knelt on my bed and pulled at my jeans until they slid to my thighs…where they stuck. We wrestled a little, laughing. Kissing. I wriggled and kicked to inch them off, while he helped.

He paused when I lay in front of him in just my bra and panties. His eyes roamed my every inch, and for the first time I could remember with him, I felt shy. My fingers twitched, itching to cover myself.

"What?" I asked.

"You're beautiful," Alex said.

Who doesn't like to hear that, especially when almost

naked? But it rang a little false to me, as if it wasn't what he meant to say. I lifted myself up on my elbows and put a foot on his thigh, rubbing.

"Aren't you going to get undressed?"

"Baby, I'm gonna smack it, flip it up and rub it down." He bumped his crotch and smacked an imaginary ass in front of him.

I watched him push his jeans off, along with the boxers beneath. His cock, half-hard, sprang free. Alex rolled on his back to kick off the denim, but was back on his knees in thirty seconds.

"Turn over," he said.

I got on my hands and knees. The bed dipped as he moved behind me. His hands slipped over my satin-clad butt. One moved between my legs, stroking. He eased my panties down.

"Put your ass in the air."

My forehead pressed the bed. I closed my eyes. I heard the sound of tearing and his soft grunt as he slid the condom on. I tensed, waiting for him to fill me. Alex took his time, using his hand to get me ready.

By the time we got to the fucking, I was already so close I came within a few strokes. He didn't last much longer. Short, but intense. I rolled onto my back, an arm flung over my face. Alex got up, used the bathroom, came back and turned off the lights. He sat on the edge of the bed.

My bedroom has no windows, so the only light came from the living room, where we'd left every lamp burning. I watched his silhouette and put a palm on his hip.

"Come to bed," I said.

I thought he was going to leave. His body tensed under my hand, and his shoulders lifted in a sigh. But then he slid under the blankets and grabbed the pillow that had become his. He faced away from me instead of spooning me the way he usually did.

In the sheaf of photos I'd shown Alex, there were many of Pippa and very few of me pregnant. I hadn't wanted to document that time of my life the way I did with everything else. Those nine months had felt like the worst sort of dream.

I chose to have her without benefit of pain medication. A natural birth. It seemed as though she'd been conceived the most natural way possible, two people getting their rocks off together without much thought at all. It seemed as though I should make every effort to remember something about this pregnancy and labor, since I hadn't made any effort in her conception.

The pains began in the afternoon, two days before my due date. My belly, stretched taut and tight, a drum against which tiny feet had kicked and little fists punched, rippled with the contractions. I went to the bathroom and discovered what the midwife had warned me would be a "bloody show." I'd stared at it for a few minutes. My body had already begun the process that would expel the life inside me, but my mind hadn't quite caught up to the reality of it.

Sarah drove me to the hospital. We were sharing an apartment for the time being, since my dad was unwilling to admit he even knew about the bastard swimming in my belly, and my mother…well, my mother and I hadn't been on good terms for a while. My brothers lived too far away. Patrick and I were not on speaking terms then, and if we had been, he wouldn't have been the one I asked.

Devon and Steven were there, waiting to help me check in and take care of all the insurance information. They didn't come with me to the labor and delivery room. I'd asked them not to, not explaining my reasons. I wasn't sure I knew them myself.

I'd had nine months to nurture this child inside me. I'd eaten right, taken my vitamins, exercised appropriately. I'd abstained from sex and hot tubs. I'd made sure to go to every single doctor's appointment, had all my shots. I'd done everything I could to ensure this baby would be born healthy. Everything but love it.

I'd thought that would be a no-brainer. All mothers loved their children, didn't they? Automatically? Even the ones who gave up their children to others to raise? I'd always held some sort of comfort from believing that my birth mother had loved me enough to give me to a family that could take care of me better than she could. My parents had never said such a thing, never convinced me she'd done it out of love rather than for the simple fact now facing me. She didn't want to be a mother.

I didn't want to be a mother. Not to this child, at least. This accident. Abortion hadn't been an option. Adoption had been the only choice for me. I'd thought it made the most sense, and that I was doing good.

When I held her in my arms, seeing the tiny dark curls and rosebud mouth I recognized from my own infant photos, I knew I hadn't made a mistake. Not in deciding to have her, or in giving her away. Not even in not taking enough pictures.

There was no way I would ever forget this.

The bad stuff happened a little later, during a frantic visit from my mother. With my belly still swollen, a blood-soaked ice pack between my legs to soothe my stitches, my hormones running wild, I was in no shape to face my mom. I didn't weep until I saw her. Once I did, I couldn't stop.

At first she held my hand, then hugged me, stroking my hair. Over and over, the way she had when I was a little girl. She'd rocked me.

And then she'd said, "It's not too late to change your mind."

My mother had always taught me to stand on my own, to make my own decisions. To stand behind my choices, face the consequences. But now she was telling me to go back on a commitment I'd made, to disappoint Devon and Steven, who'd paid for my entire pregnancy.

My mom wanted me to keep my child.

I was in no mood for kindness, had no patience for soft words. I hadn't had drugs while giving birth, but had taken whatever they'd give me for after. I wasn't slurring, but I was most definitely impaired. I let her have it with everything I had. Maybe it was too much, but years of pent-up frustration and disappointment poured out of me. Pus from a wound.

It had been very bad for a while, then slowly started getting better. And now she'd met Alex. This seemed to me to be the most significant event of all. I'd taken him to meet my mother because…why?

Because I'd wanted him to see where I came from. Who I came from. Who I was, in part. Because when I looked at him I saw a future. I saw children. A family.

I didn't want to fight with him. "Alex?"

"Mmm."

"I love you." Words whispered into darkness, as though it made them less frightening to say.

Or to hear.

"Love you, too."

But when I woke up in the morning, my fingers creeping across the pillow to find him, Alex was gone.

Chapter 15

"*I* have to go out of town. Business," Alex added. "Sorry, it's sort of last-minute."

We were eating take-out sandwiches from the Allen Theater down the street. He'd bought a kitchen table, an oversize monstrosity with a copper top and massive, carved legs. It fit the apartment perfectly.

I paused with the turkey and avocado sandwich halfway to my mouth, then put it down. I licked my mouth, tasting salt from the potato chips, and an underlying tang of bitter dread. We hadn't talked about him leaving in the night, a week had passed, and things still weren't exactly right. Something hung between us, and I didn't know what it was.

"Where are you going? When will you be back?"

"I'm going to check out one of the Hershey factories in Mexico. Should be gone about a week." Alex paused. "Want to come with me?"

I pressed my finger to my plate to lift up the bits of sprouts, but I didn't put them in my mouth. "I wish I could, but I have to work this week."

He nodded and dug back into his sandwich. "Yeah, I figured you would."

I frowned. "So why did you ask me to go with you?"

Alex looked up, still chewing. He took his time washing down his mouthful with a swig of cola before answering. "I've been known to be wrong, Olivia."

My frown stubbornly refused to leave my face. I pushed my sandwich aside. "Sorry to disappoint you. Maybe if I'd had more notice."

"I only found out yesterday," he said mildly, but with an underlying bitterness. "And it's business. Believe me, it's not like I'll be hanging out on the beach all day."

I got up to gather my garbage and take it to the kitchen to dump. My stomach had tightened into knots. I shoved the food and paper down deep into the pail, then turned to wash my hands. I scrubbed harder than I needed to, and used hotter water. It stung, and I hissed.

"Hey, hey." Alex turned the water to cold and took my hands. "Be careful. I've been meaning to tell you about that. We should have it looked at."

"Are you telling me this as your landlord or your girl-friend?"

He wrapped my dripping hands in a towel but didn't hold on to them. "What's that supposed to mean?"

"Nothing."

"Don't say nothing, if it's something." He followed me from the kitchen to the dining area, where I started gathering the plates. "Olivia, what the fuck's the matter with you?"

I turned, a plate in each hand. "Nothing, I said! Go have fun in Mexico!"

"It won't…I already told you," he said, trailing me into the kitchen again. "It's not fun. It's business."

I dumped the plates in his dishwasher and closed it, then turned to face him. "Are you coming back?"

He stopped in his tracks, stunned. "What?"

"Are you coming back?" I asked slowly, my chin lifted and my voice kept steady by sheer will.

"Of course I'm coming back," Alex said. "I just bought a kitchen table!"

My laugh startled us both. He looked surprised. I covered my mouth and looked away.

"Olivia…fuck, I'm so bad at this."

He hugged me, and I let him. He breathed against my cheek. I didn't want to ever let him go, not for Mexico, not for anything.

"At what?" I asked.

"Being this. Doing…this."

I contemplated that for a full minute as we hugged. "Being in a relationship, you mean."

"Yes."

I rubbed my cheek against his shirt and breathed his scent. "Everyone sucks at being in relationships."

His hand caught the back of my neck and tipped my head to look up at him. "I thought it would be easier."

"Than what?"

"Than not being in one," Alex said.

I ran my fingers up the buttons on his shirt. "How many have you had?"

"None like this."

It should've made me feel better. "I should be flattered."

Alex didn't answer me, but he didn't pull away. I did, though.

"I've had a few relationships," I told him. "None of them were the same. None of them were like this. And none of them were easy, either. If you…" I hitched in a breath, determined not to give in to the hysteria tempting me. "If you love someone, you just work at it. You don't run away."

"I told you I wasn't running away. It's a business trip, that's all."

"You left the other night and didn't tell me you were going." I said it, finally. "Why?"

"I didn't feel good. I wanted to go back to my own bed. I didn't want to wake you up."

Concern creased my forehead. "Were you sick?"

He hesitated. "No."

"But you didn't feel good. Because of me?" I crossed my arms, hating all of this.

"Because… Fuck, I don't know." He ran a hand over his hair. "I just needed some time alone. That's all. Is that okay?"

"It's fine. Of course it's fine. I'm not some crazy bitch who can't let you have a minute to yourself!"

His eyes got cold. "I never said you were. Don't put words in my mouth."

"I'm sorry."

"Why are we fighting again?"

I sighed. "I don't know."

"Fuck," Alex said, as though he couldn't comprehend it.

"It happens, baby," I said sadly. "People fight. Even when they love each other."

I wasn't expecting the kiss, and it took my breath away. His kisses always did, but this was different. Not lust. Not passion. A need of a different kind. He gathered me close, and though he was taller and the one holding me, I was the one anchoring him.

"Do you love me?" he asked into my hair.

"Yes, Alex. I do."

"Why?"

"I just do. It happened. I don't know why. But I think it happened the first time you kissed me."

He laughed. "That's bullshit. You don't fall in love with someone as fast as that."

I looked at him. "What if you do?"

"If you can fall in love that fast, you can fall out of it that fast, too."

"Are you afraid of that?"

He squeezed me a moment longer, then stalked away. "I don't know. Yes. No."

I wanted to know who he'd been in love with, before, and why it had ended. How long it had taken him to get over it. How many times it had happened. But I didn't ask.

He turned. "When I met you, you were still in love with Patrick."

This was not an accusation, but truth, and it still made me feel a little sick. "Loving someone isn't the same as being in love with them."

"Semantics," Alex said darkly. "Do you still love him?"

"I haven't spoken to Patrick in months, Alex! Are you really worried about that?"

"No." And I believed him, if only because so far I'd never been able to find him in a lie.

"I love you," I said. "I don't know how, or why it happened.

God knows you weren't exactly number one on my dudes to take a chance with." I held up a hand before he could answer. "But I know you're not Patrick. I know it's different with us, and I believe you when you say you don't lie."

"I never said I don't lie. I lie all the fucking time. I just said I wouldn't lie to you."

"So, what makes me different?" I swallowed all the anger and tears and everything that would turn this from an argument into the end of things.

"I don't know," Alex said. "You just are. Because I want you to be, I guess. I just want you to be."

"Then that has to be enough, right?"

We stared at each other, an arm's length apart. The distance felt much vaster. He moved first, to take my hand. His long, strong fingers squeezed mine.

"I want this to work."

I smiled. "Me, too."

"I have to go pack," he said a few minutes later, after we'd kissed and hugged and generally finished the squishy love stuff. "Want to help?"

"You don't need me to help you."

"This is true. But you could talk to me while I do it."

I stood on my tiptoes to kiss the corner of his mouth. A few days before I'd have said yes, gone with him, made love to him among the piles of his underwear and socks. Now I shook my head and squeezed his ass before giving him a little push.

"I've got stuff to do here. Call me when you're done."

He was too smart not to know what I was doing, but Alex didn't argue. He did insist on kissing me some more, following me to the door and kissing me even as I tried to go out.

"What time do you leave tomorrow morning?"

"Early. I have to be at the airport by six."

"I'll drive you," I said. "You won't have to leave your car."

"You don't have to do that. But okay." He grinned. Sneaked another kiss.

"It must be love for me to get up at the butt crack of dawn for you. You know that, right?"

"I know it," Alex said.

With Alex gone, I had a whole lot of time I hadn't noticed I'd been missing. I put it to good use, cleaning my apartment, working on the studio. I worked full shifts at Foto Folks every day and managed to squeeze in a few private portrait sessions, too, as well as snag a couple more advertising jobs. Local businesses that couldn't pay much, but a little was better than nothing and I'd vowed every cent I made was going back into the business. Live to work, work to live.

I also caught up on some reading. A few novels, but quite a bit of nonfiction. *The Jewish Book of Why. Judaism for Dummies.* A few others, nonreligious books about Conservative Judaism's principles.

I had to believe there was a middle ground, a place between nothing and…everything.

I thought I was finding my way toward it, piece by small piece. Nothing all at once, but then did anything ever happen all at once, other than maybe love? And maybe not even that.

I missed him.

Not just his mouth and hands, or that pretty, delicious cock. Not just his quirking smile and dry humor. Not even the way he said "fuck" without provocation, making one word mean so many things.

I missed the way he rapped lightly on the bathroom door before he entered, even though I wouldn't have cared had he barged in. I missed how he stopped at the store to pick up the kind of ice cream I liked, and remembered to bring in the mail but never, ever opened mine, though I probably wouldn't have minded that, either. I missed small pieces of him, and the whole.

He didn't call but sent me random, sexy text messages. Not every day. But enough.

"You have it bad." Sarah made this observation over tuna subs I'd picked up from J & S Pizza down the street.

"What?"

"Him." She pointed at my food. "You're not eating."

I patted my stomach. "Too many cookies, thanks."

She laughed. "I'm glad someone will eat them. I've baked so many pans of peanut butter blossoms the smell of them alone is enough to make me puke."

"You got it bad," I told her, without knowing who "it" referred to.

Sarah shrugged. "Maybe. But it doesn't matter. It's over. Before it even got anywhere."

A pang of guilt flashed through me. I'd been so busy with Alex, Sarah and I hadn't spent as much time together as we used to. She hadn't complained or made me feel guilty, so I knew she'd been busy with her own stuff—Sarah wasn't one to let something like that slide. I felt guiltier for not noticing she wasn't making me feel guilty.

"Do I know him?"

"No. Hell, I barely know him." Sarah scraped a finger over the top of her sub and tucked it in her mouth. "Pass the chips."

I tossed her a single-serving bag I'd picked up along with the subs, and watched her look it over. She shook her head. Tossed it back.

"Pig," she said.

"No." I grabbed the bag and looked. "What the hell? Who makes chips in lard anymore?"

"Grandma Utz." Sarah laughed. "How about the other ones? Salt and vinegar should be okay."

I handed her the other bag and studied the one in my hand. "Sorry. I should've checked."

"Not your responsibility to make sure what I put in my mouth won't send me to hell." Sarah tore open the bag and laughed. "If I believed in hell, anyway."

I put aside the chips cooked in lard—I didn't keep kosher but knew enough about it to feel suddenly like I should. "My mother would've known. She'd have flipped out, too, if I'd accidentally handed her this bag."

Sarah snorted delicately. "Well. Your mother has her own issues, don't you think? As do we all, my friend. As do we all."

She nodded sagely and ate another chip, then swigged from the bottle of cola next to her on the floor. She tipped her head back to stare at the ceiling with its bare beams. "Fairy lights."

"Huh?"

"You need some fairy lights. Maybe some netting. Make a soft light up there, up those beams and across. It will make the room seem cozier without taking away the impressiveness of the ceiling height."

"*You* are so impressive."

"All that and I can defrag your computer like a fucking

champ." She grinned. "Except you're a smart one, you have a Mac. Not much for me to do there."

We ate and chatted. Boys and clothes. Television. Books. Boys. More boys. Famous boys, not the ones we were actually sleeping with.

Sarah's phone beeped from her pocket. She didn't look at it. This was so obvious I had to comment.

"Him?"

She shrugged. "Could be."

"Wow, and you're not answering?"

"I'm not a booty call."

I looked around at our late-afternoon floor picnic. "Who makes a booty call at three o'clock on a Saturday afternoon?"

"A guy who's busy all the rest of the time," Sarah said smartly.

I sort of felt bad for the unknown dude who'd so raised Sarah's ire. It took a lot to get her riled, but once she was it took her a long, long time to cool down. "You want to talk about it?"

"Actually and surprisingly, I do not." She flicked me a look. "How 'bout you? Want to gush and squee over your perfect man?"

"Oh, he's not perfect. Far from it."

Sarah grinned. "I've seen him, Liv, and he's pretty fucking perfect."

"Sarah," I said fondly, "you love guys. All guys. Quasimodo gets you hot."

"Hey, ugly guys give the best head. Don't dis me because I am an equal-opportunity provider of cunnilingus practice."

We both laughed. "Better an ugly dude with a long tongue than a hottie with a soft prick."

"Pfft. You know it."

We laughed some more.

"When's he coming back?" Sarah asked.

"Tomorrow. I have to pick him up at the airport after Pippa's birthday party."

"Ooh, that is love. Picking him up at the airport. Hey, I get to be your maid of honor."

My laugh went a little stilted. "Yeah, that's getting a bit ahead of us, don't you think?"

Sarah paused, her hands full of paper and napkins. She shrugged and tossed the trash into the industrial-size can by the door. "Don't rule it out, is all I'm saying."

"I don't think so." Loving him was one thing. Marriage something else.

"That's what my sister said. And look at her."

"Your sister's been married four times!"

Sarah fluttered her eyelashes and clasped her hands to her chest. "And evewy time has been twuuu wuv!"

"Not exactly the poster child for marriage."

"My point is, she was burned three times, and she went back again. Some might think that makes her stupid," Sarah said. "But I think it just proves that you have to give love a chance, even if it hurts."

"Huh." I chewed the inside of my cheek. "Including you?"

"Oh, fuck no," Sarah said. "I'm running away from that shit as fast as I can."

"I got new shoes." Pippa pointed her toes, one foot and the other. "My daddy Devon bought them for me. And my daddy Steven bought me this dress."

She twirled as I took picture after picture, the camera Alex had bought me weighting my hand differently than I was used to. It made a difference. Lots of the pictures came out blurry or off center. Those were sometimes the ones I liked best.

Not Pippa. She demanded to see the pictures in the view screen and frowned if they didn't show her off to her best advantage. She crossed her small arms and shook her head until her curls flew. A moment later she was sweetness again, in time for me to take another shot.

"Livvy." Devon opened his arms to hug me, and I disappeared for the full minute it took him to greet me. He turned me, an arm around my shoulders. "I want you to meet some folks."

"Some" turned out to be everyone at the party. Devon and Steven had gone all out for Pippa's birthday, complete with a bounce castle in the backyard and professional catering. Gifts towered on a table and servers dressed as Disney characters passed trays of kid-friendly treats like chicken fingers and mini hot dogs. I took some chicken fingers, but without knowing if the hot dogs were made with pork, I passed. I wasn't quite sure why, just that it felt right.

"Leah, this is my friend Olivia." Pippa had another small girl by the hand.

Both of them stared up at me. Leah had long dark curls, big brown eyes and beautiful dark skin. She wore a pretty dress, but hers was a little rumpled and her hair bow askew. Chocolate dotted the corners of her mouth.

"Hi, Leah."

Pippa nodded. "Leah has two daddies. Like me."

I was pretty sure a lot of the kids at the party had either two daddies or two mommies. I wasn't sure what Pippa wanted me to say. If you've ever been put on the spot by a four-year-old, you'll know how I felt.

"I grew in Livvy's tummy," Pippa said matter-of-factly.

Stunned, I stuttered, "Who t-told you that?"

"Daddy Devon showed me a picture of when I was in there."

I looked across the room to where Devon was chatting with two other men. Steven was nowhere in sight. "Does your daddy Steven know about it?"

Pippa raised both eyebrows and put her hands on her hips. "He'd better! I didn't grow in his belly, don't you know that? Boys don't have the babies, they only donate the perm!"

Leah listened to all of this with wide eyes and didn't say much. I racked my brain for a memory of any pictures taken of me while I was pregnant. I knew there were a few, but nothing Devon would've had. Except...

"What did the picture look like, Pippa?"

Pippa was busy dancing and singing to the sudden burst of "Part of Your World" from the speakers. She'd already moved on. I snagged the sleeve of her dress to catch her attention.

There was only one photo she could've seen—a black-and-white self-portrait I'd taken of my swollen belly just a few days before going into labor. I'd felt huge, ripe, ready to burst. Feminine and full. My breasts had been like melons, resting on the smooth, taut drum of my tummy. My belly button had popped. My body had never been the same after having her.

Nobody had told me about that part.

"Pippa, sweetie, how did you know that was me?"

"I saw the lady," she said.

"What lady?"

"The lady in the pictures, silly." Pippa, still dancing, waved a hand. "She's in some you took today, too."

Then she was off, Leah in tow. I stared after her, then lifted my camera and thumbed the button to view the shots I'd taken today. Many were motion-blurred, a few out of focus. A couple of Pippa were clear as glass, but with a faint fuzz in the background I'd passed off as someone moving behind her.

The lady.

It had been a long time since she'd shown up in my pictures. I held my camera close, over my heart, smiling.

"Hi. Olivia?"

I turned to see at my elbow the blond man Devon had been chatting with. "Yeah, hi."

He held out his hand. "Chad Kavanagh. Leah's dad."

"Oh, hi. I just met your daughter. She's adorable."

He grinned. "I know. Devon was showing us some of the gorgeous pictures you took of Pippa. My partner, Luke, and I were wondering if we could make an appointment with you to get some portraits of our daughter."

"Oh, sure. Absolutely." I fumbled in my bag for a card to press into his hand. "Did he tell you I work at Foto Folks? So my hours are a little odd."

"That's okay. We'll find a time that works." He looked past me to where Pippa and Leah were accepting chicken fingers from a not-so-little mermaid. "Those two are quite a pair. I thought Leah was a princess. But Pippa…wow."

I laughed. "She's something else, isn't she?"

"She's a beautiful little girl."

I wondered if he knew I was her birth mother. I wondered if I should tell him, if that was bragging. Devon wouldn't care. Steven would.

"She is," I said.

"The pictures you took of her, wow. Amazing."

I smiled. "Thanks."

"How long have you been taking pictures?"

We talked for the rest of the party about photography and art, and kids and work. About life in Central Pennsylvania and how different it was to move here from other places. Chad had grown up close by but lived in California for years. I'd come from suburban Philly.

"That's a pretty necklace," he said after a while, as we watched the children gather around to pummel a piñata.

I lifted my camera to focus. "Thanks. My mother gave it to me."

"Are you Jewish?"

Snap. Click. I kept the camera to my face. "Umm…"

He laughed. "My sister's Jewish. That's why I asked."

I took a shot of a little boy in a bow tie whacking the starfish-shaped piñata as hard as he could. Not even a dent. I glanced at Chad.

"Your sister is? But you're not?"

"She converted before she got married."

"Ah."

"Sorry, it's not my business. It's just unusual. The necklace, I mean. Striking."

I touched it and stopped taking pictures for a moment. "Thanks. It was one of those gifts that sort of made me say what the hell, but then I put it on, anyway."

"I have a few sweaters like that."

We laughed. I took a few more photos of the kids as Devon, frustrated by the lack of carnage, pulled out the handful of ribbons from the piñata's back and handed one to each kid. They were supposed to all pull, releasing the candy. I thought they'd all had enough sugar, but whatever, I wasn't the one who'd be trying to peel them off the ceiling later.

"So…your mother is Jewish but you're not?"

I turned away from the candy chaos. "Long story, but yes. Sort of. I don't know."

"I'm being nosy," Chad said but without apology. "Sorry. I guess it's just something I've been thinking about lately, now that Leah's getting older. We want her to be exposed to all sorts of faiths and cultures, you know? Neither of us is really religious. I want her to have something beyond Santa and the Easter Bunny. Luke's an optimistic agnostic."

"What's that?"

"Someone who's not sure there's a God, just hopes so."

We both laughed again. I contemplated this, thinking of how sometimes friendships erupted in unlikely places and for unexpected reasons. "My dad's hardcore Catholic. My mom's become an observant Jew. When I was growing up they weren't anything. They left it for me to decide when I grew up. And now…when I want something, I can't decide what to believe."

"Really?" Chad frowned. "See, that's what I tried to tell Luke, but he's not convinced."

We both glanced over to his partner, a handsome black man with a shaved bald head and loud, infectious laugh. I looked at Chad. "You want my opinion, from my experience?"

He nodded. "Sure."

"Give her something, one way or the other. When she's grown up, she'll make her own choices no matter what you've taught her. But if you give her nothing, she might not know."

He nodded again, slowly. "Thanks, Olivia."

It was easy advice to give, though it didn't do me a damn bit of good. "I think my parents both would like it if I picked what they are, but they're both a little…"

"Fierce?"

I laughed. "Yeah. Scary."

He nodded. "After my dad died, my mom started in on church in a big way. She'd always gone, but after he passed away, wow. You'd have thought the Pope himself had sent her an engraved invitation to weekly Mass."

"Cake!" Devon shouted, and the screaming, writhing horde of children stampeded into the dining room, while Chad and I leaped aside.

"How'd she accept your sister converting?"

He shrugged. "Nothing she could do about it, right? Like you said, my sister made a choice."

"How's your mom with it now?"

"I think it helps that she likes my brother-in-law. But I know she's lit many a candle for my sister's soul." His tone was slightly mocking, a little sad. "Hell, mine, too. Not that I think either of us needs it. Hey. You should meet my sister."

My expression must have shown my bemusement, because Chad laughed. "She's not scary."

Chapter 16

*H*arrisburg International Airport is tiny and yet every single person who came down the stairs to the luggage area was not Alex. Little old ladies in Las Vegas T-shirts hugged squealing grandchildren, and suit-wearing businessmen checked their BlackBerry devices in a frenzy of thumb-typing. I hated every one of them for not being Alex.

I finally saw him at the top of the escalator and his name tried to leap from my lips. I was saved from embarrassment by the lack of air in my lungs; I'd been holding my breath. I took a few steps toward him, gave a mental "fuck-it-all" and ran.

He caught me and twirled me around, just like every sappy couple in every romantic movie ever made. He buried his face against my neck and nibbled. He squeezed me. I stepped back to look at him. It had been only a week but he looked different. A little tan, his hair mussed. Instead of the familiar long, striped scarf, he wore a colorful scarf in a woven Mexican pattern.

"For you," he said.

I draped it around my shoulders. That first kiss after being apart for a week was soft, then hard, quick turning slow. I'd been hungry for this meal, his mouth. His tongue. We were making a spectacle of ourselves but nobody seemed to care.

"Fuck, I missed you," he said.

"I missed you, too. How was Mexico?"

"Lots of tequila and Dos Equis."

"Oh, torture. What did you have?"

"Tequila. And Dos Equis."

He didn't sound teasing, and I held him off at arm's length for a moment to study him. I'd never seen him really drink. I'd never asked him why. Now I wished I had.

"And I still spent two days shitting my guts out, but I blame the fish taco."

I wrinkled my nose. "Ew. Gross."

Alex grinned and pulled me closer. "I was glad to have my own room, let's just say that."

"Alex!"

We both turned. A young man dressed in the blue uniform of the airline, his blond hair spiked and frosted, waved a long, striped scarf. He crossed the baggage area to press it into Alex's hand. "You forgot this on the plane."

"Thanks, man." Alex took the scarf. "I didn't even notice."

Blondie and I stared each other down before he backed off. Did I know for sure he was flirting with my boyfriend? Hell, yes. Did he know enough to back the fuck off?

Hell, yes.

He shot a slightly woeful look tinged with regret at Alex,

who'd turned his back after taking the scarf. Then he headed back the way he'd come, taking the stairs two at time. He stopped again on the overhead bridge to look down at us. I waved.

"That was nice of him," I said benignly.

Alex laughed. "Yeah. Cuz I so couldn't buy another one of these at Abercrombie & Fitch."

I hadn't heard him sound like that before. Smug and offhand. It wasn't flattering.

"Lots of people would be upset to have lost a fifty-dollar scarf."

He glanced over his shoulder, but blondie'd disappeared. "I figured he'd keep it. He liked it enough."

"They're probably not allowed to keep things left on the plane."

"Yeah, well, I'm pretty sure they're not supposed to offer hand jobs instead of cream with the coffee, either."

My lip curled and I took a step away from him. At once he looked contrite. He caught me before I could retreat farther.

"Baby, I'm sorry. That was a shit thing to say."

"Yes, it was!" On a few levels.

"I'm sorry." His sly, wicked "I know how charming I am" smile was back. I hadn't seen that one in a while. I hadn't missed it. "I didn't take him up on the offer."

I snatched my hand away. "I didn't think you would."

He took it back. Pulled me close. His voice softened, the smile eased into something more familiar and sweet. "I'm sorry. I was making a joke. A bad one. I'm an asshole."

It's never easy to see someone you love as less than shining, even if they admit to it. I gave him a grudging nod. He kissed me. I kissed him back.

"Fuck, Olivia, I missed you so much." His words, whispered in my ear, had heat that transferred directly to my clit. "I didn't even jerk off once the entire time."

I put my arms around his neck and turned my face to breathe into his ear. "I made myself come every single day, thinking of you."

Every muscle tensed against me. "Really…?"

"Yes."

"Fuck me," Alex said. "Christ, that's fucking hot."

I hadn't, but I was glad I'd told him the small white lie. "Take me home and I'll show you how I did it."

We didn't make it home. Alex got me off in the front seat of my car in the parking garage. The car filled with the smell of sex and the sound of our mingled groans. The weather was too warm for us to steam the windows, and I'd parked in the middle of a long line of cars everyone leaving the garage had to pass.

We sat, feigning chatter, his hand between my legs where nobody could see. His fingers in my panties, my skirt hiked to my thighs. I couldn't reach his cock without making it obvious what was going on, so he took it into his fist and pumped it slowly beneath the cover of his scarf. Nothing about his movements gave us away.

I opened my legs for him and said his name when he fucked his fingers inside me to get them wet, and when he drew them up over my clit in small, tight circles that made me wild. He kissed me just once when I was finished, when he'd come with a groan and low cry into the softness of his scarf.

"I'm glad you're home."

"I love you," Alex said.

The phone call came in on my cell as I was watching late-afternoon TV and reading my mail. I'd had the early shift at Foto Folks and Alex was off somewhere, doing whatever he did. I was thinking of taking a long hot shower to rinse away the smell of cheap makeup and get the feathers from my hair. I didn't recognize the number but picked up, anyway.

"Hi, is this Olivia?"

"Speaking."

"Hello, Olivia, this is Elle Stewart. You met my brother Chad at a party this past weekend."

"Oh, right, yes." I sat up straight, mail forgotten.

"I hope you don't mind that he gave me your number. He said you two had an interesting discussion."

"Umm…yes, we did."

Awkward silence.

"Well, I'd like to invite you to come to our house for a Passover seder, if you're interested." Elle spoke quickly but enunciated every syllable carefully. "I won't be offended if you say no, and I know it's a strange thing to be invited to by a stranger…and you might have plans to be with family…"

"I don't, actually. Passover. That's coming up soon, right?"

"Yes. Next week. I've invited a lot of people, so you won't have to feel you'd be sitting around with a bunch of family you don't know." She paused, then sounded drily amused. "Not that I want you to think your invitation isn't special."

I laughed. She sounded like Chad, her voice higher and softer, but with the same inflections. "Thanks very much for the invitation. I'll have to check my calendar."

"Oh, you don't have to answer right this second. But we'd love to have you. Dan and I, that is. My husband. He loves having guests and Chad said he thought you might be interested."

"I am."

"Good." She laughed again. "My brother is a sweetheart. He's a fixer, that Chaddie."

I was flipping through my calendar as we spoke, still not sure about taking her up on the invitation. "Am I the baby bird he found on the ground?"

"Something like that, I think. Olivia, if you'd like to bring a guest, you're more than welcome. If that would make it less awkward."

"Oh, thank you." I stopped my calendar on the date she'd mentioned. "I'd love to come. With a guest. What time?"

I marked her information on the calendar and we hung up. I sat back in my chair, still thinking of a shower. Thinking of needing so badly to be fixed even a stranger had seen it.

I wasn't sure if I wanted to ask Alex to go with me to the Stewarts' house. I hadn't been to a seder in years, but the last one had been a nightmare. Hours long, too much praying, people I didn't know making me feel stupid for not understanding how to follow along. I didn't want to subject him to that, not for what was my own personal journey. Still, when he told me he'd be out of town that night, more business, I couldn't stop feeling disappointed.

Sarah, too, was busy with her own family seder. "You know you could've come along with me, anytime."

"I know."

"It wouldn't be so bad," she said with a laugh. "I'm the craziest one in my family, and you love me."

"I'm sure it would be great. I just can't take four days off right now."

"Right, right. Well, anytime, Liv. You know it. Hey, maybe next year you'll be having your own seder."

"Riiiight."

I went alone.

I wasn't sure what to wear to a seder, and settled for a long, cinnamon-colored skirt, my knee-high leather riding boots and a soft, cream-colored silk blouse. I'd washed and palm-rolled my hair just that morning, and pulled the locks back into a thick bun at the base of my neck. I felt overdressed, but being underdressed would've been worse.

I stared up the sidewalk to the small stone house, almost identical to the ones on either side of it. A light shone from the front windows and on the porch. I shifted the bottle of wine I'd brought, gussied up with a silk bag and a gift tag.

I'd had to call my mom for advice on the wine. I could tell she was torn between glee that I was voluntarily participating in a Jewish holiday and grief that I wasn't celebrating it with her. I gave her credit, though, for not saying so to me. She gave me the names of several brands of Kosher for Passover wine and said at the end, "These people. They're nice?"

"Nice enough to invite me to their home for Passover, Mom."

"You know you could come here, anytime, Olivia."

Of course I knew it, but I didn't give her a reason why I hadn't. She didn't push. We'd hung up without acrimony.

The front door opened and a handsome, sandy-haired man looked out.

"Olivia?"

"Hi, yes." I hesitated, not sure if I should hold out my hand, if he'd be offended that I assumed we, strangers of different genders, should touch, even socially.

"Dan Stewart." He solved the issue by holding out his hand to me. We shook.

"Hey, honey, we have another guest." Dan crossed the brightly lit kitchen to give the dark-haired woman at the sink a squeeze.

She turned, drying her hands on a dish towel, and smiled. "Hi. I'm Elle. You must be Olivia? C'mon into the dining room. I just took the brisket out of the oven and it can cool while we get started."

I saw Chad right away, along with his partner, Luke, and their daughter, Leah. She was laughing, sitting on the lap of an older woman who looked too much like Elle to be anyone other than her mother. Dan's mom, Dotty, sat at the other end of the table chatting with Marcy and Wayne, a young couple with a toddler. Dan made the round of introductions as the doorbell rang distantly, and Elle excused herself to answer the door.

I was relieved I wasn't the only nonfamily member, though I did appear to be the only charity case. Chad came around the table to hug me as if I was family, though, and whispered in my ear, "I'm glad you could make it."

"Okay, everyone, let's get started so we can eat," Elle said from the foot of the table. "We do what we like to call Seder Lite—"

"Which means we get to the food sooner," Dan interjected.

She gave him a stern look. "Which means we hit the important parts without going over everything a dozen times."

"And we get to the food sooner," said Dan. "But don't cut out the four cups of wine!"

"No, never!" She looked faintly scandalized and gave him a look of pure affection.

I'd been seated next to Elle's mother on one side, with Marcy, the woman with the baby, across from me. We moved on with the seder, which did indeed prove to be light and entertaining, at least for most of us. Beside me, Mrs. Kavanagh gripped her Haggadah, the prayer book, so tightly her fingers turned white. She didn't utter a word along with any of the prayers, not even the English readings that explained the holiday. A quick glance at her eyes showed me she was reading along, but her firm-pressed lips proved she wasn't going to speak them aloud.

I'm used to feeling out of place in groups. At home and in school the color of my skin had set me apart even as I was being included. But here, I wasn't the only non-Jew, or nonwhite, or even the only nonfamily member.

Here, I felt I belonged.

"Olivia?"

I'd missed something with my mind wandering. "Beg pardon?"

Dan held up his Haggadah. "Would you like to read the next section?"

"Sure." I found the place he meant and read aloud the passage about Moses leading his people out of Egypt, and how they'd been pursued. How they'd been slaves.

Different.

I stuttered on the last few sentences as emotion welled

inside me, strangling. Mrs. Kavanagh gave me a curious look but said nothing. A song began. Dan pounded on the table and led the chorus so that even those of us who didn't know the Hebrew words could sing along. *"Dayenu." It should have been enough.* The song got faster and faster until only Dan was singing, everyone else out of breath. We finished it up with a rousing shout and much laughter.

"You always were so good at that," Dotty said proudly. "You and Sammy both. It's a shame your brother couldn't be here tonight."

Dan's broad grin got a little tight. "Yeah. Too bad."

The moment passed, subtle enough not to be awkward. I hadn't quite recovered, though, from my epiphany. I raised my glass with the rest of them, ate the hard-boiled egg and parsley dipped in salt water, followed the order of the seder until it was time at last to eat the festive meal. Then, unable to hold back any longer the burst of emotion whirling around inside me, I excused myself from the table to use the bathroom.

I ran cool water from the tap and bathed my wrists and dotted my forehead. I looked in the mirror at myself. What was I? For the first time in my life I thought I might have started to know.

I stopped in the kitchen on the way back to see if I could help serve anything. Elle, her hair pulled off her face, bent to peer into the oven, where she poked a pan of roasted potatoes and tutted.

"Can I help?"

She stood, surprised, then shook her head. "My mother will say she told me to put the potatoes in an hour earlier. And she was right. I'll just turn up the heat and they'll be ready in

another ten minutes. We'll still be eating the rest of the food.
It's fine."

"Are you trying to convince me? Or yourself?"

She laughed. "Myself. I'm glad you could make it tonight,
Olivia. Are you enjoying it?"

"Yes, very much. Thanks for having me."

She didn't seem to be much for small talk, which left an
awkward silence between us as I struggled for something
chatty to say so we weren't just staring. Elle didn't seem to
mind. She pulled out a bowl of what looked like guacamole
from the fridge and held it out.

"You could take this in while I fight these potatoes."

I took the heavy cut-glass bowl. "Sure."

She tilted her head to look at me. "It's moving, isn't it? The
story?"

"Am I that transparent?"

She shook her head and nudged the dial on the oven
higher, then leaned against the counter. "I don't think so. I
just remember feeling so lost and overwhelmed the first few
times I tried to do anything with Dan's family. I wanted very
much to fit in. They all had this secret language, these…tra-
ditions. Stories they told about what they'd done on vacation
as children. My family doesn't really have that, so it sort of
freaked me out at first."

I set the bowl on the kitchen table to listen to her. From
the dining room I heard laughter. "I can imagine."

Elle laughed gently. "Well, anyway, a Christmas ham I
could do, but how do you brag about that to your boyfriend's
parents when they're Jewish? I needed something to impress
them. They're not terribly religious, but they'd invited me for
Passover, and I decided I was going to make matzo ball soup.

Well, let me tell you something, Olivia, in the vast world of matzo balls, you have what's called floaters and sinkers. And I made sinkers."

We laughed together. "What happened then?"

"Oh, they ate them. Nobody complained. I was mortified, obviously, but Dan's family just took me in and made it all part of their joke. Not in a bad way. They made me feel at home. It was just after that I decided I really could marry him, after all. So Passover's special to me for that reason, even though I never have learned to make floaters."

"That's a nice story. Now you have one of your own," I told her.

Elle looked surprised for a second before smiling again. "Yes. I guess we do! C'mon, these potatoes are as finished as they'll get without burning. Ready to go in?"

I got the guacamole and followed her into the dining room full of family and friends.

Everything about me was buzzing, and it had nothing to do with the wine I'd had as part of dinner. I'd stayed much later than I'd planned, laughing and talking with my new friends. I'd asked to borrow a Haggadah to read at home, and Elle had given me a few books to read, too. I'd driven home humming "Dayenu."

Alex's car was in the parking lot when I pulled in, but with my hands full of books and leftovers packaged in aluminum foil, I didn't knock at his door on my way past. I tucked the food into my fridge and stacked the books by my bed, where I did most of my reading.

My life had tilted and gone off balance. Everything about tonight had felt right in a way nothing had for a long time.

The prayers had made sense. The story had spoken to me. I wasn't sure what to make of any of it, just that suddenly a door had opened inside me the way we'd opened it to welcome the prophet Elijah.

Something had shifted inside me, and for the first time, I thought I might have started to find my way.

I drifted into the shower to let the steam and heat unkink the knots in my shoulders and neck as I thought about the evening. I was very glad I'd gone tonight.

Mascara came away on my fingertips when I rubbed at my eyes, suddenly more tired now that I realized I had to get up in the morning to put a few hours of work in before I went to Foto Folks. I tipped my face to the spray and let it wash me clean. I didn't bother to shave, just rinsed off the soap and got out to wrap a towel around me.

I came out of the bathroom and screamed at the top of my lungs as a figure whirled to face me. "Shit! Alex!"

His pink button-down lay open at his throat; his khaki pants were neatly pressed and belted at his waist. He'd slicked back his hair or had it cut, I couldn't quite tell which. I saw his jacket slung over the back of my couch. I could smell the sharp tang of pot.

I took a step back from it.

"You're home." Alex didn't sound high; he didn't move like he was slow and dopey. He jittered, as a matter of fact.

"What the hell are you doing?" I pressed a hand over my chest to feel the thunder of my heart inside. "You scared the crap out of me."

"Sorry." He moved forward to kiss me. "I let myself in, heard the shower running. Figured I'd stay out here so you didn't think I was getting all Norman Bates on you."

This close, all I could smell was cologne, and I wondered if I'd imagined the odor of marijuana. I looked into his eyes, which searched mine, but weren't red-rimmed. His tongue slid over his lips and he kissed me again, and I tasted mint. Nothing more.

"You scared me," I repeated lamely.

"Sorry." He flicked the hem of the towel. "Sexy."

I clamped my arms tight to my sides to keep the towel from sliding down my breasts. I was waterlogged, exhausted, still spinning from the night and aware at the same time that Alex looked as if he'd stepped out of the pages of a fashion magazine. "Let me go put something on."

"I like you like this." He pulled me closer to search my mouth with his. His hand slid beneath the towel to find my skin warm and wet from the shower.

I kissed him and could do nothing about his roaming fingers unless I wanted to risk dropping the towel. I squirmed, laughing. "Stop it! I have to go put something on!"

"Why?"

"Because...just because."

His smile seduced me. Opened my thighs. Made me let the towel slip down so the curves of my breasts showed, the hint of nipple. His hand drifted under the towel, up and down, moving so slowly and softly I couldn't find it within me to protest.

"Come have a glass of wine," he murmured into my ear.

"Alex, I have to work in the morning. And I've already had wine tonight."

"Me, too, but so what?" We moved in a small circle, dancing, my head on his shoulder. In my bare feet I had to stand on my toes to reach it. Now I pulled away to look at his face.

"You did?"

Something like a shadow flickered in his gaze. "Yeah. Couple of glasses."

"I thought you didn't drink."

A crevasse a whole inch wide yawned between us. His hands had come to rest on my hips, and his fingers tightened there, bunching my towel. "I never said I didn't drink."

"But you never... Forget it," I told him. I scanned his face, the set of his mouth. "I thought you were at a meeting, that's all."

"I was. A dinner meeting. And then I met up with some friends. We had drinks. Is that all right?"

I wanted to step away, but his grip held me just tightly enough I'd have had to make it obvious I wanted out of his embrace. "It's fine. I'm just surprised, that's all. You hadn't mentioned seeing friends in Philly."

"I didn't know I needed your permission to have a couple of drinks or to have friends, Olivia."

I leaned in again to take a long, deep sniff. Then I did step away. "I thought I smelled pot, before."

Alex didn't look guilty, but he sure as hell looked something. "I smoked a joint."

"You drank and smoked pot and drove all the way home?"

"I smoked the joint downstairs while I was waiting for you," he said too casually.

I thought of New Year's Eve, the night I'd come home to find him holding a cigarette. The first time we'd kissed. "I didn't think you smoked."

"I quit cigarettes, but a joint's not... Hey, hey," he said as

I stepped away. "One small joint, and only half of it. It was some old shit I had floating around, not even any good."

I clutched the towel, hitching it higher, and shook my head. "Wow. Just…wow."

I turned and headed for my bedroom to pull on a T-shirt and pair of sleep pants. Alex followed, too close on my heels. I wouldn't look at him.

"I didn't know you cared," he said when I didn't turn.

I used my towel to squeeze the water from my hair, gently, so as not to fray the locks. Then I grabbed up a bottle of oil from my dresser to rub through them. I wasn't sure how I meant to answer him, only that whatever words were lying in wait down deep in my throat tasted bitter on the back of my tongue.

"I'm sorry," he said, but didn't sound it.

I turned then. "It's not that I care, exactly. Lots of people drink, Alex. Lots of them smoke pot now and then. But you never have. And I have to wonder, why now? Why tonight? I have to wonder what the hell is going on with you lately?"

This struck him hard enough to make him flinch. "Olivia—"

I held up a hand. "No. Don't even give me a bunch of bullshit for an answer. I'm not hearing it."

"How do you know it's bullshit, if you won't let me tell you?" His quirked smile wasn't warming me this time. I couldn't read his eyes. We were back to the beginning of things, and I hated it.

I stared him down, and he didn't falter. The buzz from earlier had faded and left behind foolishness. How could I have thought one dinner, a few hours, could change me? How could I have thought I might know who I am?

"I don't want to fight with you," I told him quietly, and busied myself with the array of pots and jars of creams on top of my dresser. I opened one and rubbed a dollop into my skin.

"I don't want to fight with you, either."

"It's late, and I'm tired. I think maybe you should go home."

A balloon of silence inflated between us.

"Shit. This isn't how I wanted this to go. I thought you'd come home, we'd have a glass of wine…"

I sniffed and kept my attention on the cream I was rubbing into my skin. "I told you, I don't want to fight with you."

"I'm not fighting!" He sounded exasperated.

I breathed deep to find the smell of marijuana, not sure if I was imagining it. It wasn't the drugs or the booze that had come between us, but the difference in him. Maybe the difference in me.

"Olivia. Would you look at me? Please?"

I didn't get it, at first. The small velvet box, the hopeful look. Alex sank to one knee in front of me, the box held in one palm while he opened it. Something shiny glittered inside, bright enough to send me back against the dresser, so hard I rattled everything on top of it.

"Olivia Mackey, will you marry me?"

"What?"

He got up, moved closer. The ring flashed so brilliantly in my bedroom's dim lighting I knew it had to be a diamond. Of course it was—who got engaged with something different? Alex was offering me a diamond ring and the chance to become his wife, and all I could do was stare.

"Will you marry me?" he asked again.

I looked at his face, thinking I would say no. That no

matter how fast this had happened or how deep into him I'd fallen, marriage was not the next step. That I'd taken a ring once before, and the promise along with it, and it had ended very badly.

But things were different with Alex.

"I don't know what to say…"

"Say yes, Olivia." Alex pulled the ring from its velvet cushion and held my hand. "Say yes."

I looked into his eyes and saw everything inside his gaze. Fear. Hope. Pride and love. Heat there, too, familiar and welcome. He smiled and held the ring over my fingertip, but didn't push it down.

I thought of all the reasons to say no, and none of them were any good. So I let him slide that gorgeous band of platinum and diamond to the base of my finger, where the metal warmed quickly to the temperature of my skin.

And I said yes.

Chapter 17

Alex let out a breath and kissed me, hard. I'd seen the look in his eyes before I closed mine for the kiss; he was relieved. I pushed him back gently so I could get a better look at the ring.

"You thought I'd say no?" I asked quietly as I tilted my hand back and forth to make the diamond sparkle. I glanced at him.

Alex rumpled his hair, then stuck his hands in his pockets. "Yeah."

I had to hug and kiss him again for that honesty. "But you asked me anyway!"

He put his arms around me and we rocked back and forth in our usual slow dance. "Of course I did."

"Why did you think I'd say no?"

He looked down into my face. "Because I figured there was no way in hell I would ever be so lucky as to have you say yes."

"Oh, Alex." I wanted to scoff, but his gaze told me he was dead serious. "Why would you ever think that?"

He didn't answer, just kissed me again. I opened my mouth and waited for him to feel different, taste new. I could feel the ring on my finger, a weight where there'd been none. The stone slid to the side and pressed against my other finger, not hurting. Just there. Unable to be ignored.

"I love you," I told him, and meant it.

However it had happened, it was the truth. And, over-whelmed by too much discovery in one night, I started to cry. Alex didn't look alarmed. He used his thumbs to brush away the tears slipping down my cheeks. He kissed the corner of my mouth where they'd accumulated. Licked them away. He didn't ask me why I wept, and I didn't feel I had to explain.

I took a deep breath and blinked away the blur so I could focus on his shirt buttons. One, two, three. He stood patiently as I opened his shirt and slid my hands up and over his warm, bare flesh. He shivered, though my hands weren't cold. His nipples tightened and tempted my mouth. I licked each one and listened to him sigh.

I undid his belt and the zipper. I got on my knees in front of him and slid his trousers over his hips. The front of his briefs bulged, and I pushed them down, too. His cock came free of the soft fabric and I took it at the base to hold it still while I slid my mouth over it. When he groaned, I smiled and twisted to look up at him.

He was gazing down at me. His hand caressed my hair. When I opened myself to take him in deeper, Alex's eyes fluttered closed for a second before opening again. He licked his mouth. I sucked gently and felt the throb and pulse of his cock on my tongue.

It wasn't the first time I'd sucked him, but it felt different this time. The floor beneath my knees, the weight of his balls in my palm, even the length and girth of him were all different, like a photo that's been cropped to emphasize a different aspect.

I stroked him with my hand a few times, then got up and took him to my bed, where I laid him back and straddled him. He still wore his shirt, open all the way, and I still had on my T-shirt. It rode up my thighs as I brushed my clit over his erection. I hadn't trimmed my bush in a few days, and the thick, springy curls tickled us both, adding to the pleasure. He put his hands on my hips.

I reached over and past him to my nightstand, where I'd left my orgasm-worthy new camera. "I think we should take a photo to commemorate the event."

He laughed as his hands stroked up my thighs and over my ass. "Of course."

I angled the camera, holding up my arm, as I lay my head next to his on the pillow, our bodies still aligned. Out of focus, our heads chopped off, our mouths fused, one shot after another. I didn't bother to look at them as I took them. I held the hand with the ring over my face, and the flash glared off the diamond like lightning. I held it beneath the glare of my bedside lamp and it shot rainbows onto the ceiling. I took pictures of that, too, or tried.

I gave him the camera and it became his eyes as I rode him, his cock deep inside me. I pulled my shirt over my head to be totally naked with him. I put my hand over the lens, then, and pushed the camera aside so I could see him, and Alex could see me with nothing between us.

He pushed inside me and his hands moved over me to find

all the places he already knew, but as with everything else tonight, his touch skating over my nakedness felt different. His palms on my nipples made me cry out when they never had; his thumb's sweet pressure on my clit sent new tension through my every muscle.

It took me a long time to come, but not too long. Seconds became minutes, strung together until I lost track of them. On top of him, I moved slowly, my head bent so my hair fell over my face. My palms were on his chest, and his heart throbbed under my palm.

I rocked on his cock and his hands helped me move, but didn't urge me to go faster or hold me to slow down. Light caught the diamond on my finger and that's what I was looking at when the first trembling spasm of pleasure swept over me. My fingers clutched, and he moaned at the slight gouge of my nails into his flesh.

The sound tipped me harder. My orgasm rippled through me so I shook with it. My thighs clenched his sides and my pussy clutched at his cock. His hips lifted then, pounding into me harder, and sweet pleasure rose again until I had to fall forward, exhausted.

Later, when I rolled off him and we lay side by side, staring at the dancing colors my ring made on my ceiling, I took up the camera and scrolled through the pictures we'd taken.

"Oh, God," I said. "This is so not how I'd like to remember I looked."

Face stripped of makeup, hair all over the place. My only consolation was that in most of the shots my face was blurred, or turned. Alex looked perfect, of course. He always did.

"You're beautiful," he said without even glancing at the

photos. "And it worked out okay. Believe me, I'd pictured it all going a little bit…smoother."

I turned on my side to look at him, tucking a hand beneath my cheek on the pillow. I put the other hand, the one with the ring, on his chest and watched it rise and fall with his breath. "You had it all planned out, huh?"

He nodded. "I was going to give you a glass of wine first. And flowers. I have flowers out there for you."

He shifted to look at me. "Best laid plans, huh?"

I thought of that picture-perfect proposal, but didn't regret missing out on it. Good sex and all the excitement were pressing my eyes to close, but I struggled to keep them open. "I never guessed this was coming."

He reached to brush my hair from my face, and let his fingertip linger on my forehead, then slide down the curve of my temple to my cheek and jaw before dropping it to my hip. "I know."

A yawn split my laugh. "The ring is so beautiful."

"I bought it in Philadelphia from a jeweler friend I know."

I blinked and traced a heart on his chest. "So you didn't have a business meeting tonight?"

"Nope."

I narrowed my eyes a little, thinking that a lie could sometimes be forgiven. I touched his face, and he kissed my palm. I thought I had something more to say, something profound, but I was asleep before I could say it.

We were engaged.

For the second time in my life, I called my parents, my brothers, my grandparents, to tell them all I was getting married. My voice shook and I dissolved into semihysterical laughter with every one of them. Sarah greeted the news with a predictable shriek and demands for a bachelorette party, though we hadn't even set the date. By the time I got off the phone with her, I had less than an hour to shower and get dressed for work.

Hastily, I logged onto my Connex account, which had languished in past months. I'd been spending so much time with Alex in real time I hadn't put much effort into my virtual relationships. I hadn't, in fact, even added him to my page. Hadn't even asked him if he had something as silly as a Connex account. I quickly uploaded one of the decent shots from the night before, one in which the ring and my hand obscured most of our faces, and no private parts were showing. Then I switched my relationship status from "single" to "engaged."

I stared at my updated profile page for a few minutes with a giddy grin. Somehow, even more than the ring, putting it out there like that for the entire world to see somehow made it all more official.

The girls at Foto Folks all squealed over the ring, which was twice the size of any they had. If they had envy, they hid it well, or I chose not to see it. I walked around the entire day with a silly grin plastered on my face, showed the ring off to every customer, and took some of the best damned shots I ever had there. I cooed over babies in a way I'd never done. Babies seemed more real than they ever had before. I complimented even the most garish choices for the boudoir pictures, happy for the women who'd never have thought of taking shots like this for themselves, but would do it for someone they loved.

I floated through that day, each sight of my ring sending another thrill fluttering through me. I was engaged! I was getting married!

I worked until closing and declined an offer to go out for drinks to celebrate; I endured the good-natured ribbing about how now that I was engaged I had to rush home to placate my man instead of hanging with the girls, even though it was mostly true. I promised them another time, and thought they all got it—that rushing home to be with Alex was still new and fresh and desirable. And again, if they had envy, I didn't choose to see it.

The day had been so warm it was easy to imagine summer on the way, and I slung my jacket over my arm as I went to my car in the mall's back parking lot. I tensed at the sight of a figure waiting there, but relaxed when I saw it was Patrick. I wasn't even really that surprised.

"Hi." My voice still held that floaty, giddy, silly tone I'd been using all day. I was way up there, and nobody was going to make me come down, not even Patrick.

"Can we talk?" He had turned up his collar and he hunched his shoulders, his hands jammed deep into his pockets. He rocked on the balls of his feet. He looked pale and rumpled, unlike himself.

I unlocked my car but didn't get in. "About?"

I waited for anger and got only a frown. "I can't believe you wouldn't tell me yourself."

I had no reason to feel caught out and didn't like feeling that way. I tossed my purse and jacket into the backseat but kept my keys jingling in my hand. "We haven't been exactly chit-chatting every day lately, Patrick."

"I can't believe I had to find out from your Connex page."

Naked 299

His voice was thick with grief I thought with some surprise might be genuine. "Me and five hundred of your closest friends. Jesus, Liv. I thought... Shit. I thought I meant more to you than that."

I remembered once that had been true. I stopped myself from taking a step toward him by digging my keys into my hand. "We haven't been close for a long time."

"A few months!" he retorted. "We had a fight, that's it! And suddenly I'm not on your must-call list? What the hell happened to all those years?"

"I didn't think you'd care," I said, but knew it to be a lie. I'd known Patrick would care.

"Not care?" He yanked his hands from his pockets to toss them in the air. "Not care? Dammit, Liv, how can you say that? When I have to find out you're *marrying* that asshole—"

"Hey! Don't you call him that!"

Patrick's handsome face turned angular. Eyes narrowed, mouth thinned. "You're making a mistake, that's all."

"Like the one I almost made with you, is that it?" I didn't care if my words stung. I wanted them to gouge and slice.

Patrick flinched. "He will hurt you. I don't want to see you hurt. I love you, Liv—"

"You," I said with venom in my voice, "shut the fuck up."

Patrick took a step back. In the spring, night still falls early. It had been dark when I came out, and the parking lot lamps cast pools of yellow-white light that didn't flatter him. The breeze came up, chilling me, and I wished I'd put on my jacket, but didn't bend to reach inside the car for it.

"I've always loved you. You know that." He was brave enough to try again, and though I could still taste my anger, it dissolved under the force of nostalgia.

I did not want to hate him.

"Oh, Patrick. Can't you just be happy for me, the way I've always been happy for you and Teddy?"

He flinched again and cast down his gaze. He scuffed the ground with his toe and shoved his hands back into his pockets. His voice went low and shamed.

"We broke up."

"Oh, no." Once I'd have hugged him, but now the ring on my finger made my hand too heavy to lift. "What happened?"

Patrick shot me a twisted, strangled grin. "I fucked up, that's what happened. I fucked around. Teddy found out. I was tired of lying, of being that person who lied. And I thought he'd forgive me, because Teddy always forgave me."

I wasn't sure Patrick deserved compassion, but I was able to find some pity. "I'm sorry."

"You're sorry." He snorted and kicked at the ground again. "Sorry doesn't start to cover how I feel."

He looked up at me, gaze bleak. "And then I find you're marrying that…Alex Kennedy… Oh, Liv. I promise you, he's not—"

"Shut up, Patrick," I said, but more softly this time and without heat. "I love him."

"You used to love me," he countered. "What happened to that?"

I almost wanted to look around for hidden cameras, sure I was being punked. "You know what happened."

"At New Year's you still loved me. That was only a few months ago. You don't stop loving someone that fast. Do you?"

"You can stop loving someone in a second," I told him.

His hand dropped, but he still stood much too close. "I'm sorry I ever hurt you, Liv. I really am. I'd do anything to take it back."

I backed up and pressed against the car's chilly metal. "Are you fucking kidding me, Patrick?"

"No. I'm not." He shook his head, sorrow stamped in every line of his face, the shift and sag of his body. "I know I've messed up. And I'm sorry…"

I put my hand on his shoulder because putting it over his mouth would've been too intimate. "I will always care about you, Patrick. You know that. I'm sorry about you and Teddy, and I know you're hurting. And what happened between us…it's the past. I'm not holding a grudge, okay?"

He moved closer, angling his body for a hug I didn't give at first, until it was either embrace him or push him away. It didn't last long, and when I didn't melt against him, he must've sensed my reluctance. Patrick stepped back.

"Do you think…you could ever…?"

I stared at him, then laughed. It hurt him more than anything I'd said so far; I could tell by how his mouth turned down and his lip curled. "Take you back? You are not asking me that, Patrick. Are you?"

"Teddy said it was because of you—"

"What? Teddy said…?" This sliced me. "How is it my fault?"

"Not your fault. Because of you. Because of how things happened with us, and what happened at New Year's. Teddy said I was upset by what had happened, and that's why I was doing the shit I was doing."

I stabbed the air between us with a finger. "Teddy's wrong."

Patrick shrugged. "I thought a lot about what you said that

night, Liv. I thought a lot about how that made me feel, that I was jealous of another man for getting what I could've had but didn't take when I had the chance."

I held up a hand. "I am not your sympathy fuck, okay? Because you want to get laid, or petted, or cuddled, or what-the-fuck-ever."

We both knew that not so long ago I'd have gone to bed with him if he'd asked. That I'd have tossed aside all reason for a chance at what I thought I wanted. I couldn't believe he'd ask me this now, but then, I couldn't exactly be surprised.

"I'm not interested in just a fuck."

I stared at him long and hard. "You're off boys, now? Back to women? Or just me?"

Patrick opened his mouth to speak, then shut it. He had nothing to say, or at least knew better than to say it. He hung his head. It was the only time I'd ever seen him look so ashamed.

I waited for him to speak or to turn away so I could go. He spoke.

"I'd be better for you than he is."

"How do you figure that?"

"We've known each other longer."

I laughed with twisted lips. "That doesn't matter."

He let his gaze move up, finally, to mine. He looked determined. "I don't care if you're still seeing him. I just think we should get each other out of our systems. Admit it, Liv, you'll always wonder about me."

"And you'll wonder about me?" I gave an incredulous laugh, stunned at his audacity. "You had your chance, long ago. You didn't want it then. You can't make me believe you want it now."

"I just can't believe you'd marry him."

"Why?"

"You know why," Patrick said.

I sighed wearily. "You know what, Patrick? Alex has never lied to me about who he is, or what he's done, which is more than I can say about you. I'm sorry you and Teddy broke up, and I'm sorry we're not friends anymore. Believe me, I'm sorry about that."

He crossed his arms over his gut, as if it hurt. "You know I slept with him."

"Yes, Patrick. I know what you did with him."

He shivered. "Well, maybe that's why you like him so much."

"I don't like him. I love him." I moved toward the driver's side of my car, turning my back. "Fuck you, Patrick."

"He can be a part of it, if you have to have him so much. I'd fuck him again. He's a fucking great lay. "

"What?" I whirled, my throat going tight over a surge of nausea.

Patrick shivered again. I tried to remember how much I'd loved him, how he used to make me laugh. It was hard to remember the good times just then, with all the bad staring me right in the face. But there had been good times. Patrick had been my friend. I didn't know this man in front of me, and I wondered if I ever had.

"Don't use me to make yourself feel better," I told him. "Or to prove to yourself you're something you're not. Don't be... Dammit, Patrick, don't go back to hiding who you are because you think it's easier. That somehow you can pick up the pieces with me because it's easier than moving on. Don't do that to me. Don't make me your second chance. That's not love. That's selfishness."

Patrick crumbled in front of me. "I'm sorry, Liv. I don't know why I said any of that. I just miss you so fucking much, I haven't ever gone so long without talking to you. No matter what happened to us, I never wanted us to stop being friends!"

"So you offer to fuck me and my fiancé?"

He shrugged and swiped at his face. "Everything is such a mess. I don't know what I'm doing anymore. I don't know why I'm doing it."

I'd heard that story once before, when I'd stood in front of him with the ring he'd given me in my palm. "I can't help you, Patrick. I'm sorry. You have to do this without me."

Then I got in my car and drove away.

"I could totally get used to this domestic stuff." I speared a carrot stick into the bowl of hummus before crunching it. When I kissed Alex, he tasted of garlic and oil, a little salt. He handed me the end of the loaf of French bread he was slicing. "How was your day?"

"Fine. Here. Use this." He pushed a small, shallow plate of shimmering oil toward me. "It's garlic-infused olive oil."

"Yum. Where'd you get that?"

"I made it." He tossed a smile over his shoulder before turning back to the boiling pasta.

I dipped the bread in the oil and tasted. I moaned. "Wow."

"Good?" Alex dumped the pasta into a fancy metal colander I'd never seen before.

"Delish." I looked around his apartment, noticing a few more new things. "Did you go shopping today?"

"Yeah. I went down to King of Prussia." He waved away

the steam and settled the pasta on a decorative platter. Then he pulled a crank-wound cheese grater from the counter, added fresh Parmesan and a handful of shredded mozzarella, some pine nuts and some of the oil to the pasta. "Hungry?"

"Starving. We were so busy today I didn't have time to grab much of a lunch." I watched him set out the food. "Why'd you go all the way down to King of Prussia?"

"Um, because it's the only mall worth going to?" Alex carried the platter of pasta over to the dining-room table. "Grab the salad, would you?"

This bowl looked new, too. "Crate and Barrel? Pottery Barn?"

"IKEA."

"Wow, you were all over the place." Envy panged me. "I haven't been to IKEA in forever."

He looked up. "We can go this weekend, if you want."

"I have to work on Saturday, and I still have some client jobs to catch up on."

He frowned and sat. "Shit. Can't you switch or something?"

"No, it's my Saturday to work. I told you that." I got up to grab the basket of sliced bread, and came back to the table.

Alex had already served me some pasta and salad, and I wiggled in pleasure at the service and the prospect of the food. I was lucky he was such a great cook. I had a few dishes I was really good at making, but hardly ever felt motivated enough to cook when it was just me. I was more likely to toss together premade items from the supercenter I grabbed on the way home rather than start from scratch.

Impulsively, I bent to kiss him before I slid into my seat. "Thank you."

"For what?"

"Being so wonderful."

Alex had been lifting a serving of salad onto his plate when I kissed him, and his hands stopped halfway. Bits of red and green lettuce fell onto the cranberry-colored tablecloth. He blinked. Then smiled.

"I guess I know the way to your heart." He dumped the salad and stuck the wooden tongs back in the bowl. "Right through your stomach."

I let my bare foot nudge his calf. "And other places."

He laughed. "Well, you're welcome. You're not so bad yourself."

We ate and chatted about our days. His, aside from the shopping, sounded uneventful. A conference call taken on the drive to King of Prussia, a few e-mails sent. He had more travel lined up. The job was due to finish in another month or so.

"Then what?" I ran a slice of bread through the oil on my plate and added some of the delicious, gooey melted cheese from the pasta bowl.

"Then...I find another job, I guess."

I swallowed the bread and cheese with a mouthful of good red wine Alex wasn't sharing. "Anything in mind?"

He shrugged and used his spoon to help twirl his pasta. He wiped his lips with his napkin, then drank from his water glass. Watching Alex was sometimes like watching a movie. A picture come to life. Everything he did was so fluid, but precise. I spilled oil down my front. His lips barely glistened from it.

"They might keep me on, who knows," he said.

I picked apart another slice of bread but didn't put any in

my mouth. I'd eaten too fast, and my stomach was full now though I'd touched barely half of what was on my plate. "It's nice to see you're so lackadaisical about it."

He paused then to give me his full attention. "I know how to work, Olivia."

"I know you do. I didn't say you didn't. I just meant that you don't seem worried about not finding another job. I'd be freaking out a little bit."

"I have money."

"I know you have money," I said patiently. "But...you should still have a job."

"If I don't work, I can stay home all day and be your houseboy." He ran a finger through the oil and licked it suggestively.

He was teasing, but the gesture still sent heat slip-sliding through me. "Oh, really?"

"Sure. Get me a little thong—" His voice caught for a second, his gaze flickered. He recovered with a drink of water. "You could come home to dinner every night. I'll be a regular Mr. Mom."

We'd never spoken much about children, even when I'd told him about Pippa. The thought of an infant with my curls and Alex's gray eyes seemed startling and distant, not something I'd ever wished for, but once spoken of impossible not to want.

"You do want kids, don't you?" he said.

"I guess so. Do you?"

Alex set aside his fork, then nodded. "I'd like kids. Yes. It's time, I guess. Before I get too old."

I tossed a small hunk of bread at him and he caught it neatly, then tucked it in his mouth. "You're not old."

He grinned and chewed, swallowed. "Nah. I know."

I was quiet for a few minutes as we ate. I thought of the accusations my mother had hurled at me, her words unkind but not unreasonable. "Alex."

He looked up. "Yeah, babe."

"You don't mind that our child wouldn't be my first?"

He put down his fork. He took my hand. "No, Olivia. Does it bother you?"

I shook my head. I'd come to peace with my decision long ago. I loved Pippa for being on this earth, and I was glad to be a part of her life, but I had no claims to her as a mother. "No."

His fingers squeezed. "I admire what you did."

"My mother told me no man would ever want to marry me, since I'd had a child and given it away. That men wanted children of their own. I thought she was stupid. I think she meant that it was because I was young," I said. "But even so, it was a lame thing to say."

"It was a mean thing to say, and I'm not surprised you're angry about it."

"Oh, I'm not mad anymore."

He squeezed my fingers again. "Oh, yeah?"

I laughed after a second. "Okay. Yeah. It stings. But…you don't care, really?"

Alex pushed his chair back from the table and tugged my hand until I came to sit on his lap. I put my head on his shoulder and toyed with the buttons on his shirt. I'm not small, but with Alex I always felt soft and feminine.

His hand came to rest just above my knee, and it was warm through the thin washable silk of my trousers. "I love you.

Whatever you've done before, or whatever you do in the future."

I loosened a few buttons on his shirt so I could slip my hand inside. "That sounds like a line from a romance novel."

His breath huffed against my hair. "I've spent a lot of time in airports and on planes. I've read my share of romances."

"Why me?" I asked, shamelessly angling for compliments to take away the sour memories of my mother's words and what had happened in the parking lot after work.

Alex shifted my weight on his legs. "You ate pot stickers for breakfast."

I sat back to look at his face. "That's not the answer I was expecting."

"And because you're one of the most beautiful women I've ever seen," he added. "And because your talent blew me away the first time I saw those photos you took. Because you can almost kick my ass at *Dance Dance Revolution,* but not quite. But really, it was the pot stickers."

I had to laugh at that, for how ridiculous is it that food had led to love? "Why?"

He shifted again and I got off his lap onto my own chair again. He laughed and swirled another slice of bread through the oil on his plate and handed it to me. "I've spent a lot of time around people who think their entire value is tied up in their body mass index. Men who obsess about their workouts to the point they can't talk about anything but cardio and reps. Women who think emaciation is sexy."

I raised a brow. "So in other words, you're trying to tell me I'm—"

"Voluptuous," he interjected. "Pneumatic. Curvy. Gorgeous."

I looked down at my breasts and shifted to glance at my thighs. "Uh-huh."

"My point is, none of the women—or men—I've been with for the past few years would've eaten a pot sticker for breakfast."

"Sounds like you've spent a lot of time with the wrong people."

He shrugged. "I don't have a lot of friends, Olivia. Not real friends. But I have a fuck-ton of money, and had nobody to spend it on but myself. It's easy to get caught up in a lifestyle."

I had no problem seeing what he meant. I pushed the platter toward him half an inch. "People who care about brand names, for example?"

He smiled. "Baby, for the people I was hanging with, Crate and Barrel would be slumming."

I thought of the scarf he'd been willing to leave behind and replace with another. "You won't find too much of that sort of thing here in Annville."

He grinned and shook his head. "Tell me about it. I have a serious hard-on for a really good plate of Indian food and a bookstore. Fuck, I think I'd slap an old lady with a fish to have a really good bookstore around here."

"Slap an…" I goggled, then giggled.

It was that way with him; one minute we were talking about the mysteries of life and the next he had me breathless with laughter.

"Okay, I wouldn't go that far. But I really would like a bookstore. And fuck me, a Starbucks."

I wrinkled my nose. "I didn't know you liked Starbucks."

"I don't. It's just that everyone, everywhere, has one."

"Not Annville."

"Nope. But Annville has you."

I groaned, even though I loved that he'd said it. "What romance novel did you pull that from?"

"Oh, I think it was called *Passion in the Cornfield* or something." He winked and twirled another mouthful of pasta. Mouth full, manners put aside for once, he said, "Why me?"

I'd already been compiling a list. I couldn't have asked the question, after all, without expecting to give my own answer. "Do I even need to mention that you are a GQMF?"

He laughed. "The fuck's a GQMF?"

"Some motherfucker so goddamn good-looking he could be on the cover of *GQ* magazine." I paused to give him an eye. "Which is you."

He waved his fork at me. "I'll take it. Keep going."

"I can't tell you any one thing. There was no one moment. It was just like…you were there when I needed someone, and I figured out that it wasn't just *someone* I needed, but you."

Alex licked his mouth clean of oil. "Even though I was everything you swore off?"

"Maybe especially because of that." I turned my engagement ring from side to side to catch the light. "But you were right when you said you weren't Patrick. I couldn't keep thinking every man would be him. I mean, I think I wouldn't even give straight men a chance."

His gaze flickered. "Gotta watch out for those straight men, Olivia."

"Yeah. If there is such a thing."

"Oh, they're out there," Alex said. "Sort of like unicorns, though."

"You have to be a virgin to catch one?"

"I meant horny." He laughed.

I'd wondered how to bring up my encounter with Patrick, and this seemed like the best time. "I saw Patrick tonight. He was waiting for me after work. He was angry I hadn't told him in person that we were getting married."

Shields went up on Alex's expression. Not all the way, as they'd have done once, but enough. "Oh?"

I laughed to set us both at ease and make this no big deal. "Yeah. He was all up in my face about it, like I owed him something."

"Do you think you did?"

I scowled. "No! Patrick and I have a lot of history, but I don't owe him a damn thing."

Alex said nothing, just nodded. I soaked more oil into my bread but didn't eat it. I drank the rest of my wine.

"He and Teddy broke up."

Alex shrugged and shoved food around on his plate. "Did he say why?"

I didn't want to think about all that entailed. "He says he fucked around, but he and Teddy had an agreement about stuff like that."

Alex's gaze sharpened. "It's not cheating if you both agree. It is cheating if you don't."

"Yeah, I guess so." I hesitated. "I never got it, anyway, that arrangement, but it wasn't my business. I was still surprised."

Alex shrugged once more.

"He…he was pretty upset. He said Teddy told him part of why Patrick was such a mess was because of what had happened with me—"

Alex's laugh scoured the air. "He tried to blame you?"

I didn't know if the "he" meant Patrick or Teddy. "Don't

worry, I told Patrick he was out of line, that the past was over and that I wasn't interested in figuring out what had gone wrong."

Alex put down his fork very carefully. "He wanted to get back with you? What the fuck is that about?"

The cold vehemence in his tone set me back a bit. "He was talking out of his ass, Alex. He's upset. And there's always been this tie between us. I think he thought I'd be there for him again, the way I always have."

"That's shitty."

"It is," I agreed, and reached to put my hand on his. "But I'm not interested. Even though he offered up a *Playgirl* fantasy of a nice little threeway—"

Alex took his hand from mine. "What?"

"Patrick seemed to think that because you and he...had done whatever...and he and I—"

"No." One word, but there was no mistaking the finality in it. "Never."

"I don't think he meant it, Alex." I tried to sound gentle and ended up sounding unsure.

Alex shook his head, eyes dark with what didn't seem like anger but something else. "I don't care if he did. It's out of the question. I don't share. Not ever. Not with anyone."

"Okay," I said. "I'm sorry I said anything. I wasn't interested in that, either."

He looked at me, and his gaze cleared a little. He took my hand and pulled me across the table to kiss me hard. Our teeth clashed and he eased up enough to stare into my eyes.

"I love *you*," he said. "No arrangements. Just you."

His response was a little scary, a little flattering. I got a little tingly. I kissed him, more softly than he'd kissed me.

"I don't want anyone else, Alex. Just you."

He didn't smile. "If he comes around you again, I will kick his ass."

I wasn't sure Alex was speaking literally, but I touched his face gently. "You're jealous? You weren't before."

He kissed my hand. "He didn't want you, before."

Alex got up to clean off the table, and I followed. The moment passed. In another few he had me laughing again, and I put it from my mind.

Chapter 18

I had a ring on my finger and no wedding date, no plans for a dress. No idea where we'd have the ceremony or the reception. What seemed more important than the wedding was the marriage—and it was almost as though we already had that.

We didn't quite live together, but with the outside doors locked and the doors to our individual apartments kept open, we moved back and forth between the floors the same as if we'd turned the whole building into one house, the way I'd dreamed of someday doing.

I went to work most days and came home to find dinner waiting for me, or plans made for going out. Alex always treated, and I'll admit that it was nice to be courted like that. Flowers, dinner dates, small, silly gifts he bought to make me smile. I'd never had a boyfriend who worked so hard.

"You didn't have to," I said when he presented me with a silky, pretty nightgown I'd commented on in a catalog.

"Just say thank you," Alex said.

I ran the silk through my fingertips, thinking of how I really needed to work on my Web site, post some photos to my blog, edit the pictures I'd taken at the workshop. I'd spent two shifts at Foto Folks to cover another photographer whose son had gone in to have his wisdom teeth removed. I was tired and hungry and horny, and I didn't want to do more work. I wanted to make love, have a snack, curl up in front of the big-screen television Alex had put in my apartment because I had a better couch.

"Put it on," he suggested.

I didn't have the willpower to resist him. I shrugged out of my work clothes and let the silk fall over my head. It swirled around my thighs when I turned in a circle. The silk whispered on my skin.

Music played, something sexy. A little Sade, "No Ordinary Love," a little "Glory Box" from Portishead. It was his playlist, not mine, slinking from his fancy iPod Touch docked in a set of Bose speakers that had somehow made their way into my apartment, too. Good music for seduction, though does it count as seduction when both of you know the only place you're going is to bed?

I didn't think he'd gone to work that morning, but he still wore a button-down shirt, a pair of dress trousers. No tie, the first few buttons undone to hint at his chest. He'd slicked his hair back from his face. He watched me with a knowing smile as I swiveled my hips.

I took off my panties, and his eyes gleamed. Alex sat in the high-backed leather chair and pushed the footstool out of the way to give me more room to dance in front of him. I swayed to the music, letting it fill me.

I never looked away from his eyes.

Something faster came on, and I gave him a show, shaking my tits and ass. Rubbing my butt on his lap—on his erection, which I could clearly feel through his pants. The fact that he was getting hard from this performance, which felt half silly and half sexy, turned me on more than the dancing did. I inched the silk over my thighs, giving him a hint of bush, then let it fall back as I turned to look at him over my shoulder. I tossed my hair, stuck out my ass. I put in a couple porn-star moves, just for fun, and we both laughed, but his breath caught.

I leaned in with a hand on his shoulder, face-to-face, our mouths open but not kissing. I let my tongue flick his. Soft. Fast. My nipples got tight and hard, poking the silk. The nightgown's thin straps fell down my arms as I leaned, and my breasts threatened to spill out over the top.

I turned and sat on his lap, my head on his shoulder, my face tipped so I could see his jaw and the tip of his nose. He hadn't touched me once, playing along with the whole stripper fantasy, I guess. I rocked my ass on his cock, slowly, straddling his thigh. The silk had gotten tucked between my legs, and with every push-pull of my hips it rubbed my clit.

We weren't silent during this. He told me how sexy I looked, and how much he wanted to touch me. To fuck me. I told him how much I wanted to taste his prick. Sex words, not always coherent. Sometimes said just for the effect of saying them, like shock value. Titillation. It didn't matter; I knew we both meant it no matter how ridiculous it sounded.

I lifted my ass just enough. "Unbuckle your belt. Take out your cock."

He did. I slid onto him, still facing front. The silk lifted and puddled down around my hips, covering his lap. I leaned forward a little, my hands on his knees and mine kept close together to make a nice, tight fit, and so I could keep my balance.

His cock rubbed my G-spot at this angle and I gave a low cry. "Touch my clit."

His hand came around to do as I'd commanded. I pushed myself up and down, slowly, in time to the circling of his finger. I closed my eyes, my body already shuddering. The nightgown shifted, exposing my left breast to the air. My hair fell over my face.

I couldn't think of a title for the picture I imagined we made. I couldn't think of anything but the desire building between my legs. I moved a little faster.

"I'm going to come," he warned. "Fuck…Olivia…"

"Another minute," I begged in a sex-rough voice that broke on the words.

Faster. Harder. His hand moved just right. He made a low, guttural noise I knew meant he was coming, and I toppled into orgasm, too, at the sound of it.

With pleasure fading, I discovered my toes were cramping from pushing so hard on the wooden floor, my thighs shaking. I felt bruised inside and a little chafed from the angle, though not necessarily in a bad way. I pushed off his lap and stood, wincing at the slow, hot trickle down the inside of my leg.

Alex grinned at me, his clothes barely disheveled. "That was worth way more than a handful of dollar bills."

I tossed a pillow from the couch at his face. He deflected it at the last second, though it mussed his hair. "Smart-ass."

"That's me."

I smirked and padded to the kitchen to grab a dish towel from the drawer to take care of cleanup. Then I drew a glass of cold water from the tap and bent to look in the fridge for something to eat. Alex came up behind me, his hands on my hips. His crotch bumped my ass.

"Oh, sorry," he said, not sorry at all. "I didn't see you there."

I turned, hands full of lunch meat and mustard. "Watch it, buddy, or I'll make your sandwich with the wrong kind of cheese."

He gathered me against him, anyway, for a kiss, not minding the cool glass jar digging into our bellies between us. Then he let me go. I made food, which we ate, and he cleaned up the dishes while I showered. By then there was no way I could fool myself into thinking I'd do some actual work. Not when I couldn't even convince my feet to head up the stairs to the studio, where I always tried to work so as to make it like a real job.

Instead, while Alex showered and did whatever he did in the bathroom that took him so long—he spent more on moisturizers and hair care than I ever did—I powered up my laptop and curled up on the couch with it. I checked for a Connex profile for Alex, but nothing came up. He either didn't have one or he'd set it to private, unsearchable. I updated my page with a smarmy, selfish status update, "Good lovin', good eatin', now chillin'." I checked Patrick's profile, which hadn't changed. He still listed himself as dating Teddy. Teddy's profile had been deleted.

I wasn't going to let myself get sucked into that drama. I skimmed over a bunch of posts from friends I rarely saw, and checked out Sarah's latest photos. She had a bunch of her with some cute guy, dark hair, lots of tattoos. I commented to one with a simple question mark. She'd know what I meant.

Then, with the patter of water still coming from the bathroom, I checked my e-mail. The usual stuff from my brothers and their wives. Mostly jokes, a few pictures. A forwarded angel chain letter piece of junk from my dad, along with a superreligious Jesus prayer at the end. I deleted it without replying. And an e-mail from my mom.

I was reading it for the second time when Alex came out with a towel around his waist and one wrapped around his head. He might have been trying to be funny or was being completely un-ironic; that was one of the things I loved about him, never being able to tell. He was absolutely so unapologetic about everything he did.

"What's up?" he asked, concerned.

I hadn't realized I was frowning until I smiled. "It's an e-mail from my mom. She wants to come visit me."

"Okay." He whipped the towel off and dried his hair vigorously, tipping his head to each side and shaking it to get water from his ears. He stopped to look at me. "Is that bad?"

"It's not bad, just...unusual."

"Huh." Alex tossed the towel over his shoulder and put his hands on his hips. "Well, at least it's not bad."

"She doesn't come here because it's too long a trip to make in one day, she's always said, and because she can't stay here in my house, because she can't eat."

He nodded as though he understood, but said, "Why not?"

We hadn't ever really delved into the hows and whys of my

mother's transformation from cultural Jew to full-on observance. "Not kosher."

"Couldn't you make her something kosher?"

"Even if I bought kosher food, the plates and silverware aren't kosher. Hell. I guess the air isn't, or something."

It had been a sticking point, not just for me, but with my brothers, who all lived so far away. "It's important to my mom."

Alex frowned and came to look over my shoulder at the message. "More important than seeing her kids?"

"I guess so."

"You know, it seems to me that God cares less about what you put in your mouth than how you treat the people you're supposed to love," Alex said. "And besides, she could always bring her own food. Eat on paper plates. Right?"

"She could have, she just never did."

"But now she wants to, right?"

"I don't know about the food," I told him with a wave at the computer. "She just said she'd like to come visit for a day or two, overnight."

His hand squeezed my shoulder. "So tell her when she can come."

I didn't have to look at my calendar to know I had no time off in the next few weeks, and that she wouldn't come on a Friday or Saturday, since that would interfere with her Shabbat. "I don't know, I'll have to see if I can take the time off work, but shit, I really can't afford to do that, Alex."

"Olivia, baby," he said into my ear before he kissed it. "You don't have to worry about any of that stuff. Is it money? Don't worry about that, I told you before."

I shifted on the couch to look at him. "I have to worry about it. I have bills to pay."

He smiled and shrugged. "You know, when we're married…"

"But we're not married yet." I was being stubborn and didn't care.

It would've been very easy to let him make me his Cinderella. I didn't have some sort of misplaced feminist pride about bringing home the turkey bacon. It would hurt him if I gave my reasons—that I wasn't going to bet on this horse until it crossed the finish line—so I kept quiet.

He shrugged again. "Your mom can still come. I'll be here when you're at work."

"Really?" I eyed him. "You'd entertain my mother?"

"My future mother-in-law," he pointed out. "Sure, why not?"

I chewed the inside of my cheek. "Okay."

As I typed my reply to her, outlining the few days that might work, my e-mail dinged with a new message. My jaw dropped when I read it, an invitation from Scott Church to participate in his next gallery show. I thought at first it was a blanket invite to all the people who'd taken his class, but he'd mentioned a specific photo.

"Alex, look at this."

Wearing his Batman sleep bottoms, Alex bent over my shoulder. "No fucking way! Baby, this is awesome!"

I high-fived him haphazardly. "I don't get it…"

"He wants you to hang one of your pictures in his show. Fuck yeah." Alex pumped the air with a fist and kissed the top of my head. "I knew he'd pick you."

"Wait a minute, you sent him one of my pictures?"

He jumped over the back of the couch and landed beside me, jostling my laptop. "Yeah. I saw the notice on his blog."

"Wait a minute. Back up. You read Scott's blog?"

"Sure."

Huh. Somehow I'd missed that. "And he posted a notice about what, exactly?"

"Anyone who'd taken one of his classes should send in a picture to be considered for his next show at that Mulberry Street Gallery place. It's in September or October."

"And you sent in one of my pictures without asking me?"

He sat back a little against the cushions. "Are you mad?"

"No." I looked again at the invitation, which listed all the details of the show. "I guess not, since he accepted my picture. But I wish you'd told me."

"I wanted it to be a surprise."

I lifted a brow. "Well, it sure was. How did you know which photo to send?"

"You gave me that whole disc. I picked my favorite," Alex said, and buffed his fingernails against his bare chest. "It's one of me. Of course."

I laughed because I knew he was serious. "Okay, Mr. Vain."

"Your work deserves to be in a gallery show, Olivia."

I closed the laptop and put it on the footstool to kiss him. "You love me. You're supposed to think nice stuff about me."

Alex cupped my face. "I wouldn't say it if it wasn't true."

I believed him, which made it all the nicer.

He kissed me, then looked into my eyes. "You should quit Foto Folks and that other job. The traveling one. Spend more time on your own work. Get your business off the ground."

I shook my head so slightly my hair barely moved. "I'm

not quitting my job. Not now. I can't let you…keep me like that."

He sighed. "Fine. But after we're married, will you consider it?"

"After we're married, I guess I'll consider a lot of things," I told him with a waggle of my brows.

He took my hand and linked our fingers. My diamond, still so bright and pretty there were times I had to sit and stare, flashed. Alex touched it with a fingertip. We smiled. We kissed. But neither of us pulled out a calendar and talked about a date.

Sarah looked tired. She toyed with her salad, poking at the croutons and spearing a cherry tomato but not eating it. She yawned and put aside her fork. "Eh, fuck it."

I'd devoured my own half sandwich and cup of soup, and thought about heading up to check out a brownie from Panera's selection of homemade treats. Then I put a hand on the curve of my belly, calculated the hours I'd have to spend working off dessert, and settled for a refill on my iced tea.

"I like this one." Sarah pointed at the brochure I'd pulled from my bag. She was on a break from her job and I was on my way to work at the mall. "I like the graphics."

"I like that one, too." I studied the front of it, then flipped it over. "I've got some nice stock shots I can use for the back, but if you're free this week, I'd like to take some more. Sarah?"

She wasn't listening. Her eyes, thickly framed today with black glittery liner, widened. She looked past me, toward the entrance and the long line of people waiting to order.

"Shit," she said in a low, very non-Sarah voice.

I started to turn to see what had her so spooked, but she hissed at me to freeze.

"What's the matter with you?" I demanded.

Her mouth thinned and she ducked her head, then put her elbows on the table to press her face into her palms. "Fuck."

"Sarah, what's wrong?" I twisted in my seat though she'd told me not to, but still couldn't tell what had upset her.

She looked up at me. "It's him."

"Him, who?"

She frowned and shifted her chair behind the pillar, blocking her view. Or the view of her—I wasn't sure. "Some dude I've been seeing. Not important. Maybe he'll leave."

"The one on your Connex page?"

"Not anymore."

"Damn, girl, you've been holding out on me."

Her smiled seemed more natural this time, though still a little strained. "You've been a little busy, muffin. I didn't want to harsh your buzz. Besides, there's nothing to tell. You know me. One guy, another guy, whatever."

I made a face. "That's so not you."

Sarah dated a lot, and freely, and it was true she wasn't always serious. She was…friendly. Sarah loved easily and it wasn't always romantic. She wasn't a prude, but she didn't bed-hop, either.

"His name is Jack," she told me.

The way her voice caught on that single syllable told me a lot.

"Aw, honey. What happened?"

She shrugged fiercely and wiped at her eyes. "Nothing. That's the problem. Nothing is happening."

A wide-hipped woman in a flowing dress, her makeup too

thick, her jewelry too flashy, passed us with a much younger man behind her. His baseball cap hid his hair and his long-sleeved shirt covered any tattoos, but the way Sarah looked told me everything. He stopped at our table, a dead, full stop as though someone had suddenly nailed his feet to the ground.

"Sarah." Longing dripped from his voice, but she pretended she didn't hear.

His gaze caught mine for a second, both of us embarrassed, and he moved on as though he hadn't spoken. I saw him talk to the woman, his hand on her back and her greedy gaze devouring him. She didn't look our way, but nodded and got up to move to the other side of the room, behind a wall so we couldn't see.

"Do you want to leave?" I asked.

Sarah stabbed her salad again. "No. I'm not letting that fucker ruin my lunch."

I was sure he'd already ruined it, but didn't say so. "Do you want to talk about it?"

"Jack," Sarah said, "is a whore."

"Oh, my God." I remembered our conversation from a few months back. "You weren't kidding?"

"No. He fucks women for money."

"Oh. Wow." I had nothing more to say about that.

Sarah drank angrily and tore a hunk of bread into increasingly tiny pieces. "At first, you know, I was like, whatever. It's just a job, right? God knows I'm no virgin or anything. I've fucked dudes for reasons other than love."

"Well…I think everyone does, sometimes."

She shook her head and stared at the mess on her plate. "And I don't care that he did it, Liv. I really don't. I just care that he keeps doing it."

Her voice broke, and I wanted to pet her. Sarah was the hugger, and she needed one now. I had to settle for taking her hand and squeezing it.

"I'm sorry."

She squeezed back, then withdrew it to wipe the crumbs from her palms. She looked up at me. Her smeared mascara made her look even more tired.

"I know a lot of women who wouldn't be able to get past that he did it at all, you know?"

I thought of the first time I saw Alex. "Yes. Boy, do I ever know."

She nodded, her expression serious. "Yeah. You do. So I can...not forgive, because I don't think he did wrong. But I can put whatever he did before me aside, because you know, it was before. And it's not everything he is. But...I can't be with him if he still does it. You know?"

I thought of the airline steward's hopeful eyes and Alex's bad joke about the cream for the coffee. "I understand, absolutely."

Sarah smiled. "I know you do."

"So why didn't you talk to me about this before, dumbass? God, how long has this been going on?" I studied her. "You look like shit, by the way. I didn't want to say so before, but since we're being all honest and stuff—"

"Fuck you, Olivia," Sarah said, but she was laughing. Some color had come back to her cheeks. She actually ate a bite of bread. "I don't know. I didn't want to weigh you down. I didn't want to talk about it because I just... Shit. It's different with him, that's all."

She looked very sad and very small. "Or at least, I thought it could be."

Sarah had seen me through many a bad date and derailed relationship, but I'd never seen her this way before. "I'm sorry."

She heaved a heavy sigh. "It's okay. I'll get over him, just to piss him off."

We laughed. When we left, I looked for a glimpse of the man who'd tried to break my friend's heart, but he must've left from a different door.

My mother arrived the next week with several grocery bags full of food, and not only so she'd have something to eat. She'd brought me plastic containers lovingly stuffed and labeled, a year's worth of dinners to shove in my freezer. I burst into tears when she handed me a container of homemade chicken broth, the same she'd always made for me during college to take back to school.

My mom hugged me and rubbed my back the way she'd always done. She'd brought her own plates and silverware, but didn't say a word about my microwave or oven not being kosher enough to heat up the food she'd brought. She stayed for three days.

I don't know why I was surprised she got along so well with Alex. I knew how charming he could be. I came home from work every day expecting to find him in his place downstairs, where he was sleeping during my mom's visit, and her wearing a judgmental frown. I waited for the lectures. But my mom loved him.

I walked through the door one night after getting off the early shift, thinking of suggesting we go to the movies or something, since it was her last night there. I came into the kitchen to find my mom and Alex bent over a vat of bubbling chicken stock.

"It's the seltzer," my mom was explaining. "That gives it the lift. Oh, Livvy, hon. Come here and be our taste tester."

She held up a spoon of broth with a giant matzo ball teetering on it. She blew to cool it, then held it out. I looked at Alex, who was smirking with pride and leaning against the counter. "Did you make these?"

"He did," my mom said. "I helped just a little. But he's a good cook, that one."

"I know." I took the spoon and bit into the matzo ball, which was perfectly soft and had just the right hint of spices. "Mmm, definitely a floater."

"What do you know of floaters?" my mom teased. "Grab some bowls. Let's eat this soup before it gets cold."

We ate soup and played round after round of cards. Then my mom excused herself to take her nightly shower, advising us with a wink she'd be in there for a while.

"Is that so we don't bang on the door?" Alex asked.

I laughed as we cleaned up the kitchen. "No. It's so we can canoodle."

"Ah." Disregarding the mess, he pulled me into his arms. "I didn't know anyone did that anymore."

I kissed his chin and then bit it lightly. "We don't have time for a quickie."

"It's been three days," he murmured into my ear, his hands roaming. "A quickie's all it would be."

A hiss of breath, a kiss, a touch. It was like that with us. A flame. I leaned into him. I heard the pipes squeal as my mom turned on the shower. I did entertain the idea of dropping to my knees and giving him a quick blow job, but just for that moment being hugged up against him was so sweet, so perfect, I didn't want to move.

"I want to go home," Alex said against my hair.

"Now? Okay." I nestled closer. "Wait until she gets out of the shower?"

"No, Olivia. Not downstairs." His hands moved in circles on my back. "I mean home, to Ohio."

I pulled away. "To your family?"

He lifted my hand with the ring on it and tipped it back and forth to catch the light. "Yeah. I think I should introduce you, don't you?"

My heart turned in my chest. "Yeah. I guess I should meet them before we get married."

He laughed without sounding happy. "Memorial Day weekend? We could drive up Friday, come back on Tuesday."

I didn't want to say no right away, but calculated the time off in my head while I stalled him with a kiss. Alex knew what I was doing. He let me kiss him, then pulled back enough to say, "When's the last time you took a vacation?"

"Oh, so a visit to meet your family is a vacation?"

Alex bit down on a grin. "Well, it'll be a trip, I can guarantee that."

Chapter 19

$\mathscr{S}$o it was decided. I made the arrangements to take the days off, finished up all the work I had for my personal clients, and rebooked the few portrait and modeling sessions I had. It meant working a lot of hours for a couple weeks, but Alex didn't complain about not seeing me as much.

He was quiet about a lot of things. Preoccupied. I chalked it up to the impending visit, since I knew his relationship with his family wasn't very good. I tried asking him about it.

"You'll understand when you meet them," he said.

"I'd like to understand at least a little before that. So I can be prepared."

We were on the couch, spooning while we watched some random series of home improvement programs. I couldn't see his face, but his arms tightened around me. His breath blew hot on the back of my neck.

"Let's just say this mask of sophistication I wear didn't come about naturally."

I snuggled a little closer. "Does anyone's?"

He chuffed against the back of my neck. "My dad's a drunk who doesn't drink anymore. My mom's a doormat. My sisters, God bless 'em, were the sorts of girls who had their names written on bathroom walls. Well, fuck, I guess I had mine written on some, too."

"In high school?"

That finally earned a laugh. "No doubt."

We were quiet for a minute while we watched some perky, bubble-breasted brunette describe how she'd made "original art" from a collection of milk jugs, a pair of candlesticks and an old throw rug.

"You know I will still love you no matter what your family's like," I said as the show mercifully cut to commercial.

He squeezed me. "I hope so."

I shifted to face him. "I mean it, Alex. I don't care if your family's awful. I'm glad you're taking me to meet them."

His brow furrowed and he looked as though he meant to say something, then changed his mind. He shook his head a little.

"What?"

"Nothing."

For the first time, it seemed as though he was hiding something from me. I studied him. I stroked the hair back from his face. "You can tell me."

"Nothing," he said again. "It's nothing."

And because he'd never given me reason to do anything else, I believed him.

★ ★ ★

Sandusky was a long-ass drive from Annville. We made it in nine hours, pulling into town about three in the afternoon. My legs were stiff and I had to pee like crazy, and my stomach was rumbling because all we'd had to eat was a couple of doughnuts from a rest stop.

We didn't go straight to his parents' house the way I thought we would. First we went to check in at the large old hotel located right on Lake Erie in the heart of Cedar Point Amusement Park. Alex had made the arrangements, and I was surprised at his choice, but he only grinned as we took our bags up to the suite overlooking the water.

"If you're going to do the park, you really have to stay onsite," he said.

I cocked an ear to listen for the rumble of a roller coaster. "Are we doing the park?"

"You don't think I brought you all the way not to ride the tallest and fastest roller coasters in the country, do you?"

I laughed. "I guess not."

He stretched out on the bed and beckoned me with a come-hither pout. "Let's try out this mattress."

"Don't we have to go to your parents' house?"

"Not until Sunday."

I crossed to the bed, but didn't let him pull me down. Both of us knew my resistance was more for show than anything. I crossed my arms. "I don't really want to ride a coaster with your love juice oozing down my thighs."

Alex made a face. "You are soooo classy."

"I'm serious."

He sighed and looked put-upon. "Can I just eat you out until you come all over my face?"

"So long as you wash it right after," I told him sternly.

I loved the glint in his eyes. "It's a deal."

"I might even suck your dick at the same time," I offered archly.

He fell back onto the pillows, both hands clutched over his heart. "Yessss!"

"Hold that thought, tiger. I'm going to use the bathroom and freshen up a little."

"Hurry," he said, with a leer so blatant it should've been silly but wasn't.

"Yeah, yeah. Give a girl a minute or two."

"I'm counting."

Laughing, I went to the bathroom and availed myself of the facilities, then grabbed a washcloth to do a quick freshening. A nine-hour car ride hadn't done much for my sense of sexy. Over the sound of the water running, I heard the distinctive jangle of Alex's iPhone—he was the only man I knew who used sound clips from *The Wizard of Oz* as his ring tone. And, considering most of the men I knew, that was saying a lot.

He cut Glinda off in midtrill. Through the cracked-open bathroom door, I heard the low murmur of his voice, then a laugh. Also low. Deep. A sexy laugh.

I froze at the sink, my fingers wet and soapy, and water clinging to my eyelashes. I blinked to clear them, and turned off the water. I could hear his voice, but only pieces of words. He wasn't talking to his parents; I could tell that much. There was no denying the dip and cadence of his words or the implication in them.

I stood at the door, listening without opening it. I knew

better and did it anyway. You never hear anything good when you listen at doors.

"Fuck you, man," Alex said. "No, fuck you twice. Fuck you with something hard and sandpapery. Right. Whatever. Yeah, I know it has. Yeah. Well, good. It'll be good."

For other women with other boyfriends, the simple "man" would've been enough to chase away any fears...but of course, it only created some for me. My hand slipped on the door and it opened. Alex looked up.

"Yeah, we'll be there," he said, sounding subtly different with me as his audience. Or maybe my imagination put that butch accent in his tone. "Yep. See you then."

He slid his finger across the phone's face to disconnect the call. "That was Jamie, my best friend from high school."

"Oh?"

I guess there are always moments when you realize for the first time you don't really know the person you love. Something beyond the giggly checklist you go through in the beginning of a relationship—favorite color, favorite food, shoe size. When you first realize you could know all those things and a lot more and still not truly have a clue about the person you've decided you don't ever want to live without.

"Yeah." Alex hesitated, maybe realizing he'd never mentioned this friend before. "I haven't seen him in a few years."

"He's still here in town?"

"Yeah. He invited us over for a barbecue on Monday. I told him we'd go."

"Sure, of course. I'd like to meet your friend."

"Awesome." Alex tossed the phone onto the bed and headed for me with a familiar grin. "Now...about that business with the oral sex..."

We didn't make it into the park for another couple of hours. We spent Saturday at the park, too. We rode every ride, sometimes twice, and ate our fill of amusement park junk food. I hadn't seen Alex act the part of tour guide before, but it was clear he was proud and excited to show off to me the machinery he'd worked on and the bathrooms he'd scrubbed back in the days of his teenage employment at the park. He was different here, the way I guess we all are when put back into a place we've left.

And he had stories to tell. It was the most expansive Alex had ever been about his past, and I gobbled up every scrap he offered. Realizing there was so much I didn't know made me all the more determined to learn all I could.

We walked hand in hand on the midway, lost a roll of quarters in the arcade. Had our pictures taken in the photo booth, me laughing on his lap. Kissing. He won me a stupendously crappy stuffed frog with great goggle eyes and a crown.

"Should I kiss it?" I said.

"I'm the only prince you'll ever need, baby."

It was a very good day.

Early Sunday, when it was still dark, I woke to the muffled sound of something nasty happening in the bathroom. I sat up in bed and felt the empty spot beside me. I heard the toilet flush and the water in the shower turn on. It ran for a long time, so long I was just about to get up and check on him, when it turned off. Alex came into the dark room a few minutes after that and slipped into bed next to me, naked.

"Are you okay?"

"Too many loopty-loop rides and ice cream." He sounded a little hoarse and exhausted. "I'll be okay."

"Can I get you anything?"

"No."

We'd made love the night before and he'd been fine. I turned to press the back of my hand to his forehead, checking for heat. My own stomach turned at the thought of a virus shared with a kiss.

"Do you feel better?"

Surprisingly, he croaked laughter. "I'll be okay, babe. Really. I promise. I just need to get some sleep."

I yawned, not knowing the time other than it was early. "How long have you been up?"

"I haven't slept."

"Oh, honey." I shifted in the sheets. "That sucks."

"Yeah." Another croak masqueraded as a laugh. "I'll be okay. I think I can sleep, now. A good yark always does that for me."

I wrinkled my nose. "Ew."

He turned on his side, away from me. "Sorry."

"It's okay. I'm sorry you don't feel good. Sure I can't get you anything?"

"Nah, I'm fine. Really. Just…" He hesitated and cleared his throat. "My stomach's just shot to shit, that's all."

I got it, then. "Your parents?"

His body shook a little, from a shiver or a nod, I couldn't tell. "Yeah. Fuck."

I put a hand on his shoulder. "We don't have to go."

"Yeah," Alex said soberly into the darkness. "We do."

I thought I understood, though my heart went out to him that it had made him so nervous he was sick. It didn't do much good for my peace of mind, either. "Do you want to talk about it?"

"Not really."

I understood that, too. I rubbed his back in gentle circles and listened to the sound of his breathing finally get soft and slow as he fell asleep. Then I was the one with a churning stomach, staring at the blackness, unable to sleep.

"This is it." Alex pulled the emergency brake, though we weren't on a hill, and turned off the ignition.

We sat in front of a small but well-kept bungalow on Sandusky's main street. It had a narrow driveway leading to a detached garage, a small front porch and a side door. Gray stone walls, door and window frames outlined with black. A black slate roof. The door had been painted red.

Alex made no move to get out of the car. I didn't, either. I looked through the front windshield at the tiny house. The curtain at the front window twitched.

"Babe, we can't sit here forever."

"Fuck," he muttered. "Yeah. I know. Let's go."

"Wait a minute," I told him, and waited until he'd turned to me. I took his face in my hands and kissed his mouth. "It's going to be fine."

Alex looked grim. "I do love you, Olivia."

"Good." My smile couldn't tempt one from him, but I tried.

He sighed. "Let's go."

We went to the side door. Just before he pushed it open, Alex grabbed my hand. Hard. I winced and tried to ease his grip, but he wasn't watching me. He pushed open the door and we went into a small, cluttered kitchen filled with steam and the scent of good things baking.

A skinny woman with a head of blowsy, faded hair pulled

off her face with a stretch headband turned from the sink, where she'd been scrubbing at a pot. She wore a stretched-out, pale yellow shirt, the hem unraveled and untucked from a pair of baggy white walking shorts. Her hands were red and raw, her arms and face freckled and bare of makeup.

"A.J.!"

I saw where he got his wide grin, and his deep gray eyes, too, when the woman moved closer. Alex looked quite a lot like his mother, though I had a hard time believing he'd ever have allowed himself to look so haggard.

"Ma," he said in a cool, distant voice nothing like her adoring tone. "This is Olivia."

I stepped out from behind him with a smile on my face. I wasn't expecting a warm embrace and was, in fact, hoping for nothing more intimate than a handshake. I didn't even get that.

What made it worse was that she'd moved toward me, arms half-open, then stopped. "Oh...hello."

I saw her gaze travel over my face and linger on my hair, pulled back today with the locks twisted into a braid. Then she glanced at my hand, caught tight in her son's.

I've had my share of curious looks, especially from people who've met my parents first. Sometimes it's been the other way around. I've been judged on the color of my skin before I ever opened my mouth, and not always by white people. But I'd never, until that moment, been so awkwardly and uncomfortably aware of another person's reaction upon seeing me.

"Mother," Alex said sharply. "This is Olivia. My fiancée."

"Oh...yes, of course. Olivia." Mrs. Kennedy, who still didn't have a first name to me, put on a smile. She wiped her hands over and over on the dish towel she grabbed up from the counter "Come in! Come in. Dinner's going to be ready real soon. I'll have to call your dad. He's down in the basement. Come here, A.J., and give your mom a kiss."

He moved dutifully forward. Her fingers scrabbled at him, striving to keep him close a moment longer. He pulled away gently. Her eyes skated over him, drinking in the sight with such painfully obvious pleasure I didn't want to see it.

"You two go into the living room. Your sisters are there. With the kids. They'll be so happy to see you. Let me go get your dad."

"Okay." Alex took my hand again. "C'mon, babe, let's go say hi."

I swallowed hard and lifted my chin, girding myself for more stunned looks, but Alex's sisters, at least, didn't seem as shocked as his mother. He had three, all much younger. Tanya, Johanna and Denise. All of them had multiple children, ranging in age from late teens to drooling toddler, and I got the impression there were other kids missing. Not a husband in sight, though Johanna and Denise both wore plain gold wedding bands.

Alex greeted his sisters with easier affection than he had his mother, and they in turn hugged the breath out of him and slapped him around a little in the way younger sisters can do to older brothers. I knew that from experience. I hung back, not wanting to interject myself into the flurry of their questions, but Alex turned and drew me forward, my hand in his. He didn't abandon me.

The older kids gave perfunctory greetings and went back to reading or texting or playing their video games, but the three youngest crowded around me with wide eyes. The littlest, a diapered girl in a smudged yellow sundress, climbed up on the sofa beside me and touched my hair over and over.

"Trina, get down offa her," Denise said, but made no other move to get her kid off me.

Alex scooped up the girl and flubbered the side of her neck until she squealed, then handed her to her mother. "Change her diaper, for God's sake."

Denise rolled her eyes. "Yeah, listen to you, like you've ever changed a diaper in your life. How about you, Olivia? You got any kids?"

I looked around at the pack of children and then at her. "I… No."

Tanya reached to ruffle Alex's hair. "Maybe you will soon, huh? Big brother gonna be a daddy?"

"Yeah, you'd better get caught up," Johanna told him. "Hell, even Jamie's got a kid now. I seen him at the mall a couple weeks ago. You still keep in touch with Jamie, don'tcha?"

"Of course he does," Denise said with scorn. "Do you even think he'd be back here just to see us?"

She said it like a joke, but we all heard the weight of truth in her words.

"Yeah, I knew Jamie had a kid," Alex said. "His name's Cam."

"Well, well, well," said a booming voice from the back of the room. "If it's not the whattaya call it…prostitute son?"

"Prodigal, Dad," Tanya said under her breath.

"And his blushing bride-to-be." Mr. Kennedy moved into the room on feet that looked too small to support his bulk. He was short of hair up top, but the growth sprouting from his ears and eyebrows made up for that. "Livvy, is it?"

"Her name's Olivia, Dad," Alex said to him. To me, "John Kennedy."

"Just like that idjit who got his head blown off." John Kennedy must've been warned by his wife, because although his roving gaze picked me thoroughly apart, he didn't look as surprised as she had. "Welcome, girl. We've been waiting for the boy to bring someone home for a long time. Hell, we're just glad you're a girl, right?"

His knee-slapping *hyuk-hyuk* was the only laughter. All of Alex's sisters found other places to look, and Alex said nothing. I cleared my throat.

"It's nice to meet you, sir."

"Sir? Sir, yet? Nice manners on her, son. But you don't have to call me sir, Livvy, just call me John."

"Her name's Olivia," Alex said tightly. "Not Liv."

His father looked at him. John Kennedy was a lot less stupid than he was acting. His smile tightened chapped lips at the corners, and he fixed his son with a deep, solid stare.

"I heard you the first time."

"Umm…dinner's ready…" said Mrs. Kennedy, who still had no first name. "Let's all go eat, okay?"

John patted his giant belly. "Yes. Let's do that. C'mon, Liv—Olivia. You come sit next to me."

It was hard to tell if this was an honor or a punishment. John Kennedy talked my ear off for the entire meal. He had a lot to say about many topics—religion, politics, newspaper columns. Taxes. There was a lot wrong with this country, in John's opinion, and all of it appeared to be the fault of many people who were not John Kennedy.

"You a vegetarian?"

His question surprised me, interrupting as it had a diatribe against a local chain department store that apparently no longer carried his favorite brand of cigarettes. Startled, I glanced down to the end of the table where Alex was entertaining one of his nieces with a magic trick. I looked at my plate, where most of the food was gone.

"No."

John pointed with his fork at the small slice of ham I'd taken for politeness but hadn't touched. "You're not eating that."

"Dad, for fuck's sake—"

"Hey!" John drew down those heavy brows and stabbed the air with his fork. "Watch your fucking mouth."

Some of the kids giggled. Alex didn't. He put down the saltshaker he'd been trying to make disappear.

"She doesn't have to eat anything she doesn't want to."

"John," said Mrs. Kennedy timidly, "the ham is very salty. Maybe Olivia just doesn't care for it."

John reached over and ground his fork into the small slab of ham on my plate and lifted it to his mouth. He took a bite, chewed, swallowed. "Ain't a damn thing wrong with that ham, Jolene. I'm just wondering if Livvy don't eat ham for some reason."

I clutched my hands in my lap to keep anyone from seeing how they'd suddenly begun to shake. "No offense meant, Mrs. Kennedy. I'm sure it's delicious."

"Huh. I thought maybe you weren't eating it because you were one of them moose-lums."

"Dad!" Alex shoved back from the table, but I cast him a look.

"I'm not a Muslim, Mr. Kennedy."

He eyed me. "Good. Cuz I won't have a goddamned Muslim at my table."

Across from me, Johanna groaned and dropped her head into her hand. "Dad. Good Lord."

"What's a moose-lum?" asked one of the smaller kids.

Nobody said a word.

John shot me a grin filled with crooked, yellowed teeth. "Just so long as you ain't one."

I wanted to stand up then and show him the necklace my mother had given me. I wanted to proudly proclaim I was a Jew, just to see if that would piss him off. I wanted to own who I am. But I caught Alex's gaze and his angry slash of a mouth, and I knew the only thing standing up for myself would do was cause a lot of trouble just then. John would probably say something incredibly rude, and from the look on Alex's face, I thought he might just punch the old guy in the face.

"Delicious mashed potatoes, Mrs. Kennedy," I said as serenely as I could.

The collective sigh of relief couldn't be ignored, but John didn't seem to notice. He got right back to his constant stream of complaints against society. This time, he added jokes. To be fair, he was an equal-opportunity bigot, a modern-day Archie Bunker tempered with a mutated twist of political correctness. John Kennedy didn't say "Polack," he said "Polish guy." He didn't say "Chink," he said "Chinaman." And he never once, in a whole slew of ethnic jokes, said the word *nigger*.

I think we were all waiting for it. I wouldn't have been shocked to hear him say it. I'm not sure I'd even have been angry—but never having been called a nigger to my face by someone who meant it with derision, I'm not sure how I would have reacted. We all just waited for it. I'd felt out of place before, one dark face in a roomful of pale skin, but I'd never been so on edge about waiting for it to be pointed out.

In the end, it wasn't a black joke that got the biggest reaction. We'd all finished dinner and were picking at the apple pie and ice cream. John had already put away a huge slice and was on his second.

The first gay joke slipped in between a rant about gas prices and cigarette taxes. At the second, I glanced down the table to see Alex's reaction. He was staring at his plate, at the ice cream melting over his untasted pie. His hair had fallen forward, so I couldn't see his eyes.

Nobody had laughed at any of the jokes, but that hadn't stopped John from continuing. The third faggot joke was about gay marriage. That's when I looked up from my plate.

"I don't think that's funny."

Dead silence except for Mrs. Kennedy's squeak. I didn't look to see what Alex was doing. I kept my gaze focused on John's face.

He studied me intently, and I wondered for whose benefit all those jokes had been made, anyway. His eyes gleamed with dark and nasty intelligence and justification. He thought he had the right to feel the way he did about the blacks, the queers, the spics and chinks and hymies. He didn't seem to notice he was as much a stereotype as any one of the groups he was brutalizing with his poor sense of humor.

"Well, now," he said with a leering grin. "I guess I don't find faggots funny, either."

And he left it at that.

In the Kennedy house, women cleaned up after dinner, while the men retired to the basement to watch television. Alex stayed upstairs until one of his sisters chased him off.

"Get out of the way," she said without pulling any punches. "We want to get to know your Olivia."

"Will you be okay?" he whispered as he kissed me.

"I will," I assured him, with a look into the kitchen where the other women were working. "It's okay."

"I'm sorry." He sounded defeated and looked pale. He hadn't eaten much.

I touched his cheek. "Baby, there are all sorts of people in the world, and some of them are assholes."

He smiled at that and kissed me. "I love you."

"I know you do. Go." I pushed him toward the basement door. "Go…bond."

"As if," he said with a glower, but went.

Away from her husband, Jolene Kennedy proved to have a much better sense of humor, even though she didn't tell many jokes. She had a pretty laugh that rang out in the tiny kitchen as she let her daughters push her into a chair to play with her grandchildren instead of hand-washing all the pots and pans. I pitched in, no stranger to kitchen work, and found that Alex's sisters might have been sluts in high school, but they were pretty decent mothers and daughters for all that.

And they loved their brother, that was clear. They told me stories about him—how he'd always been there when they needed something. A ride, some money, advice. He'd moved away when they were very young, and still had managed to be a large part of their lives. Maybe more than my own brothers had, and we were closer in age. Their stories fit a piece into the puzzle of the man I loved, and I saw another picture of him.

I excused myself to use the bathroom, the only one in the house, in the upstairs hallway. When I came out, John was waiting. I stepped aside to let him pass, but he countered with a step in front of me.

My heart pounded, but I refused to let him see he'd intimidated me. "Excuse me."

"So, you're gonna marry our boy?"

"I plan to. Yes."

"In a church?"

I stared at Alex's father, whose gaze dropped to the necklace on the outside of my blouse. "We haven't decided yet."

His gaze roamed all over me. "You know, I can't say as I'm surprised he picked you, Livvy. You are awful pretty for a black girl. I've had a taste or two of black girls myself, though don't you let on to Jolene."

I tasted bile but kept my chin high. "Excuse me."

He didn't move. "You full black?"

"What?"

"Are you full black," he repeated, as though I were stupid, or deaf. "I only ask because you got some white features to you. And you ain't so dark, you know?"

Oh, I knew all right. I swallowed the surge of acid and looked him in the eye. "I love your son, and he loves me. It has nothing to do with the color of my skin, you racist asshole. Now let me by before I kick you in your nuts."

John blinked, then grinned, but didn't move. "Sassy, ain't ya?"

I moved closer, my mouth twisted in a sneer. "Get out of my way."

His fingertip shot out and flicked my necklace. A point of the star stung my throat. "So. You'll get married in the church? Yes or no?"

I pushed past him without answering. John followed me

down the stairs. I found everyone in the living room. Alex was laughing with Tanya. It was the most relaxed I'd seen him since we arrived. He shot me a smile that faded quickly.

"Don't walk away from me," John said from behind me.

The room froze. I'm sure all of the people in it had heard his tone before, judging by their reactions. Johanna went visibly pale. Even the teens looked up from their video games and cell phones. Alex took a step forward.

"Thank you for lunch, Mrs. Kennedy," I said clearly. "I think it's time we left."

"Girl, don't you walk away from me when I'm talking to you. I asked you a question."

"And I gave you an answer," I said calmly, though my knees were shaking, my guts quaking. "We haven't discussed it yet. And frankly, it's for me and Alex to decide. Not for you."

"What's going on?" Alex asked.

"I asked your girl here if you were getting married in the church, and she won't answer me. I just want to know," John said. "I mean, doesn't an old man have a right to know if his only son's going to get married the right way or the wrong way? Or should I just be glad he's getting married at all?"

It was not the first time Alex's father had teased with such a comment, but this time, Alex responded. "You mean that I'm not a faggot, right?"

John laughed heartily, the same false *hyuk-hyuk*. "No son of mine's a cocksucker."

I found Alex's gaze with mine and tried to send him strength, but this was not my battle. It probably never had been about me at all. He looked at his dad with an expression so blank it might have been on a doll.

"We're leaving now. We'll let you know about the wedding. But don't expect it to be in a church." Alex looked at me. "C'mon, babe, let's get out of here."

I thought John might shout after us, but nobody said a word as we left. Nobody even offered a goodbye. We left in total, utter silence unbroken until we got in the car.

Then Alex let loose. "Stupid motherfucking shit-heel asshole!"

He jammed the car in Reverse and we smoked into traffic. He clutched the wheel so tightly his fingers turned white. I said nothing, just let him rant. I didn't point out that he sounded a lot like his dad.

He didn't stop until we got to the hotel parking lot. Then he turned off the car and drew in a deep, hitching breath. He didn't look at me.

"I'm sorry, Olivia. I'm so fucking sorry."

I stroked his hair and let my hand rest on the knotted bunch of his shoulders. I squeezed. "Honey, I don't care about your dad being a prick. Really."

He looked at me. "He was baiting me."

"Yes. He was." I hesitated, thinking of the conversation in the upstairs hall, and wondered what might happen if I told Alex the other things his dad had said.

"I should've told him."

I worked at the knot in his shoulder. "Told him what?"

Alex shook his head. "I don't know. That he was right. I am a cocksucker."

"That's not all you are."

I took my hand away and put it in my lap. His heavy breathing filled the air between us, but I had nothing to say.

No comfort to give. This was a shaky bridge over a treacherous drop.

He flashed me a look. "But I love you. I want to marry you. That's what matters."

His words lifted me a little. "Yes, that's what matters. To me, anyway."

He nodded as if we'd come to an agreement. "Good. Right. And fuck him, anyway, that old man. He's a fucking twat. I fucking hate him."

His voice broke. I touched his shoulder again, unsure what to do. Alex shook his head, blew out a breath, swiped at his face. He gave me a smile that didn't quite reach his eyes.

"You kicked his ass, though, didn't you?"

My laugh scratched my throat. "I've faced assholes before."

"I'm sorry."

"Honey," I said solemnly, "don't be sorry. If anything, I'm glad we went. I'm glad I met your sisters, and your mom, and your nieces and nephews. You can't help who your dad is."

"Now you know one reason why I never fucking come back here."

"No kidding," I teased, trying to lighten the tension. "With that, do you need any others?"

He didn't answer, and I wondered if there were more reasons than his bigoted, homophobic father. Alex kissed me, though, soft and sweet, and I didn't bother to ask him about anything else.

Chapter 20

*M*onday morning, Memorial Day, was bright and hot by the time I woke. I heard the rush of water in the bathroom again, but this time Alex emerged with a grin. I burrowed under the pillow. We'd stayed up very late doing all the sorts of things people do in hotel rooms, and some of those things twice.

"Wakey wakey, eggs and bakey!" He jumped on the bed and drew back the sheets to expose my warm naked body to the chilly, air-conditioned air.

"Five more minutes."

"C'mon, Olivia. We're going to miss the party."

I pulled the pillow away to look at him. He'd slicked his hair back, but it would fall over his eyes as soon as he dried it. He'd shaved. I smelled cologne. Water still sparkled on his eyelashes.

"You are way too cheerful for a dude who got only a few hours of sleep."

He kissed me, though I kept my lips closed tight to imprison my morning breath. "You, on the other hand—"

I pinched his nipple and, laughing, he grabbed my wrist. "Watch what you say."

"My love, you are an angel of the morning."

I grumped a few more seconds, then sat up. "If you loved me, you would bring me Starbucks in bed."

Alex raised a brow. "Is that so?"

"That is so."

He leaned close, but didn't kiss. I saw my reflection in his deep gray eyes. "I'll be back in five minutes."

I smiled. "Now that's what I'm talking about. Service."

Alex laughed again, already pulling on a pair of jeans and a T-shirt. "Get your ass out of bed, Olivia."

I groaned as he left the room, but hauled myself from the too-soft bed and padded into the bathroom. I took my time in the shower, luxuriating in the steady stream of unending hot water. I flossed and brushed and tweezed and shaved, for good measure. With a towel wrapped around me, my face a dark blur in the steam-covered mirror, I could admit to myself I was more nervous about meeting Alex's friends than I'd been his family.

By the time I got out of the bathroom, he'd returned with two huge cups of coffee and a couple of scones. He'd also laid my clothes out for me on the bed—panties, bra, a sundress I'd packed but hadn't expected to wear. Even my sandals had been set out.

"What's this?" I took the coffee and sipped.

"I want you to wear that."

I studied the outfit. "It's a little dressy for a barbecue."

"But you'll look so fucking hot in it."

The dress, pale blue with an embroidered design of red and gold flowers, had come from India. Light, filmy fabric, short but full sleeves, a hem that hit me just above the knee. I'd worn it only a few times, but I liked what the color did for my skin and eyes. I liked the sandals, too, flat, with crisscross straps. I'd intended to wear a pair of capris and a camp shirt.

"Are you sure?" I took off my towel and stood naked in front of the mirror. I cupped my breasts, then ran a hand over the curve of my belly. My ass. "It's not a fancy party, is it?"

"I doubt it. But who cares? You'll look beautiful."

I looked at him in the mirror. "You want to show me off?"

"Of course." His grin held not even a speck of apology. "Who wouldn't?"

I turned to face him. "What are you wearing?"

"Why? You want to show me off?"

I laughed and moved to pull on the pair of pale blue panties and bra he'd set out for me. "Matching underwear. How very queer eye of you."

I'd meant it lightly; if we were going to spend the rest of our lives together there was no point in pretending I didn't know about his past. It sounded harder than I'd meant it to, and when I glanced up at him, Alex was frowning.

"You always pick out panties that match your clothes," he said.

I put my arms around his neck. "I do. Thank you."

Mollified, he let me kiss him. He let me do a little more than that, too, but I stopped before his cock did more than twitch in response to my stroking. I laughed when he groaned in protest, and went back to the bed to pull the dress over my head. It fell around my thighs like a butterfly kiss. When I turned from side to side, the fabric flowed around me.

"Gorgeous." Alex sounded more like he was admiring a painting or a vase than me, and I shot him a careful look he didn't notice.

I'd gone to my last high-school reunion with a man I wasn't dating on my arm. Pure eye candy. Sarah had hooked us up— he was a general contractor she knew from her renovation work. He had muscles on his muscles, abs you could wash clothes on, the chiseled features of a god. I invited him to the reunion for the simple reason that he'd look good on my arm in front of people whose opinions hadn't even meant that much. I hadn't ever been eye candy myself.

"How long's it been since you've seen your friend?" I asked casually, moving to the bathroom to start putting on makeup.

"Couple of years." Alex tugged off his T-shirt and rustled in the suitcase for a familiar pink button-down.

I watched him through the open bathroom door as I pulled out powder and mascara. Alex could take as long to get ready as I could. Longer, sometimes. I watched him run his fingers through his hair and shake it out. Pull on his shirt. Leave it untucked, button up the buttons, then undo a number of them. He pulled a belt from the suitcase and ran it through the loops on his jeans, tugged the buckle shut. Tucked the shirt.

I thought maybe Alex was more nervous about meeting his friends than he'd been about his family, too.

I smoothed scented oil into the fine stray hairs at my temples and pulled my locks back in a loose bun, with a few escaping. I glossed my lips and dusted my skin with glittery powder. I was finished and he was still fussing.

I went into the bedroom and took his shoulders to turn him from the mirror. I looked into his eyes. And I kissed him, not because I understood his anxiety, exactly, but because I didn't have to know his reasons. I only had to know how to ease them.

He rested his forehead on mine, his eyes closed. We didn't say anything. When he opened them, he looked better. His arms around me felt good and right and strong, as if nothing could ever go wrong between us.

"Let's go," he said.

The Kinneys lived in the smallest house on a long, lakefront road lined with large, expensive-looking homes. Their tiny yard backed right up to the water, though, which must be nice for the summer. I could see the amusement park across the lake, and a large metal spit took up a lot of space in the backyard. The smell of roasting meat hit me the second I got out of the car.

So did the music and laughter. Party noises. Summer sounds. I felt suddenly shamed I hadn't brought anything, not even a platter of store-bought cookies we could've picked up from the grocery on the way over. Alex assured me it was all right, but that didn't stop my hands from needing something to hold when he led me along the crushed stone path and into a bright, cheerful kitchen. I'd forgotten my camera, proof of how nervous I was.

"Jamie, you jumping muthfucka."

I'd never heard Alex sound so fond. The man who must've been Jamie turned from the kitchen island, where he'd been setting a platter of hamburgers. My first thought was that he was handsome, far better looking than Alex in a pretty sort of way—deep blue eyes, brows darker than his sunbleached hair, with the planes and angles of his face aligned just right. My second was that they might have been brothers, the way their very different faces managed to pull identical expressions.

And my third?

That Jamie, Alex's friend, his good buddy since junior high, hadn't been expecting me at all.

It wasn't the color of my skin but my entire presence that set him back a step, his hearty grin freezing in a grimace so brief it passed before I should've seen it. He stepped forward at once as though he'd never recoiled. He held out his arms.

I was a voyeur watching their embrace, which lingered a little too long, but broke apart just a bit too abruptly. Jamie's face had flushed when they pulled apart, slapping shoulders and punching biceps like adolescent boys. I couldn't see Alex's eyes.

"This is Olivia," he said, reaching a hand to snag me, pull me close. "My fiancée."

He didn't stumble on the words, and with his hand in mine the world that had shifted a little beneath my feet grew solid again. Alex tugged me to his side, his arm sliding around my waist. "Olivia, this is Jamie. My best fucking friend."

"Olivia," Jamie said solemnly. "How the hell did this bastard ever trick you into saying yes?"

And then…it was all right, so far as I could tell. Whatever had passed between them remained there. Jamie pumped my hand thoroughly and slapped Alex's back a few more times as they traded insults.

"Everyone's here," Jamie said. "Come on out in the back and say hi."

"Everyone?" Alex asked.

Jamie laughed and clapped his shoulder once more. "Yeah, even my mom. Make sure to give her a hug."

Alex glanced at me. "His mom loves the fuck out of me."

"Fuck yeah, she does."

I blinked a little at the f-bombs being dropped all over the place, but laughed. "What's not to love?"

Jamie gave me another solemn look. "What's not to love, indeed?"

Outside on the back deck, small groups of guests with plates of food in their hands greeted us. They all knew Alex. None of them seemed as surprised as Jamie had that I was there, or that he introduced me as his fiancée. I also got the impression most of these people might have known him long ago, but not that well.

"There's Anne," Jamie said from behind us as Alex led me down the short flight of steps to the yard. "She's wading with Cam."

Alex's hand tightened in mine. "Let me introduce you to Jamie's wife."

Anne Kinney wasn't paying attention to anything but her son as he kicked and splashed in the shallow water at the lake's edge. She wore faded jeans that looked as if they might have been her husband's, rolled up to the calf and belted tight around her waist with a bright scarf. Her red hair hung in a long wavy braid down her back, and her striped oxford shirt was wet from splashing.

"Go with Grammy," she said as we walked up, and the little boy took off in the opposite direction, toward an older woman in a large sun hat who held out her arms to catch him.

"Anne."

She turned slowly at the sound of Alex's voice, as if she

had all the time in the world, and when she saw him, she smiled. "Hello, Alex."

Unlike her husband, Anne didn't seem to be surprised to meet me at all. She wiped her hands on the seat of her jeans and looked from me to Alex. She raised a brow.

"This is Olivia," Alex said. "My... We're getting married."

"Congratulations," Anne said.

She sounded as if she meant it. She did not step forward to hug him, the way Jamie had. Nor did she hold out a hand to shake. She didn't touch Alex at all.

"Olivia," she said warmly, "did my husband get you something to drink or eat? No? What a brat. C'mon, let's find something before that pack of locusts he calls a family eats it all."

And just like that, she took my elbow and led me off toward the house.

"Don't worry about Alex. He'll be with James," she said with fond resignation. "Those two together are a force of nature. It's best just to stand out of the way."

In the kitchen she pulled cool bottles of cola from the fridge and handed me one. She unscrewed the top and drank back hers with a gulp. I took a little longer with mine, gave a dainty sip. I hadn't said much.

"It was nice of Alex to bring you," Anne said quietly.

Outside, the music played and the party went on. People laughed. I heard the rev of an engine and a baby's cry. I looked out the bay windows overlooking the deck. I could see Alex and Jamie standing side by side at the railing, both holding beers. The wind blew Alex's hair off his face. He was laughing. Had I ever seen him laugh like that? Stand like that?

Had I ever watched him lean toward another person the way I thought he'd only ever lean toward me?

"They've been…friends…a long time?" I said at last.

"Oh, yeah. Since junior high." Anne crossed her arms over her belly, hands cupping her elbows. She looked out the window, too. "They are very, very good friends."

Before I could say more—uncertain if I even wanted to— the back door opened and a younger woman tumbled through it with Anne's son squirming in her arms. "Mama, this stinky little boy needs a change."

"Thanks, Claire. My sister," Anne said, as Claire heaved the boy over her shoulder and spanked his diapered bottom fondly. "Claire, have you met Olivia? Alex's fiancée."

"No fucking way," Claire said.

"Fuggingway!" a small voice crowed from over her shoulder.

Anne sighed. "Claire."

"Sorry." Her sister grinned and turned the boy right side up on her hip. "Change this kid, gross. Olivia. Hello."

She held out a hand and I shook it. She studied me up and down, checking out every inch. I wasn't sure if I'd passed inspection until she let out a low whistle and shook her head.

"You're *marrying* Alex?"

"That's the plan," I said as lightly as I could.

"Claire!" Anne sounded exasperated.

An impish face peeked at me from behind his hands. He had blond hair like his daddy, his mother's fair skin. He had big gray eyes. I looked at him for a very long time.

"What?" Claire shrugged. "Sheesh. Any woman who agrees to marry that guy has to have a sense of humor, at least."

I laughed, not feeling judged. "I try."

"See?" Claire made a face at Anne and wiggled the boy on her hip until he giggled. "Look, I'll take this Mr. Stinkybutt here and change him, okay? Am I forgiven my social fox pass?"

"Fox pass!" the little boy cried, laughing.

"Faux pas," Anne murmured, and rolled her eyes. "Yes, please change Cam's diaper. Thank you."

"Nice meeting you, Olivia. Don't let anyone here scare you off. We're not a bad bunch."

"I'm not scared," I said.

Claire took Cam back down the hallway and I could hear their laughter even out here. Anne tore a paper towel from the rack and used it to wipe up some barely there crumbs from the counter. She tossed the towel in the trash and drank another gulp of her soda.

"How old is your son?"

"Cam's almost three."

Outside, Alex and Jamie had disappeared from the deck.

"I'm starving," she said. "Let's go outside and get something to eat, all right? And I'm sure someone's doing something crazy, like playing lawn darts or getting ready to sing karaoke."

My own stomach rumbled, and I thought eating, if nothing else, would give me something to do, since I'd been abandoned by my boyfriend. "Food would be good."

"C'mon," Anne said. "I'll show you where it is."

I've been to parties where I knew every person and had an awful time, and to ones where I didn't know a soul and had a blast. This party was a mix. I didn't need Alex by my side every second, but I spent more time waving at him from across the yard and watching him play lawn darts or drink beer after beer than I did talking to him. He didn't ignore me—he checked in on me every hour or so, and I saw him looking for me a few times. But he wasn't with me.

He was with Jamie, whom everyone else called James.

The other people at the party were all very nice. They included me in their conversations as if they'd known me for years. Some of us set up a rousing game of Balderdash, one of my favorite board games, and we all laughed a lot. Claire and her husband, Dean, took me out on the little sailboat while their daughter Penny stayed behind with Anne's parents. We ate a lot, danced a bit, even sang a little karaoke.

Darkness fell, and someone lit a few tiki torches along the edge of the water and some paper lanterns strung along the deck. Guests with small children began to leave. The crew for the pit beef came to clean up, and I helped in the kitchen, bundling leftovers with Anne. We worked well together, side by side, saying little. Frankly, there wasn't much to say.

And finally, Alex and I were the only guests remaining. Anne had put Cam to bed an hour before, and we'd finished in the kitchen. She'd just turned on the television, and I blessed her for it—we could both watch something stupid together and not have to speak. She'd handed me a glass of iced tea and poured one for herself when Alex and Jamie at last stumbled in from outside.

"Baby," Alex said.

I'd never seen him drunk before. His eyes shone with it, and his cheeks were flushed. His mouth looked wet and soft. He'd unbuttoned his shirt nearly to the waist, and had somewhere lost his shoes. Jamie didn't look much better—his hair was stuck with sweat to his forehead and his shirt bore grass stains.

"What the hell have you been doing?" Anne said. "Wrestling?"

"Fucker tried to jump me for the last beer," Jamie said. "Had to kick his ass."

"Fuck you, fucker," Alex said, and added a two-handed one-finger salute. "You stole the last dinner roll."

"We have more dinner rolls," Anne said drily, and tucked her feet under her on the couch. "They're in the fridge. Help yourself."

Alex put a hand over his heart. "Anne. You're a goddess." He looked at me. "Baby…baby, where've you been all day? I missed you."

He tripped on the two stairs leading to the sunken living room, and hit the love seat beside me ass first. Laughing. He put his head on my shoulder to look up at me with those big gray eyes. "Baby, hi."

I touched his face. His skin was hot. He kissed my palm and I took my hand away, awkward at this sudden display of affection in front of his friends. "Hi."

Alex sat up. Jamie had gone to rustle around in the fridge. I caught Anne's gaze, staring after her husband. She didn't look upset, exactly. More as if she was resigned. And definitely not surprised.

"Bring me one of those rolls, fucker," Alex called.

"Fuck you, dick, come get your own. I'm not your fucking servant."

"Fuck you, ya shit-kicker," Alex said, and settled farther into the love seat next to me. "Baby, will you get me a dinner roll?"

"Baby," I said tightly, "maybe we'd better think about heading back to the hotel."

"No, no, you can't go yet." Jamie turned from the fridge, his face a picture of dismay. "You just got here! I'm about to crack open a bottle of Jameson!"

Both men cracked up laughing. Anne and I did not. She sighed. I felt my every muscle go stiff.

"James, Cam's sleeping," she said.

Jamie put a finger to his lips. "Right. Sorry. I forgot. We'll go outside. C'mon, you fucking cocksucker, get your pansy ass out on the deck so we can drink this shit."

Beside me, Alex stirred and sat up straight. I thought for sure he would take offense to Jamie calling him a cocksucker, but he only laughed and nudged against me. "We'll go in a little while, baby. Okay?"

I bit down on my tongue, hard. There's a fine line between being firm and being a bitch, and I was about to cross it. I was even considering making a scene. I'd spent hours here, being ignored, making nice with strangers. Watching my fiancé act like an idiot with a guy who stood too close to him.

"James," Anne said quietly, like a warning.

I didn't want to be grateful to her, but I was. I stood. Alex stood, too. He held on to my arm, maybe for support, maybe just to prove a point.

"One drink," he said. "Then we'll go. I haven't seen Jamie in a long time."

If he'd kissed me, that would've been the end. But he didn't. He just gave me a look he knew I couldn't resist, and I guess I wasn't as interested in being a bitch as I'd thought.

"I love you," he said into my ear, in too loud a voice to be a whisper, though he seemed drunk enough to think that's what he'd done.

Then he and Jamie went out onto the deck, leaving me and Anne to stare at each other across the coffee table. She clicked off the television. I could hear laughter from outside.

"Sorry," she said. "It has been a long time since they've seen each other."

"A few years, Alex said."

She hesitated, then nodded slowly. "Yeah. I guess it has been that long."

My fingers curled into fists, not from anger, but because I had nothing else to do, nowhere else to put my hands. I had no pockets. I didn't want to be here.

Another burst of laughter filtered through the back door and turned both our heads. Anne sighed again. I tried a sigh and it caught in my throat. She looked at me, then, eyes narrowed.

"They can both be such dicks," she said.

Her words surprised a laugh out of me. "You think so?"

"Oh, God, yes." She stood. "It's bad enough when they're just talking on the phone, or through the damned Xbox. And don't get me started on the Connex tags. I swear they're both fifteen years old."

"This is… I haven't seen him like this."

She nodded after a second. "You want some more tea? Piece of cake? I saved some."

"I can always eat cake. Yes." I followed her to the kitchen, where she pulled a chocolate cake from the back of the fridge.

She cut slices while I poured some tea, and we stood at the island where we could both lean and look out onto the back deck, where all I could see of the men was the bright cherry light of a cigarette being passed back and forth. I cut my fork through the thick chocolate icing, but I didn't eat it.

"They're always like this?" I asked.

Anne licked icing from her fork. "I think if they saw each other more often in person, they would not be. Because James isn't like this with anyone else."

"Alex is…different here."

"They've been friends a long time," she said, not for the first time.

I turned to her. "So, what should I do about it?"

She licked more icing and put down her fork. "Do you love him?"

The question didn't come off as insulting the way it might have from someone else. "I do. Very much."

"Then you should know…"

"I know enough," I said.

Anne gave me a long, steady look that made me think she knew a lot more about me than should've been possible on such short acquaintance. "Then you could do what I do with James."

"Which is what?"

She looked out through the glass again as more laughter sifted in the open windows. "You can love him even though sometimes he acts like a dick."

And then I knew.

It was in what she hadn't said. In how she hadn't touched him, not even a handshake earlier. It was in how she'd watched Alex with her husband, both men being boys, and how she'd been so kind to me. And suddenly, sickeningly, it was in a pair of big gray eyes in a toddler's face.

In the kitchen, everything stopped.

It was a very quiet showdown, and I wasn't sure whether to draw or hold my fire. I wished desperately for my camera, which I'd left behind in the hotel room. Behind the lens this all might have seemed like just another party. Just another group of people. Anne and James might have been an average married couple. Their son might not have looked like my lover.

But I didn't have my camera. Everything was right there, punching me in the face, over and over. I drew in a quick, sharp breath.

"I think it's time for us to go."

"Olivia," Anne said quickly, but I was already moving toward the back door, yanking it open.

Alex and Jamie weren't kissing, but it would have been better if they were. I could've ended it there with that as a reason. But they weren't kissing, they were simply sitting side by side on a big lounge chair, their shoulders touching and their soft laughter speaking of intimacies I didn't want to hear.

"Alex."

He didn't look up at first, and in the long seconds before he did I considered just leaving him there. Then his eyes turned toward me, and he smiled. I saw love on his face, and I wanted to smack it off.

"Let's go," I said.

"But, baby…"

"Now."

Neither he nor Jamie said anything, but Alex got up. I heard Anne's footsteps behind me pause in the doorway, but she didn't speak, either. I had no quarrel with her, or with her husband, and I'd have said so out loud if pressed. In the quiet

I heard Cam's faint cry, and Anne went back inside the house to take care of him. Jamie got off the chair and followed us to the car, where I slid behind the wheel and stared straight ahead while the men said their goodbyes.

I seethed as I drove back to the hotel, but with Alex saying nothing in the passenger seat, I bit my tongue bloody. He disappeared into the bathroom when we got back, pissed forever, and then stumbled into the bed without undressing or brushing his teeth. I stayed in the shower a long, long time, and when I came out, my stomach knotted and twisted, I spent the night in the armchair with the spare blanket from the closet to keep me warm, and no pillow to cradle my head.

It was a long, long drive home.

Chapter 21

We got home late and went right to bed. I left Alex sleeping there the next morning when I woke early and went upstairs to catch up on everything I'd put on hold for the weekend. I lost myself in the soothing minutiae of touching up a series of photographs I was using in a brochure for a local day spa. I'd taken several shots of Sarah in various poses and superimposed her on different backgrounds, trying to give the impression that spending money at this particular spa was the equivalent of a deluxe vacation at an exotic resort. Compared to the vacation I'd just had, anything looked exotic and luxurious.

I was scheduled to work at Foto Folks for the evening shift. I had a mound of laundry to take care of, errands to run. My week to organize. The thought of it, the list of simple tasks I wouldn't have thought twice about last week, now paralyzed me with indecision. I stared at my computer monitor and my fingers tapped the keys, but I couldn't focus.

I believe it's possible to look back and pinpoint the moment when something good turns to shit in front of you. I know for a fact it's also possible to know it's going to happen even before it does. I didn't want this to end. I didn't want to lose Alex—and I didn't want to give him up.

But I knew I was going to.

He brought me coffee, and I almost said nothing. He kissed the top of my head and nuzzled my neck, and I almost said nothing. I closed my eyes and felt his touch, heard the soft whisper of his breath. I pulled away.

His sigh turned harsh. Resigned. "You're pissed off."

I clicked carefully with my mouse to close my project. A dialogue box popped up. Changes have been detected in your document. Do you want to save? Yes or No.

I'd spent a few hours working on this piece, and it was still crap—worse off than it had been before, as a matter of fact. Time wasted, but a lesson learned.

I clicked No.

I swiveled slowly around in my chair to face him. "We need to talk."

Alex's eyes narrowed the tiniest amount, followed by the smallest tightening of his mouth. He nodded, though, and pulled up the straight-backed chair to sit in front of me. He hadn't yet dressed or even showered, and his rumpled hair and low-hanging pajama bottoms invited my caress.

Everything about him still seduced me, and I had to look away.

"I'm sorry," Alex said. "I know my father is an asshole. I'm sorry."

My breath actually hitched at his words, my throat closing so tightly I thought for a moment I wouldn't be able to breathe. My head whipped up so fast my hair slapped my cheeks. I thought he was fucking with me, but one look at Alex's face told me he really had no clue.

"I don't give a flying fuck about your dad, Alex."

"So…then what are you pissed off about?"

I stood to get away from him. To move. To give my body reason and focus, so I didn't give in totally to anger. I faced him, but from a safe distance. He couldn't reach me—I couldn't touch him.

"How could you take me to that house, to meet those people, without telling me the truth?" Each word bit out, jagged and sharp. "How could you stand there and introduce me to her without telling me in advance who she was?"

I'd seen him be many things, but never stupid. Even so, no matter what else he was, Alex was still a man. And any woman who's ever had one knows how smart men are doesn't have much to do with their IQs.

"Who?"

"Anne," I said tightly.

His face went a little blank—not as much as I'd seen it in the past, but enough to show me I'd poked him someplace tender.

"Anne is Jamie's wife." He put the emphasis on "wife."

"And Jamie," I said. "Christ, Alex. Did you think I wouldn't see? Did you really think I wouldn't figure it out?"

"Jamie's my friend." He didn't look away from me, though the intensity of his gaze made me wish he had. "My best friend."

"And what about her? Anne? What is she?" Without

waiting for him to finish, I stepped forward. He retreated. "You took me to their house and you pushed me in front of her without telling me you'd slept with her, and then you dropped me to run off with your BFF. Do you know what an idiot I felt like? Do you even understand why it might have been important for you to tell me that hey, by the way, I fucked my best friend's wife?"

His mouth opened. Then shut. Alex straightened, his shoulders going impossibly broad as he put his hands on his hips. "I'm sorry. It wasn't like…that."

I pulled in a breath that hurt my throat. "What was it like, then?"

For the first time during our conversation, he dropped his gaze.

I stepped back, my stomach sick. My heart sore. "You…love her."

"No," he said at once. "Not anymore. And not like you."

I swallowed bitter bile. "Is that supposed to make me feel better?"

"Yes!"

I could've stretched out my hand and he his, and we might've touched. But we didn't. Vastness stretched between us, and there was more to come.

"That you loved another woman you've never mentioned, not once. You gave me a laundry list of just about every other person you ever fucked, but you never once mentioned her. The one you *loved*."

"I just…" He shrugged, looking helpless. He scrubbed at his hair, making it wild. "Does it matter who I loved first, so long as you're who I love last?"

This went deeper than an ex-girlfriend. "Does your bestie know you fucked his wife?"

"Yes. He knows."

I swallowed again, hard. Alex had told me many times he would tell me the truth, if I asked, and I'd spent too much time not asking. "Look at me."

He did. Many times I'd seen my Alex with blank eyes and smile, putting on a face for the world. He didn't do that now. He gave me everything I hadn't asked for, and I couldn't pretend I didn't see it.

I thought of two men, standing too close for friendship. I thought of Anne, whose gaze had followed them, knowing and accepting...and loving despite what she knew.

I could not be that woman.

And I could no longer not ask.

"The three of you?"

He nodded. "Yes."

"For how long?"

"A few months. Years ago. It's over, Olivia. I swear to you, it's over."

I knew that without him telling me. I'd seen it in Anne's face when she'd looked at him, and heard it in her voice when she'd told me to love him anyway.

"Why didn't you tell me?"

He ran a hand through his hair. "Because I didn't think you'd understand."

"Is she the reason you didn't go home for so long?"

He opened his mouth and I waited for the lie, but then he nodded. "Yeah. The shit with my family isn't ever going to go away. But what happened with Jamie..."

"And Anne," I said, my tone challenging him to say her name in front of me.

"Yes. With Anne. I didn't think I should go back. But then I met you, and everything seemed different. Olivia," Alex said, "I love you. I want to make a life with you. And I don't want to never see Jamie again...but...I won't, if you don't want me to."

I couldn't ask him to do that. I swallowed again, my throat sore from holding back screams and tears. "You should've told me anyway. I'd have been upset, but it would've been better than finding out the way I did. I felt stupid, Alex."

"I know. I'm sorry. I'm really sorry."

I believed him, but that didn't matter. I looked at the ring sparkling on my finger and twisted it back and forth from underneath with the pad of my thumb. I wouldn't have minded crying, but though I felt the tears in my throat, behind my eyes, nothing would come. I looked at him with clear eyes—nothing blurred, nothing out of focus. I saw Alex for real, with nothing but truth between us.

"Do you love him?"

He hesitated again. "Yes. But I never fucked him, Olivia. I swear to you."

"Do you want to?"

He moved closer then. "No. Not anymore."

"Does he want to fuck you?"

"Jamie," Alex said, "knows when to stop. Look, Olivia, Jamie and me...we're a pair of douche bags when we get together. I know we can be fucktards."

I'd seen them together and knew there was something more than friendship between them. There'd always been; it seemed there would always be. And unlike Anne, I wasn't sure I could ever just watch it happen.

"Is Cam yours?"

Alex said nothing, though his jaw dropped. He shook his head and ran a hand through his hair to cup it at the back of his neck. He paced. "No. How... Fuck, no. That boy's Jamie's, through and through."

"He looks like you."

Alex whirled to face me. "He's not mine."

"Are you sure?"

"I'd have to count the months," he said, his voice on the verge of sarcasm, "but yeah, I'm pretty sure. And even if he were mine, Olivia...that kid isn't my son."

My breath caught on a small squeak. "How can you say that?"

"You of all people," he said, "ought to know."

Then the tears came, sliding down my face in thick, wet streaks. Alarm twisted his features. This time he was the one who moved, I was the one retreating.

"Olivia—"

"I can't do this, Alex. I thought I could. I thought it wouldn't matter to me, but it does."

His breath hissed out. "I don't understand."

I took the ring off and held it in my palm. He stared. I watched his throat work as he swallowed, hard, and his mouth slipped open, wordless. He made no move to take the ring, and it glittered and shone on my palm the way it had on my finger.

"I thought it would be different with you. I wanted it to be."

"It is different with me," Alex said in a low voice. "You know it is."

"Not different enough." I put the ring on the desk. I crossed my arms tight over my stomach, gripping my elbows. It was the way Anne had stood in her kitchen, and I understood why.

"You're breaking up with me?"

Everything about him went hard. His shoulders, his jaw. His eyes went to ice. His fingers curled into fists at his sides. "Because of what someone else did to you? Because of the lies someone else told you? I should fucking pay for someone else's sins?"

It was my turn to say I was sorry, though the words slashed my throat and left the taste of blood on my tongue.

"I never lied to you," Alex said in a stiff, cold voice. "You knew everything about me. And I thought…I thought you would understand. You, especially, would understand."

"Because I loved Patrick," I said flatly. "You thought I could love another gay man? That it would just be that easy?"

"I thought," he said, "that you could love *me*."

"I would always wonder," I told him, "if I was…enough."

I wasn't proud to see my words had broken him. Alex took a step backward, toward the door. The hem of his jeans dragged on the floor. I couldn't stand to look at his naked feet.

Everything about us was suddenly, terribly naked.

He paused with his hand on the door. "Fucking men doesn't make me gay any more than fucking women makes me straight. You can either trust me or you can't. There's nothing I can do but love you, Olivia."

"I envy you," I said. It wasn't what I thought I was going to say.

"Why?"

"Because you know exactly who you are. And I have no idea who I am."

"But how could you ever think you aren't enough?"

"Because I've never been enough," I said. "Never enough of one thing or another. I don't know how to be enough, Alex. I don't know who I am, or who I should be."

Alex crossed to the desk, where he picked up the ring. He put it in my hand and closed my fingers over it. "Then let me help you find out."

Shadow and light. Truth and lies. I didn't want this to end, and neither did he.

"You don't have to choose, you know." He said this into my ear before kissing my throat, my collarbone, the slopes of my breasts. He tugged a nipple between his lips, and I sighed. "You don't have to be any one thing, Olivia."

"I'm not sure I could be if I tried." I ran my hands through his hair, always just a little too long. "But what about you?"

He smiled and pushed himself up on one elbow. He ran a hand over my naked belly. "I choose you. I've been an asshole for most of my life, Olivia, but I swear to you I will be a faithful asshole."

I laughed and cried at the same time. My ring flashed as I ran my hand again through his hair. "I do trust you."

"Good."

"But the rest of it...about getting married in a church, or..."

"We'll get married wherever you want to get married. Whatever you decide. I'm easy that way."

I gave a playful peek at the cock tent made in the sheets. "You're just plain easy."

"Yes." He kissed me softly, then a little harder, hands roaming.

I stopped him long enough to cup his face, to look into his eyes. "Remember when you said you thought this would be easier?"

"Yeah."

"I'm sorry it's not."

Alex traced a pattern on my belly with a fingertip, then laid his hand flat upon it. "I'm not."

"No?"

He shook his head and looked at me. "Nope. Nothing worth having is easy and all that shit."

"You're such a philosopher."

He kissed my belly in the place he'd just traced. "Let's just say I spent a lot of time fucking up. I don't want to do that anymore. I want to make this work with you."

"I want to make it work with you, too."

He kissed me again, lightly, just over my belly button. "It's a deal."

"I like that," I whispered. "Do it again, a little lower."

He obliged. Then lower still, until he nuzzled at my thigh. He nipped. He laughed. He licked my clit and made me squirm, then held me still while he kissed and stroked and sucked. But he didn't let me come.

That he saved for when he was inside me, propped on his hands to keep from crushing me. I tasted sweat when I kissed him. It tasted good.

Later, when we had finished but weren't done—I thought maybe we'd never be done, Alex and me, and that was just fine—I rolled onto my back and stared at the ceiling, where once he'd pointed out the shape of an angel.

"I love you, Alex."

He sounded sleepy when he answered. "I love you, too. It's going to be all right, Olivia. No matter what happens. Okay?"

He was sleeping when I crept from the bed and grabbed my camera from its loyal place on my dresser. He didn't move when I took the first photo, or the second. He shifted, though, when I crawled back on the bed and held the camera at the end of my arm, pointing down, clicking to capture whatever moment this was.

There were shadows, so we were half in dark and half in light. And there was a blur to the corner that might have been a woman's shape, if you looked closely enough. There were layers in this picture and many things to see.

He opened his eyes and kissed me, and I put the camera down to let him.

I didn't have to decide if I was one thing or another. If I was both and neither. Everything and nothing. It's okay to struggle to find our place in this world and the person who will take us for who and what we are. Sometimes we dress ourselves in layers that only get peeled away in the end, to leave us as we should be.

Naked.

★ ★ ★ ★ ★